Barbara Ewing is a New Zealand-born actress and author who lives and works in London.

Also by Barbara Ewing

Strangers
The Actresses
A Dangerous Vine

THE TRESPASS

Barbara Ewing

A *Time Warner* Book

First published in Great Britain in 2002
by Time Warner Books

Copyright © Barbara Ewing 2002

The moral right of the author has been asserted.

A CIP catalogue record for this book is
available from the British Library.

ISBN 0 316 86057 3

Typeset in Palatino by M Rules
Printed and bound in Great Britain by
Clays Ltd, St Ives plc

Time Warner Books UK
Brettenham House
Lancaster Place
London WC2E 7EN

www.TimeWarnerBooks.co.uk

To Bill
across the distance

Forgive us our trespasses
As we forgive them
That trespass against us

ONE

As dusk fell the lamplighters with their ladders hurried along the main thoroughfares, dodging the crowds, climbing upwards like monkeys, lighting the gas lamps. Then, as it got darker, lights began to glow all along the River Thames.

The Palace of Westminster flickered as servants turned up the lamps for the honourable members. Then fires and lights appeared one after the other on the boats of every kind that crowded the river, and the small craft of the lightermen darted in and out of the shadows. On the wild, swarming, noisy bridges the cabmen lit their lanterns; it was high tide and the passing flashes of hundreds of vehicle lights caught and then lost the darkening water as it slid up the muddy shore and snaked down shadowy waterside alleys. Horse-drawn cabs collided sometimes with horse-drawn omnibuses, and horse-drawn coaches, and carts and barrows: horses stumbled, coal capsized, fruit and vegetables rolled under iron wheels, barrow boys yelled and laughed, ladies screamed, drivers swore and shouted. Pedestrians pushed and shoved their dangerous way through the horse dung and the dust; many took the dimly lighted route over the new Hungerford Bridge where people were the only traffic, although farmers often herded skittering cattle that way, across to Smithfield Market to have their throats cut.

(Some of the inhabitants of the city seemed not to need light at all, seemed to know their way round the narrower streets and watery alleys on the hot, late-summer evening: hurried down unlit paths and even along the soft, muddy riverbank that seeped into the city at high tide; turned right or left into a passage or a doorway where a dim candle, or a whisper, showed the way.)

The moon rose, a thin sliver of light. Stars came out, night fell on London, changing the yellow-grey water of the river to black velvet, hiding the acrid, dark smoke billowing from the chimneys, shadowing the spires of the great churches and palaces, so that the city looked – almost – beautiful.

So that you could not see the refuse from the cesspits, the privies, the common drains, the dusthills, the nightcarts, the infirmary, the workhouse, the burial grounds, the slaughterhouses, the tripe shops, the gasworks, the cotton factories, the dyeing works, the tanneries that all flowed through the sewers into the Thames. You could not see the animal carcasses, the pig manure, the horse dung, the human excrement, the arsenic from the sheep-wash, the metallic salts, the dye, the road scrapings, the white lead, the urine wash or the human corpses that had been dumped there, in the water.

And, silently, all night long, from the great cesspool of the city – the River Thames – the polluted, infected water went *back* again, through official waterpipes, into the water system that fed the inhabitants of London.

'Gentlemen,' the Prime Minister said.

For a moment he was silent, and his mouth turned downwards. He put on his spectacles, looked again at the paper in front of him. 'Gentlemen, the death toll from the new cholera epidemic is already over two hundred and fifty persons per day. Our hospitals are badly overstretched, our burial grounds in London are already full to overflowing, literally overflowing. It is important that all the usual precautions are taken and it is up to us—' he paused, 'not to alarm the people of London, but to alert people, as I am now alerting you, that once again the epidemic is suddenly no longer confined to the – ah – to the poorer parts of our metropolis.' He heard the rustle and the coughing of the men who did not want to believe that an epidemic could touch them, saw one or two feeling for a cigar in the pocket of their waistcoat (a fine cigar, a symbol, a talisman against what happened to other, lesser people). The Prime Minister raised his voice slightly. 'As happened last time, the disease seems suddenly to have jumped barriers, appeared in places where it has – ah – not been expected. Most of the deaths previously were reported south of the river but this week I have to inform you that the cholera has been reported in Marylebone. And I very much regret to have to tell you that one of our honourable members has just informed me of the death of his own fourteen-year-old daughter.'

The rustle and the coughing rose to a kind of roar as the honourable members looked about them in dismay – dismay, and something else the Prime Minister saw: a kind of terror. *Who? Who? Not one of us? Not the Cholera?* The Prime Minister took off his spectacles abruptly and left the chamber.

He got out his own cigar as he reached his large office overlooking the river. He wished he could go home. 'Very well,' he said to the man hovering, 'send them in.'

The group of businessmen: the planners, the speculators, the lawyers, the bankers, had been waiting in one of the rooms at the end of the long corridor. They crowded in. Some of the men were smiling and rubbing their hands together as if in a kind of jolly supplication, slightly awed to be in the great man's grand room in the rebuilt Palace. But some of the men were assured and energetic, a hundred times more energetic than their Prime Minister. The world was changing, and expanding, and they knew it was theirs.

The curtains had not been drawn, the Prime Minister liked to look out over his city. The large and small jostling boats on the water were hundreds of dark, flickering shapes. Even businessmen paused for a moment at such a sight: their beautiful river. Drinks were brought on a silver tray, a servant poured whisky.

'Gentlemen,' said the Prime Minister again. A wave of weariness suddenly swept over him, how tiring this all was, how he longed to be home; he drank the proffered glass quickly. 'Gentlemen, I have been, of course, advised of your plans. It is true that the traffic in London now is at an insufferable, indeed quite unacceptable level, sometimes I wonder—' his appearance in the chamber still on his mind, 'if it is not the traffic itself that is bringing these intolerable epidemics into our great city. They tell me that, despite your new railways, upwards of five thousand horses pass through Temple

Bar each day: the congestion, not to mention the – miasma – has become quite insupportable. But . . .' He refilled his own glass. 'You know of course that yours is only one of a number of proposals that Parliament has been inundated by, and you also know that a Royal Commission has already recommended that there should be no further railways built in the central area.'

The gentlemen stirred and coughed, one made as if to speak, but the Prime Minister raised his hand. 'Yes, of course, your proposition is different. However I still find it unusual and rather a shock to the mind to think of trains underneath our city. *Underneath* our city. A circular tunnel underneath our city, some of you suggest. Have you considered the number of local parishes and urban bodies that would have to be drawn together for such a scheme? Good God, have you any idea how difficult it is to approach such a large number of local authorities about anything that affects the city as a whole? You are, I believe, planning to excavate under a built-up area of London. Have you thought how our houses, our homes, this very building, could be affected by your building *underneath* them. One has visions of our great capital collapsing into the bowels of the earth as you tunnel! And I cannot help but think that to persuade the people of this great city to travel under the ground may present you with problems also.' But his interest suddenly flagged. 'Gentlemen, I would be happy to at least hear further ideas on the subject; I understand that you will be dining tonight with some of the honourable members and further discussion will be held with them and perhaps another report could be submitted . . . yes . . . yes . . . thank you, gentlemen, forgive me, I am afraid that there are others like yourselves waiting, and then Her Majesty . . .' He always used the Queen as an excuse.

The businessmen thus dismissed – some disheartened, some openly critical, some understanding the long process required – walked, murmuring to each other, back through the wide halls in twos and threes, past the heroic figures along the walls.

'Mr Chadwick is waiting to see you, Prime Minister.'

The Prime Minister's shoulders literally sagged. 'That truculent, arrogant individual. Does it have to be now? He was here only last week.'

'He says it is most urgent, Prime Minister.'

'Yes, I expect he does.'

'He is with another doctor, sir.'

The Prime Minister sighed, trapped. Could he never escape from the medical men and the General Board of Health? 'Then bring more whisky.'

Two more gentlemen were ushered into the Prime Minister's rooms, introductions effected. The crystal glasses tinkled like small bells.

'Well, Mr Chadwick?' said the Prime Minister wearily, looking openly at his watch.

The thin-faced man wasted no time. 'I hear it's one of your own this time?'

The Prime Minister drained his glass, considered pretending to misunderstand, dismissed the idea. 'The daughter of one of my members, yes.'

'Listen to me, sir. What d'you expect in London? How often do I have to come and see you and go over and over the facts? When will you be prepared to understand that it is necessary to spend a large amount of money on the sanitation of this city, that we will never solve this problem otherwise? I have prepared reports for you on the overcrowding and sanitary conditions of the poor. I have prepared reports for you on the grotesque overcrowding of the burial grounds in central London, how the actual height of the ground is rising as more and more bodies are interred on top of one another, on the stench, on the miasma of death and disease that covers us. I have prepared reports for you about the totally inadequate sewerage. Better sewerage is absolutely vital.'

The smaller man beside Edwin Chadwick suddenly interrupted in a low, violent, hardly controlled voice.

'Prime Minister. I want to say something else. I am a doctor. Everywhere, every city I've looked at, not just London, it is the water. I've said it till I'm blue in the face in all my reports. The Water Companies are more interested in profit than purified water. They are making huge profits providing water to Londoners from the Thames, largely unfiltered, yet there are two hundred sewers running from this city straight into the river!'

'It is the miasma,' repeated Edwin Chadwick, his voice rising, 'not the water itself perhaps, but the effluvia that rises from it, the stench, the inhalation of the odours caused by decaying animal matter that allows these terrible diseases to spread.'

'How are we to make decisions if even you people cannot agree!' The Prime Minister's voice rose in a kind of exasperation and frustration. 'I am as disturbed as you gentlemen about the new epidemic in our city and I have any number of people telling me what causes it but no clear picture of how to cure it. You talk about the money required for this and required for that. But have you any idea at all of the preposterous amount of money that would be needed to build a new sewerage system and drainage underneath this city? The population of London would rise in mutiny – as they have done in earlier times – at the amount of taxes that would be required for such activity. For there is still no definite proof that water is the cause!'

'People don't *want* there to be proof,' snapped the smaller man. 'Water companies don't want there to be proof, builders don't want there to be proof, landlords don't want there to be proof, commissioners of sewers don't want there to be proof. But all the dead bodies carried away on the carts every night in London – they're the proof! And now you are finding that disease is no respecter of classes. Listen to me, Prime Minister. It is a truism that we could not live without water. Water is as necessary to us as air. Is the next thing going to be private Air Companies charging us for the air that we breathe? When people congregate in their thousands and thousands as they do in London, it is essential to public health that water is abundant, and available, and where possible free, not sold to yield thirty per cent interest to greedy, profiteering members of private Water Boards. It must be supplied cheaply by the state. The water companies should be municipalised, controlled, and for public good not for private profit—' and Edwin Chadwick broke in.

'Prime Minister. There must be, no matter what the cost there has to be, one central body to arrange proper sanitary arrangements, the abolition of cesspools, the construction of drains, the construction of new sewers . . .'

The Prime Minister stood up. '*Gentlemen!* I agreed to see you because I thought there might be something new. You know very well that last year we passed a Public Health Act yet nothing we are doing seems to make any difference. It is not yet clear what is causing the return of the cholera. The water belongs to the Water Boards and good men run those boards, many of the honourable members of the government of this country are directors of the Water Boards. And what is more I am not entirely convinced that it is the job of the state to cure all the ills of the country. I am sorry, Her Majesty is waiting . . .' And Edwin Chadwick, and his companion, found themselves being ushered from the large and elegant room.

It was the second man who spoke back into the room as they left, again low and violent, just loud enough for the Prime Minister to hear every word: 'Sir. Your family has I believe done many things for this country. It is said you have met Napoleon, and I have heard that you have written a five-act play, as yet unperformed. These are interesting matters perhaps. But, I promise you, you will go down in history as Prime Minister of a country where people were forced, and required by businessmen to *pay for the privilege*, to drink their own shit.'

The Right Honourable Sir Charles Cooper, MP, left the restaurant in the Strand, listened for the particular sound of a cab-horse's hooves that heralded a closed hansom cab rather than an open gig, and hailed one out of the darkness. He directed the driver to Bryanston Square and his tall, brooding figure disappeared at once inside the cab. He wished he could direct it to an even better address, Berkeley Square, or Park Lane. But Bryanston Square (although not to be compared with Berkeley Square) was better than Clapham. He lit a cigar, held a handkerchief over his nose as the cab edged its way through the crowds. It was so unseasonably warm for the time of year, the smells were worse – surely by the very end of August a little respite could be expected. He had been dining with the men who wanted to build an underground railway. Charles Cooper was not convinced that there was enough money in it. His main loyalties at the moment were towards the Water Boards where he had much money invested: an underground railway could interfere with Water Board property. There were enough problems underneath the city, as he well knew. He had listened and barked with the businessmen as expected. But as the wine had flowed and the men's voices had risen, his thoughts were else-where. He went over again the Prime Minister's words about the epidemic.

Sir Charles Cooper had a daughter also. Bryanston Square was a stone's throw from Marylebone.

He would send her to Kent, to his brother's farm, until the danger from cholera had subsided. He could not bear it. But it must be done.

He pulled his watch from his waistcoat; in the darkness of the cab he could just make out that it was well after midnight, too late to arrange things tonight, no need to hurry home, although he could of course, even at this hour, talk to his daughter if he so desired. (But no, perhaps – not tonight.) He shifted uneasily inside the cab as a hundred visions kaleidoscoped across his mind: suddenly he abruptly knocked on the roof and told the driver to turn off and head for St Martin's Lane. Mrs Ballantyre's house, in a narrow street nearby, was free of cholera germs, he was sure of that, she had had the place cleaned and disinfected twice a day since the epidemic began; she had told him how she soaked her curtains in chloride of lime and her sanitary arrangements were better than many a finer house.

A whisky, and a girl, before bed. He stretched his legs in a kind of dull, automatic, physical anticipation. Mrs Ballantyre's girls were young. They knew the kind of thing that pleased him.

But as the horse trotted up along one side of the new Trafalgar Square and turned past the church it had to stop. A crowd had gathered from a narrow street nearby, halting the traffic. Above all the other noises of the city night he could hear a woman screaming over and over but there was nothing unusual in that, in this area.

'Pass on, pass on.' Sir Charles bent his head out and upwards to shout at the driver.

But the way was completely blocked and the driver was silent, staring at the commotion. A cart was collecting dead bodies. The woman who was screaming would not let the body of what seemed to be another, older, well-dressed woman go and her arms tried to hold the body back from the cart drivers; her skirt and the skirt of the dead woman were torn, dragged in the mud and the muck of the street. Through the gathered, murmuring people several other bodies were being carried from other doorways, wrapped in threadbare blankets or old pieces of clothing and passed up to the top of the cart and somewhere a child was crying as if its heart had broken.

Suddenly one body began to slide off the top of the pile; the crowd watched fascinated as it slid slowly downwards. A hand emerged from a shirt and seemed to move and for a moment there was total, mesmerised silence. Then one of the drivers snorted angrily and swore, jumped up on to the cart with the falling body and with his feet pushed the pile of bodies down. And the woman in the mud-stained skirt, tussling with the other driver, screamed again: *No, no, no!* Finally the driver on the top of the cart jumped down and kicked her. She fell to the ground, across the body of the older woman.

The Right Honourable Sir Charles Cooper pulled back into the darkness of the cab in shock. He had recognised the dead woman.

'Leave them, leave them,' shrieked another woman in the crowd whose shawl covered her nose and her face. 'They're only tarts.'

Another woman shouted at her, 'Could be you next, missus, whether y're a tart or not!'

As the last of the other corpses was piled on to the cart one of the nightmen pulled at the dead woman, the other pushed her screaming companion away from the body. With an impatient, upward heave they threw this last body on to the top of the pile, and the older driver kicked the other woman again for good measure as her cries became at last discordant and broken. Then he got on to the front of the cart with his companion and whipped his horses away through the milling, suddenly parting, people.

Someone was weeping harshly, big, jagged sobs. 'God have mercy,' someone muttered. Other voices joined in, low and resigned, as people moved at last. 'God have mercy on their souls.'

But out of the darkness a man's angry voice called, 'There ain't no God, you fools.'

'Pass on, pass on,' called Sir Charles Cooper hoarsely, once more directing the driver to the safety of Bryanston Square, and he found that he was sweating with fright. He passed his white handkerchief over his forehead several times in an effort to calm himself but he felt his heart beating too fast beneath his coat. He saw again, in disbelief, the body *of someone known to him* being roughly thrown up on to the cart: the torn, muddy skirt, no blanket even to give the body dignity. He knew very well that this woman had a fine house of her own as well as the house she ran off St Martin's Lane. Mrs Ballantyre had been, whatever her profession, a lady. And then he remembered where her fine house stood.

In Marylebone. Where, this week, the cholera had been found.

Actually, Sir Charles Cooper had two daughters.

In Bryanston Square his elder daughter, Mary Cooper, was reading, in bed, the new novel 'Vanity Fair', and laughing. She came to the end of a chapter, closed the book so she could savour the pages she had read. From somewhere she heard a clock strike, realised how late it was, turned down the lamp. She was entranced when someone described the human heart in a way that she understood, confirmed a world she knew. Part of her listened for the roll of carriage wheels as she lay smiling into the darkness. She knew their father was not home yet, and so lay between waking and sleeping: waiting. Her smile slowly disappeared as she came back to her own world: her sister would be waiting also.

Mary clasped her hands.

> Dearest Lord, help me. Help me, and guide me,
> in thy infinite goodness and wisdom and mercy,
> to care for everyone in this family.

She had the odd habit, when she was alone, of praying with her eyes open: in the hope that she might one day see God, and therefore his advice would be clearer. But all she could see tonight were the cornices on the ceiling, and the shadows everywhere: the shadow of her favourite picture on the wall, an engraving of the Mona Lisa; the shadows of the water jug and the washstand and the big mahogany wardrobe. These shadows she knew.

(*But in the spring something had happened, something had changed, in Bryanston Square and it lay there in the air of the house along with the smells and the sounds, unspoken but there in the air, another shadow, dark and waiting.*)

Mary stared at the ceiling and spoke again to God.

> Dearest Lord, who knowest all things.
> Please guide me.

At last she closed her eyes, and her thoughts drifted away from this house to the house she had lived in long ago. She was not sure if all women conjured up their mother when they were preparing for sleep: she was now a middle-aged woman herself, after all. But her path was precarious and her mother was the only guide she had: if she lost her memory of her mother she feared she would lose her way. When she was nine years old and particularly overcome with religion she had informed people most fervently that she was named after the Virgin. Her laughing mother had said to her, one day in the rose garden, that she would tell her a secret, which she must keep close to her heart. She had been named after a heroine, but she was a secret heroine. Her mother had named her not after the Virgin Mary, nor after any ancestors in her family with the name of Mary, but after a writer of the previous century called Mary who had thought a lot about women: Mary Wollstonecraft, whose books Mary would read when she was older.

Mary Cooper was a lot older now, almost thirty, and she had read the books, found them (out of print now) in a second-hand bookshop. Mary Wollstonecraft had defined the difficulties, certainly, but had not counselled for the unspoken.

It was harder and harder now, to see her mother in her mind. She could still hear, if she listened carefully, the rustle of the skirts and the birds that sang in the early morning in the rose garden. But Elizabeth Cooper's face had become indistinct, merged with the roses, and the other sisters, and the croquet on the grass on the warm summer afternoons.

Sometimes still though, if she listened very carefully, Mary heard her laughter.

In the next room Harriet Cooper also lay awake in the darkness. She was seventeen years old.

She listened, alert to every sound. And the clock on the table, ticking monotonously, was always there in the background, a dull, unvarying sound measuring the days. And the nights.

It was very late now: she heard a clock chime from the direction of Oxford Street, then she heard the nightcart clattering over the cobblestones in the mews. While their Aunt Julia was staying, just after the new water closet had been installed next to the dining room and unaccustomed water had flowed downwards, the old cesspit under this house had overflowed: a catastrophe of odour and discharging drains and questionable mud that nobody in

Bryanston Square, not even the ladies, could ignore, although naturally they pretended to do so. Workmen were called in, the ladies did not of course acquaint themselves with the details and took an extended trip to Brighton until the work was completed. The nightmen still came to the house in the night; what they did there in the darkness Harriet did not know.

Someone passed along the Square singing rather unsteadily:

> Be it ever so humble
> There's no place like home.

and then the voice faded into the distance. Harriet suddenly got up, went to the window and opened it, trying to find some breeze, some freshness in the still, warm night.

(*I am there*, Mary had said as she kissed her goodnight, *I am always there*.)

There was an oak tree in the Square. The tree was stunted, it was true, covered in specks of black soot, unable to reach properly upwards to clearer air, but an oak tree with green leaves in the middle of London nevertheless and Harriet thought of it as her own. Her room was the corner room; it looked out not only over the Square but also over the mews where the horses were kept and the grooms lived and the servants came and went: a bustling lane full of life and voices and the whinnying of horses and the sharp sound of their shoes on the cobblestones. The servants kept all the windows of the house fast shut almost always, to try to keep out the black dirt, and the eternal sounds, and the worst of the malodours of the city. But the black soot still found its way inside the windows, like the smells, and the sounds, of London. This was the only house Harriet remembered: she had known the sounds and the smells all her life, they were part of her. By these things she measured her days.

Early in the morning she would hear the clanking pails of the milk carriers from the farms and the calls of the costermongers on their way to Covent Garden. Then she would hear the servants going downstairs to light the fires and heat the water. (Lately, since she got back from Norfolk, it seemed there were always servants, everywhere in the dark, heavy house. She felt sometimes spied on, trapped; often now she would come across a footman, or a maid she had never seen before, just in the next bend of the staircase, just inside a door.) Then, after the servants, the horses would begin to pass by in the street, and the rumble of carriage wheels became louder, and all the morning clocks would chime and church bells would be rung. Before too long, in among the calls and the carriage wheels and the bells, a barrel organ would start up, or a violin: 'Home, Sweet Home' or 'Nearer My God to Thee' would be heard over and over again, wafting along from the corner, breaking off sometimes in the middle of a bar and then starting up again, faster and faster, driving many inhabitants of the Square to distraction. Then somebody would send a footman down to the street to shout, or to pay the musician to go somewhere else and play his tune. (Mary sometimes said, laughing, that the street musicians made their living not from playing but from *not* playing the music.) The Square would remain music-free until another music-maker set up somewhere, not far away. Sometimes it was a German band with tubas and cornets, playing a mixture of polkas and hymns.

And sometimes, in the early evening, a gull would cry over, surprising the city dwellers, reminding them that their river led to the sea.

And even with the windows tightly closed no-one could be unaware of the heavy smells of the street. Cesspits and drains and horse dung and smoke. And the outside smells mixed with the inside smells: of people, of chamber pots not yet emptied, of cigars and port, and the eternal, inescapable smell of meat being cooked in the basement that clung to the chairs and the hard sofas and lay hidden in the long, heavy curtains. Always the mixture of smells wafted upwards through the big, dark house, lingered in the curtains of Harriet's bedroom also and drifted across the pillows; it was in the coverlet as she knelt to say her prayers. Sometimes, in a kind of shame, Harriet would actually smell her own long hair, wondering if it too smelt of mutton and cigar smoke and something emanating from the drains. But her hair smelt of soap, and she would suppose that it was inside her nose that the smell lingered, that it was part of her.

Harriet Cooper stood now by her window in the night, tall and tense and thin. Tonight she had heard the new sound that everybody recognised. A bell rang as the cholera cart passed, with the dead bodies. For a moment Harriet knelt down beside her bed.

Almighty and Everlasting God, have mercy
on those who have died of the cholera.
Dear God, please have mercy on their souls
and bring them everlasting life.

Amen.

Approaching wheels could be heard in the Square: their father's
cab rolled up to the door, stopped, clattered off back to Oxford
Street. And then a door banged. And then there was a silence, as if
he was deciding something. And then Sir Charles Cooper came
right up the stairs of the house in Bryanston Square. Harriet Cooper
turned the gas lamp up as high as it would go, so that there was
light in her room.

She stiffened as his steps came nearer and nearer and then hesitated outside her room: adrenaline pumped into her legs and arms
and her heart beat hard against her ribcage. Outside her door there
was silence. (*But she knew that Mary too, just along the passage, would
be waiting for the next sound. I am always there, said Mary.*) Then after
a moment there was a knock and the door opened into the room
where the gas lamp shone.

He stood in the doorway, surprised at the light.

'You are still awake, Harriet?'

'Yes, Father.'

He closed the door and leant against it.

His younger daughter was not in bed, she was sitting very
upright on a chair, beside an unlit fire. She was in her nightdress
but had a shawl wrapped tightly about her. Her feet were bare. *She
was so beautiful.* (He saw again the body of Mrs Ballantyre being
thrown up on to the cart.) There was a long silence while he
regarded her from his hooded, blank eyes. She felt her heart pounding, she felt perspiration run down inside her nightdress, but she
remained quite still, unconsciously gripping the arms of the chair.

'What have you done today?'

She could smell the cigars, and the whisky. 'I have been reading,
Father.'

'I thought we had agreed that your reading should not take pref-
erence over your social duties which your Aunt Lydia has arranged
for you. You were to press some flowers for your album, I believe,
and inscribe their Latin names.'

'Yes, Father, I finished that.' *Damn it, she would not even look at him.* He wanted to shake her hard. He wanted to hold her. *I must hold her again before I send her away.* He moved towards her with a little, involuntary groan, whispering her name over and over, *Harriet, Harriet*; behind him the door opened gently.

'Good evening, Father,' said Mary. 'Have you had a very busy day? Is there anything I could get for you?'

The Right Honourable Sir Charles Cooper, MP, stood in the middle of the room, a daughter on either side. They could hear him breathing; but if he had listened for their breath he would have heard – almost nothing.

Time stopped, although all three of them heard the old clock ticking, there in Harriet's room.

Then he turned on his heel and left.

They heard him walk down the stairs again, to his own room on the floor below, where their brothers had rooms also. They heard him call for Peters, his man, who would bring him his very last whisky. Their ears strained, alert to every sound; at last they heard the door of their father's bedroom close in the distance. The sisters exchanged no words; swiftly at last Mary kissed her sister and went back to her own room.

In the night, Quintus the dog barked somewhere. Chasing the rats perhaps that congregated near the overflowing cesspits under the elegant houses in Bryanston Square.

It was their father's decree that breakfast was an early meal. They were all, of course, in the dining room next morning as always: the Right Honourable Sir Charles Cooper, MP; his two sons, Richard and Walter, his older daughter Mary. And Harriet. (And Quintus the dog, who knew how to keep out of trouble.) And the twelve servants, who always assembled for prayers. Sir Charles read from a small prayerbook, all said *Amen* and then breakfast was served around the long, formal table and Quintus sat somewhere between Mary and Harriet, under the table, waiting for donations.

Eating kidneys and bacon chops, Sir Charles observed his youngest daughter. His handsome, dangerous face was completely blank: his face never showed his feelings. *I must send her away.* Very slowly, aware, or unaware, Harriet buttered her toast. She never looked at him directly, not ever now, and his heart ached; obliquely she spoke, answered, acquiesced politely in whatever was discussed. Just sometimes he saw her face light up, become animated at something she and Mary were discussing. He would intervene and the light would go from her face and she would speak quietly again, nod in agreement with whatever was said

(*And all the time, something shimmered in the shadows, dark and waiting.*)

Sir Charles pushed away his plate, his face still expressionless, his thoughts agitated, knowing she must go. *I must send her away.* And who could know from which danger in the dark recesses of his mind he was sending her.

By the time Harriet was fifteen she had had several governesses, she could read aloud most pleasantly, she could play the piano delightfully, her handwriting was exquisite. However her father was perfectly well aware that she had, thanks to having a much older sister who was an unsuitable influence, read far too many books than was healthy for a young girl. He was therefore amenable that his sister Lydia, who had lived with them in London from time to time after his wife died, take charge of the fifteen-year-old's more essential education: the education of a young lady. Harriet had therefore been required to go with her Aunt Lydia to Norfolk, and then be placed, by her, in a recommended Academy for Young Ladies. When Harriet's letter, smuggled out of the Ladies' Academy, had arrived in London, begging her father to take her away, *I am learning nothing, Father, but lists*, Sir Charles had been furious, blamed Mary for putting ridiculous and unsuitable ideas into her younger sister's head. 'I want her a lady fit for my drawing room, not a bluestocking!' he had shouted at his oldest daughter and he had written sternly to Harriet, saying she must stay.

After almost two years under her aunt's watchful eye Harriet was returned to London, not as a pretty girl, but as an extraordinarily beautiful young woman. It was a strange beauty for the times, because something about the intensity of the face took away from what was normally considered beautiful: interfered with the serenity and placidity and quietness that were considered a woman's greatest assets. But something about the beautiful intensity was mesmerising, and unforgettable. Everybody commented on the change: her brothers were shy with her, her father inscrutable. Then Aunt Lydia insisted that she herself would stay in London to launch Harriet. Social calls were made, cards were left, all the things were done which young women of Harriet's age did, but from which the elder daughter, Mary, had on the whole (in the circumstances) been excused. Dinners and balls were attended and arranged: Harriet seemed to shimmer and gentlemen had secret bets that they could encircle her tiny waist in their hands. Mary was expected to dress in ballgowns and not to dance. Her brothers, who had their own activities in card rooms and other parlours, were expected to be in attendance. The idea that all his sister Lydia's activities would inevitably lead to – were for the express purpose of – marriage taunted Charles Cooper, haunted him. Every member of the family heaved, for different reasons perhaps, a sigh of relief when Aunt Lydia, her launching activities completed for the moment, returned to Norfolk in the spring. (*But then, in the spring, something had happened, something unspoken.*)

Mary limped over to the sideboard to fetch more milk, observing that the new maid had not seen that her father would want it; always Mary tried to keep the dining table calm; always she smiled. Mary Wollstonecraft had indeed defined the difficulties, but had not counselled for patriarchal dining tables.

Exasperatedly now her father said, 'You should not leave the table, the maid should do that, hurry up, hurry up,' and Mary patiently came to his side with the milk (motioning gently to the scurrying girl) then walked with her ungainly gait back to her place at the table, smiling calmly at everyone.

Her father looked away. *Deformed. Deformed. Deformed.* He never got over it, never. He had tried to insist that Mary be put away into some sort of asylum when they realised that the ugly, misshapen foot would never be normal: it was the only time in his married life that his wife Elizabeth had not deferred to his wishes. Elizabeth, the laughing Elizabeth, who never raised her voice, who ran his household smoothly, who brought money to the marriage (which he in turn had used to clever enough effect to obtain first profit, then a knighthood, then a seat in parliament), had turned into some sort of screaming madwoman that he did not recognise, she had threatened to kill herself and he had believed her. So the deformed Mary stayed at home and Elizabeth had become herself again: not once ever again was the matter referred to and sometimes Charles

Cooper wondered if he had only dreamed of the wild hair flying, the hands flailing at his body.

More births had transpired after the trauma of Mary's birth: he acquired two sons (and two more, stillborn) but in his heart he longed for one beautiful daughter. When Harriet was born and the midwife had come hurrying out calling for more basins and towels, he had gone into the room blank-faced, being told it was a girl, half-expecting another cripple. Two perfect, tiny feet filled him with an overwhelming, overpowering tenderness. Clumsily he tried to hold them in his hand, they were so small he feared they might break. He held the beautiful, perfect baby girl gently, fearfully, he had never before held a baby in his arms. He was stroking the perfect feet with one finger, when they came to tell him that his wife was dead.

His son, Richard, was trying to get his attention.

'The railway, sir. Will the underground railway go ahead?'

His father pushed back his chair. 'I have my doubts. I can see how they make it sound attractive, when the city is so crowded, but think of the problems! Think of the districts to be brought together, and then think of what is already under the city, think of railway lines hitting drains and sewers and gas pipes, is that what we want? They propose tunnelling under central London – do we actually require a railway under this very house? Think of the noise! And most of all think of the cost. I am a good speculator, as you know to your advantage, but I think money could be lost in this foolishness. I am supposed to report to the Prime Minister this afternoon. As if there weren't enough to do, running the country.' And then he stared at both of his sons. 'You work for one of the Water Companies, thanks to me. Ask them what they'd think of trains running over their pipelines. Harriet—' and she lifted her head slightly at the sound of her name, waiting yet not looking (*like a colt* he suddenly thought) '—you are to go to stay with your Uncle William until this epidemic is over, you will be safer there than in London, London is not safe.' (And he saw again the body of his old friend Mrs Ballantyre being thrown up into the nightcart and then he saw Harriet in her white nightgown and the two pictures rearranged themselves over and over in his mind.) He repeated the words more loudly than he needed to, 'London is not safe. I have already sent word of your arrival.'

Her quiet voice: 'With Mary?'

'Not with Mary,' he said, 'she is required here, obviously. The large carriage is ready, you will go this morning, one of the maids will accompany you on the journey.' He did not mean his voice to sound harsh. 'There is a wedding coming up in that family, is there not? That will amuse you.' *She must know how hard this was for him, how much he would miss her. He could not even bear to say goodbye.* He stood abruptly. 'You will write to me every day.' Then he formally kissed her cheek, the way he always did, and left the dining room. The two young men rose also.

'Goodbye, Harriet,' they said. Richard and Walter, who had once found all their world in their sisters, took their cue from their father these days: they largely ignored Mary (although she had brought them up and they were fond of her), were bemused by the new and beautiful Harriet. These days they were men of the world (because their father had arranged positions in it for both of them) and they had business to attend to.

The new maid, Lucy, having nervously cleared the dining room under the instruction of a footman, passed the door of the dark, wood-panelled drawing room; saw the two sisters arm in arm, leaning together, looking out of a window and over Bryanston Square. Their bodies rocked together almost imperceptibly, as if they were comforting each other.

TWO

'Now, my dear Harriet, you must tell us all about London. Not about the cholera, of course. Have you seen Her Majesty? Have you been to the Ballet? Did you know that Alice's wedding gown has come from London, for I insisted upon that. Tell us *everything.*'

Harriet's Aunt Lucretia sat on her brightly covered sofa surrounded by her daughters, Augusta, Alice the bride-to-be, and Asobel. Her husband and their two sons were still in the dining room with the port bottle. Augusta served tea in dainty floral cups that seemed to Harriet to match the floral sofa and the floral wallpaper, and Asobel, who was eight, stared at her London cousin with interest.

'We went to the Drury Lane Theatre when we were there last,' her aunt continued. 'Have you been there? The orchestra was magnificent; I felt the conductor improved Beethoven's Fifth Symphony immeasurably – shortened it, made it more to my taste somehow. And tell me have you heard – oh the delight of her – the Swedish Nightingale?'

'I was in Norfolk,' Harriet answered gravely.

'Ah yes of course, I had heard. For your education. Our two girls went to a Young Ladies' Academy for three months to have *their* education and I must say it was worth every penny. They have returned infinitely more ladylike. Their father said to me he hardly knows them with their genteel ways. Tell me, my dear, what did you learn?'

Harriet considered her answer for a moment. 'There were many lists and catechisms we had to learn by heart,' she said. 'About whalebone, and umbrellas, and what Queen Elizabeth the First thought about silk stockings.'

'Good heavens!' said Augusta. 'We learnt those things by heart too.'

'All very useful I am sure,' said Aunt Lucretia, 'but of course I meant the social side, the feminine skills.'

'We studied "Etiquette for the Ladies: Eighty Maxims in Dress, Manners and Accomplishment",' said Augusta.

'How to Carve, When to Wear Gloves, When to Pay Calls,' said Harriet dutifully.

'Exactly!' said Aunt Lucretia. 'Alice, show Harriet your album!'

Alice obediently showed Harriet the marbled album. Inside the other girls at the school had written suitable sentiments or verses, or made small drawings. A round childish hand had laboriously written:

> To my dearest Friend Alice
> Shall I compare THEE to a summer's day?

next to a pressed violet. And a teacher, a Miss Spence, had written some sort of quotation:

> Whatever may be the talents and energies of a woman
> they must be shaded by sweetness, veiled by
> modesty, or else much of what the eye looks for and the
> heart expects in woman, will be wanting.

The doors burst open and the gentlemen joined the ladies.

'Now, my dear Harriet,' said Uncle William, 'you must be tired after your long journey but shall we have a song before you retire?'

'Oh yes!' cried Asobel, clapping her hands and running to her father. 'A song with the piano. May I play, Papa? I have been practising!'

'Asobel!' said Aunt Lucretia.

'Asobel!' said Augusta.

'Asobel!' said Alice.

'How long is it since you were last here?' enquired Cousin John, bending over his cousin and taking her floral teacup. He knew very well it was three years, he had not by any means forgotten his cousin, but she had become extraordinarily beautiful. It quite threw him.

'It is three years, I believe,' said Harriet. 'Mary and I were with you in the summer then.'

'And Cousin Mary taught me to read and she has got a funny leg and cannot walk properly.'

'Asobel, it is time you went up to the nursery,' said Aunt Lucretia, ringing a bell beside her.

'Asobel, bring me my tea,' said her father, but his oldest daughter Augusta took the tea to him, put it on one of the tables beside his armchair, moved the bowl of wax fruit to one side.

'My dear Harriet,' said her uncle, 'have you been warned about the mad rooster?'

'I beg your pardon, Uncle William, I do not believe I have.'

'It is a magnificent specimen or we would have removed it long ago. But it appears to be deranged; it crows in the dead of night. Do not be alarmed.'

Harriet smiled shyly at her uncle. 'There are more alarming sounds, I think, in London. I will not be alarmed by a deranged rooster.'

'Well, well, my dear. London is a difficult place at the moment. We are glad to have you here with us.' There was a moment of silence. Harriet felt them all regarding her, knew she should say something; her uncle, seeing she seemed unable to speak, filled the space.

'Have you observed our new painting?' He indicated the very large gilt-framed painting of Augusta, Alice and Asobel that hung next to the painting of Queen Victoria. Harriet had indeed observed it. The painter had caught the girls' expressions; Augusta slightly supercilious, Alice vivacious, Asobel mischievous, but had made them all look nevertheless like cherubs: very pretty and rather plump.

'It is very – agreeable,' said Harriet shyly.

'Indeed it is,' said William with great affection. 'My own girls.' And he gave a large sigh. 'Soon our happy family is to be dispersed but—'

'Oh Papa,' cried Alice, and she ran to his side and knelt beside his chair, 'I am not going far, you will gain a son, not lose a daughter,' and she looked as if she would cry.

'There, there, my dear, I know, I know,' and he kissed her, and the blood rushed, unbidden, to Harriet's face. She saw how easy they were with each other and yet she felt her heart beating wildly.

'You will agree, Harriet, that the artist has painted my girls very well.'

'Indeed, Uncle William, they are – angelic.'

'Now where is our music for Harriet?' said her uncle, still holding Alice's hand.

'Come then, Augy,' said Cousin Edward. 'Harriet will have to endure us,' and he grinned at Harriet. Edward was their favourite cousin: he was rotund and earnest and kind, a younger version of his father. Edward had ridden to meet Harriet's carriage in the small town near the farm. She had recognised his stocky figure riding towards them in the distance, and as he got nearer his round, amiable face was wreathed in smiles of welcome.

'Do not call me Augy!' said Augusta to her brother but she got up dutifully and went to the piano and she and her younger brother began to sing one of the popular songs of the day:

> I dreamt that I dwelt in Marble Halls
> With vassals and serfs by my side
> And of all who assembled within those walls
> That I was the hope and the pride

and Alice sat prettily, still holding her father's hand, and Aunt Lucretia whispered loudly over the singing to tell Harriet all about Alice's intended, and the wedding dress.

*

Dear Father,

I am now arrived at Rusholme. Uncle William and Aunt Lucretia and the family are all well. They have made me very welcome and send their greetings to you.

> *Your obedient daughter*
> *Harriet Cooper*

Harriet sat at a small table by the window, reminded of her childhood, before the gas was connected at Bryanston Square, by the flickering shadows the candle threw on to the walls of the room as she dipped the pen into the ink bottle. There was no prospect of gas at Rusholme but Uncle William, who forbade so little, forbade paraffin lamps in the house, having seen a neighbour's house burn to the ground. In vain Aunt Lucretia spoke of 'progress', and 'civilisation', not to mention the dangers of candles also – but her daughters too preferred candles, hating the smell of paraffin in other houses. And so, all over Rusholme, soft candlelight flickered. The Right Honourable Sir Charles Cooper, MP, disliked immensely coming back to the country and the places of his childhood, but both Harriet and Mary, who had paid many visits here when they were younger, thought of Rusholme with a kind of exasperated pleasure: it was old-fashioned, it was inconvenient, there was an outside privy and lots of barking dogs. But Rusholme had a kind of unkempt charm that they loved. There were wild climbing roses at the front of the house and blackcurrant bushes grew in unchecked profusion everywhere and an ancient walnut tree stood outside the window. In order that Mary could get about more easily Uncle William had taught them to ride like their cousins: upright, side-saddle, elegant. Some years ago a gravel drive had been put in for the carriages and the horses, and Grecian statues had been placed on the lawns. But the drive had become somewhat overgrown, and the statues last seen were covered in moss and arms had fallen off, around which wandering hens sometimes pecked and cackled.

My darling Mary,

I am here, in the room we always have, the one that looks over the roses and the walnut tree and the fields in the distance. I cannot say how I feel being here except that you cannot imagine how much I miss you already. I find being parted from you so difficult, and yet, of course, I am glad to be here also. I tell myself every hour that you will at least be here for Alice's wedding, surely.

Our cousins John and Edward and Augusta and Alice and Asobel seem much the same except that Asobel is eight years old now, and is very 'energetic' (that is the word I have heard the family use several times this evening). Uncle William and Cousin

Edward are kind, just as they always were, and Aunt Lucretia has become rather grand.

These are only first impressions after not being here for three years.

Father must allow you to come to the wedding at least.

Please write to me and tell me that it will be so, and please look after yourself, my dearest sister. There is no point in me being safe from the cholera and you not.

God bless you, my dearest Mary, and keep you safe. I am writing this by candlelight and the shadows flicker on the walls as they did when I was little.

From your loving
Harriet

PS Give Quintus many loving pats from me. I hope he is getting plenty to eat without me there to spoil him.

*

'She is very – solemn – is she not? Do you think it is all part of her training to be a lady?'

'Now, my dear.' William Cooper always pulled off his own boots and was exerting a great deal of energy in this task. 'It is a long journey from London. The poor girl is probably exhausted.'

Lucretia Cooper, already lying flat in bed, adjusted her night-bonnet to be more comfortable, trying not to move her face muscles. Her face was covered in Rowlands Kalydor, whose claims she knew by heart: *it imparts a radiant bloom to the cheek; its capability of soothing irritations and removing cutaneous defects, discolorations and all unsightly appearance render it indispensable to every toilet*, and she had it on good authority that Queen Victoria lay in bed with her face smothered in Rowlands Kalydor also. 'I hope she does not think just because she has been made a lady in Norfolk by your sister that she is above her country relations. We are the gentry here. I hope she understands that.'

'My dear Lucretia.' The boots off, William padded about, looking for his nightshirt without his spectacles. 'She may be a little serious but she has turned into a – a rather beautiful young lady, no question about that. I expect Charles has plans for her. A good marriage. Ah—' alighting upon his nightshirt.

'William, please do not mention the word marriage. Every time I think of what has to be done before the wedding I am quite over-come. Alfred's family will be expecting so much and I have told you over and over again that we need more help in a matter of such vital importance as our joining with one of the most important families in the county. Yet your brother Sir Charles seems not to be coming, your sister Lydia says Norfolk is too far – how shall we look, family-less? And we should have double the amount of ser-vants, as I have often made clear to you – how you expect me to manage with only five, one of whom is busy with the horses most of the time and one of whom (I mean the new girl) is an obvious imbecile, I cannot imagine. And how do I know if the few servants we do possess understand everything that is required? I have sent an invitation, by coach, to Lady Kingdom. We must make plans for Augusta, William, and Lady Kingdom is the mother of the two most eligible young men in England. But what if she accepts and we are found wanting!' Again she adjusted her head. 'Harriet has become extremely attractive, I agree. Uncommonly, actually. But as I said: solemn. I do not approve of young girls being too solemn – I do not think it is good for them. I do not remember her as *solemn* and I do hope it is not a matter of feeling she has some advantage over us just because she comes from London. Do you suppose they teach that odd solemnity at some of the Ladies' Academies? Our own girls are not odd in that way, I am glad to say. Well. If we are led to believe that she thinks she somehow surpasses us in any way we shall soon make sure she understands that we have *friends* at *Court!*' But William was already asleep.

Harriet lay awake.

Her body, so used to being alert, tense, waiting for any sound, relaxed slightly.

She listened to the silence.

THREE

Dear Father,

   The September weather continues fine.

   Aunt Lucretia has great hopes for the wedding day.

   She of course hopes to see Mary here then, and so does Uncle
William.

   I have not yet met Alice's intended but he is the son of a
neighbouring landowner and Aunt Lucretia seems very pleased.

   I do hope you will allow Mary to come for the wedding.
Everybody here would be very pleased to see her.

Your obedient daughter

Harriet Cooper

My darling Mary,

   I miss you and think of you always. Mary, how did you educate
me, past what the governesses thought I should know? How did
you know where to start? I have begun giving Asobel lessons –
you taught her to read when we were here three years ago and now
she is eight – lessons of the kind you used to give me when I was
small, and find I am enjoying immensely having something to <u>do</u>
each day. It makes the days seem less long to have something
regular as part of them. It began because the family were finding

her 'energy' so exhausting And as the weather continues fine, and as there is a summerhouse at the end of the garden, we are able to work outside which is very enjoyable and I believe Asobel likes it too. I am teaching her to add and to multiply and to divide, and her favourite book is 'Robinson Crusoe', so off we go, Asobel and I, on our journeys to the wild islands every morning. And a book of English poetry, all our favourites, Shelley and Herrick. I try to find easy bits in 'The Rise and Fall of the Roman Empire'.

I talk to Asobel about many things, the way you talked to me. How lucky I am, my dearest sister, to have had you teach me, so that I can begin, at least, to teach someone else.

Surely Father will let you come to the wedding? Write and say you are coming soon. Cousin Edward asks me every day if you shall. Surely Father will agree to this one thing?

From your loving sister
Harriet

PS A hug for Quintus. Tell him I miss him too.
PPS There is a very mad rooster here. Nobody seems to know what to do about him. He crows only in the middle of the night!

*

In London Mary always spent part of each morning with the servants, arranging everything to her father's liking: the food, the flowers, the fire in the chill, dark drawing room summer and winter. Occasionally there was a social call to make or receive, but not many. Mary was, because of her foot, because she would never marry, often excused. Always she was at home ready to greet her brothers and her father on their return from their busy lives, always ready to attend to their wishes. Twice a week she took her father's smaller coach to St Paul's Church in Covent Garden, there with other worthy ladies to dispense goodness to the poor who crowded the church door on Tuesdays and Thursdays.

Once, Mary had lived for teaching Harriet.

Mary had just turned thirteen when her mother died. And the thirteen-year-old had grasped and understood something: that Elizabeth Cooper had, despite difficulties of which she never spoke, loved life: had been curious and humorous and gay. As well as educating her daughter as best she could, she had encouraged

Mary to laugh at things, to question things, to enjoy being alive and to thank God for the privilege. *Being a cripple did not matter.* And so, somewhere in the mind of the bereft little girl was the thought that it was her duty to pass these things on to the small bundle that lay wrapped in a beautiful shawl while the sisters and the servants wept, and the undertaker was called.

Sir Charles did not marry again. Instead he threw himself into his multifarious business activities as well as his parliamentary ones: doing deals, acquiring property, buying shares. Up and up the Victorian ladder: a strict, remote figure to his four children. He was especially harsh with Harriet, made her stand in front of him while he questioned her minutely. His four children, but especially Harriet, feared him excessively. Nurses and nannies passed through the big house they moved to in Bryanston Square. The boys were sent to school; Harriet was taught to sit very straight and to honour her father and brothers.

And there was Mary, dutiful Mary, who sat just as straight as Harriet, and had begun to run her father's house, as was expected of her. But, like a secret agent, dutiful crippled Mary infiltrated the nurses and the nannies and later the governesses. She encouraged Harriet to question things, as she had learnt from her mother. She read to Harriet from books that would have sent governesses into a dead faint. Through Mary's chaotic but earnest and joyful teaching Harriet became familiar with Mary Wollstonecraft as well as the Bible; John Stuart Mill as well as Instruction Manuals for Young Ladies; Dante, Dryden and Doctor Johnson. Copies of 'Punch' or the 'London Magazine' lay hidden under the cushions. Harriet learned from governesses that she must be ladylike but she had a second, secret education that was catholic, haphazard (and most unsuitable). Mary knew very well the danger: that because of the books they had managed to read, unchaperoned, in the musty, unused second-floor drawing room they had somehow glimpsed worlds that did not belong to them, yet the limitations of their actual lives faced them every day when their reading was over. Often they became bewildered, sometimes they would simply laugh – Mary would lean back on the hard horsehair sofa and say, 'I don't know, Harriet!' in answer to a question. 'But,' and her eyes would sparkle, 'aren't we lucky to have the chance to even think about it!' and sometimes the grim, dark hallways of the house in Bryanston Square would echo with their laughter.

And then it had been decided that Harriet must become a young lady.

Now most afternoons Mary would read. Her mind would fill with questions, and sometimes answers: she could often feel the energy of her thoughts wanting to break out of her head. And when the dark house was silent with that still, chill silence of an empty house with too many servants she would sometimes slip a shawl over her head and quietly go out through the mews and into the bustling London streets to try to release the energy that had built up inside her. Young ladies did not walk alone, but with a shawl and a limp Mary felt oddly safe, looked around with curiosity and familiarity and delight at London, her own city. People took no notice of her, would never have considered for a moment that she was the daughter of a member of Her Majesty's government. Almost always on these walks she visited her friend Mr Dawson of the Dawson Book Emporium, a second-hand bookshop in Oxford Street. They spoke with excitement of new books, and old; Mr Dawson lent her more books from both categories, discussed with her what she had been reading, tried to answer her questions. Sometimes he told her of the Working Men's Clubs where he taught, how the working men who had had no education were trying to rectify matters, and Mary began to understand that the world *would* change and that, one day, women too would be able to learn.

And then last week Mr Dawson had told her about the Ladies' College that had opened in Harley Street: Mr Dawson saw Mary's eyes, how they flashed fire to hear the news; and then how they darkened in unusual despair that she was not one of the lady students.

'Anyway,' she said to Mr Dawson, and he saw that she smiled wryly, trying to make light of it, 'I suppose I would be too old.'

Sometimes if her foot was particularly painful she would sit with her books in the big, silent house, alone for hours and hours. She would read and read: her books were her salvation. Sometimes Quintus the dog sat with her dutifully for a while, but he soon got bored and disappeared to explore under the house again.

This afternoon, listening to the slow, slow ticking of the clock, thinking of the Ladies' College in Harley Street, Mary wondered what would happen if she screamed.

Dear Father,

The preparations for the wedding are continuing. Will Mary be coming, Father? Everybody here is very much hoping to see her.

I offered to give a few lessons to Asobel, the youngest daughter; you will remember her, Father, she is now eight years old. I am so pleased to be doing something useful and I am enjoying it very much and I wondered, Father, if it were possible for me to perhaps do something like this when I come back to London. I like so much to feel useful, and I know there are young girls like Asobel in the families of some of our friends whom I could help. It is only a few very basic lessons. Also, they wish her to be a little more ladylike and think that I can impart some London manners. She seems not to have much to do and everyone else is so busy.

I am sure Mary is looking after you well. I do so hope, Father, that you will spare her for the wedding, everyone is hoping so much to see her.

> *Your obedient daughter*
> *Harriet Cooper*

My darling Mary,

Your letter came last night and with it the news that Father has said you may come to the wedding and at once my heart beats differently. Suddenly, what a lovely day it is today and I feel so happy. I am only half, without you. Hurry here, my darling, and stay as long as you can.

Oh, the dramas of this Wedding! The scenes at the dinner table! The chatter! And because we do not talk like this at home I find it so hard to join in, I am never sure what to say; all the laughter and arguments: 'That is ridiculous,' says Augusta, her favourite expression – imagine saying that at Bryanston Square! You will see when you get here that Aunt Lucretia is quite beside herself that the big local landowner's son has been snared, only the <u>youngest</u> son, but nevertheless . . . She is rushing about like a thing possessed arranging dressmakers and guest lists and *ordering the servants to do impossible things, you remember how she is. I thought the cook would have an apoplexy this morning (something about quail cooked inside chicken) and now the newest maid has actually run away (this was a very brave or a very foolhardy thing to do when any work, they say, is so hard to come by for the people in this neighbourhood). So you see it is not only the rooster that is deranged.*

There is much excitement about a marquee that is being put up behind the house. It is to be used for refreshments and, I believe, a band! Some local men have been employed to put this enormous thing up and it seems a difficult task. One cannot help noticing how thin most of the men are, they seem undernourished. Cousin John (you will remember he is predisposed towards portentousness) explained to me that unemployment in Kent is the highest in the country and the farm can get as many cheap labourers as are required at any time. I feel sorry for all the working men in Kent who will work for Cousin John when he inherits the farm, I fear he will not be kind and care for them and their well-being in the way a Squire should, in the way Uncle William does.

We continue our lessons in the summerhouse, I have persuaded Aunt Lucretia that a little fresh air will help Asobel to concentrate. As long as you are teaching her to be ladylike, says Aunt Lucretia distractedly(!) But I enjoy it so, truly, to be doing something useful and I plucked up my courage and asked Father if I might do something like this in London. I think it would change my life, to DO something. And always of course I think of how I could earn some money of our own. For that would give us freedom.

Yesterday I heard Aunt Lucretia berating one of the maids (the one who afterwards ran away) for allowing to be seen – not her own – the maid's – leg, but the leg of a table! 'Cover it! Cover it!' she cried, dreadfully shocked, and the poor girl had to pull a great white tablecloth down over the offending limb. For one amazed moment I thought she was covering the table legs because the latest fashion has decreed that they are rude, but it transpired that one of the legs was damaged; I believe nevertheless that long table-covers are part of our Aunt 's new grand style. When I went to my room I lay in bed and I had visions of all the chairs and tables coming out from under their heavy cloths at night and showing their ankles and dancing.

I send all my love to my dearest sister and cannot wait until I see her dear face. My love to our brothers also. And to that little rascal, Quintus, I miss him too.
            Harriet

PS Of course, being sent here so hurriedly I have not a suitable dress. Will you send or bring the primrose silk, for I expect that will be the most suitable. What shall you wear? I like your blue dress best.
PPS Is Walter still gambling at cards?

On Old Quebec Street, just where it runs into Oxford Street, a man and a woman stood beside a small handcart, handing out tracts headed 'Education For All' or 'The Betterment of Life for the Working Classes'. A woman with a shawl over her head limped nearer and smiled at the couple, took one of the pamphlets, began talking; over and over the dreaded word 'cholera' could be heard.

The following afternoon the couple, the limping woman, and several others could have been seen in Seven Dials, entering crowded alleys where the sun never shone, walking under lines of grey, wretched clothing that hung between the rotting houses; they passed wild, filthy children who fought over one marble in the excrement that lay everywhere and stared up at the gentlefolk who were trying to make their way through the broken cobble stones. By the standpipe a gentleman paid a penny several times for three buckets of water; the men carried the buckets into dark rooms, the ladies carried disinfectant and soap.

Down in the summerhouse Harriet read to her youngest cousin. Already Asobel had her favourites and asked again and again for 'the sleepyhead poem', and Harriet's voice, and the cadence of the lines, drifted out across the sunny morning.

Two of the local workmen brought in to raise the marquee were waiting for the arrival of some rope. They were reclining on a grassy bank in the sunshine; they had been discussing the abnormality of this Indian summer; when the voice that they could hear but not see began reading they stopped talking and listened.

Get up, sweet slug-a-bed, and see
The dew bespangling herb and tree!
Each flower has wept and bow'd towards the east
Above an hour since, yet you not drest!

'I am not a slug-a-bed, Harriet.' Asobel's voice was high and clear across the garden. 'I get up as soon as my eyes pop open.'

A whistle recalled the workmen to their duty: the rope had arrived.

Harriet and Asobel turned to 'The Life and Strange Adventures of Robinson Crusoe of York who lived Eight and Twenty Years Alone in an Uninhabited Island'. This was Asobel's favourite book, and the second time she had had it read to her; she directed Harriet to where they had reached the day before. 'The raft! Robinson Crusoe is building a raft. Please, Harriet, do hurry and begin.'

We had several spare yards and two or three large spars of wood, and a spare top-mast or two in the ship: I resolved to fall to work with them and I flung as many of them overboard as I could manage for their weight, tying every one with a rope, that they may not drive away. When this was done, I went down the ship's side, and pulling them to me, I tied them together at both ends, as well as I could, in the form of a raft, and laying two or three short pieces of plank upon their crossways I found I could walk upon it . . .

'Oh, he is very clever,' said Asobel, 'oh, I wish it could be me. I wish I could live on a desert island.'

'You may be lonely,' said Harriet.

'Why?'

'Well, he is the only person there.'

'Oh, do you not *know*?' said Asobel scornfully. 'He is going to have lots of pets – parrots and dogs and cats and a darling little goat kid, and then he will meet Man Friday.'

'Ah,' said Harriet, smiling, and read on.

But in the middle of the adventures Asobel began fidgeting and moving in her chair.

'I know it is hot but try and sit still, Asobel,' said Harriet. 'Ladies always sit still.'

'Why?'

'They just do. You read to me now.'

Asobel read slowly and carefully in her high, piping voice, every now and then asking for elucidation. Harriet could hear the birds in the trees outside and in the distance the men calling as they pulled up the marquee. Then she heard Asobel's skirts and petticoats again, scratching and catching on the wooden chair, and the little girl pulled at her bodice again and again as she read. Her tight little boots kept banging against her chair and her reading became more and more exasperated, and interspersed with sighs.

Finally she stopped reading and said, 'Harriet?'

'Yes, Asobel?'

'Harriet, can I ask you a question?'

'Of course.'

'You will not be angry?'

Harriet smiled at the little round earnest face looking up at her. 'I do not suppose I will be angry.'

'I am not meaning to be rude, or not like a lady.'

'What is it, Asobel?'

Asobel took a deep breath. 'Harriet, what is the water that runs down me?'

'What do you mean?' Harriet looked alarmed.

'See, you are angry. I thought you would be.'

'No, Asobel, I am not angry.' Harriet sat up even straighter.

'Harriet, I am so hot. My dress scratches, and my stockings and my petticoats. And water runs down me under my arms and sometimes past my waist. What is it?'

Harriet cleared her throat very slightly. 'Asobel, there are many things that ladies do not talk about. Not at all. Not ever. If I discuss this with you you must not discuss it elsewhere.'

'Even with Mamma?'

'Particularly with Mamma. She would say what I am saying: ladies do not talk about this. But what you mean is *perspiration*.'

'*Perspiration?*'

'Yes.'

'Is it dirty?'

Harriet cleared her throat slightly again. 'No, it is not dirty. It is perfectly natural. But it is just one of the things that happens when – when a person is hot. But ladies never, ever mention it, and you must not mention it again.'

'Do men have *persip – perspiration*? Or only ladies?'

'Everybody has it. But nobody, ever, talks about it.'

'I thought it meant I was sick.'

'Why?'

'Because it is – funny.' And Asobel wriggled slightly disconsolately in her chair in the summerhouse.

'Read on now, Asobel.' And Asobel sighed and then began to read again of the adventures. She had secretly decided that she was going to be a sailor when she grew up, not a lady.

Later two of the workmen passed near the summerhouse. They were hauling huge metal poles across the grass.

'Harriet, look!' Asobel whispered. 'They are – they are perspirationing.'

Harriet gave her such a warning look that Asobel at once sat demurely, her hands clasped in front of her as she had been taught.

But later the younger of the workmen who had been listening to the poetry, John Bowker, ventured past the summerhouse. There was nobody there: cushions and chairs and a table sat neatly and silently in the sunshine.

In London in the sunshine Mary, wearing a light shawl instead of a hat, limped her way to Hyde Park, crossing where the road had been cleared a little by a sweeper, giving him a penny and a smile; her skirts nevertheless caught excrement and leaves as she walked. She loved the Park, never tired of it, the green grass and all the trees – even though the miasma around the Serpentine drifted towards Oxford Street. A band played today as it did so often, jaunty tunes wafted on the afternoon air; fashionable coaches rattled by. A woman was selling ginger beer, Mary bought a twopenny glass, sat on one of the iron seats in the sunshine. She was tired: she had walked to Harley Street, had stood outside the Ladies' College.

She listened to the band; now they were playing a polka, the new craze, her fingers tapped in time to the music. She watched the fashionable and unfashionable passing by, and the ginger beer tingled on her lips. In a few days she would turn thirty. Half her life was perhaps over. If she did nothing now her life would stretch endlessly onwards through the other half, and nothing would change. For Harriet's sake she must always be near; nevertheless on her thirtieth birthday a difference must be made at last. And her thoughts turned again to the Ladies' College in Harley Street, her heart's dream. She closed her eyes in the warm sunshine.

Her mother had known that Mary's salvation was to be through reading books. Her eyes had sparkled with her plans for Mary's education: 'It will be my education too'; daily they had read and talked and planned for Mary, when she was nine, when she was ten, when she was eleven. And her mother told her of meeting an old, old lady of the most impeccable background, Lady Arabella Stockton, who had known Mary Wollstonecraft, known her trials and tribulations, but also her shocking ideas: her belief in the rights of women. She had met the old lady just before Mary was born: 'It was my first confinement and I was very frightened; after meeting Lady Stockton I prayed every evening and every morning to God, that he would grant me a girl, and I got you, my darling. When you were born I knew that what I might not have for myself I could give to you. And I called you Mary.' And so all that time, of the rose garden and the rustling skirts of the sisters and the echo of laughter everywhere, the mother and the daughter were conspiratorially reading and planning and questioning and laughing – you could teach! you could travel! you could write books! – and it mattered not one jot that she was a girl who would not marry, being a cripple.

Mary's attention was caught by a balloon in the sky above Hyde Park: people rode in these nowadays, waved through the hazy sunshine to the earthbound. She looked up in amazement as she always did, and waved back even though she imagined they could not see her. An elderly man in black was slowly walking by, but staring upwards also. Mary looked at him carefully; she had seen him several times, and she recognised him: it was the old Duke of Wellington, England's greatest hero. He lived nearby and often walked in the Park. He was all alone, still staring, as Mary had been, up into the sky at the balloon floating by and the people waving. And Mary thought that despite all his history, and all his battles, the Duke of Wellington seemed just as amazed as she.

All over London, people stared upwards, wondering what the world was coming to.

Next day the workman John Bowker watched, when he could, the comings and goings of the summerhouse. Suddenly Asobel was called urgently up to the house: the dressmaker had arrived.

John Bowker approached the summerhouse with his cap in his hand. He saw the young lady look up in surprise to see him there; she half-rose: he thought she looked frightened.

'Excuse me, miss,' he said gently. 'I don't mean to interrupt you, or alarm you.'

She sat down again, reassured perhaps by his voice, but said nothing and seemed ready to spring up again at any moment.

'I wanted to ask you to help me.' The words came out in a rush, seemed to surprise the young man as much as they surprised Harriet, but he hurried on. He tried not to notice how extraordinarily beautiful she was, close to. This was his chance, and nothing else mattered.

'I need to send some letters. I can read quite a bit, I went to a school for a little while but I can't write, I haven't used a pencil since I left school and the letters have to be neat-like, it wouldn't do if they was untidy.' But all the time, because he saw that he had alarmed her in some way, even in his enthusiasm and his nervousness he tried to speak quietly and he did not move from the door of the summerhouse. Harriet saw that his shoes were worn and his jacket looked as if it belonged to someone else and she could definitely smell him. But there was such earnestness and enthusiasm in his face that she felt herself relaxing. She still had not spoken but now she nodded, to show he might go on.

'I need to go away,' he said. 'You couldn't understand, miss, but there is no work for us here. I used to help on farms but the farms have got machines now, to do what we was used to doing. I was the best there was with a scythe but now they've got them threshing machines, even down here. I came back this late summer, I'd heard there might be work at the harvest but we wasn't needed. There's nothing here for us and so some of us want to have a new chance and go to a new country. We could start again, maybe even – they say it is so – own some land of our own,' she saw how his eyes lit up, 'build things for ourselves, make our lives begin again.' He forgot she was afraid, stepped into the summerhouse. 'There's new lives to be had in Canada and Australia and New Zealand, all these new places we've discovered, these new parts of Great Britain. We've heard that some of the countries are paying men like me, I mean offering to pay our fares if we work when we get there. What we've heard is they might pay for us to get on the boat and just sail away and start again, can you believe that? And we've heard that countries are giving free land, acres and acres where no-one has been. So we need to write to find out if they'll take us, people like us. I went up to the Church and asked the Vicar if he would help me but he didn't know me and asked me if I had family, and I said I had my mother and sisters and he said I should stay and look after them, but what use am I to them like this, without proper work? If I could go there – Canada maybe, it's a bit nearer than them other places – I could work and work. I wouldn't mind the work and then, when I'd made my way, they could come too.' His eyes shone. 'I've got all the addresses, me mates have already got them things, the Brochures. And one of them has got a handbill, it blew off a building in London and he brought it all the way down, walked with it, to show us.'

'Harriet, Harriet, Harriet!' Asobel came running down the lawn.

'Do not run, Asobel, ladies do not run!' Aunt Lucretia's voice floated down to the summerhouse.

John Bowker at once moved outside the summerhouse but he kept his eyes on Harriet.

'Bring the addresses tomorrow,' said Harriet.

Only for a moment did the little girl stare at the strange, shabby man touching his cap, turning away. 'Harriet, we are having peach dresses, what do you think, *peach* dresses, it's called peach but it's a sort of pink, well sort of like peaches.' She tumbled into the summerhouse in excitement.

'Sit down, Asobel,' Harriet said in her severest voice. 'Breathe in and out quietly until you are calm.' Then as Asobel's breath came slower at last, even though her cheeks were still as pink as peaches, Harriet smiled. 'Now tell me,' she said.

Asobel took one more deep breath and considered her words.

'Actually I am going to be rather beautiful,' she said.

'I think perhaps it is time for multiplication,' said Harriet.

*

Dear Father,

I have just received your letter and the copy of 'The Women of England: Their Social Duties & Domestic Habits', by Mrs Stickney Ellis, which you enclosed. I understand you to mean that young ladies do not work and that it would be quite unsuitable for me to think of working with other children.

Thank you for agreeing that Mary should come to the wedding.
The family here is so much looking forward to seeing her.
Your obedient daughter
Harriet Cooper

*

'What exactly do you want the letters to say?'

Asobel had gone, with much sighing and complaining, for her afternoon rest. The workmen had been dismissed because the marquee was ready but John Bowker had found Harriet in the summerhouse.

From his pocket he took the brochures he had spoken of, and a larger tattered notice which she guessed to be the treasured handbill: he handed it to her with immense care. She saw:

FREE PASSAGE
EMIGRATION TO CANADA
For Mechanics, Gardeners, Agricultural
Labourers, Domestic Servants
Of good character.

'I want you to tell all of them, all the countries that Britain owns, that I'm a hard-working, all-round agricultural labouring man of twenty and that I want to go to their beautiful country and work hard and make something of my life.' He looked uncertain. 'I thought I should say beautiful country to each of them, and it's not a lie, they are beautiful to me. And that I need my fare paying. And that I'll work like a nigger and be a credit to their beautiful country.' He had to step across to the table to hand her the brochures.

'Are you sure you want to leave England?' said Harriet shyly, not yet looking at the brochures. 'It is – it is very beautiful here also, where you live.'

'No, miss, it is beautiful where you are, not where we are. And anyway, it will still be English, Her Majesty is still the Queen after all. We own these new places.'

'Where do you live?'

'In Canterbury. Like I said, I walked down here because I heard there was work. But there was none – bar putting up this marquee for a couple of days. I'm staying just in the town here. With a friend.'

'I do not think you gave me your name.'

'John Bowker, miss. Twenty years old and hard-working.' He took a deep breath. 'Will you? Will you write these for me, miss?' He looked at her as if his life depended on it, was aware then that he was standing too close, that she had partly turned away, *I've been lifting them canvases this morning, I'm maybe none too clean*, and he moved back at once to the summerhouse door. He had taken the handbill back again. 'Then I'll go to London. Most of them offices are in the Strand. I'll take it to them. I'll go every day till they give me an answer.'

LAND AVAILABLE, said the brightly coloured brochures.

'Have you been to London?'

'We walked there, year before last, we'd heard about the work on the railways. But I wasn't used. I worked at Smithfield for a while, being a country man I had some skills. But not for long, it's a right brutal, disgusting place is Smithfield Market, I was becoming disgusting meself. I walked back again, to Canterbury.' Harriet stared at him. It had taken many hours to come here by her father's coach.

'Yes, of course I will write the letters,' she said at last. 'Shall you come tomorrow?'

'They've laid us off, miss. Could I come to the servants' door?'

Harriet thought for a moment. 'No, I shall walk to the town in the afternoon. I have done that several times. I could meet you by the clock. You will need to sign the letters yourself, can you do that? I could not sign them for you.'

'Course,' said John Bowker stoutly. 'I can write me name, of course I can. I'll wait by the clock tomorrow then. And – thank you, miss. You could change my life.'

'You change your own life, I think,' said Harriet. 'Sometimes other people help you.'

Neither of them had noticed Cousin John coming towards the summerhouse. He looked in amazement, and then anger, at John Bowker.

'What the devil d'you think you're doing here, bothering Miss Harriet? How dare you! Get out of here!' and, in the doorway of the summerhouse, John Cooper struck the other man across the shoulder. 'Get out of here at once!'

'John.' Harriet had risen, blushing. But John was still pushing at the workman, named John also. And Harriet saw that John Bowker began to raise his hand too, and then, with an incredible effort it seemed, he let it go. He said nothing as he turned and walked away across the grass, carrying his precious handbill. He did not run.

'My dear Harriet, whatever were you thinking of? You do not speak to the workmen.'

Harriet had pushed the brochures under some books. 'He – he only wanted to ask me something.'

'What? What did he have that he could ask you about?'

For a moment Harriet considered telling him the truth, which was so simple. And then she did not.

'The time, I think,' she said vaguely, picking up the books, putting the brochures inside them.

'Whatever would your father say? Or my father, for that matter? That is how a girl's reputation is quite ruined if anyone had seen you, Harriet.'

Harriet looked at him curiously, did not answer. He took her arm to lead her back to the house, at the same time firmly taking the pile of books from her. He thought, vaguely, that he might, one day, marry his cousin Harriet. She was extremely quiet, and obviously pliable. And beautiful. He glanced at her. She seemed in some way cast down. 'Never mind, Harriet, we shall say no more about it.' He did not notice that she shrank from his arm under hers as they walked up the lawn in the late-afternoon sunshine. Across the grass in the distance a gay marquee with lots of little flags waited silently, ready for the celebration.

That night Mrs Lucretia Cooper had, during dinner, an attack of neuralgia and an attack of the vapours, both at once: after the soup but before the mutton.

Around the polished oak dining table (covered right down to the legs, a white, stiff double damask tablecloth) the Cooper family had just begun dinner. William was standing, in the process of carving. The maid was just removing the soup plates when there was such a piercing cry from the far end of the table that the maid dropped a plate on Cousin John who sprang to his feet protesting angrily while at the same time looking at his mother in alarm. The screaming went on at the other end and everyone else spoke at once so that a great cacophony of sound rose to the candles in the chandelier.

William Cooper shouted, 'STOP!'

He hardly ever raised his voice, so that when he did everybody was so surprised they became silent immediately.

'What *is* it, Lucretia?'

She was now half-lying back in her chair with her napkin to the side of her face so that both Alice and Augusta rose to go to her. She did not answer her husband but sobbed.

'Mamma?'

'Mamma dearest?'

'What *is* it, my dear?' said William Cooper.

'It is the Wedding,' sobbed Aunt Lucretia at last. 'Things will never be ready, we will be shamed before the whole County, not to mention Sir Marmaduke Miller's family to whom we are to become joined in matrimony. What if Lady Kingdom should come, the mother of the most eligible young men in England? There will not be enough food. The gowns are not ready. I cannot manage, William, I cannot manage and my neuralgia is not to be borne and a cholera epidemic lurks in the bushes.'

Alice looked quite pale and distressed to hear all this but nevertheless with her sister Augusta patted her mother, telling her it would be all right, that the maid was bringing her laudanum, that there was almost no cholera in Kent and anyway only poor people got cholera.

'There have been poor people *here*!' cried Lucretia. 'Putting up the marquee. Leaving their germs. And the band – how do we know where the band has been?'

'But my dear, you engaged the band, it is the farmworkers' band, I pay for the trumpets, you said you heard them at the Church fete.'

'But I don't *know* them!'

Asobel observed her mother's display with interest, but quite dispassionately as if she was somebody else's mother altogether.

William Cooper, once he saw that the young women were in charge of his wife, continued to carve the mutton. The maid had, in the general disturbance, skipped providentially away from Cousin John who now mopped at his trousers absent-mindedly as he asked querulously down the table: 'It will all be all right, won't it, Augy, I mean everything will be in time and what not and so forth?'

'Of course it will, John,' answered Augusta. 'Do not be ridiculous.

Mamma is only tired and who is to blame her with so much to be done. And do not call me Augy.'

Alice suddenly burst into tears and had to be comforted by the others. The meal proceeded rather haphazardly and afterwards, seeing that Aunt Lucretia was about to have another attack and was mentioning cholera and bandsmen again, Harriet felt it best to excuse herself and go to her room.

She sat at her window, just the way she so often did at home. There was neither the all-pervading smell of meat nor the smell of the streets. Nor the bells of the midnight carts taking away the bodies. Here she could smell lavender and the grass and the roses. The cesspool to which the servants carried the waste was far down past the main garden; only occasionally did something unpleasant drift towards the house. She stared out across the farm. It was very beautiful in the fading light and there was the slightest chill to the air and she realised with surprise that it was, really, autumn. Bundles of hay leaned together, shadows in the distance. The poplars lining the long drive moved slightly in the small breeze, she heard a horse snort and stamp its feet from the stables and she gave a small sigh of pleasure as she again caught the scent of the last roses of the summer. But she knew it was not the scents nor the sounds nor the country shadows that calmed her of course but something else. *I am not afraid, here.*

She turned at last into her room and pulled out the brochures and read them carefully. Each place sounded like paradise: 'cheap land', 'temperate climate', 'all welcome', 'assisted passage'.

On the table there was a quill pen, some ink and sheets of paper, a seal, and a wax taper. She sat beside these and thought of what John Bowker had said, how he would walk to London with the letters. And then she began to write.

> *To the Agent for the Canada Company:*
> *Dear Sir,*
> *My name is John Bowker. I wish to present myself for your consideration as an assisted immigrant to your beautiful country. I am a fit, hard-working labourer of twenty years and am free to travel at any time. Please advise me if my journey is possible.*
> *I remain, Sir*
> *Yours faithfully*

She stared again at the Canadian brochure. All that space and freedom to begin a new life. Just for a moment she closed her eyes and saw herself and her sister, sitting on a Canadian mountain. Then she pulled herself together, drew another blank page towards her and wrote:

<u>To the Agent for the New Zealand Company:</u>
Dear Sir,
    My name is John Bowker . . .

When she had finished the letters for John Bowker who wanted to have a new life, she picked up the book her father had sent her, flicking from page to page.

> . . . the highest aim of this writer does not extend beyond the act of warning the women of England back to their domestic duties, in order that they may become better wives, more useful daughters, and mothers, who by their example shall bequeath a rich inheritance to those who follow in their steps . . . in her intercourse with man, it is impossible but that woman should feel her own inferiority; and it is right that it should be so. She does not meet him upon equal terms. Her part is to make sacrifices in order that his enjoyment may be enhanced.

Then for a long time she sat quite still. Afterwards with a supreme effort she picked up her pen and dipped it once more into the ink.

My dearest Mary,
    If I tell you I have been writing letters all evening you will wonder if my circle of friends has become somewhat enlarged. (Yes, I have written to Aunt Julia, TWICE!) But I have been doing a good deed for one of the workmen here who cannot write and who wishes to travel to a different country and start a new life. Cousin John hit this man for speaking to me in the summerhouse.
    But dearest Mary, imagine! Imagine if <u>we</u> were free to just decide to travel like that, to the other end of the world. The climates they say are temperate and a new life is to be had for

everyone. How we would laugh as the ship pulled away, to Canada say, with you and me on board. We will find gold. We will take Quintus, of course. (You will see I have got quite carried away by my charitable labours.)

It occurs to me as I write that the serving maid here (who tonight spilt soup on Cousin John's trousers while Aunt Lucretia was having hysterics), or indeed any of our maids at Bryanston Square, could go to any of the new countries. They would know what to do, they would obtain work, they would make their own living. But what should we do, you and I, who are only trained as 'help-meets'? Father sent me 'The Women of England: Their Social Duties & Domestic Habits': I knew in my heart that he would never let me be a governess, or do anything at all.

I have now met Alice's intended. He was here last night for a small musical evening. He is exactly as you would expect – but quite handsome and Alice is almost beside herself with joy and expectation. Alice sang 'Then You'll Remember Me' and then the intended (Mr Alfred Miller) sang 'Home Sweet Home'. Uncle William asked me to play the piano so I gave a feeling rendering of 'The Loreley Waltz' by Johann Strauss that everybody is whistling, and Uncle William wiped away a tear, a satisfactory evening all round as you can see.

And lastly but most importantly, tomorrow is your thirtieth birthday and I am not there to celebrate with you. The cholera seems very far away. I pray for you, my dearest sister, that you shall be happy and healthy for thirty years more, and that we may not be parted much longer.

Your loving sister
Harriet

PS And yesterday I learned something more from Asobel (who is of course the source of all my knowledge here!). Aunt Lucretia has a friend who is employed by the Royal household. In what capacity I do not know, a wardrobe mistress perhaps to the Queen from what Asobel spoke of. But she writes regularly to Aunt Lucretia about how things are done at Windsor and the like and of course that would explain the floral wallpaper and the wax fruit, which delights have not yet come to Bryanston Square in such profusion. And the very long tablecloths!

FOUR

In London, on the day of her thirtieth birthday, Mary Cooper asked to speak to her father's lawyer, Mr Frith. He was coming out of her father's study where he sometimes went over papers even though her father was at the Palace of Westminster.

She offered him tea in the drawing room; he placed his top hat in the hall.

'Ah,' said Mr Frith, 'this is an unexpected pleasure, Miss Cooper,' and he leaned back in the chair by the fire, his eyes watching Mary carefully, how she limped as she poured from the teapot into the china cups and brought the cup to his side, how ugly the limp made her, an old maid to her bones. Her father said that she spent her life reading books. How very much he disliked women who didn't fit in to the scheme of things.

'Mr Frith,' she said, without any preamble but with her warm smile, 'I am thirty years old. I know my mother wanted to make provision for me because of my disability. She wished part of her own inheritance to come to me, if I was unmarried, when I was thirty.'

Mr Frith smiled also. 'My dear Miss Cooper.' And then he sipped his tea for some moments before he went on and the summer fire spat in the grate. 'My dear Miss Cooper. Your father, as you know, became of course the arbiter of all your mother's money when they married and her money belongs to him. You have your dress allowance, and your pin money for your no doubt worthy charitable activities. Whatever else, if I may be so bold as to ask, would be the needs of a young lady like yourself, who has all her happiness provided by her father?' He sipped his tea again, still watching her carefully.

'I believe my mother thought it important for women who did not marry to have money of their own. It was my mother's wish, Mr Frith.'

Mr Frith smiled again. 'My dear Miss Cooper. Much water has passed under the proverbial bridge since the very sad day of your mother's demise. Your father, as I am sure you realise, has your best interests at heart at all times: I am sure you know and understand this. If you have any other little expenses, your father, I have no doubt, will provide. What is it, my dear, a new gown? A piece of pretty jewellery that has caught your eye? What can I arrange for you? Say the word.' And he smiled benevolently.

'Mr Frith, I do not want you to "arrange" for me in that way. I understood from my mother before she died that my father had agreed that the money was to come to me as it was unlikely that I would marry. That it was mine.'

Mr Frith put his cup down firmly on the small table beside the chair, and stood.

'Miss Cooper, if I may be blunt, nothing in the world is *yours.* Now I am, if you will excuse me, an extremely busy man. Your mother's money is safe where it is and wisely invested and I do not think you should be worrying your pretty little head about matters that do not concern you. Your father will always provide for you of course, and should anything happen to him your brothers will do the same. Your father, as I say, always has your interests at heart: only the other day he and I were reminded that you were about to turn thirty – indeed I believe the day is today and I do give you my very best wishes. Your duty, Miss Cooper, is to make your father happy, and he in return takes all the worries of the world from your weaker shoulders. That is how it will continue. Now if you will excuse me . . .' and he moved into the hall where the footman waited to hand him his hat.

'A final word, Miss Cooper. It is a well-known fact, my dear, that women's brains are smaller than men's and should never be troubled by manly things.'

Mary flushed on her thirtieth birthday, the footman smirked very slightly as he opened the front door, and Mr Frith disappeared into the grey, hazy afternoon.

Harriet picked up her bonnet and a small basket.

'I shall go for a walk,' she said to her aunt and Augusta and Alice, who were sitting in the drawing room with the curtains partly drawn, looking exhausted.

'Walk!' repeated Aunt Lucretia in amazement.

'Oh heavens!' said Alice.

'That is ridiculous,' said Augusta.

Needlework sat untouched; all three of them were wearing gloves, to keep their hands white.

'Unless of course there is something you wish me to do?' added Harriet hurriedly.

Her aunt gave a limpid wave. 'No, my dear.' The clock ticked loudly and Aunt Lucretia sighed, picked up a fan decorated with bright flowers and fanned herself languidly. 'We are only resting. Preparing ourselves for what is to come.' Then she remembered her duty. 'But I do not think a young girl should walk alone, it is not proper. We cannot spare one of the servants at the moment of course.'

'I shall not go far, Aunt Lucretia,' said Harriet.

'It is not proper,' repeated her aunt, but droopingly.

'May I go, may I go, may I go?' Asobel rushed into the room from nowhere with her own bonnet in her hand, ribbons trailing across the floor. 'Let me come too, Harriet!'

'Asobel!' said Aunt Lucretia.

'Asobel!' said Augusta.

'Asobel!' said Alice.

'Really Asobel, you are becoming more and more of a nuisance,' said her mother. 'It is too hot, you are not going with Harriet, you will lie down in the nursery and conserve your strength for the wedding day, or I shall not allow you to be a flowergirl at all. If Harriet means to be foolish that is her own business.' And Aunt Lucretia lay back in the sofa in the darkened room and closed her eyes.

The little girl stood at the front porch waving disconsolately as Harriet became a smaller and smaller figure in the distance. She sat down on the steps in the sunshine and dejectedly plaited the ribbons of her bonnet. The voices of her mother and her sisters floated out from the drawing room.

'I do not understand why Harriet is so *solemn*,' Lucretia complained. 'She used to be a perfectly pleasant little girl. It is as if she thinks she is better than us.'

Alice, too exhausted almost to speak as she lay among the cushions on the chaise longue, said, 'But she is pretty, isn't she? I expect she will easily find a husband.'

'As if that is everything,' said Augusta, who was hunched in the other corner of her mother's sofa.

'Augusta, do not sit like that, it will spoil your figure.'

'Actually, Augy, you know finding a husband *is* everything,' said Alice. 'You just say things like that because it is me who is getting married and not you.'

'That is ridiculous,' said Augusta and immediately burst into tears and threw herself against the back of the sofa, spoiling her figure even more.

'I shall go mad,' cried Lucretia Cooper, 'if you girls do not stop your endless bickering! As if we did not have enough trouble, and tomorrow her sister the cripple arriving; I am sure cripples are bad luck at weddings. Do you suppose there is some way we can ask Mary not to come?'

'Noooooo!' Asobel came running in from the porch. 'I love Mary. She taught me to read. I love her like I love Harriet. Please don't ask her not to come, Mamma, how can you be so horrible about her and Harriet and so cruel,' and she burst into tears and threw herself on her mother's lap.

'I have never heard that cripples are bad luck,' said Alice and burst into tears also.

Lucretia Cooper with a supreme effort of will pulled herself upright from the sofa and surveyed her weeping daughters. She gave a loud, large sigh. 'Girls, girls. We are all far too excited and overwrought. We shall order some wine, even though we are expecting no visitors,' and she rang the little bell on the table beside her. 'And some Madeira cake. It is my own fault and only because I am so exhausted. Of course we all love Mary and she is not really a cripple, she has a small limp only. And I do believe that Harriet is only quiet because she is shy. She has been extremely kind.' Asobel sat up, mollified, and her mother continued: 'Augusta dear, you must not cry, you want to look your best at the wedding and remember, Lady Kingdom may come and you have only two more days to prepare yourself to look beautiful. As you will, in your elegant new dress. Alice, it is not like you to be so unkind to Augusta, who has been immensely kind and generous and helpful to you in your good fortune and I am sure you regret such unkindness with all your heart.' And then she gave a little scream. 'Oh good heavens, Donald, you startled me, I didn't hear you come in. Where is our wine?' But the butler handed her first a letter from his tray. She opened it immediately, and gasped.

'Oh my dears, such good news. We must inform dear Harriet the minute she returns, she will be so pleased. A message to say Sir Charles will be accompanying dear Mary.' And Lucretia Cooper's demeanour suddenly improved visibly. 'My dears. It will do a great deal for our side to have the Right Honourable Sir Charles Cooper as one of the family, they must not think all is on their side.' She positively preened. 'Now where is Donald with the wine?'

Harriet passed the stables. Edward was trying to calm a dog whose leg had obviously been broken; the leg hung, useless, as the dog tried to crawl away. Edward made calming, crooning noises; one of the grooms arrived with some saplings, laid them down on the ground and then knelt beside the dog also, and held its head.

'Oh Edward! What has happened?'

'She got kicked by John's horse. I'm going to try and mend the leg, I can make a splint from one of these saplings. Keep out of the way Harriet, the dog will try to bite.' She moved away but saw Edward lift the dog gently, talking to it all the time; then he suddenly grabbed the leg and tried to straighten it; the dog screamed in pain, reared for the groom's face, its teeth bared. She heard Edward's calming voice, and the dog's cries, fainter, as she walked on into the shimmering afternoon.

She took the short cut to the town through her uncle's fields; in the distance her uncle and her cousin John walked with a horse in the sunshine. In each field the wheat stacks stood tidily together, except for one field that was still to be harvested. She skirted the golden, waving stalks so as not to damage them; her skirt caught in the brambles and the bushes of the hedges at the side of the fields.

In a little more than an hour she saw the high steeple of the church. The small town was bustling: it was market day. Voices shouted their wares: turkeys, rabbits, ducks' eggs, kaleidoscopes, lace, tin soldiers. A friend of her uncle's recognised her, bowed, raised his hat. Harriet smiled demurely, bowed also, did not stop. John Bowker was standing, as he had said, under the clock. It struck a quarter to three as she walked towards him. The moment he saw her he smiled in relief and removed his cap. She felt rather shy, decided she would return at once, lifted the cover of the basket and took out the letters and the brochures as she approached him.

'Good afternoon, miss.'

'Good afternoon, John Bowker. I have written the letters for you.' And she handed the bundle of papers to him.

In his enthusiasm to take the letters he took her gloved hand with them, felt her pull away, startled. He apologised at once, blushing slightly as he realised what he had done.

'I hope – I hope the letters will change your life as you wish,' and Harriet began to turn back the way she had come.

'Miss – Miss – *Harriet* – I heard Mr John use your name – Miss Harriet, have you got just a bit of a minute more to spare?'

Harriet looked puzzled. 'What do you mean?'

'My friend – he has a room just near here, he wants to travel too and he cannot write, please, Miss Harriet, it would take such a short time.'

She felt embarrassed, as if he should not have asked for more: he sensed this and blushed again.

'Miss Harriet, this is life and death for the likes of us, and a few minutes for you, else I wouldn't have bothered you.' He looked quite desperate. She half-looked about her.

'All right,' she said at last, but reluctantly. 'But only a moment.'

As if he understood at once that she might not like to walk with him, he moved slightly ahead of her, looking back now and then to see if she was following, holding his letters and his brochures carefully in front of him. Hens ran across her path and a huge cauliflower rolled out of a doorway. She avoided both of these impediments and the rabbit carcasses hanging from a nail and the blood that dripped from them and followed John Bowker round a corner and away from the main street down a narrow alley. Suddenly the streets were mean and dark, harder for the sun to penetrate. Doorways here looked darker and dirtier at once; the people who lounged in them made her feel uneasy and she wished she could go back. Backtracking down another narrow alley John Bowker slowed down and waited for her. Ahead of them stood several old hovels in need of much repair and what looked like a crumbling barn.

'It's just here, Miss Harriet.' And he whistled. A shock of red hair appeared at a small hole in the wall of the barn, disappeared again immediately. Then, the red-haired person appeared from one of the dark doorways, grinning.

'This is Miss Harriet,' said John. 'This is Seamus.'

Harriet nodded politely. But Seamus put out his hand and smiled and smiled and looked as if he might cry. Harriet extended her gloved hand.

'You came then, miss,' said Seamus. 'And we're the lucky ones, in the name of God we're that. Come in. Come in.'

He was Irish. She had been warned so often about the Irish rogues that had come to England after the failure of the crops in their own country; sometimes in a carriage she passed groups of men near where the new railways were being built, angry-looking and sullen and dangerous. Her heart beating very uncomfortably, Harriet was escorted through a doorway into the dark barn. She saw that there were puddles round the entrance but someone had put an old piece of wood down for her to walk across to where it was drier, further inside. There seemed to be shadowy people everywhere; she held her skirts up, kept passing people who leaned out of her way; she let out a muffled scream and almost lost her balance as something large ran past.

'It's only Porky,' said Seamus soothingly. 'Come in now, won't you, come in.'

There was a box in the corner of the dark space, and a stool. On the box were four cups and a teapot. 'Sit on the little stool now, will you, I'll just get the hot water,' said Seamus and he ran out of the barn again. Harriet sat gingerly and looked around, clearing her throat nervously. The only light came from the doorways, from the small hole whence Seamus's red hair had materialised, and chinks of daylight could be seen through cracks in the old walls, but in the gloom it was clear that there were many other people in the barn. Some sat on the ground, some leaned against the walls and suddenly there was a scurrying, scraping sound, as if *rats* busied themselves in dark corners. Harriet drew her petticoats around her in horror. Pieces of wood hung from the roof at odd angles and the walls appeared to be caving in slightly and there was a strong, unpleasant smell: from the walls, from the mud on the floor, from the people. There was a pile of filthy, mud-covered blankets in one corner. She had the strong feeling that the whole barn could fall down on top of her at any moment; it made her feel slightly dizzy. John Bowker stood by the doorway, still holding his letters so carefully, and nobody in the barn spoke but she could hear all sorts of different breathing sounds, and people sniffed and coughed without talking. She was terrified.

'Is Seamus a – a workman – like you?' she asked John Bowker in a high, nervous voice and the sound seemed to echo among the coughing and the breathing and the movement and the silence.

'No, no. He does all sorts of things. He's a navvy. He makes honey.'

He must have been able to see the surprise on Harriet's face. 'Not here of course. He came here because of his sister. He works as a navvy in London most of the summer, builds the railway lines. They came across from Ireland because of the famine. But what he really wants to do, see, he's got these fine bees in a hive and he reckons he could take them wherever we went and that honey would be in great demand.'

'Would there not – would there not be bees *there*, wherever you went?'

'He wants to take his hive. With the queen and that. To be sure of the finest honey. That's right, Rosie, isn't it?'

From the pile of blankets a tiny voice answered. 'Fine honey would be the thing, miss. That's what we was thinking. I'll be helpin' him, sure.'

Seamus bustled back with a jug of hot water. 'I been keeping this on the fire out the back for an hour or two,' he said. 'In case you could come. You'll have a cup of tea, miss?'

Harriet still stared in horror at the pile of dirty blankets where the voice had come from. She thought very quickly. 'If you would not mind I would rather not,' she said. 'But – but thank you.'

Seamus looked crestfallen for a moment, poured the water into the teapot nevertheless. 'What – what was it you wanted me to do?'

'Let me just give Rosie a cup of tea, and I've got her a little bit of quietness to go in it,' said Seamus.

'Quietness?'

But he seemed not to hear and he took one of the cups across to the blankets and bent down and murmured encouragingly to the small voice inside them.

'We want to go to Australia,' he said, returning to the box. 'Me and Rosie. That's my sister. When she's better. A whole new start where the weather's better for Rosie and where there's land for the asking. I can make honey and Rosie'll help me. She's such a fine worker, been a farmworker when there was work. Clearing stones. I should think there'll be a lot of clearing stones in Australia, what do you think, miss? I thought I might get myself taken as a thief,' he said, and he gave a little bright half-laugh but to Harriet it seemed full of sadness. 'But I might have made a mistake and got sent to Newgate, and I needed to be sure Rosie could come too. John here said you might be kind enough to write us a letter. You're sure then, are you, about the tea?' and again he looked disappointed at her refusal, stared at his little carefully prepared display of cups and the old teapot. 'Well, I've acquired the paper and the pen and the ink,' he continued after a moment, 'for I knew you'd not be carrying them, not expecting me and Rosie to be wanting your help as well. You'll write us the letter? Will you?' And again, when he stopped talking in his cheerful, engaging manner his face looked as if it would cry. 'Just one short letter, that's all we want. The Vicar won't help any of us, we've tried him, and we don't know who else to ask. And then John said he'd found you. Here now—' and he moved the teapot and the cups carefully on to the floor and from a corner produced the paper, '—here's the writables.'

Harriet felt as if all the other people in the room, all the snuffling and coughing and smelling people, were watching her. She flicked her eyes nervously across to the pile of blankets, then leant on the box where he'd placed the pen and ink and began to write as quickly as possible.

To the Agent of the Australia Company:
Dear Sir . . .

'I do not know your name.'
'Seamus Link.'

Dear Sir,
   My name is Seamus Link and I wish to present myself . . .

'And Rosie Link.'

. . . and my sister Rosie Link as assisted immigrants to your
beautiful country . . .

When she had finished writing, Harriet said, wanting desperately to go but fearing she had appeared rude when she had refused the precious tea, 'Do you really mean you will try to make honey?'

'Oh yes,' said Seamus, 'I've got my Queenie and my nucleus and my sweetened water and my pollen pod. All safe in a box, all waiting for the signal to go. Such sweet Irish honey we'll make them, will we not, my Rosie?'

There was no answer from the blankets and Harriet rose at last.

John Bowker walked her back across the piece of wood over the mud and into the air. She felt she had been holding her breath, breathed in now, gratefully, even though the alley was narrow and dirty and the people lounging stared without smiling. He led her back down the first alley and into the second one. Just before they reached the main street Harriet stopped.

'Thank you, John Bowker,' she said. 'I can manage from here.'

He understood at once and did not press to come any further. 'Thank you, Miss Harriet,' he said. 'If our lives change it will be because of you.'

'No,' she said to him again. 'We change our own lives.' But she had to ask him. 'Does Rosie have the cholera?'

John Bowker looked shocked. 'Is that what you thought?' He looked at her oddly. 'I wouldn't have taken you where someone has the cholera, miss,' he said sharply. 'I ain't that much of a fool.'

'But – she—'

'She was sick long before the cholera. She has a lump in her stomach. It eats her. There's almost nothing left of her. It's the cancer. They thought they had an aunt in Kent, they walked here when Rosie began to get ill. But they never found the aunt and then Rosie wasn't well enough to move again.'

'Oh. Oh – I am so sorry.'

'Me too, I'm sorry,' he said fiercely. He seemed then to be going to say something else but he did not, seemed to be somehow disappointed in her. He added formally, 'Thank you for helping us, miss. We are very grateful.'

'I am glad.' She could not quite leave. 'Was that – excuse me for asking – a *pig* in the barn with all the people?'

'That's Porky. He's our savings.'

'I beg your pardon?'

'He will pay for our expenses, when we sell him.'

'Oh. Oh yes, I see.' Still she stood there. 'Excuse me for asking questions but a lot of things were – new – to me. What's the – the – "quietness" he was giving to Rosie?'

'Oh, he meant the Godfrey's.'

'The Godfrey's?'

'The Godfrey's Cordial. It will help her to sleep. It's like poppy tea and that.' She tried not to look shocked.

'Will Seamus really *take* bees? All that way? Surely there will be bees in Australia?'

'He wants to take some of his hives. He says they're special bees.'

'On a ship?'

'On a ship. When Rosie dies. The doctor says it will be a very short time now.'

'But—' Harriet's face paled. 'He included her in the letter.'

'Of course. Do you think we would arrange all this around her without including her?' He still spoke stiffly, and it flashed through Harriet's mind that Rosie might have been his girl.

'I am so sorry. I must have seemed rude. I thought it was cholera. In London we think everything is cholera. I was – sent here – into Kent. To get away from it.'

His face softened again. 'If you don't mind me saying so, as we won't meet again – I'm thinking you're too beautiful and too rich for the cholera to get you, miss. It gets us lot, not you lot, and that's why we're going. Where it'll be more equal. Goodbye, Miss Harriet. We'll always remember you as our letter-writing—' he paused for a word, '—angel.' And he turned and went the way he had come, without looking back.

She walked quickly through the town and back along the dusty road to her uncle's wheatfields. She thought of her sister Mary, still in London where it wasn't safe, and was filled with such a longing to see her that her body actually shook as she passed the harvested bundles. When she got back to the house her aunt and her cousins were sitting looking more exhausted than when she left them. All three waved once more a limpid arm; they still wore their gloves.

'My dear!' said Aunt Lucretia. 'Such splendid news! Your father is coming down tomorrow also, and honouring us with his presence at the wedding!'

Down by the summerhouse Asobel was chasing butterflies with a small net.

FIVE

When the maid brought in the hot water next morning, placing it, with a smaller jug of cold water, by the basin on the washstand, Harriet was sitting by the open window. A pair of peacocks were running across the grass: a brown, neatly stepping peahen and a male with his bright feathers displayed for all the morning to see.

'Sun's still shining, miss. Only has to last till tomorrow and we'll all be happy.'

'Yes,' said Harriet.

Asobel, grasping her butterfly net by one hand and Harriet by the other, was waiting on the steps when the carriage at last arrived. As the black horses clip-clopped delicately along the overgrown drive Asobel felt her cousin's hand tighten on hers so much that it hurt. She did not cry out but looked up at Harriet's face. Asobel was only eight but recognised some urgent expression there that she had never seen on anyone's face before. And then her cousin let go of her hand and flew (it seemed to Asobel) down the steps and to the carriage door. The driver was already there; he helped Mary step heavily down and then Harriet threw her arms around her sister. For just a short moment they stood there, quite still, and Asobel did not understand the feeling of desolation that came over her. Then the two sisters moved away from the coach and Asobel saw her Uncle Charles, of whom she felt quite scared, alight also.

Her mother and her father and sisters and brothers had heard the coach and stood on the steps also, waiting to greet the guests, and Donald in his butler's uniform directed luggage.

'Harriet,' said the Right Honourable Sir Charles Cooper, MP. Asobel saw Harriet turn from Mary and give a small curtsey to her father, her eyes downwards. He stepped towards her and she stood very still as he held her shoulders and kissed her cheek.

Lucretia Cooper bustled forward. 'Charles, my dear, how good of you to make the time. You will add to the *lustre* of our happy occasion,' and the brothers shook hands, and the cousins bowed and bobbed and everyone was swept in through the doorway.

Asobel stayed silently by the coach, not looking at the doorway, biting her lip.

'Asobel,' Mary called.

'Asobel,' Harriet called.

The little girl turned and rushed up the steps. 'Hello, Cousin Mary,' she said, 'you taught me to read, how's your foot?'

'Hello, little Asobel, my foot is splendid. Won't you come and help us unpack? Harriet has told me what a fine reader you are now. I have brought you a present.'

Alice and Augusta still stood in the hall. They liked Mary, they greeted her pleasantly. But neither could help remembering what their mother had said about a cripple at a wedding.

But their younger brother Edward had no such qualms. He bounded over from speaking to his uncle and kissed Mary on the cheek, his eyes shining with pleasure. 'I say, Mary, this is a treat,' he said joyfully. 'Shall I carry you upstairs like I used to try to when I was a boy?'

Mary laughed. 'And dropped me, Edward, as I well remember! I can walk quite well, I just take a little longer. But I will meet you in the drawing room later, I have brought—' and she lowered her voice conspiratorially, '—the old chess set,' and Edward grinned. Mary and Edward had played chess together since they were children, when Edward had suddenly understood that his older cousin could not run and play like the others. They had both become experts. Chess was not really a game played by elegant women, it was rather too cerebral, as Mary was often told, but she smiled, and played, and won. Now Mary turned again to her cousins. 'Will you show me your wedding gowns?' she asked, and Alice and Asobel, and even Augusta (who had a particularly beautiful dress to compensate for not being the bride) squealed in delight and ran up the stairs. Harriet, as she always did, walked behind Mary as she leaned on the banister walking slowly upwards, Harriet asking questions, chattering, making her sister's slow journey seem entirely natural. Harriet looked back once, briefly: her father and her uncle had already disappeared into the study.

For the rest of the afternoon the polished brass doorknocker on the front door never stopped banging. Flowers arrived; Lucretia's sister and her family arrived from Nottingham and had to be revived after their long coach journey; the dressmaker arrived to make final adjustments to the wedding apparel. The Vicar arrived to have a final conversation with Alice about her duties as a wife, followed by a final conversation with her mother about the choir, accompanied by wine and Madeira cake. Outside the servants moved chairs and tables into the marquee, the band rehearsed 'Home, Sweet Home' and several of Strauss's waltzes, and Lucretia Cooper kept rushing out and looking at the sky.

Dinner was a huge affair with Sir Charles Cooper and Mary and the large family of Lucretia's sister. The nieces, exuberant girls from Nottingham, giggling and screeching despite their mother's protestations, were excited beyond redemption at the prospect of such a large and romantic event. Even during grace there was a ripple of heavy breathing and excitement in the air. Cousin John looked at the Nottingham girls sourly, he felt they were making far too much noise; looked then across at his other cousin Harriet, so quiet, so restrained and – yes, it was true – beautiful. He would look further into the matter of marrying her, when he was ready. Charles Cooper, handsome (Lucretia proudly observed) in his white cravat and dark, tight-fitting jacket, drank his brother's ale and remembered how much he hated the country; grimly observed his nephew staring at his daughter. Observed how beautiful his daughter looked, her face animated and open as she listened to her sister and reported something across the table to the small child.

Harriet felt her father's look. She did not look at him directly at all, but something left her face and she became quite still, her hands in her lap.

After the consommé of lobster and the fresh turbot William Cooper stood at the head of the table, holding his – already much replenished – glass. He welcomed the guests at some length and then proposed a toast to his daughter Alice who was – and he found a large handkerchief and blew his nose noisily – leaving the bosom of the family where things would never be quite the same again.

'Oh Papa!' cried Alice, much moved herself.

'Don't cry, Papa,' said Asobel sensibly. 'I'll still be here. And Augy and the boys.'

'Don't call me Augy!' hissed Augusta.

'Yes we'll still be here, sir,' said John, wishing to appear jovial in this company. 'You shan't get rid of us so easily as you did Alice.'

'You'll all marry and leave me,' said William Cooper, 'I shall simply be alone.' For just a split second, Harriet saw, he seemed to exchange glances with his younger son. But then the moment was gone and he looked dramatically and dolefully around the table, bringing out his handkerchief again, warming to his theme. 'You'll all leave and I shall remain here alone!' and then Lucretia began to cry also, saying, 'You have forgotten me, William. You have forgotten your Wife!'

'No-one must cry,' Asobel said quite crossly. 'This is a Happy Occasion.'

'Go and give your Mamma a kiss, and then me,' ordered William Cooper and Asobel ran round the table kissing as she was bid and everybody laughed and clapped and the toast to Alice proceeded in elderberry and dandelion wine, followed by partridge, mutton, beef, rabbit and four extremely large fruit pies covered in cream from Uncle William's own cows.

Both were in their long cambric nightdresses; the corsets and the gowns had been unlaced and put away. Mary had a shawl around her shoulders and the two sisters sat on the large, soft four-poster bed. The room was filled with the scent of the big yellow roses that Harriet had picked from the rambling garden. Automatically Harriet took Mary's twisted, damaged foot in her two hands, rubbed it gently.

'Well?'

'Well.' In the companionable silence they settled, relaxed; at last they were together again. Mary breathed in the scent of the roses, sighed, leant back on the pillows.

'Whenever I smell roses,' she said dreamily, 'there it comes again. I see our mother and her sisters playing croquet. All those blue muslin dresses with their big sleeves, and the hats with ribbons trailing.'

'That is exactly why I picked the roses,' said Harriet, and she was smiling. 'So that you would tell me again.'

'All that laughter, and the sun shining. It is actually a small part of my memory of her – yet it is the one that is always there, waiting for me. Mother was not even good at croquet!' And both the sisters laughed a little; Mary lay back on the bed, closed her eyes; Harriet, still massaging the foot, stared down at the face she loved more than any in the world.

After a few moments Mary opened her eyes. 'Oh I'm so glad to see you, darling, I have missed you so in London. But you look well, it is – good for you to be here.' And a tiny look of understanding flashed between the two sisters and was gone. 'And I have enjoyed your letters – I even read little bits to Walter and Richard, and we all remembered The Journal. Why not begin again, write as you used to? It was such fun to read, like Mother's.'

They still read their mother's youthful diaries, carefully preserved: all addressed TO THE DEAR READERS OF MY JOURNAL. The pages told of dancing in the Cremorne Gardens, seeing the Diorama Show in the Park; descriptions of dashing vicars and trips to Brighton with her sisters, and the Duke of Wellington's victories over the French.

Mary had encouraged Harriet to write the same kind of diary to entertain her brothers and sister: so stories appeared of a visit to the Museum when a small yelling boy got stuck in a big vase; of a visit to a Mesmerist when Aunt Lydia got so mesmerised she had to be revived with brandy; stories of a new puppy called Quintus who ate shoes. But at the Academy for Young Ladies in Norfolk Harriet had been shocked to find that her thoughts for THE DEAR READERS OF MY JOURNAL were seized, read, commented on, and destroyed by her governesses, in the name of propriety.

And then, of course, spring had come.

'No,' said Harriet shortly. 'I'm finished with journals. That is for children.'

Mary closed her eyes again. After a moment she said, 'Augusta has a beautiful gown but she does look so – dissatisfied. She is in a difficult position, being the eldest sister and unmarried – I suppose she is upset.'

Harriet shrugged. 'It matters to her so much. Asobel informed me once in the summerhouse that at first they were not going to let Alice marry until Augy did, but Aunt Lucretia was frightened they would lose such a catch as Mr Alfred Miller. And Asobel said to me quite seriously: "I suppose they think Alfred is a fish, Harriet."' Both sisters laughed again and Harriet's normally serious face changed completely, opened up, *like a flower*, Mary thought. *It is not lost then. I have been afraid she had forgotten about laughter.*

Up and down the deformed foot Harriet's hands smoothed and pressed gently. 'It is so swollen. Does it hurt badly?'

'It has come a long way,' said Mary dismissively. 'Has Augy a young man?'

'I do not believe so. I think Aunt Lucretia has had wistful hopes for years, as has every family with daughters, of the two eligible sons of the Kingdom family seat – but I understand that success has eluded them so far in that rather illustrious direction.'

'Good heavens, one hears of the Kingdom brothers in London! But that would be out of the question, surely?'

'Well, the country seat is nearby; perhaps proximity breeds hope. Aunt Lucretia has known Lady Kingdom for many years apparently, as has Father, they tell me, and the groom's family is acquainted also – I believe Lady Kingdom's presence is even hoped for tomorrow. But no sons, the sons are mostly in London.'

'Poor Augy.' And both sisters were quiet for a moment.

'Mary.' Harriet was looking down at Mary's foot but she did not see it. 'Mary, do you suppose the world is divided, not just into rich people and poor people, but into contented and discontented people, no matter what their position? Augusta has always seemed dissatisfied, even when she was a little girl. Do you think – is it possible – that it is something deep inside us, not the things that happen outside us, that is responsible for our – our demeanour? I do not—' Harriet hesitated very slightly, 'I do not speak of myself,' and a shadow flickered for a moment on her face, 'but of you. You have so many things in your life that might – that might make you much more dissatisfied than Augy. But when I bring you into my head, when I am thinking of you, I see you laughing at things and having a kind of joy.'

For a moment Mary was silent. She loved her younger sister so much but, since the spring, she seemed to have lost the art of comforting her. Mary knew she had, over the years, somehow passed on to Harriet (as well as the memory of the rustling skirts and the laughter in the rose garden) the kind of natural *joie de vivre* that the handsome, uniformed Charles Cooper, who had seemed to promise so much, had dimmed in his wife but not extinguished. Mary knew it was there, in Harriet.

'I think you have it too, darling, somewhere inside you, that joy of living. Our mother was like that, and we are our mother's daughters. It is just that—' and Mary's voice was suddenly low, '— oh darling, it is just that—'

Immediately Harriet's face went blank and she interrupted. 'Are Richard and Walter well?'

And Mary acknowledged the interruption with a tiny nod. They could not speak of what was always so heavily on their minds. 'As much as one can gather. Richard, poor boy, hardly acknowledges my existence so it is difficult to know how he is, exactly. He seems to be involved in a lot of business, like Father, but Richard gets harassed, I am not sure that he manages as well as Father hopes. And I know Walter is getting into trouble at the gaming tables, I have tried to talk to him, but he will not speak of it. I expect Father will have to deal with it, eventually. I think he feels a little gambling will make a man of Walter, but I fear it is more than a little.' Both girls fell silent.

'And the letters you have been writing for workmen?' asked Mary finally.

Harriet recounted to Mary her experiences in the barn at the back of the village. 'I was frightened.' Still her hands went backwards and forwards over her sister's foot. 'Are you shocked?' she asked, when she'd finished her story.

'At you? Or at the room?'

'I never saw anything like that before. Of course we see poor people all the time in London, you cannot not see them, but I think – I think my eyes slide over them somehow, so as not to see, not to have to think about their lives. But I had not, ever, been into a place before where they actually lived.' Harriet's face was very serious. 'Have you heard of Godfrey's Cordial?' she asked at last.

'Yes. It is treacle, and water, and spices, and opium.'

Harriet's eyes opened wide. 'How do you know that?'

Mary answered her obliquely. 'You know when I go on my walks round London, it is as if, because of my foot, people do not quite notice me, do not bother me. I always wear a shawl over my head, instead of a bonnet, and I think that makes people not see me, just as you say you do not see the poor. It is as if crippled people only exist in the lower classes: there is no such thing as a crippled lady. No, no – *do not* feel sorry for me,' (for she felt Harriet stir) 'I think I am *lucky*. You know very well,' and she tickled Harriet to make her smile, 'that I think I am lucky that I have managed to escape from much of the calling and the entertaining that young ladies like us are supposed to be involved with,' and Harriet made a face. 'At least we are only very minor young ladies,' Mary added wryly. 'Imagine what we would have to go through if we were *royal*! But,' and she sighed, 'I'm afraid Father hates to feel he is a minor gentleman. That is why of course he was so incensed at the idea of you becoming a governess.'

'I only wanted to *do* something,' Harriet flashed angrily.

'Father strives at all times to be a real gentleman. It is not enough just to be rich. A gentleman's daughter does not become a governess: governess is a rude word in the society he aspires to. It would reflect so badly on *him*. Likewise a gentleman's daughter does not have a real education, even if she is crippled and has no prospect of marriage. She will run his house: that is what she has been educated to do. An over-educated daughter would reflect badly on *him*.' There was a silence in the room: Harriet felt some sort of odd tension in her sister who she knew so well.

Mary moved her foot. 'Give me your hairbrush, Harriet.'

And Mary began to brush her sister's hair, as she had always done.

'But you haven't told me how you know about Godfrey's Cordial,' said Harriet.

'Well, it is just that when I walk I get to know people, and they tell me things. The draper's wife in Great Cumberland Place. The bookbinder in the same street – he has shown me the paste and the paper. And I often stop at the Oxford Street Apothecary and wave at him, not because I am ill but because I love the red and blue bottles in the windows and all the lozenges and powders and perfumes. And I took you once, remember? to see Mr Dawson, the second-hand bookseller in Oxford Street where I almost always stop. I love the smell in his shop, that wonderful smell of books. And lately – lately I have been – I have been elsewhere. I say to the servants that I must make a call on Lady Fitchings or Lady Murray. Sometimes I ask Peters to fetch me a hansom cab.'

'Peters is still there?' Harriet's voice was tinged with distaste. Peters was a new manservant their father had hired: both girls felt that he listened at doors.

'He's still there. There is no point in saying anything to Father, you know how he absolutely insists on hiring the servants himself. Although,' and Mary gave her quick, warm smile, 'one of them I do like, one of the maids, a young girl called Lucy. She is so keen and earnest and she polishes things that have already been polished but when I point this out to her she says she does it "for luck". She's very fond of Quintus.'

'Oh Quintus, I miss him so – how is Quintus?'

'He is still chasing rats. And Lucy sings to him!'

'*Sings* to Quintus?'

'She has a beautiful high, clear voice. I heard her singing to him that she dreamt she dwelt in marble halls with vassals and serfs by her side.'

Harriet laughed.

'And another time I heard her telling him about Spitalfields!'

'Was he interested?'

'Yes, he did seem to be so. He was wagging his tail and he appeared to be smiling. And Lucy can read a bit. She reads to him, very slowly.'

'What does she read?'

'Stories of suspense from penny journals: *And then just as darkness fell over the moors the Lord of the Manor appeared before her in the gloom . . .*'

'Does Quintus enjoy the stories?'

'He *loves* them, his ears prick up and he breathes heavily.'

Harriet giggled. 'And then what happened on the moors?'

'Just as the Lord of the Manor appeared it said *to be continued next week!*'

Laughter pealed out of the bedroom and along the hall.

'But darling, Peters. There is something so odd about Peters, the way he creeps about. You know, Harriet,' Mary stopped brushing, tapped her sister's shoulder to get her attention, 'the other day, just before morning prayers, I looked at the servants. They never stand in a group, quite. They stand apart from each other a little as if they do not quite like, or trust, each other. And for a moment, in their black and white uniforms, they reminded me of a chess set,' and Mary began to laugh again, 'the white starched aprons and caps and the black jackets of the footmen and the butlers, and Peters' white gloves. I would have liked to push them around a board, the new maids are the pawns, Peters is a thin, suspicious bishop *to be continued next week . . .*' As the laughter subsided she added, 'Father is the King, of course.'

'Where do you go in this hansom cab that Peters orders for you?'

Mary paused for just a moment before she answered, made several brushing strokes. 'I go to Seven Dials.'

There was a sudden, frightened silence in the room.

'No, Harriet darling, listen to me. The cholera epidemic is worse than we suppose. People like us can perhaps be of use.'

'Mary!' Harriet turned right round, looked at her sister. 'Have you been going into poor people's houses right where the cholera is found?' Her voice rose wildly in alarm, she saw again the hovel in the town and the small voice coming from the pile of blankets. 'Mary, how could you be so *foolish*, what are you thinking of? You could put yourself in danger,' and she threw her arms around her sister and held her, almost weeping. After a moment Mary gently disengaged herself, but still held her sister lightly.

'Dearest, you have only been away three weeks. I have only been twice.' She took a deep breath and went on. 'Harriet, it is not enough just to *be*. I cannot think that God has allowed us to come into his world just to *be*. We are the lucky ones—' she felt Harriet stiffen, '—I mean by that that we do not starve and suffer so, the way many people starve and suffer not a mile from Bryanston Square. It is money only that separates us. Our mother taught me – and perhaps I have not taught you well enough – that it is our duty to help people less fortunate than ourselves, to think of people other than ourselves. My darling, I would stifle if I had to live like Alice or Augusta. I have been extraordinarily lucky in some ways. But I must live my life and now, in some way, be *useful*.'

'What do you do?' said Harriet in a small voice.

'Simply taking chloride of lime into some of those dreadful, dreadful places is something – although it is hard to know if it is any use. Everything is so – so absolutely filthy, everything smells so poisonous. There are water standpipes in some of the alleys but they are only turned on for a few hours and it is a penny for three buckets and so often they cannot even afford that. It is shameful, *shameful*. No wonder people seem so worn down, so hopeless. Often I do not think they even take in what we are saying – I believe they think of us as intruders. But sometimes there is some-one who will listen, one of the women. Maybe it does a tiny piece of good.'

'But the cholera!' Harriet's voice rose again wildly. 'All those terrible smells, those odours, those diseases – they *cover* you, you could so easily be infected.'

Mary sighed. 'I was almost sick the first time I went, but I stopped myself. I would have been so ashamed to be sick because of the smell in someone's home. And we don't know that it is the smell of everything that carries the disease. Many people believe that it is the water, not the smells.'

'But how can you take that risk? How could you, at this time above all others? What if something happened to you? Yes, yes, I know I am thinking of myself too,' she said, her voice muffled in Mary's shoulder. 'But you are my life. I could not have gone on without you.'

'Ssssssh.' Mary rocked her sister for a moment and then gently pulled away and took her hand.

'Harriet, we take precautions of course. Some of the men who come are doctors – even though they are so busy some of them give half a day a week to be in these terrible places, and I am sure they are not foolish. I am thirty years old and so far all I have ever done is take some disinfectant and a few cakes of soap to poor people, that is all! I suppose it is a little more use perhaps than the gestures we make as Ladies of the Church. But I want to be properly *useful*. That is not only my duty, but what I believe in. I cannot believe that my life forever is to be looking after Father!'

'And the Godfrey's Cordial,' said Harriet finally.

'They give it to their babies to make them sleep, and who can blame them. If they give the babies enough, they are no longer hungry. If they give them a little more, sometimes the babies – do not wake.' She saw her sister's horrified face. 'We live in a different world, Harriet. But after all, Aunt Lucretia has her laudanum.' And Mary began the long, smooth brushing again, and for a while that was the only sound in the room.

And then there was a knock at the door. The knock they knew. They glanced quickly at each other. Mary saw the colour drain from her sister's face as the knock was repeated, more insistently.

'Come in,' said Mary pleasantly. As long as Mary was there Harriet would always be safe. This was their pact.

Their father stood in the doorway. They saw at once that he had been drinking. His handsome face was flushed and his cravat was undone.

'Harriet,' he said. 'Harriet.'

'I am just doing her hair for tomorrow,' said Mary calmly. 'She must look beautiful for the wedding.'

Silence. Just the sound of his breathing.

'Have you everything you need, Father?' said Mary.

The Right Honourable Sir Charles Cooper, MP, stood a moment longer in the doorway. Then he turned and left.

There was only silence now, in the bedroom that was scented with the open yellow roses. Harriet's face was pale and blank as she stared at nothing. Mary's face, unseen by Harriet, looked deeply troubled as she brushed the long, dark hair. *I have been responsible for Harriet, guided her life. But I do not know now what to do or who to turn to.*

Outside, mistaking the time, the mad rooster crowed. Two of the dogs barked briefly and were silent and the thatch on the roof stirred and settled. In the light from the candles the two women were caught for a moment in the mirror on the wall opposite, like a tableau. Harriet looked down, her face almost hidden. Mary's face in the mirror was unreadable.

But Mary was thinking that what Charles Cooper had never been able to destroy in his wife, he seemed almost to have killed, in the spring, in his youngest daughter.

SIX

At three o'clock in the morning a small but insistent rain suddenly became a downpour. Within an hour mud had formed along the driveway, through the stables, about the cesspools. Lucretia Cooper could be heard crying loudly. Servants ran along corridors. At five-thirty the rain stopped. At six o'clock the servants brought immense amounts of hot water to all the rooms, filled tin baths, brought jugs of cold water. Rays of sun appeared. In the stables the two grooms were cursing the mud that lay everywhere, brushing the horses, tying white ribbons in their manes. Servants ran from the kitchen to the dining room and back again, cursing their masters who of course wanted breakfast ('Kidneys on a wedding day!' the cook expostulated) before the wedding feast could be dealt with, and the dog with the splint on his leg, who should have been outside where he belonged, was happily making do with three legs and yelping and barking and getting in the way. Augusta and her mother, half-dressed themselves, were supervising Alice's hair and her voluminous petticoats and her wedding veil and her wedding posy and her state of mind, while Asobel ran from room to room in her peach flowergirl's dress, seemingly demented. At seven-fifteen Alice had hysterics and maids ran hither and thither for smelling salts and liquorish and laudanum drops. At eight o'clock the brothers William and Charles Cooper, with various sons and nieces and aunts, were still eating breakfast: the brothers discussed politics and ate kidneys while messages kept arriving for William that he was required by his wife; the visiting nieces ate toasted loaf, giggled and excused themselves. Mary and Harriet were dressed and downstairs, helping with great jugs of white flowers that were to be placed in every comer of the entrance hall. Seeing Asobel at one point about to end her life by leaping over the staircase in her stiff little petticoats and the starched, filled bodice that lay under her peach dress, they repaired with her to the summerhouse and the three recited

> Get up, sweet slug-a-bed, and see
> the dear bespangling herbs and tree!

and saw the uniformed bandsmen unpack their instruments from their cases in the morning sunshine, polish the trombones and the cornets with big red cloths; the first notes filled the garden rather unsteadily.

Somehow, just before ten o'clock, as some villagers wearing bonnets waited virtuously at the very back of the church to see the gowns, and some stood in knots by the churchyard to wave to the Squire and his family, all the Coopers had been transported to the church in the gleaming carriages by the white-beribboned horses. The church was full of guests (including, to Lucretia's delight, the illustrious and powerful Lady Kingdom of the eligible sons); the groom and his family were there as required at the altar; the vicar stood smiling in his white surplice, and finally Alice and her father walked down the aisle and Alice promised to love, honour, obey and give all her worldly goods to her husband.

In the end it was a perfect Indian summer day and long after the wedding feast and the toasts were concluded the sun still shone on the marquee, the little attached flags still fluttered in the breeze and the ladies sat in the shade and were brought more lemonade by the servants. Alice and her husband had departed for Ryde (where Lucretia hoped they might catch the eye of Her Majesty), deciding to do most of the journey on the railway (despite Lucretia's forebodings), and it was generally agreed (very many times) in the relaxed aftermath of the wedding that Alice had looked beautiful and that she and the groom made a delightful couple. The extremely magnificent Lady Kingdom, who had been accompanied by a large clerical gentleman (who Lucretia knowingly assured anyone who was interested was a distant Kingdom relation, and whom Asobel had gleefully dragged Harriet to observe as he staggered somewhat in the gentlemen's side-tent where alcoholic liquor was dispersed), had long since sailed away in her carriage, but not without looking sharply and somewhat patronisingly at the assorted young ladies through a rather terrifying lorgnette. The band in the marquee, hired till the last guests had taken their leave, was now repeating some of its repertoire: 'I Dreamt that I Dwelt in Marble Halls' and 'The Loreley Waltz' had been heard a number of times.

Harriet and Mary had at last taken off their bonnets and were sitting under the oak tree with their cousins John and Edward and Augusta and Asobel. Cousin John, flushed by the wedding and the wine, regarded his cousin Harriet and thought how beautiful she looked in her primrose gown and suddenly wished he might be going to Ryde also. He leaned back in his chair with his legs crossed, and looked slyly at Harriet, and imagined how it might be, in Ryde, as night fell. Asobel was exhausted and began winding herself around Harriet, not whining exactly but letting out a soft, plaintive humming.

'Asobel,' remonstrated Augusta irritably, but Harriet did not complain, rested Asobel against her knee, settled her comfortably. Then from the corner of her eye she saw her father walking towards the group.

'Your legs have gone all stiff, Harriet,' said Asobel in a tired, sing-song voice.

Cousin Edward, seeing his uncle, jumped up at once. 'Sit here, sir, sit here,' but Charles Cooper directed his attention to his daughters.

'I have received a message, I must return to London at once. Come along, Mary.'

And Mary, with a quick glance to Harriet, began to rise.

'Father.'

She so seldom addressed him directly that he was almost startled. 'What is it, Harriet?'

Harriet rose. Asobel, almost asleep, did not complain, but leaned with her arms around Harriet's skirts.

'Father, am I to be here for some time yet?'

'Of course. Until there is some sign that the epidemic is receding. Unfortunately such a sign has not yet been observed.' His voice was severe as he looked at his beautiful daughter. *Did she not understand what torture this was for him?*

'Father, may Mary stay?' She saw his face close. 'Just one more day?'

'Oh yes, Uncle Charles,' said Asobel sleepily. 'Just one more day. I haven't played with her properly yet and I love her.'

'Asobel!' said Augusta sharply.

'*Please*, Father.' Her oblique glance was gone, she focused on his face.

There was a pause.

'I expect I am needed at Bryanston Square,' said Mary, retying her bonnet.

Cousin Edward stepped towards his uncle. 'I have to come to London tomorrow on business, sir. I would be very pleased to escort Mary back to town.'

Charles Cooper saw that all the faces were turned towards him, that Harriet's eyes seemed to brim with something: tears, or anxiety. Or love?

'Very well,' he said, 'if Edward is to be travelling. Come, Harriet, I wish to speak to you before I leave.'

The cousins saw Harriet, who suddenly seemed to shimmer in the pale primrose dress, obediently lift Asobel away from her and step in silence across the lawn. Her father took her arm and drew his daughter close to him. They saw the father and daughter walk past the roses towards the waiting carriage while the band reprised a love ballad.

In the early evening Harriet and Mary and Augusta and Cousin Edward played cards. Asobel had been put, protesting loudly, to bed; Lucretia and William Cooper and various relations sat in combinations around the drawing room recounting the day yet again to themselves, gossiping about family matters. Cousin John was outside somewhere, smoking a cigar. Everybody was drinking negus, everybody was tired, but nobody wanted to end the perfect day and anyway it was not yet quite dark.

'It was a great success,' Lucretia repeated. 'At last we have entertained Lady Kingdom, and who can tell,' and she cast a significant glance at Augusta, 'what this may lead to.'

'Four hearts,' said Cousin Edward.

'My only worry is the railways. The stationmaster at one of the stations has been apprehended for embezzlement, parcels are being stolen from carriages, who knows who is in charge?'

'But my dear Lucretia,' her sister offered, 'Her Majesty after all recently travelled from the Highlands to Gosport, a journey of six hundred miles with only stops for the boiler to be replenished. Her Majesty was loud in her appreciation of such a journey. It is the modern way.'

'Five spades,' said Augusta.

'You are right, I expect. Her Majesty was indeed full of praise.'

'What are you doing in London tomorrow, Edward?' asked Mary idly.

'Avoiding the cholera, I hope, Eddie,' said Augusta sharply. 'I do wish you would not go.'

'Come, Augy, I shall be home before you miss me.'

'Please take enormous care.'

'I will, I will, dear Augy,' Edward answered and for once she did not say: 'Do not call me Augy' or 'That is ridiculous' and Harriet, who had hardly spoken since her father left, saw how Edward smiled at his sister, and she at him. *They are fond of each other*, she thought to herself in surprise. When she was younger, and often alone with her brothers and with Mary, writing TO THE DEAR READERS OF MY JOURNAL to entertain them, there had been warmth and teasing among them, but now, older, her brothers seemed to become more and more like their father, and older sibling relationships remained a mystery. Over the cards she saw that Augusta's face still wore the supercilious expression that seemed to have become part of her, but she looked drawn too, as if this wedding of a sister who was younger had been even more of a trial than they had guessed. Harriet with an effort put her own, darker thoughts away; she smiled at her cousin.

'I like so much your gown, Augusta,' she said. 'You looked lovely today.' And was surprised again: her cousin blushed at the unexpected compliment, then her eyes filled with involuntary tears, then in great embarrassment she put her hand up to her face and gave a half-stifled sob. Her brother and her two cousins all leaned towards her across the card table, as if to shield her from the rest of the room.

'Don't, Augy,' said Edward quietly. 'We all understand.'

'Stop!' hissed Augusta in despair, and it seemed that she was going to burst into tears completely at this mortifying invasion of her privacy but somehow with a supreme effort she regained her composure. The card game continued all this time and the older people went on congratulating themselves on the success of the wedding.

Edward said suddenly, 'It is not quite dark. Will you all come outside with me. I want to show you something.' The three women, surprised, obediently got up from the table, picked up their shawls from the back of the chairs.

'Are you going to bed already, my dears?' said Lucretia.

'No, Mamma. We are just going to get a breath of air,' called Edward as he led the three women outside. Lucretia's voice echoed after them, '*Such* a success, such a *success*!'

Edward led them, slowly so that Mary could keep pace, past the summerhouse and into the further fields. The chill in the air was notable now and the girls pulled their shawls tightly around them.

'Autumn. It is really autumn,' said Mary, gazing about her in wonder at the difference from London. All the wheat was harvested now; the neat sheaves leaned against each other, strange embracing patterns in the dusk, and a bright full moon shone down, lighted their way. They had to cross a stile; Edward helped Mary who stumbled against the step, the other girls lifted all their petticoats and climbed over and into another field.

'Here we are then,' said Edward. In one corner of the field a clearing had been made. A small, strange edifice stood before them. They all stared.

'It's a bit dark,' said Edward, 'but you can get the idea. What do you think?'

'It looks like a room, with a roof on,' said Augusta dubiously.

'Bravo, Augy! It *is* a room with a roof on! Look, you can walk in,' and he took them round to the other side where a door swung open.

'But what *is* it?' asked Harriet. Mary, who was still breathing heavily from her exertions over the stile and was leaning on her sister's arm, said, 'Have you built yourself a house, Edward?'

'Yes! Look, look!' Inside the house was a candle which he lit and they saw he'd made a small bed and a table, but at that moment a fieldmouse, disturbed, scurried under their feet and the girls screamed. Edward seemed exasperated at their silliness. 'No, but *look*!' He led them outside again: they held their petticoats and looked for more mice. Edward had acquired an old kettle, it stood on some iron bars with small pieces of wood underneath. Edward cleared his throat proudly. 'I made everything myself.'

He made them come and sit inside the room. The three girls sat very uncomfortably together on the wooden bed, squashing against one another in their wedding gowns. Edward sat on the table beside the candle, shadows flickered across his face. With the best will in the world none of the three girls quite knew what to say. They couldn't imagine what Edward meant by showing them this. The candlelight threw strange shapes on to the roof.

'Are you leaving home, Edward?' enquired Harriet finally.

'*Yes!*' cried Edward.

'But Eddie, that is ridiculous, why *on earth* would you want to live here?' Augusta looked around her disbelievingly. 'You are so comfortable at home.' She pulled her shawl more firmly about her, looked around again.

'No, no, I won't live here! I've just been practising. I'm going to Canada.'

Harriet's head snapped round to regard him. 'Why is everyone going to Canada?' she asked, puzzled.

'There's no *work* for us,' said Edward.

'But – you have the farm,' said Augusta and her voice sounded suddenly fearful.

'John has the farm. You and Asobel need income from the farm. None of us has got a proper job of work, none of my friends. It's all right for Richard and Walter,' naming Harriet's and Mary's brothers, 'Uncle Charles has got them positions with the Water Boards, because he is an influential man. But it's London where everything happens, not here.'

'Perhaps Father could get you a position also,' said Mary.

'I don't want to work for the Water Boards. What ever would I do? I would require them to clean the Thames, for a start. I considered going to California where the gold has appeared but I fear it is a dangerous, reckless life and I am not, perhaps, a very reckless person. But I know about land, and working the land, a little anyway, and these colonies are promising good land to people like us, they want us there. That's why I'm going to London tomorrow, to visit the Canada Company, and the Colonial Land and Emigration Commission, see if they'll have me. And so—' and he gestured towards the walls and the roof of his little building, 'I thought I would teach myself to build a house, in case I have to later. Some of the lads in the village do building work. They gave me advice. About how to join bits together. See?' And he took up the candle and showed where the roof met one of the walls. 'I came down here this morning after the rain stopped and it was almost completely dry in here.' And in the candlelight they saw a big smile on his face as he studied his handiwork.

'Well?' he said, turning back to them at last.

'Yes!' said Harriet and Mary almost simultaneously.

'But Edward. I will miss you so and I will never see you again.' And Augusta burst into the tears that had lain behind her eyes all day. She sobbed and sobbed, apologising. Mary put her arm around her on the small cramped bed.

'Don't cry, Augusta. It was a lovely day. It will come for you too. And Canada isn't so far away these days, lots of people are going there and making a new start.'

And Edward said: 'You could come to Canada too, Augy.'

Augusta's sobs hiccoughed at last to a surprised halt. 'Whatever do you mean?'

'There must be hundreds of men like me travelling to somewhere else to get away from here. They won't be the boring chaps, the settled chaps, like Alice has acquired. They'll be more like me.'

Augusta gave a half-laugh.

'But it's *true*, Augy. I was thinking about it in the church today. Lots of men like me. Full of energy and plans.' He waved his arms about in enthusiasm, throwing more strange shadows on the walls. 'And when we have established ourselves, bought our land, built our houses, we shall all want wives, shan't we? Lots and lots of energetic and extremely handsome chaps like me,' and all three girls laughed. Edward had so many good qualities but he was not, exactly, handsome.

'Does Papa know? Will he give you money?'

'To start me off? Of course. He wants to help me.' And Harriet at once remembered the look at the dinner table that she'd seen pass between father and son. 'He remembers the trouble he and Uncle Charles had about the farm before Uncle Charles got married.' It was Uncle William who had told the girls the story when they came to stay three years ago: their father, Charles, was the younger son and there were some dreadful months – after the war, after Napoleon had been trounced at last by the Iron Duke, before he met his future wife and her fortune – when it seemed as if the dashing, still uniformed Charles Cooper might have to become a clergyman.

'I need money to start off,' Edward went on, 'it would be too difficult otherwise.' (And Harriet thought of John Bowker and Seamus and Rosie and the pig that represented their savings.) 'Father knows I am going to London about all this tomorrow. I was just waiting until Alice was safely married. And who knows? I may make my fortune and all the family could join me.'

'Harriet! Edward! Where are you?' Cousin John's voice called them from far across the fields.

'Well. You have seen it now anyway,' said Edward proudly. 'We had better go back.' The girls stood up from their cramped seat. Edward saw them safely into the field and then blew out the candle and shut the door of his little house behind him.

They all adjusted their eyes to the night; the moon shone brightly. Edward took Mary's arm and helped her back over the stile.

'Harriet! Edward!' John's voice sounded angry, and in the distance they saw the light of a lantern moving in the darkness.

Augusta giggled. 'He has his eye on you, Harriet. He thinks you're in the summerhouse with Edward!'

'I am his cousin!' said Harriet angrily. 'Both of you.' She sounded upset, her sister caught her tone.

'Come,' said Mary. 'Let the four of us link arms, if you do not mind going slowly, and we will present a united front.' And as the four young people strolled across the last, ploughed field before the house and the garden Mary said to Edward, 'I think it is a wonderful idea. A whole new country,' and Augusta said, 'Did you mean it, Eddie, about me coming – but Mamma and Papa would never allow me to go.'

'One step at a time,' said Edward.

And Harriet remembered for the rest of her life her sister Mary, who could not dance, suddenly half-waltzing with her crippled foot as she held the arms of the others. She sang *one step at a time* and the others joined in. So that Cousin John's jealous lantern heard them before he saw the shadows of all four of them come into view. They sang *one step at a time* to the tune of Johann Strauss's 'The Loreley Waltz' that was all the rage, that summer of the cholera.

In their bedroom, Harriet again took Mary's foot in her hand. It was ugly, but Harriet did not ever think it so: it was her sister's foot, that was all. 'Your foot is so swollen, Mary.'

'Never mind, darling. It was worth it. Oh – it was a lovely day, everything. The family are right to be so pleased. And imagine, we walked to Edward's little house in the moonlight, it was like going to Canada already! We can never walk like that in the night in London, it would not be safe, of course.'

Harriet held the twisted foot that had tried to waltz, rubbed it gently.

'It is so strange to me, to see a family,' she said slowly, almost dreamily, 'where people talk to each other and like each other and do things together. Were we *ever* like that?' And then with a great effort she said, 'Were you like that when you were young, before I was born – like a happy family – you and Walter and Richard and Mother and – Father?'

Mary did not answer for a long time and in the darkness they heard the rooster crowing. The dogs barked briefly in reply and in the distance some sheep called at the full, bright moon.

At last Mary said, 'A little, I think. We had lots of wonderful times with Mother, of course . . . Mother and all her sisters,' and Mary gave a small sigh, 'well, I have told you about that, so often. I suppose in a way I am not surprised Father would not see the sisters afterwards. They were too much like her. For so long I asked for them, I missed them so, but they never came. He would not allow it. But when Mother and Father were together it was – it was always pleasant, Mother made everything pleasant, but – but it was never like it is here at Rusholme.' Mary chose her words carefully. 'I think Father was always – a difficult man.'

Harriet seemed to look down at the foot in her hand but she did not see it. Very abruptly she said, 'Why did she marry him?'

'Harriet, how can we know those things? She never, never spoke of it. She spoke to me of many things even though I was so young, but never that. She never criticised him. Perhaps her parents arranged the match because he seemed so – energetic, he must have seemed to be a new and coming man, all that energy and ambition. Perhaps – perhaps she loved him.'

Harriet's voice was suddenly so low Mary hardly heard her. 'Do you suppose, ever, ever, we could go?'

'Go?'

'To Canada. Or one of the new colonies. Start a new life. Start all over again.'

Mary too spoke in a low voice, as if their father was somehow near, although they knew he could not be. 'You know he would never agree to your leaving.'

Harriet was silent for a moment and then the words burst out of her. 'But what is my life to *be*? I must get away from him.'

'How can we? Without Father we cannot even get to Kent, let alone across the world.' Mary pulled her shawl around her shoulders. 'Without Father's permission we cannot do anything. I did not write about it but – Mr Dawson, the bookseller, told me something extraordinary. A Ladies' College has been opened.'

'*A Ladies' College?*'

'Yes. And I decided that more than anything in the world I would like the chance to go there, and study, and solve some of those questions that you and I could never answer.'

Harriet gasped. 'Learn in a real school with real teachers?'

Mary nodded.

'Now, when you are already old?'

Mary laughed a little at her sister's words. 'I know. But Harriet, you were educated in an Academy for Young Ladies and you told me that the biggest lesson you learnt was to, at all times, *smile*. I do not care how old I am, if only I could be educated properly! Do you know what they teach in Harley Street? English Literature, Theology, Natural Philosophy, Maths, Ancient and Modern Languages.' Harriet could not miss the longing, and the pain, in Mary's voice.

'Would Father allow you to go?'

'I am thirty years old. I should be able to take some decisions for myself. But I cannot get any financial independence from Father. And he would never agree, of course, to my going. So no, I cannot go.' And she repeated their fate: 'Without Father's permission we cannot do anything.'

In the silence they heard an owl hoot out of the darkness, and then the rooster crowed again.

Finally Mary, recovering, choosing her words carefully, said, 'Harriet darling, all the social calls and the Ladies' Academy, and Aunt Lydia's connections, they are all because you will be, eventually at least – and surely Father would not prevent you – expected to marry . . .'

'Why do you prescribe for me what you should loathe yourself!' Harriet's voice flashed across the bed.

'Cannot have myself,' her sister answered wryly.

'I will not get married,' said Harriet and her voice was low and cold. 'Nobody can make me, not Father, not even you. And tell me, Mary, who would marry me, if they knew our life?' She breathed in and out and tried to calm herself. And she began to half-sing, as if a nursery rhyme she had learnt long ago had come into her head.

> The Married Englishwoman
> Has no right
> To own Money or Home or Property
> She may not have custody of her children
> Nor refuse any wish of her husband.

Mary persisted. 'But then Mother's money would at least come to you, as a dowry. It is a large sum.'

'And it would go straight to my husband.' Harriet gripped the foot hard in her hand without realising it.

'Perhaps – perhaps you will meet a man who will allow you to keep part of your money . . .'

'I do not want to get my freedom from Father by marrying another man! How would that be freedom?' Her fingers pressed into the foot and Mary felt the tension in the fingers, felt them press the foot in the wrong way, hurting. 'If only Father would let me go away for good and make something of myself, like Edward is doing. If only I was a man. If only I could be a governess to someone's children. If only I could have just a little money of my own and *get away from my life.'*

'Harriet my darling, leave my foot now. Let me brush your hair.'

'As he got into the carriage—' Harriet swallowed at air and her voice rose in hysteria, *'he said he would be waiting for me!'*

'Let my foot go now, darling.' Mary spoke deliberately slowly and calmly. 'You are hurting me.'

Harriet suddenly looked down, saw her own nailmarks there, let the foot go at once. She stared at her sister, appalled.

'I am so sorry, Mary.'

Mary smiled, moved her foot. 'We are only tired,' she said.

'I am so sorry, Mary,' repeated Harriet humbly. 'And I am so very sorry about the Ladies' College.'

Mary took her sister's hand. She was silent for a long moment, and then she spoke. 'If anything ever happens to me, Harriet, take all the jewellery and sell it. You will find it in the second drawer in my room. All Mother's jewellery is there.'

'Nothing is going to happen to you ever, Mary. Ever, ever, ever. If anything happens to you, I could not live. I would kill myself.'

'Nothing is going to happen to me, my darling. Go to sleep now.'

Aunt Lucretia Cooper took to her bed the following day as soon as her sister and her nieces had departed for Nottingham. The depleted family stood on the steps to farewell Mary and Edward on their journey to London.

William Cooper and his younger son muttered together over last-minute arrangements while John stood rather superciliously by; Harriet held Mary tightly.

'Take great care, Mary, wherever you go,' whispered Harriet. 'You know I cannot live without you.'

'Come along now, come along,' cried Uncle William at last.

Edward half-lifted Mary into the carriage and ran round to the other side. Mary leant out of the window and waved to her sister.

'We shall be together again soon,' said Mary. 'Enjoy yourself, my darling.' And the driver flicked the whip and the black horses trotted neatly down the overgrown drive with their heads held high and Cousin John felt glad that he would have his beautiful cousin to himself and Asobel took Harriet kindly by the hand, intending to, at last, show her how to catch butterflies.

SEVEN

Mary was aware, as she walked slowly over the broken stones (embarrassedly holding a handkerchief against the noxious stench of the alley, ashamed that she felt so hot and faint), that the little girl was following her. If Mary went into a house with her soap and her chloride of lime, the girl waited and then followed again, the eyes in the dirty face with its sores and running nose staring only at Mary in a fierce fascination.

Once Mary stopped and turned and smiled. 'What is your name?' she said to the girl. But the girl would not, or could not, answer; wiped dirt from her nose and continued to stare, unsmiling.

The man walking with Mary carried a bucket full of water, they knocked at another half-open door, entered the dark, fetid room.

The noise and the smell informed them of what was happening. In a dim corner a woman was vomiting over and over again and crying out in pain at the same time. Her family stood about her: fearful and knowing and incapable; they turned dull eyes to the visitors. The man with Mary was a doctor; quickly he went to the woman where she lay on some sacking, used the water he had to try and clean her, called for more.

Mary grabbed one of the young boys by the shoulder and picked up a bucket.

'Quickly!' she cried. The standpipe was not far, Mary limped hurriedly behind the boy with money to pay for the water; did not see now the little girl, still staring.

There was a queue for the water. In her panic Mary pushed the others away; they looked at her in open hostility as she tried to help the boy to pump the water out. She stared at the fresh water from the pump, then turned away, almost vomiting herself, to see brown particles swirling in it.

By the time they got back to the room the woman was unconscious, lying in her own vomit and excrement. The doctor held her pulse; Mary approached with some soap and a wet cloth, attempted to bathe the woman's face, trying not to breath in the stench, felt the coldness of the skin, saw the faintness of the breathing and the way the face changed so that it seemed to have become suddenly old. Around her the family stood as if paralysed: Mary saw tears pouring down a young girl's face as she stood there silently: futile, wretched and bereft. Frantically Mary tried to clean the woman but there were no towels, no cloths but the one she had brought, no blankets. And then she saw that the face had changed again, there was a blue tinge about the lips and the nose. She looked up at the doctor who shook his head. 'The blue is the fatal sign,' he said quietly. 'It is the cholera.'

Within minutes the woman was dead, and the doctor stood. 'There is nothing else we can do,' he said to Mary. He turned to the family, who seemed so passive, unenergised, dull. 'It is the cholera,' he said. 'I am so very sorry. We were too late. You must burn everything, and you must wash the room with the disinfectant we shall leave with you. The cart will come for the body.' He gave one of the men some money.

The doctor led Mary outside, saw that she tried to take breaths of air but there was little air, in the alley. A kind of screaming came now from the room they had left, as if the family could only show grief when the intruders had gone. Mary looked back in horror.

'Come now,' the doctor said. 'That is enough for today. We can do nothing else.' He gave Mary his arm. As they walked, someone threw something from an upper window, wrapped in newspaper. It hit Mary's arm, fell open just ahead of them. The newspaper was smeared with human excreta. Mary's face turned bright red, the two stepped round the newspaper but said nothing. The same little girl followed them as they moved through the broken pavements and the crowds of people towards Tottenham Court Road, not speaking. Mary could hardly take in what she had known that afternoon.

Just as they came out to air and barrel organs and carriages and laughter Mary felt again the eyes of the little girl and she turned again and tried to smile.

'What is it?' she asked gently. And she felt in the pocket of her mantle and gave the girl a penny. The girl took the coin, but almost without interest, and then she spoke at last as the gentlefolk turned away, pointing at Mary's foot.

'Have you got the LEPORASEE?' she called out.

As they came at last to Oxford Street and the doctor helped Mary into a hackney cab, advising her to wash carefully and rest, he remarked wryly, 'It is beyond me to understand how a child like that could know the word *leprosy*.'

'Ah,' said Mary, smiling brightly, 'I expect they have been visited by a missionary, who told them of the suffering of the children of Africa.'

She alighted from her cab at the corner of Bryanston Square, tried to calm herself as she walked, from all the things she had seen. The sound of a piano being played in one of the houses in the Square drifted downwards. Someone was playing, not very well, 'Song without Words', but the music caught at her heart as she walked towards her father's house and tears came to her eyes as she saw that the leaves had fallen now, from the oak tree in the Square.

It was Edward, full of schemes and plans for emigrating, staying with his relations at the house in Bryanston Square, who saw Mary return, saw her pale face and her shaking hands.

'What is the matter, Mary?' he cried, deeply alarmed. 'Are you ill?'

She shook her head. 'No, I am not ill. But I have been with people who are ill and it is so – so – terrible.' And she burst out in a kind of rage, 'Eddie, why does nobody do anything about the cholera?'

Edward would have liked to suggest that there was no-one better to ask than her own father, who was responsible for much of the water in London. But he was a well-brought-up young man and suggested instead to Mary that she should take great care, for it was said that the cholera had not yet properly abated. And that when she was rested he would very much like a game of chess.

Harriet and Augusta took Asobel to see Edward's little home-made house. They walked over the fields; the rays of sun beaming down through the heavy, wild clouds looked like a picture from The Child's Illustrated Bible. Harriet thought a man with a long white beard should appear in the clouds immediately, and smile upon them. Edward's house looked even more un-workmanlike in the daylight, the straw of the rather oddly shaped roof seemed as if it might fly off at any moment, but Asobel was enchanted. She wanted them to build a fire, she wanted to sleep on the wooden bed, she wanted Harriet to continue her lessons here now that the summerhouse was too cold. While she ran about exclaiming, Augusta and Harriet sat once more on the uncomfortable bed.

Augusta stared discontentedly around the shack. 'He is ridiculous building this – this *thing*, I don't know what he imagines. Surely there will be towns in Canada, and proper houses. Mamma will not hear of me going of course, nor Papa either. They say he must make his fortune first. But that could take years and years.'

'Do you want to go?'

'I do not know. It depends on what is there, I mean whether there would be suitable society for Edward and me to feel at home.'

'Do you mean like in England?' asked Harriet. 'I should not think it would be like England.'

'Mamma and I have begun calling again,' said Augusta, 'and of course we wonder if such customs will be properly established in Canada. She is to ask you to come with us, by the way, Harriet. I heard Papa say that your father was not happy about you giving lessons to Asobel, and that they were to cease.' If she noticed that Harriet had paled she did not mention it.

Asobel charged in. 'It is raining,' she cried gleefully. 'We will have to stay,' and indeed the rain followed her in through the doorway.

'We must go back,' said Augusta.

'No, I want to stay here and have an adventure like Robinson Crusoe,' said Asobel excitedly, and she pushed and pulled at the door to try to close it. 'Now we shall all sit here and tell stories and

I will be first, now, *once upon a time* . . .' and she launched into a fantastical tale about witches and weddings and castaways and footprints in the sand and journeys across the sea and shipwrecks and rafts. Augusta stared dejectedly at the rain and Harriet, blank-faced, stared at the rain also; saw how things would be now because her father decreed it: making calls and talking of nothing. The rain came in under Edward's door and started snaking along towards them, turning the floor of the little house to mud.

'If Canada is to be like this,' said Augusta, 'I will certainly stay at home,' and she firmly brought Asobel's story to a swift conclusion and shepherded everyone back to civilisation, over the stile and through the fields, as the rain continued to fall.

Three very bedraggled young ladies ran up the stony drive and into the hall where Aunt Lucretia hardly scolded, so delighted was she with the message she held in her hand that said Edward was close behind it. And immediately there was a great rush of hot water for tin baths and hair-drying and dressing so that by the time the carriage actually arrived everybody was already waiting by the door and peering into the rain.

Edward catapulted out of the carriage like a man possessed, unwilling to wait for one of the servants to bring an umbrella, carrying an armful of papers and a round parcel and calling for Donald to bring in a pile of books. Dripping rain, Edward kissed his mother, shook hands with his father, extricated himself from Asobel and said, 'I have so much to tell you all.' And then he handed the round parcel to his youngest sister. Inside the wrapping, astonishing and delighting Asobel so much that she was reduced to awed silence, was an exquisite, beautifully painted china globe of the world.

At the dinner table, after a long grace in which William, thanking God for the food, managed also to thank Him for the safe arrival of his younger son from London; after Lucretia had asked for news of London society; after Cousin John had launched into a long discussion about some cows with his father; then at last Edward was allowed to speak. He was so excited he kept swallowing air, choking on his ale, and his neck and his face got redder and redder. None of them had ever seen him in such a state.

'I have bought some land,' he announced.

'You have *already* bought it, was that wise?' his father queried, shocked. 'You are not in Canada yet.'

'I am not going to Canada. I have decided to go to New Zealand. I have bought some land – not bought it exactly but I have purchased a Land Order entitling me to select from land already purchased from the natives by the New Zealand Company. Only a hundred acres to farm to begin with,' he added quickly, seeing the looks of consternation on the faces around him, 'and a small town section as well. In a place with a name to please you,' he said to his mother. 'It is called Wellington, after the Duke.'

'But – but you were set on Canada. Where is New Zealand? It has savage natives, I have read of them, and fearful earthquakes.'

'The earthquakes are seldom severe, Mamma, and the fighting with the natives is over now. Everyone gets along splendidly. There are many missionaries there, I have heard, who have had a softening effect on primitive hearts. And I have it on good authority that a painting of Queen Victoria was earlier this year presented to a group of native chiefs in Wellington by the good offices of Earl Grey himself, among great celebration and feasting. This does not sound like savage natives, Mamma, you must surely agree.'

'But surely New Zealand is the furthest colony of all?'

'It is, Mamma. It is the furthest, but it is also the most likely place for someone like me to make my fortune. And bring you all there,' he ended triumphantly, 'to live with me.'

Asobel gave a scream of delight. But Lucretia, clutching her breast, began to weep loudly. Augusta went to find the laudanum and to Harriet's dismay Uncle William, who still looked shocked and uneasy, suggested they leave the painful subject until the ladies had retired to the drawing room.

She and Augusta and Asobel sat drinking tea with Aunt Lucretia, who refused to discuss the matter further; she instead informed Harriet that her previous 'morning activities', as she called them with a significant glance at Asobel, were to cease – 'Certainly we do not want your father to think we are taking advantage of your kindness,' she said querulously but rather vaguely on account of the laudanum. 'You must come calling with us tomorrow on old Lady Kingdom who noticed you, and asked after you, at the wedding.' Asobel, understanding, burst into loud cries and was sent to bed, still weeping, still clutching her globe of the world.

But later that evening, when Aunt Lucretia had been persuaded that bed was the best place for her also, Cousin Edward brought the pile of books into the drawing room.

Even Cousin John was caught up with the excitement, while Augusta and Harriet, who had not yet heard anything of Edward's plans, were anxiously waiting their turn. The books were laid out on the tea table, which had been cleared of its flowered cups and saucers. First Edward opened a book and showed everybody a map of New Zealand. He cleared his throat and read:

> New Zealand consists mainly of two large islands called Northern and Southern. It is 95,000 square miles, approximately the same size as Great Britain and far surpassing it in soil and climate, reminding us rather of Italy and the Bay of Naples.

And then with a triumphant flourish he opened a large green book and carefully opened up a long, large, folded engraving.

'This,' he said, 'is the town of Wellington!'

The first impression was of nothing more than sky and sea and space. But the artist had done his best. Fragile little sailing vessels could be seen sitting at anchor on the enclosed, calm harbour that was surrounded by hills. Tiny long canoes were pulled up at various places along the shore and small houses with some sort of thatched roof were dotted about. There were some small wooden jetties, they saw that a post office and two or three hotels were indicated, while beside a wooden flagstaff a group of oddly attired natives who did not, Harriet observed, look very savage, sat on the ground and listened to a white man telling them something. But everything was dwarfed by the sea and the immense sky that stretched out past the hills into infinity, and Harriet felt an odd, spacious loneliness emanating from the drawing.

'This,' Edward repeated in excitement, 'is the town of Wellington where I am to have a small plot near *here*, and *here* – just off the map – is where I may choose my farming land.'

Augusta looked devastated. 'That is a town?' she said. 'That – that *dust-hill* is where you are going?'

Nothing could dampen Edward's enthusiasm. 'I think it looks wonderful,' he said, 'with all the basic amenities that would be required, and as it is several years since that drawing was executed I expect it is bigger and more civilised now.'

Cousin John had quite forgotten to look supercilious. 'Would the land be suitable for farming? It looks very hilly.'

'I am coming to that,' said Edward joyously. 'Now won't you all sit down and let me read something more to you? Listen, listen,' and he began to read from another book, choosing the bits he thought most interesting for his listeners, skipping anything unsuitable:

> It is impossible to conceive a state of the seasons
> more favourable to agriculture . . . bad harvest
> weather is unknown . . . there is much sunshine
> all through the winter and although weather
> charts mention gales they should rather be called
> fresh breezes . . . On the basis of all the rivers
> which flow through hilly country the soil bears
> the richest alluvial character and in some valleys
> the pure black or brown sandy loam lies in so
> thick a stratum as to appear inexhaustible . . .
> indigenous timber grows to a towering height in a
> perfection equalled by that of few other coun-
> tries . . . so many wonderful native trees for
> housebuilding and furniture-making . . . many
> beautiful native flowers and birds . . . there are no
> snakes, frogs, or toads of any kind . . .

'and Father, look, there is a lot of information about sheep, they have been brought across from New South Wales, they are developed from Spanish merinos and fleeces are *twice as heavy* in New Zealand because of the superiority of the food and the climate. And I am reliably informed that there are doctors and a hospital and even a cricket club! And Mamma will feel better when she knows that there is an English Church and a Scotch Presbyterian Church and others besides. And, Father.' Edward's eyes shone. 'You heard that bit about native timbers for building – there are already sawmills in all the main settlements! That, surely, is civilisation!' And Edward threw himself at last into an armchair, triumphant and exhausted.

Harriet was sitting forward, her eyes almost piercing him with her hunger for more information. 'Edward, you are so lucky,' she said. 'It will be a tremendous adventure,' and her cousin grinned back at her, nodding, and grateful too for some enthusiasm somewhere.

'Why did you change from Canada to a place like New Zealand which has savage natives as Mamma said, and is so far away?' Augusta spoke sulkily.

Her father, who was sitting beside the fire and pulling on his pipe in a distracted manner, answered gruffly. 'He met up with those gallivanting rascals Chapman and Lyle when he got to London, and got carried away by their hair-brained schemes.'

'Now, Father,' said Edward pleasantly, 'Chapman is not a rascal by any stretch of the imagination, nor does he gallivant, and you are only against him because he speaks out against the Water Boards in London and you feel that he is criticising Uncle Charles – I do beg your pardon, Harriet. And Lyle is his oldest friend. They had already been to the Canada Office and the Australia Office and the New Zealand Office and the Colonial Land and Emigration Commission and had got as much information as they could before I arrived. A lot of the really important facts they got from an emigrants' outfitters in Cornhill; they heard news of the latest ships arriving and leaving, and the difficulties of some places over another. And all their enquiries and our subsequent enquiries showed us that New Zealand seemed the most suitable place for us to go and try our luck. As for the natives, we believe there was a little trouble about land purchases earlier but all is apparently settled now and as I say the church missionaries are no doubt a civilising influence. It is after all 1849 – the settlers have been there for well over twenty years, as you can understand by the kind of civilisation already apparent.'

'Civilisation!' said Augusta.

'When shall you go?' asked Harriet.

For the first time her cousin looked a little nervous and his eyes flickered to his father uneasily.

'He says he will go almost at once,' said William Cooper, 'which is of course out of the question. I will not answer for your mother if she thinks you are to depart across the world before the festive season.'

'At once?' whispered Augusta in shock, tears springing to her eyes.

'Do not treat your mother as foolish, Edward,' said William. 'She loves you very much and will be devastated to part from you which is only natural. She has – some ways with her that perhaps we smile at. But that maternal love which she has for you in large measure is a valuable thing and not something to be treated lightly.'

'But, Father, I know Mamma loves me dearly, as I do her, and I do not wish to hurt her. But I have told you why it must be so soon. We agreed, you and I, that I would wait only until Alice was married. Chapman and Lyle and I have been lucky enough to secure a cabin which somebody else cancelled just as we were making enquiries, on the *Miranda*, which sets sail in three weeks. Listen to this, Father: "This well-known, remarkably fast sailing barge, 480 tons, carries an experienced surgeon, most excellent accommodation." If we go then we will perhaps reach our destination before the summer there is quite over and so may be able to settle ourselves while the weather is still to our advantage, and then be able to prepare the land to plant the wheat that you know I have planned to take with us from our farm.'

'You said the weather was wonderful all the time,' said Augusta angrily. 'Please, Father, do not let him go so soon, please!'

'How long does the journey take?' asked Harriet quickly.

'It is an average of one hundred to one hundred and twenty days.' There was a stunned silence. 'It is perhaps fourteen or fifteen thousand miles.'

'One hundred and twenty days on a ship? That is four months!'

'But of course there will be plenty to do on board. I shall study, and learn up about all the things I need to know when I get there.' But he turned again to his father. 'Father, you must understand that I need to seize this chance? There was no cabin available for us on the succeeding ship, the *Amaryllis*, which goes three or four weeks later and we would have less chance of catching the weather. We were extremely fortunate to get the cabin on the *Miranda*.' His father remained silent, his chin sunk into his chest.

'Papa. What else should I do? There is nothing for me here, you and John know that, and our circumstances are not such that I could allow myself to be a burden on the family. And I could not bear to have to live in London, I could not wait to leave there. I find the atmosphere stifling, it may be considered the centre of the world but the fogs are coming down and the cholera is still seen everywhere.'

Harriet's heart contracted.

'The carts are still collecting bodies at night,' Edward continued, 'and I felt a kind of fear in people, that it has again crossed boundaries, that it is affecting all sorts of people, not just the poor. One poor fellow was taken ill in the Emigration Commission, it was terrible to see, one moment he was enquiring about travelling to Australia, the next minute he was collapsed and vomiting.'

Augusta made a faint sound of disgust but Edward seemed not to hear.

'They called a doctor but I fear there was nothing to be done, one felt it by the terror of the people around.'

Harriet could hardly speak. 'And Mary,' she whispered, 'is Mary well?'

Edward suddenly focused on his cousin. She was so pale he thought she might faint and she twisted her hands together in a way terrible to see.

'Oh Harriet, I am so sorry,' he said, 'I did not mean to frighten you. Of course Mary is well, I spent much time with her and discussed my plans with her. She has sent you a letter, I should have given it to you the moment I arrived. I will fetch it immediately.' And he left the drawing room at once.

Augusta moved swiftly to her father. 'Papa, he cannot go. You must forbid him.'

But John answered first. 'If we are to properly dominate these unruly places, people of our own calibre must go. Edward may just as well be there as here. And good may come of it.'

The Squire stared into the fire. 'If I was young I would go myself,' he said sadly.

When Harriet said goodnight to her uncle and her cousins she took with her to her room not only Mary's treasured letter, but, with his permission, one of Edward's volumes. She lit a candle and sat at the small desk holding Mary's letter in her hand but not opening it, for fear of what she might find there. She stared at some pages of

Edward's book; then she picked up the pen and dipped it into the inkwell.

Dear Father,
I have been told of your wish that I do not teach Asobel any more. Tomorrow we shall call on Lady Kingdom whom I believe you spoke to at the wedding.
The weather has turned now, and the summer has gone.
Your obedient daughter
Harriet Cooper

And then, at last, she opened Mary's letter.

My dearest Harriet,
I think of you there, safe at Rusholme, and I am glad. The country air suits you, darling, you looked more beautiful than ever, but I couldn't help wishing with part of myself that you would soon be restored to me. But that of course is selfish and we know it is best that you are there.
We have seen a lot of Edward in London and I am most interested in all his plans as I know you will be too. Dinner at Bryanston Square has been a much gayer occasion with him here. Our brothers gather their frockcoats about their persons and say Edward is mad but I believe he is right to go, and brave. Father says the British government has not been much interested in emigration and the wrong class of person has hitherto travelled and given the wrong impression of the British Empire.
I have been able to maintain some of my visits to the poorer parts of the city and I feel, truly, that I am going to another world, not the world of the great British Empire with our proud dominion over the oceans. Sometimes I sit in the drawing room at Bryanston Square and I have to pinch myself to remind myself where I was only a few hours before. I think if people knew how it was, only a few miles away, they would choke on their beef. And I think again; it is only money that divides us. Oh Harriet, surely people should care more than they do! It is said that the number of deaths is, thank God, at last declining but the newspapers tell us that the death toll has reached almost 50,000. Fifty thousand people dying: can you

conceive of it? But of course a large proportion of them are poor and miserable, and so people like us are able to close our minds to the figures. Sometimes I think the Queen or Prince Albert would have to be taken before people would be shocked enough to take action.

And yet the results of the cholera are there in front of our eyes. You know how Father prefers to go to St Paul's Church in Covent Garden on Sundays. Last Sunday we had to come home. The stench, oh Harriet, they had – someone had – left the crypt open and you could see (and smell) the pile – it was a great jumbled pile, spilling over – of shrouds and ill-made coffins. Everybody was clucking and holding their noses and complaining and leaving, no thought for the dead at all in God's house. Surely, surely it is hypocritical to speak of our Lord in one breath and not notice what is happening to people just a few streets away in the same city. How can Father not even think about this? I am well aware of the rumblings about the Water Boards in some quarters. If I stopped to think how our family has prospered I would go mad; instead I go to Seven Dials with my soap and my chloride of lime. I do not wish to be thought of as a kind, rich lady and I am well aware of the almost impossibility of having any true relationship with any of these people but I do think what we do counts for something, however small.

Harriet, when people are dying of cholera, their faces turn blue. I never thought to see such a thing, to be so near to what most of our acquaintances try to ignore.

You will worry about my health, yet I tell you again and again that I take great care. I want to live, not die, for life after all is sweet to me. But you must understand that I would a hundred times rather be doing this than calling on the other ladies of London. Please think of that, my darling, when you think of me.

With all my love, and may God bless you and keep you, my darling.

Mary

PS I almost forgot. A whale has been found in the Thames. It was killed of course before it could find its way back to the sea and its captors are charging a penny to view . . .

At first, although she started several times, Harriet was unable to reply, so great was her fear for, and her anger at, her sister. The candle was almost burnt down; she found a new one and lit it from the old as she used to do when she was younger. She watched the flame, and the shadows flickering on the wall. *How could Mary do this?*

But at last she picked up the pen and dipped it carefully in the ink. She bent over her paper and then the words poured out as if she could not stop them.

Dearest, my dearest Mary, always remember how much I love you and need you. I only get angry at what you are doing for my own sake, because I get frightened yet I see how much it means to you and I wish I was brave like you and part of me, even when I am so frightened, is proud of you because you are not like an ordinary sister but an extraordinary one. Perhaps, when I return, I could try to come with you, perhaps that would be a way to make some sense of life. Oh if only we could go and join Edward. He showed us a picture of this new country and there was such – space – in it. How I would love to be planning such an adventure as he is, I feel I could face any hardship, any deprivation, if you and I were together, and away from Father; that I would be happy at last.

The sound of the pen scratching so fast along the paper stopped for some time, then started again, but slower.

Aunt Lucretia has informed me that Father has said that I should no longer teach even Asobel; it is not a suitable activity for a lady.

I have here one of Edward's books, and have been reading the instructions about what emigrants should take to New Zealand:

'A Mackintosh sheet to spread under your blankets proves useful on exploring parties. A Mackintosh airbed, too, has been found useful. The Bishop of New Zealand once used one as a canoe while on an expedition through the interiors.'

It is all a dream of course, my dearest sister, I know that. Father will never let us. Dearest Mary, I love you very much. Please please, take every possible care. I cannot live without you.

From your loving sister
Harriet

And then she knelt down beside the big four-poster bed with the soft feather mattress.

> O Lord, from whom all good things do come:
> grant to me thy humble servant, that by holy
> inspiration I may think those things that be good.
> Lord, forgive whatever thy eyes have seen in me
> that displeaseth thee and guide me to be grateful
> for the many things in life that are beautiful.
> I do not mean to be a selfish person.
> Watch over all the people in this house through
> the silent hours of the night and may grace and peace
> be with them all.
> And most of all, dear Lord, please guide the life
> of my dear, dear sister Mary, help and protect her
> in all that she does, and keep her safe.
> For the sake of Jesus Christ our Lord,
>
> Amen.

EIGHT

The calling on Lady Kingdom was postponed, owing to the indisposition of Lucretia Cooper, to whom William had, while dressing that morning, confided Edward's early departure plans. The servants, Augusta, Asobel and Harriet all visited her in turn with warm gruel, and lozenges, and tea, and camphorated oil, but Lucretia lay with her back to them all and was silent. The doctor was finally called and reported that Mrs Cooper would not speak to him either. He and Uncle William shut themselves in the study with some cider. Asobel, holding her globe, listened outside the study for some time, until Harriet, observing her, at once suggested a walk to 'Edward's Little House', as it had come to be called. As they walked through the fields Asobel suddenly said, 'Harriet.'

'Yes, Asobel?'

Asobel looked up at her cousin and Harriet saw that her face was pale.

'What is it, Asobel?' she asked, concerned.

'I have been thinking a great deal.'

'About what?' asked Harriet kindly.

'I am very worried about Eddie's ship.'

'Why is that?'

'You remember in "Robinson Crusoe" when the big storm with

those waves comes, and the boat is cast upon the shore and every-one drowns except Robinson Crusoe – could that happen to Eddie?'

'Oh, no,' said Harriet decidedly. 'Edward will be travelling on a much bigger ship than Robinson Crusoe did. And that story was in the olden days when ships were not so reliable perhaps. Everything is much safer now.'

'Do you promise?'

Harriet said, and behind her back as they walked she crossed her fingers, 'I promise.' And then she told Asobel about the Mackintosh Mattress Canoe, a story Asobel received with delight and wove at once into one of her own long, rambling but fanciful narratives, and they sat on the narrow bed and watched for fieldmice and talked of Edward's exciting plans.

'Why won't Uncle Charles let you teach me any more, Harriet?' Asobel asked later as they walked back to the house under a stormy sky. The wind was rising, it blew their dresses in front of them as they walked and snatched at their hair, and long grey and yellow clouds seemed to race past just above their heads. 'My lessons are the best part of my day. This world here,' and she pointed at all the countries on her globe, 'I need you to teach me about it.'

Harriet was discomforted, hardly knew how to answer without making a criticism of her father. 'I expect my father – I expect every-body – thinks you should have a proper governess, who would educate you properly, someone who knows a great deal more than I do.'

Asobel was not fooled. 'I would not think Uncle Charles cares one inch about my education,' she said rudely. 'What does odicted mean?'

'*Odicted?*'

'The doctor said Mamma took too much laudanum. I heard him telling Papa. I heard them talking in the study. He said she was becoming odicted.'

'Young ladies never, *never* listen at doors,' said Harriet, shocked. 'Those are the actions of a lesser person. You must never do that again, Asobel.'

'How will I find out anything?'

'People will tell you what they want you to know.'

'People never tell girls anything. He said she must stop taking so much laudanum or she will become odicted.'

'Addicted,' corrected Harriet automatically.

'Addicted. What does that mean?'

'It means – having too much. Wanting too much. But I expect you misheard.'

Asobel gave her cousin an old-fashioned, eight-year-old look, but said nothing further.

In the house the silence of Lucretia unnerved everyone. A dramatic reaction to events they were used to: silence they were not. When, on the second day, Uncle William came in from the fields and found his wife had still not come down he took off his boots and went upstairs with heavy footsteps.

He came back down looking most uneasy. A brief, sombre grace was said to which he added *'and God bless my dear wife Lucretia'* and the meal began, but conversation was muted and Edward's normally cheerful demeanour seemed cast down at the pain he was causing his mother. Asobel's high spirits were subdued and Augusta threw many reproachful glances at her brother while Uncle William and Cousin John discussed the price of wheat in a desultory manner. The atmosphere was not helped by the cold October wind which blew through the farmhouse and rattled at the windows as the candles flickered and danced.

And then suddenly Lucretia appeared. She was wrapped in an unsuitable garment for the dining room and clutching her bosom. The three men rose in unison and Augusta moved at once to her mother's side and helped her to her usual place at one end of the damask-covered table. Asobel cheered up visibly and watched everything with great interest.

'My dear—' said William Cooper heartily, but she raised a hand.

'Edward. Come to me,' she said in a tremulous voice, and her younger son rose and moved to her. Harriet saw that his expression was a mixture of affection and embarrassment and determination; the emotions chased each other over his round, earnest face. His mother looked at him for several moments in silence.

'I do not want to lose you, Edward,' she said. 'Whichever way I look at it I know I am losing you. You are leaving England and travelling so far away from us that I cannot even picture your journey in my mind no matter how hard I try. You will board a ship that is to sail into almost unknown seas and an unknown world. It is impossible to understand when we may see you again and it makes my heart ache so much. Without you here, somewhere near us, we will be – so very lonely. You will have children of your own one day and then you will understand.'

'Mamma,' said Edward firmly, but his voice shook a little all the same. 'New Zealand is on the other side of the world, but it is not the *end* of the world. I need not be there forever. And all my investigations have shown me that if I work hard there is every chance that I could make a better life – and for my children should I have them – than I could ever make here. John is to run the farm, and be with you always, and I must find another way. You and Father have always known that,' and Harriet saw that John, always so confident and assured, was slumped slightly as he heard his fate told by his younger brother. The lights still flickered in the wind, casting shadows around the room. Lucretia was quiet again for a moment, and everyone could see that she was struggling to remain calm.

'Tell me,' she said, 'how long will a letter from you take to reach us?'

Edward wanted to make things sound positive, yet did not want to dissemble. 'They advised me that there is a mail service, Mamma. But I think a letter would take many months. Perhaps five or six. I understand mail from New Zealand goes to New South Wales first, and the ship may take four months to return to England.'

'That is such a long journey, it would have been much easier if you had gone to Canada,' and Lucretia gave a tiny sob which she at once contained. 'It must be the longest journey in the world.'

Edward was silent.

'Ships have – foundered on that long journey. I have seen paintings of waves reaching right over the ships, and all lost.' Although it was clear that she was making an enormous effort to remain composed, Lucretia's voice shook and her daughters turned pale and Asobel said 'like Robinson Crusoe' in a small voice, looking at Harriet.

Edward looked quite pale himself. 'To my knowledge, Mamma, for some years now the ships have in most cases eventually reached their destination safely, they have learned of the dangers of those oceans, and how to battle with them. Some of the ships have done the journey many times, the *Miranda* has certainly sailed to New Zealand before. And there are ports of call they can make, should the vessel become unsafe. There are many ships coming and going to the southern Pacific Ocean and I think it is a deal safer than it used to be. Certainly nobody spoke of disasters.'

'Nor pirates?'

Edward smiled. 'No, Mamma, I have heard nothing of pirates.'

'You say the barbarians there, the natives, are no longer savage?'

'I believe that there were battles initially. But as I told you the other evening the missionaries have been a calming influence.'

'Are there churches there, apart from the missionaries, who we know are often of a different class.'

'Yes, Mamma, a fine English church in Wellington and more besides.'

'And Wellington of course is named after the dear Duke.'

'Yes, Mamma.'

And then Lucretia Cooper surprised them all. 'I happen to know,' she said, 'that Her Majesty has taken a great interest in New Zealand. She is of course Queen of New Zealand also, and you will be under her protection as a citizen of Great Britain and that gives me comfort. It will be,' and her voice trembled again, 'terrible for us to say goodbye to you, Edward, to see the sails of the ship becoming smaller and smaller as we wave and never know how long it will be before we see or hear of you again.' Harriet felt something pricking at the back of her own eyes and, looking across the table, saw a tear trickling down Asobel's small cheeks, though she made no sound as she stared at her mother and her brother. Edward too was swallowing hard.

'And so I think, my dear,' continued Lucretia, nodding at her husband, 'a glass of brandy for everyone to drink the health and welfare of our dearly loved son.' And Harriet acknowledged that, even though she still clutched her heart in a dramatic manner, there was something heroic about her aunt, whose tears glittered behind her over-bright eyes and did not fall.

NINE

The preparations were tremendous.

Harriet read all the books Edward read, joined in the many fevered consultations about what should be taken to the other end of the world.

'It says here,' she said, 'that there is no water for washing clothes during the whole of your voyage, and that you must take changes of linen, and air your clothes when you reach the sunshine of the tropics. Also that finery is superfluous.'

Edward grinned. 'Don't tell Mamma.' He was labouring over a huge crate of farm tools and implements outside the barn.

'It also says here that ladies should take their pianos.'

This time Edward laughed aloud. 'I shall wait for Augusta to bring the piano. Though it would be nice to come home from ploughing fields to hear such a thing.' Into the crate he loaded axes and knives and chains and hammers and many many nails; also a hunting gun which he wrapped carefully in an old linen, and some gunpowder.

'Or a bugle or a cornet,' continued Harriet, 'which, it says here, "will be heard to advantage among the echoes of the beautiful mountain scenery".' But even as they were laughing her face became thoughtful again. 'Edward, seriously, what will happen when you arrive, describe to me what they have told you, how you will choose your land, and build your house,' and Edward would go over again what he had been told. Always Harriet fixed him with her beautiful, piercing eyes, drank in the knowledge, about a journey that was not, of course, for her.

Asobel ran towards them from the house. 'Harriet, Harriet,' she was calling. 'It is time to call on Lady Kingdom, Mamma says.'

Harriet, her hair untidy, wearing her oldest dress, looked shocked. 'Do you mean now?'

'Mamma says so.' Most reluctantly Harriet put down the book, and the rope that for some reason she had been holding.

'But it's all right,' cried Asobel, 'I'll help Edward,' and she ran around the barn, jumping over saddles and candles and various boots. Her voice echoed back up towards the house after Harriet, 'Eddie, do *please* let me bang in some nails. Also, Eddie, should you wish to know, I could tell you how to build a raft.'

The Squire's coach and the Squire's coachman were used to the country lanes. Lucretia Cooper, her elder daughter, and her niece were conveyed at speed past the empty hopfields and the autumnal hedgerows; the passengers swayed together in a most disagreeable manner as the wheels caught in the ruts and cracks in the road, but Lucretia and Augusta were used to such transport, they merely screamed a little at the biggest bumps and shouted extremely loudly, to be heard above the rattling of the carriage. Harriet was regaled with stories of the London-based Kingdom brothers: handsome, rich, and most of all unmarried. Lord Ralph, the heir, was a man-about-town who had not yet taken up his seat in the House of Lords; he was so handsome (they assured Harriet) that women swooned in his presence. Sir Benjamin, the younger brother, well, one knew not much about Benjamin except that he was handsome also, fair where his brother was dark; he was apparently immensely clever and had something to do with something scientific (they were not sure what). It was also said (Lucretia added this still loudly but rather dubiously, as if doubting its authenticity) that he was interested in *birds*. Augusta's hat was a picture of cascading ribbons and fluttering feathers that were lifted sometimes in agitation, by the breeze of their journey or the content of their conversation.

At last the carriage rolled more sedately up the impeccable gravel drive; very elegant poplars lined the route and two liveried footmen (looking somewhat grander than the Squire's only butler-footman, Donald) bowed and opened the carriage door to help the ladies to descend.

It was cold in the large, high-ceilinged drawing room. The three visitors shivered a little in their morning dresses and pulled their shawls more tightly around their shoulders. Lady Kingdom, appearing almost immediately, was an imposing figure dressed again in black. Her husband, Harriet had been informed loudly in the coach, had died in 1839 but Lady Kingdom had never returned to more frivolous attire. A lace cap almost covered her greying hair and she looked at her guests severely. But severity could not dampen Lucretia's excitement at being there. In her element, she exchanged views with her hostess on the success of Alice's wedding and the vagaries of the weather and the fecklessness of servants; later they got on to old lace. Augusta joined in occasionally, as tutored at her finishing school, with a little word and a smile or a charming laugh. Harriet was conscious of steel eyes boring into her; she had no interest in the world in joining in and sat with her hands in her lap and a polite smile on her face, wishing they could perhaps have tea after the erratic coachride. When the conversation turned to a neighbouring family whose son was in unmentionable disgrace she looked covertly about her, feeling it might not be noticed. The drawing room had none of the adornments of her aunt's more cluttered house. Here it was more like Bryanston Square, dark and sombre; a very large gloomy painting of a long-ago battle dominated one plain wall; from another a man she presumed to be Lord Kingdom stared down at them: as Harriet looked at him his grey eyes twinkled. In surprise she looked more carefully. Paintings of important men were always serious, befitting their importance, but something about the eyes broke the severity of the portrait (and indeed the room). She was still observing the picture when she found herself addressed.

'Tell me, Miss Cooper,' said Lady Kingdom without any preamble, 'who was your mother? Your father's father was of course known to me, the previous Squire,' (Harriet thought she heard slight disdain in her tone) 'but I know nothing of your mother's family.'

'My mother died when I was born, Lady Kingdom,' Harriet answered politely. 'She was Elizabeth MacDonald.'

'From Scotland then?' Lady Kingdom sounded disappointed.

Lucretia was having none of this. 'From Scotland originally perhaps,' she said. 'But Sir William MacDonald, the judge, Elizabeth's father, had lived in London all his life like his father before him.'

'Ah.' Lady Kingdom's countenance brightened a little. 'Was he not a brother of Sir Richard MacDonald, the eminent royal adviser, who knew my father well?' Receiving affirmation, she asked more questions about family connections. It was clear that they were better than she had feared. She was aware of the need of personable young girls in the county, if her sons were to be entertained. Then she rang a bell beside her. Almost at once two maids appeared with tea which Lady Kingdom poured herself, into exquisite but fragile cups.

'You must do me the honour, my dear Lucretia, of bringing these two young ladies back to me on Friday evening,' said Lady Kingdom as she held her cup delicately. 'My sons shall visit from London. They will be glad of such charming company.' Harriet's heart sank but Augusta blushed with pleasure and Lucretia beamed.

'How kind, Lady Kingdom, how kind.' Lady Kingdom was silent. 'How kind,' said Lucretia again and then for some time there was just the tinkling of the cups as they were replaced carefully on their saucers, and the rustles of the petticoats and the dresses in the cold room.

In London, Harriet knew, they would now move on to talk, at least fleetingly, of a book, or a concert, the business of the visit having been concluded. Lady Kingdom seemed to have no such subjects of conversation and soon she rose, and the visit was over, and the coach once more rattled down the long, immaculate drive. From the coach Harriet thought she caught a glimpse of the rotund clerical gentleman who had accompanied Lady Kingdom to the wedding. He was, seemingly, preparing a sermon across the lawn for he appeared to be addressing nobody, or the trees, in rather an eccentric manner. But the others were too excited to notice so Harriet sat back in the corner of the coach as it made its clattering way up the valley and along the lanes back to Rusholme.

There were no cards or music that evening: there were seldom cards or music now; rather everyone seemed to be looking at books about New Zealand. Edward or Harriet often read aloud to the family as Uncle William stoked the fire and Aunt Lucretia ordered the servants to bring glasses of negus.

> There is no occasion whereon there is so great a temptation to relax good habits, as at sea (*read Harriet*) especially on a long voyage. Amongst Passengers, negligence of persons is almost universally conspicuous. Men neglect to shave themselves for days together. Women, to whom personal appearance is really important, neglect themselves.

'Good heavens,' said Augusta. 'I am relieved we are going to visit Lady Kingdom again, where negligence of person would not be contemplated.'

Cousin John, alerted that the young ladies had been invited back to meet the sons, looked stern. He was not at all happy about Harriet going elsewhere in the district. He suddenly interrupted her reading and engaged her in conversation about her finishing school in Norfolk. The answers he received were short; even John could see that the subject was uninteresting to her. But he had watched Harriet with her crippled sister: he asked her if she had news of Mary, and his cousin's face brightened and softened at once. 'I have had a long letter from her, she is very well,' said Harriet and she smiled at John instinctively so that his heart felt quite touched and he determined to speak to her next day.

Edward glanced across at Harriet from his book. Again he saw in his mind Mary, shocked and pale, coming into the house at Bryanston Square the day the woman in Seven Dials had died of cholera. He knew how close the sisters were. But if Harriet knew of Mary's secret life she gave no sign. She merely smiled once more at Cousin John and returned to her volume.

But next day when John found Harriet as usual reading one of Edward's books in the empty drawing room he said to her: 'Cousin Harriet, I would like you to take a turn about the garden with me.'

She looked up in surprise, and something else: alarm perhaps. Obediently she laid the book on a table and put on her bonnet which was lying beside her. She was going for a ride with Augusta: the groom was preparing the horses, fastening the side saddles.

'Do you know,' she said to John as she tied her bonnet, 'people should take shoes with special cork soles, otherwise they will not be able to walk about the deck of the ship, for the sea washes over in storms and everything is covered in water.'

He did not notice that she flinched as he took her arm. Aunt Lucretia, glancing out of her bedroom window, started in surprise at what she saw: a young couple walking along, arm in arm it seemed, past the blackcurrant bushes. She frowned to herself, turned back to William in disapproval, but he was already gone back to his study after his afternoon nap. In the distance, down by the barns, Edward banged in nails.

Then Cousin John began. 'It is very pleasant to have you staying at Rusholme, Harriet.'

'Thank you.'

'I have been very glad to see more of you.'

'Thank you.'

'Do you like Rusholme?' She nodded gravely but a tremor of suspicion entered her heart. 'I have always liked coming here and everybody is so very kind. But – I miss Mary very much. I find it difficult to be apart from her.'

'Ah.' He supposed brides always missed their sisters, look at Alice in tears on her wedding morning, but no doubt greatly happy after her time in Ryde.

'I will be so glad when the cholera epidemic is over, I believe the number of deaths is now declining daily,' said Harriet firmly.

'Ah.' Then he broached his immediate concerns. 'You are invited to spend the evening with Lady Kingdom and her family?'

'Yes,' said Harriet shortly.

'I feel I should perhaps warn you.' He paused. 'The younger son, Benjamin, will cause you no difficulty: I believe he has an interest in the sciences. He is rather vague and fond of birds; I don't think he would notice a young lady, actually. However, Ralph, the elder son, has – quite a way with – ah, with the ladies. I believe he is – something of a blackguard. I have heard stories of his rather dissolute life in London, nothing I could impart to you, of course. But I feel it is my duty as your cousin to warn you about him.'

And Harriet gave a little laugh in relief. 'Oh Cousin John,' she said. 'You need not worry about me. Lady Kingdom's sons shall not find an entrance to my heart, neither the scientist nor the black-guard, I can assure you.'

'You do not understand how concerned I am for your welfare.' John was determined he should be taken seriously. 'Ralph is quite wild and undisciplined. There have been several stories . . . I should not tell you this but I understand he is involved with—' Cousin John's propriety made him stumble, '—with a young lady who is in the—' now he cleared his throat embarrassedly, '—in the *corps de ballet* of Taglione, or Cerrito, or Grisi, one of these foreign extravaganzas!'

Harriet glanced up at her cousin, surprised. 'A ballet dancer?'

'A woman of the chorus,' said John dismissively. 'And foreign. And I happen to know that the young lady concerned,' and he could hardly articulate the words, 'goes by the name of *Mimi*.'

'Then I will not interest him at all!' said Harriet, trying not to laugh. And seeing that they were near the house again and that the horses were waiting with the groom, she looked up at him, smiling again and disengaging herself gently from his arm. 'I do appreciate your concern for me,' she said. 'But I think perhaps it is Augusta to whom you should speak.'

'Why of course,' said John, confused. 'I was to speak to her also, of course.'

So that when Lucretia, hovering, anxiously asked her son if he had enjoyed his walk with his cousin he answered shortly, 'I was merely warning Harriet about the reputation of one of the Kingdom brothers. You must warn Augusta.'

Lucretia smiled in relief. 'I think Augusta can look after herself,' she said. 'She is older and more sensible than Harriet. And it is my personal opinion that all Lord Ralph Kingdom needs is a sensible wife.'

Once more the Squire's carriage catapulted through the country lanes, swaying backwards and forwards as it raced towards Lady Kingdom and her two sons. Augusta was flushed and pretty, Lucretia was even more voluble than usual in her excitement, talking again of the qualities of Ralph and Benjamin as if she were an intimate of their most secret lives. So they did not notice if Harriet was pale and even more silent than usual; she would a hundred times rather have been back at Rusholme listening to Edward's meticulous planning with his father and his brother for crossing continents than facing an evening with unknown young men and empty conversation. The swaying of the carriage and the idea of the evening before her made her feel physically ill.

Tonight they were escorted to another room in the grand house. Lady Kingdom was attended by two young men; elsewhere, looking rather small in the large space, several other young people sat in little groups beside card tables. There was a very large grand piano, shiny and gloomy, in one corner. There were too few people for the room, conversation was stilted and the same general air of chilliness that had permeated the drawing room continued here, and no gentleman twinkled from the high bare walls although another extremely large battle was seen in the distance and a portrait of Queen Victoria. Harriet looked about hopefully for the large clerical gentleman who spoke to trees, but he was nowhere in sight. She sighed inwardly. She was reminded of interminable Norfolk evenings with her Aunt Lydia; wondered then if Aunt Lydia, growing up in this area with her brothers Charles and William, had first got her taste for these dull, constrained evenings at entertainments in this grim mansion, long ago.

Lady Kingdom motioned to the Coopers graciously; they were introduced at last to the famous sons. Harriet observed that it was true they were a handsome pair: Lord Ralph dark and suave with black hair and heavy, brooding brows. He spoke easily and his wild, exciting eyes seemed to be deep pools of promise wherein young ladies probably often drowned. Sir Benjamin was a fairheaded, somehow stiller version of his elder brother: his blond curls may have been a trifle wild but with a little flicker of recognition Harriet saw that he had the same deep, amused grey eyes as his father, in the portrait.

Lord Ralph bent low over Harriet's hand, an action that turned many girls rather faint. Harriet retained her equilibrium. She smiled and bowed her head to the gentlemen automatically, as she had been taught a hundred times. Aunt Lucretia and Augusta made little breathless sounds of pleasure. Harriet was aware that she was being scrutinised but could not speak. Her shyness was found charming by the young men, who had already been apprised of her beauty and saw that it was so; she was offered an arm and led to a card table and found herself playing whist, partnered first by Lord Kingdom, and then by the son of a bishop whose voice was high and who laughed a lot somewhat unnervingly in the rather silent room. There was conversation: Harriet heard about the weather, shooting, the countryside, the Swedish nightingale, riding, hunting and horses in general. Supper was served: the rotund cleric appeared and said a rather long grace. After supper one of the young ladies played several Beethoven pieces and Harriet heard Aunt Lucretia's voice echoing out from the corner where the chaperones sat, speaking of hats. A little scatter of applauding white gloves ended each number. Then another of the young ladies rather daringly offered to sing a new number for which she had just acquired the sheet music. She sang 'Yes! I Have Dared to Love Thee' bent rather swooningly over the piano, glancing occasionally at Lord Ralph Kingdom who leaned back in his chair with his legs thrown out in front of him. Harriet saw that Sir Benjamin's eyes twinkled slightly.

Finally the carriages were at the door and the sprinkling of guests slipped out into the night and were carried away. Harriet leaned into a corner of the Squire's carriage in relief and closed her eyes but was forced to open them again by Lucretia's excited talk.

'You girls were a *great* success, you were of course much the prettiest there though I say so myself, both partnered in cards by young Lord Kingdom, such a successful evening and it was noticeable that you were paid the highest attention, the Belles of the Ball in fact!'

The belles of the small card table, Mary would say, thought Harriet.

'And I have decided that with Edward's sad leaving coming upon us so soon,' Aunt Lucretia went on, 'we should ourselves hold a Departure Party!'

In her room, in her nightgown (a sight her sons had never seen), Lady Kingdom allowed her maid to brush her hair (her only indulgence). She closed her eyes.

She had always known of course that her elder son was – she chose her thoughts carefully – a little wild. But tonight her thoughts slid past her imposed boundaries to something it was necessary to face: there was something reckless, something extreme about Ralph which she feared and which seemed to be getting worse. It was imperative that she get him settled. A person in Lord Kingdom's position: money, property, impeccable lineage, the House of Lords waiting for him, should be able to sew wild oats of course but should not be *extreme*. Lady Kingdom literally drummed on her dressing table, a most unaccustomed sign of agitation. She impatiently waved her maid away: she could not think properly if there was somebody else in the room, fussing about.

She stared at herself in the mirror. She was the head of the House of Kingdom and it was imperative that she urgently find her elder son a suitable wife. Last year they had been within a hair's breadth of disaster: there had been a duke's young wife, a whisper of duels. Now there was this ridiculous involvement with ballet dancers. The gathering of intelligence about her sons' activities was part of the duties of the Reverend Cornelius Boothby (her second cousin twice removed) who, despite his unfortunate fondness for alcoholic beverages, had some talent for obtaining information. Last night he had told her that he had been reliably informed, never mind the *corps de ballet* and foolish little Mimi Oliver, that the *prima ballerina*, Fanny Cerrito herself, was believed to be throwing herself at Ralph and there had been public trouble at the theatre. It was well-known that the famous dancer, although most talented, was quite mad, and old, and a foreigner. Lady Kingdom found she was shaking with rage. The Kingdom name must not be sullied in this way.

She breathed deeply, endeavouring to calm herself. Tonight she had observed that Ralph had been greatly taken with the very quiet, and in truth very beautiful, Miss Harriet Cooper. Miss Cooper was not at all suitable, her family was not of sufficient pedigree at all despite the mother's fine family line and the eminence, these days, of the father. But what was Lady Kingdom to do? Ralph's downfall was his ridiculous and oft-repeated belief that he was in love: she must try and turn that weakness to her advantage. Harriet Cooper was modest and quiet: it was important that a respectable girl be urgently found over whom Lady Kingdom could have complete control. Lady Kingdom continued to breathe deeply.

This was not what she would have chosen, but Miss Harriet Cooper might have to do.

Next morning at breakfast Edward's Departure Party was discussed. Asobel was delighted and asked if she might wear her peach flowergirl's dress. Even William seemed to think Edward's departure merited being celebrated in this way. John asked Harriet if she thought there should be dancing and Lucretia began fluttering at once at the short time left to arrange matters. Edward himself smiled amicably at every suggestion but it was clear that his mind was elsewhere and he soon excused himself and went out into the barn where his packing boxes were being stored.

Lucretia, Augusta, Asobel and Harriet all followed him at once to give advice and assistance. Furniture, they had discovered, was not to be provided in the cabins on board the ship. Beds, chests of drawers, tables – if they could be used inside the cabin on the voyage they could be carried free of charge.

'Any bed, so long as it is thin,' said Edward. 'The cabins are extremely confined, in fact I can sleep on one of my boxes. Any old table. Small. But I can use one of my boxes for that too.' But his mother and his sisters wanted furniture suitable for his house in New Zealand, not *boxes*, and arguments ensued.

'There will be no room in the cabin,' said Edward in exasperation, 'and I do not want to spend money on storage.'

Lucretia announced that she had read in *The Times* about Ayckbourne's Float, a portable life preserver that could become as small as a handkerchief, and had urgently sent for one. Augusta carefully packed a Palmer's Patent Lamp. Harriet read aloud from several 'Emigrants' Handbooks': one mentioned the importance only of 'strong and useful clothing'; another insisted that a gentleman would need seventy-two calico shirts with dress fronts and twelve pairs of dress kid gloves.

'I am a farmer!' insisted Edward. 'It is the farming clothes that will be of the most importance.' Lucretia and Augusta pursed their lips, talked about the importance of clothes for a gentleman and folded embroidered waistcoats and silk cravats and kid gloves carefully.

Harriet read on:

> opportunities will occur on the voyage of catching rain water as it runs from the sails; the emigrant's wife should always take advantage of this as it will add materially to her own comfort and that of her husband, to wash as much as possible of a limited outfit.

'What will you do, Edward,' said Asobel, appalled, 'without a wife?'

'I will manage,' said Edward firmly.

They packed packets of Price's Patent Candles, matches, little cloths they had embroidered, books – 'You must still *read*, Edward,' said Harriet firmly – pens, even paper although Edward told them paper would be available in the new colony. Ten pounds of soap was insisted upon by Lucretia.

Edward baulked finally at a rather large painting of Queen Victoria; he agreed nevertheless that an artist from Canterbury should be contacted, to make (at some expense) a smaller copy of the painting of Augusta, Alice and Asobel which hung on the drawing-room wall.

Asobel had got it into her head that he should take a doll that she had loved since she was small. When Edward said no, spoke of space in the boxes, and the unlikelihood of old dolls being useful in his new life Asobel burst into tears.

'You don't understand,' she said woefully, looking up at her brother, 'I want you to take Lizzie because she will always make you think of me.'

Edward gave a small sigh and pushed at his hair so that it stood on end. 'Then of course I will take her, thank you,' he said and the battered Lizzie, whose gown had once been so elegant, was found a place next to a new Bible beside some of the soap and a comb. He also suddenly grabbed from a cupboard his old, child's cricket bat, his first cricket bat, and pushed it down one corner of a box. His mother now burst into tears.

'Mamma, whatever is the matter?'

'I saw you slip in your first cricket bat! You are thinking of your children! You will settle and marry there and have children there and never return!'

'Mamma, I took the bat as a memento, that is all, just – just something of mine from home. You know I always kept it. But I will leave it if you prefer?'

'No, no. But promise me I shall see my grandchildren!'

'Edward, you cannot get married without us being there!' Augusta looked as if he had just told her he was marrying tomorrow. 'We would want to know her, to check that she was suitable!' Edward, who had been trying very hard to remain calm, looked as if it was just possible that he might explode.

'It says here,' said Harriet quickly, 'that as in other countries where there are aborigines, bright beads and materials are good things to trade in – *baubles*, it says here.'

'I have bought my land,' said Edward. 'I would be embarrassed to trade for such a thing in baubles. And please, all of you, remember I am not going to the moon. There are already many stores in Wellington where no doubt daily requirements can be procured.'

'Don't you give Lizzie to anyone at all,' cried Asobel, 'for land, or anything. I will check, when I come, that she is living with you.'

Suddenly Harriet, unable to contain her own fears, asked Edward if the idea of the long sea journey frightened him. Lucretia put her hands to her mouth in horror at the subject being mentioned; Edward stood up from the boxes.

'I do not think you should be frightened, Mamma. I am not a fool. I know very well that ships have been lost and the oceans are wild and almost unexplored, and that Pacific storms are tempestuous and dangerous. But hundreds of journeys are without incident. Hundreds! And you know the *Miranda* has taken the route before. If one does not venture . . . I heard of a ship that foundered only one day outside Liverpool! The journey will be part of the adventure,' he concluded, smiling at all the women who loved him. 'I am in God's hands and I believe He will protect me, if it is His will.'

Edward and his father then locked themselves in the study, together with John, for financial discussions, from which the women were of course excluded. Harriet overheard the odd sentence about gold and stocks and bank drafts, mourned that she was not a man, could not enter these interesting dialogues, wanted to ask how everything was arranged, but knew of course it would be a great impertinence to do so. She knew nothing about money, had none of her own, took something to church but hardly ever held money, actual money, in her hand. She longed to know if English money was currency so far away, supposed it was if Queen Victoria owned the country: would Edward pack money in his luggage, nail it into one of his boxes, take it in a special bag? She was ashamed of her rather odd curiosity, knowing this was not women's business. The three men then came out of the study and went back to the barn: sorted wheat seeds and barley seeds, and even flower seeds, packing them with delicate care. Harriet, on the periphery, tried to understand their farmers' art. The possibility of taking small trees: apple trees, cherry, roses, was discussed but rejected, considered impractical on the long journey; sometimes Harriet found herself thinking of Seamus and his bees.

Asobel heard Lucretia ordering the coach to take her and Augusta to the town to find an artist to copy the painting and to 'make arrangements for the Departure Party' so she dragged Harriet off to the drawing room to 'read' – this was their compromise most days after the ban on teaching; they had gone back to 'Robinson Crusoe' with renewed vigour now that Edward was about to have what Asobel envisaged as similar adventures. The globe always sat beside them now, adding reality to their stories. Nobody in the world, Asobel maintained, knew where New Zealand was better than she.

Later, their mind full of adventures, they went back and sat on Edward's boxes while he packed and hammered and nailed outside the barn.

Asobel stared at the growing number of containers. 'The boat will sink, Eddie,' she proclaimed in worried tones.

'This is the last of the big boxes,' said Edward. 'Better to think of things now than when I am thousands of miles away.'

Harriet read aloud:

> The Colonist who is anxious to carry with him the
> memorials of the Fine Arts of the Old World can
> purchase at the British Museum casts in plaster
> of the antiquities contained in that institution.

Edward was fitting in a rake and a pitchfork.

'To put on the piano, these plaster casts? When you all come to visit me you will be able to bring the accoutrements of civilisation with you.'

'Eddie, what I want to know is,' said Asobel with great concentration, holding up her globe, 'will you be going along past other countries so that you can see land all the time in case anything goes wrong? Or will the boat have to go away from the land and be by itself in the middle of the sea?' She had actually made a chalk mark across the world to show how Edward's ship could get to New Zealand by almost always, with a few oceanic exceptions, travelling along beside land.

Edward did not laugh, but explained to her gravely. 'We must go out into the open sea to catch the wind,' he said, 'and to take the shortest time possible. If we crept along beside the land, as you have marked, we would take years to get to the other side of the world.'

'But you would be sure of getting there,' said Asobel, 'because people could see you from the land and come and get you if anything happened to you.' Her little face looked up at him anxiously.

'I shall write to you, and then you will know that we got there safely and that I am already building a house for you.'

'Shall we come really, *really*, Eddie?' Asobel asked.

'I don't see why not,' her brother answered, 'as long as I have built you a house so that you would be comfortable.'

'And Harriet?'

'Harriet of course. And Mary. And Augusta and Mamma and Papa. All of you.'

Asobel asked again, 'Really and truly?' and her small, grave face stared at her brother.

'Why do you doubt it?'

'Because it seems like a dream, that you are going to cross the world, and I cannot think it in my head that we will ever come there because I know adults don't always tell children the truth and sometimes when I think about you going so far away I feel funny because I think I will never see you again,' and Asobel burst into tears once more. Edward stopped hammering and picked her up and put her on his shoulders although she was really far too big for him to do that now. He wandered into the barn with her and talked to her about what was in the boxes and how he would, indeed, build her a house with everything that he was taking.

Harriet sat on the last big box, watching them. Asobel's little petticoats caught round Edward's shoulders in an extraordinarily unladylike manner that seemed to affect neither of them and soon Asobel's infectious, uncomplicated laughter came floating back out of the barn.

It was night. Harriet was in her nightgown. Her father had placed himself on the edge of her bed in such a way that she could not move. With both hands he was holding, stroking it over and over again, one of her feet. And then he moved towards her, whispering her name. And then he kissed her mouth.

TEN

Lucretia found she had no trouble acquiring young men for Edward's Farewell. All the suitable young men in the surrounding area, including Lady Kingdom's sons – 'My dears, they are to come down from London again especially!' – were interested in talking to Edward about the proposed journey; many were envious of his plans, and all were full of advice for his new life. Lucretia, remembering the success of the wedding, wanted to put up a marquee again. But she was persuaded by her husband and her elder son that it would be far too large for the small gathering that they were planning and that it was now almost November and a storm would turn a marquee into a mud bath. Instead it was agreed the servants would remove the furniture from the hall and bring in the piano so that there could be dancing after all and Cousin John looked forward immensely to – his head said *dancing with Harriet* but something else somewhere inside him said *pressing his cousin to him in the candlelight*.

Alice returned from the Isle of Wight and visited almost every day. When her husband came too she clung to him and looked pretty, and pale, and fragile, like a wife: different from the unmarried girls around her. And she *was* different. She had acquired something the others did not have, a prestige. For she was now in charge of a house, in charge of servants, her life fulfilled, her dreams come true. She was A Married Woman. But she also had a tense, white look about her eyes, as if she had suffered a shock of some kind.

And sometimes she and Lucretia closed themselves in rooms – only briefly (for Harriet saw that her aunt kept these private moments as short as possible), and sometimes Harriet saw that when Alice emerged she had been weeping. Just once, Lucretia whispered shortly about Alice's 'dark duties'.

There was a great deal of laughter and squealing when the carriages arrived, for the rain poured down and the ladies had to be escorted under umbrellas as they ran inside; gentlemen manfully dashed the rain from their own shoulders with insouciance. In the house, fires were burning brightly in almost every room and the light from the candle lamps shadowed and dipped, caught in every fresh draught from the door. William and Lucretia Cooper welcomed everybody as they came in; servants took mantles and shawls and umbrellas. Asobel, under the strictest instructions to behave like a young lady, was rushing about like a demented peach-dressed cherub as the ladies she was supposed to emulate sat in small groups giving little high laughs of excitement and anticipation.

Lord Kingdom made at once for the beautiful Harriet Cooper. 'I wish to engage you in the first and last dances at least!' he said, bowing low to her. Cousin John, who was standing next to Harriet, looked thunderous.

'This is not a ball, Ralph,' he said, but the young lord was smiling over Harriet's hand, which he had somehow managed to clasp in his.

Aunt Lucretia had, after much ado, engaged a pianist and a violinist who had come all the way from Canterbury and were already ensconced in the hall playing a particularly soulful version of 'I Dreamt that I Dwelt in Marble Halls'. They had even been given permission (after many requests from the girls) to play, later in the evening, a polka or two, even though Lucretia, taking her cue from what she had heard of the feelings of Queen Victoria, pronounced it a little vulgar.

There were only perhaps thirty young people and their chaperones but the hall was small enough to look excitingly crowded.

Harriet and Augusta found themselves at one point seated next to Sir Benjamin Kingdom of the unruly curls, the younger brother, who confirmed to them that he was interested in the science of geology and that he did sometimes study birds, but usually extinct ones. And that, in both disciplines, information was to be found pertaining to the history of the world.

'The whole world?' asked Harriet curiously.

'Some birds fly to other summers,' said Sir Benjamin, 'and some do not. Their remains,' (Augusta wrinkled her nose at the word *remains*) 'could tell us much, just as rocks do. There is reason to believe that the world is more inter-connected than we perceive,' and the grey eyes smiled. 'You should meet my friend Charles Darwin, who also studies birds. One day he may persuade us that even we in Great Britain are connected to, indeed are descended from, lesser beings than we imagine.'

'That is ridiculous,' said Augusta automatically, and then she gave a small gasp and put up her hand to her mouth. 'Oh, I do beg your pardon, Sir Benjamin, I did not at all mean to say that. But God made us, and we know from whence we come.'

'If God exists,' said Benjamin gravely.

Both girls looked at him in amazement. Just then the two-piece orchestra struck up a waltz and both girls were immediately claimed. But as she stood in obedience to the other gentleman's bow, Harriet turned back for just a moment to Benjamin, who had of course risen also.

'Do you not believe in God? There *must* be a God who protects us in this world. There *has to be*.' She could not believe what she had just heard, leaned back towards him to hear his answer above the music, staring at him with intense concentration.

'It is perhaps a matter at least for conjecture,' he said gently. 'Anyone who has been involved in geology, anyone who has seen ancient fossils embedded in rocks that must have been there for millions of years, would perhaps acknowledge that the existence of God as we have known him needs to reconsidered.' And as he watched her beautiful face, so intense, so absorbed in his answer, so utterly *listening*, he suddenly saw clearly something else: his words had elucidated from her a quick flash of utter desperation which jolted him like a knife blow. And in that instant, as he caught that swift, anguished look as she listened, he had what he later had to explain to himself was a premonition, even though he didn't believe in premonitions: *something, some action of his, would change this girl's life.* Harriet was whisked away.

Benjamin was thrown enough by this odd experience to stand on the steps outside and smoke a cigar in the rain.

There Edward found him. 'Ah, Ben, all this social intercourse is not much to your liking!'

'Indeed, I am enjoying it very much,' said Benjamin, throwing his odd thoughts and his cigar into the night rain. 'What a wonderful adventure you will have, Eddie. Well worth a celebration!'

'Come and see my packing,' said Edward and the two men disappeared through the rain into the barn where Edward proudly recounted the contents of the boxes, the facts of the New Zealand climate, the farming possibilities and the terrain of the new country. Benjamin listened, asked questions, fascinated by Edward's comments on the extraordinary length of the journey, until Asobel ran to find them because more guests had arrived.

'I do envy you,' said Benjamin, 'and I do wish you much success.' He almost mentioned Harriet, and then did not. He clapped Edward on the shoulder most amiably, saying, 'I shall look for news of you,' as they walked back to the house.

Later, dancing again with Lord Ralph, Harriet said, 'Your brother Benjamin seems not to believe in the existence of God.'

'Oh of course he does,' said Lord Ralph, his dark eyes smiling down at her. 'He was merely trying to shock you. You cannot be a Kingdom and not believe in God. And I believe in God, Harriet Cooper, because after all only God could have made someone as beautiful as you.'

And because she somehow felt relieved at his answer, and because he was so very handsome and spoke so obviously meaning to charm, just for a moment Harriet could not help but be charmed, and she looked up at Ralph Kingdom and smiled.

The beautiful brief moment turned itself into an arrow, and pierced his heart.

The Squire spoke to the musicians, who stopped playing. In the silence William Cooper cleared his throat in a friendly manner. Everybody turned to him dutifully and Harriet saw his dear, round face, an older version of Cousin Edward, beam at the assembly.

'Welcome to Rusholme,' he said. 'You will all know that we have invited you here to make your farewells to our son Edward who shortly leaves us to travel to New Zealand. My dear wife and I are, as I am sure you can imagine, very sad to see him go. But we are nevertheless very proud—' William spoke quite gruffly, so moved was he, '—that Edward will be in the tradition of a long line of British explorers – for that is what he is, surely – taking our world to the rest of the world, as it were. Edward, as a farmer, is to take with him the very essence of our farm here in dear old England: the wheat seeds, the barley seeds – and will plant that very seed from Rusholme in a foreign land. In that way Britain expands to countries less fortunate than our own, and Her Majesty's influence spreads far and wide, silencing barbarians.'

There were many cries of 'Hear, hear' at this point and a tear was perhaps surreptitiously wiped from several eyes and the rain poured down outside. The Squire put up his hand.

'As has been said by a wiser man than me: THE SUN NEVER SETS ON THE BRITISH EMPIRE!' Then he turned to his younger son. 'We shall miss you greatly, dear boy,' he said, 'and we must trust God to keep you safe. But let us hear proud things of you.'

There was now much applause and further cries of 'Hear, hear!' and the musicians, quite overcome with emotion themselves, struck up 'God Save the Queen'. Everyone sang lustily, *happy and glorious, long to reign over us,* and all still stood erect for a moment as the last notes died away, thinking of Edward sailing so bravely to one of Her Majesty's far-flung dominions. The Squire, almost in tears, nevertheless gave a sign to the musicians, who now broke into a polka; William Cooper bowed to his wife and to the surprise of their children, they began to dance. Cousin John immediately led Harriet, despite the looming presence of Lord Kingdom, who merely bowed good-naturedly to Augusta, who nearly fainted in delight. Alice and her husband then took to the floor, Alice's tears and fears forgotten for this time. The stone floors of the hall rang with the dancing feet and the bright and cheerful music, while in the dining room the damask-covered table was set out with the finest cold collation the Squire's farm could provide.

Afterwards, riding home with his brother, Benjamin Kingdom spoke thoughtfully. 'Although the sun never sets on the British Empire I wonder if this wholesale emigration will prove to be a good idea. It is one thing to discover a new country, surely the most exciting thing on earth, and I do envy Edward his journey. But to colonise it may be another matter. Mr Gladstone has his doubts, if I remember. He believes that colonisation is a melancholy story, that wherever settlers from people in an advanced state of civilisation come into contact with the people of a barbarous country the result is always somehow dishonourable.'

'It is progress, Ben,' said Ralph. 'History has shown us that you can never halt progress.' But his mind was elsewhere. They did not hurry in the night. The rain had almost stopped. The horses trotted quietly down dark, chill lanes. 'Miss Harriet Cooper is extraordinarily beautiful,' said Ralph at last.

'She is,' said Benjamin quietly. 'She was quite the most beautiful girl in the room. In that yellow gown.'

'Ah Ben, you see, you notice worldly things occasionally,' said his brother wryly. Benjamin did not answer.

'But—' Ralph's horse turned down a long valley, sensing home, but Ralph held the reins tightly, did not let the animal have its head. Benjamin's horse followed, similarly held; there was the sound of bridles being shaken and pulled in the darkness. 'But – she made me feel as if there was a thin, invisible wall between us. As if,' again Ralph hesitated, puzzled, 'as if she were unreachable.'

Benjamin smiled across at his brother. 'I cannot believe you have not had your usual success! Perhaps she is in love with her cousin John, I see he danced with her often.'

'No, I watched her. She was the same with him as she was with me.'

'My dear Ralphie, you "reach", as you put it, more women than any man I know, and no doubt you will reach Miss Harriet Cooper if you put your mind to it! Mind you, if Mamma knew the half of it – of your activities in London and your latest interest in *corps de ballet* and Mimi Oliver – I believe she would disinherit you at once and you would have nothing to offer Miss Cooper!' Both brothers laughed. They knew very well of course that the Reverend Cornelius Boothby, their mother's distant relation, kept their mother informed of their activities: they derived much enjoyment from setting him off on wild-goose chases. Once they got him as far as Stoke-on-Trent before he realised that he had mistaken a lecture on fossils for an assignation with a woman: he never reported that particular journey to Lady Kingdom. This week they had managed to inform him that the glorious Italian ballerina, Fanny Cerrito, had shown Ralph favour; the Reverend Boothby had been informed (by a friend of the brothers) of scenes of jealous uproar during a performance. The Reverend Boothby was not aware that Fanny Cerrito was most respectably married. So the brothers laughed together safely down the dark country lane: they were both terrified of their mother, in their way, but Lady Kingdom could not disinherit her son, of course; more than that, Benjamin Kingdom lived in a world of books and rocks and birds. Should his elder brother be removed in any way as heir to their deceased father, Benjamin would be most extremely inconvenienced.

'But I say, Ralph,' and Benjamin's voice suddenly rose with enthusiasm in the darkness, 'I should like to go, like Edward, to the farther reaches of the world. I mean, to make discoveries. Europe is so known to us, in comparison. What secrets would we find in the African interior, I wonder? Or that of Australia? What islands of the Pacific are still waiting for their mystery to be unfurled?' and they let their horses go at last and galloped the last mile, and young ladies with invisible walls around them were not discussed again on that journey.

Yet Ralph Kingdom, leaving for London and Mimi Oliver early next morning (formally kissing his severe mother goodbye, bowing politely to the Reverend Boothby, leaving with no regret the cold, high rooms of his childhood), drew up his horse as he turned out of the valley. He hated returning to this country seat, somehow it chilled his blood: he wanted to be back to the warmth of his life in London as soon as possible. But in the grey morning he sat for several minutes with an unaccustomed feeling in his heart; looked back across the fields to where Rusholme lay, unseen in the distance, and thought again of the beautiful girl in the pale yellow gown, surrounded by something she had erected between herself and the world.

Several hours later, having gone over some estate accounts for his mother, and dealt with some trivial matters with the Reverend Boothby, Benjamin Kingdom too set out for London and his home near the Regent's Park. He was to meet with Isambard Kingdom

Brunel (a distant relation) and talk of bridges; the prospect of such a meeting filled him with excitement and delight. But when Benjamin rode out of the valley he impulsively turned his horse back towards Rusholme, galloped past the empty fields in the grey morning. He was passionately interested in all the new sciences. He totally believed that his friend Darwin would soon prove to the world that old certainties could no longer be relied on. He certainly did not believe in premonitions.

Yet as Rusholme came into view, as he sat there on the ridge looking down across the fields to the house, his horse breathing heavily from their ride, he felt it again, even as he tried to push it away: it was his brother Ralph who had perhaps set his wild heart on Harriet Cooper, Benjamin accepted that as he must: he was the younger brother. But he felt absolutely certain that *something*, some action, some decision of his, Benjamin's, was to change Harriet's life.

He shook his head in a kind of puzzlement, and then suddenly, because life almost always amused him, he laughed at himself. *This may just be another version of courtly love!* he thought, smiling, and, glad to be alive in this exciting world, he turned his horse and galloped off towards London and his life.

ELEVEN

On the last Sunday all the Coopers attended the morning service at the little church where Alice had been married. The congregation sang loudly.

> Speed thy servants, saviour speed them
> Thou are Lord of wind and waves
> They were bound, but thou hast freed them
> Now they go to free the slaves.

Rather as if, Harriet thought, Edward was a missionary not a farmer.

Then the vicar, who had visited for wine and Madeira cake the previous day, fixed his eyes first on the ceiling of the church, then on the tombstone of Edward's grandfather; finally on Edward himself.

'Today we say farewell to one of the young men of our parish who is preparing to make a new life in another country. We countenance him to place God before all things, to travel in the spirit of the Lord, to at all times honour our country, our Queen, and our God. To impart to all whom he may meet the word of God, and to remember that God above sees all things no matter where we may be and will call us to account on judgement day.'

As the vicar went on, at some length, about Edward's Christian duties, Edward sat with his head bowed. Harriet wondered what he was thinking: how he was feeling to leave the security of Rusholme where he and his family had always lived. The congregation stood and sang one more hymn to calm the traveller:

> God moves in a mysterious way
> His wonders to perform
> He plants his footsteps in the sea
> And rides upon the storm.

*

Back at Rusholme the painted copy of the cherubic picture of Augusta and Alice and Asobel was one of the last things to be packed into the cases and boxes that now stood in the hall. It was wrapped in a big farmer's coat and some blankets, to keep it safe from harm.

'But I shan't forget any of your dear faces,' said Edward, his face full of emotion as they sat around the dining-room table on the last evening. Yet it was hard to be sad: the cart was piled high with his worldly goods, the horses were already groomed for tomorrow's journey. Despite the cholera the London Coopers as well as the Rusholme Coopers would travel to Gravesend to see the *Miranda* and farewell Edward. The family was in such a state of high excitement that somehow the grief of the parting, the uncertainty of the long journey into the unknown was able to be pushed to the back of their minds and William Cooper filled the glasses.

'To Edward and his future on the other side of the globe!'

'To Edward!' called the Cooper family, and recalled family stories and laughed, the way many families meeting, or parting, do.

Edward felt things most keenly when, one last time, the gentlemen joined the ladies for tea. He had always been surrounded by loving women; for a moment he wondered when such domestic warmth would be his again. Conversation languished at last: it was high time for Asobel to be in bed, for the ladies too to retire in preparation for the early start; there were tears in the air.

Harriet surprised them all by asking a strange, unexpected question in the tentative uneasiness.

'How do you *feel*, Edward?' she asked at last. Her voice was odd, and her face was filled with a kind of naked, curious intensity. 'About leaving everything behind that you have ever known.'

The Cooper family looked embarrassed: it was not a question a lady asked a gentleman. Lucretia frowned as if Harriet had made a large social blunder.

But Edward had repeated her question: 'How do I feel?' How he felt was not something he was at all used to discussing but he rubbed his face; he would like an answer himself. He looked at all his family, all the familiar faces, and the room where the fire had been lit, and his mother's flushed cheeks from the wine, and the wax fruit, and the shadows made by the candles on to the painting of his sisters that he had had copied, and the bright, delicate teacups. For just a moment he faltered, they saw, and then something else, some other energy, crossed his face.

'I feel—' he hesitated and then gained courage, 'I feel so *lucky*! To be part of a generation of men from our great country who are taking our heritage and our Queen and our God to the further reaches of this world about which there is still so much to discover! It is as Father said, I am a kind of explorer. I will be working on land where no man has ever been – is that not an amazing thought? I will be building a life with all the things I have learnt, I am twenty years old and there will be, God willing, adventures in my life that I cannot yet conceive of. Although we do not know when we shall meet again I am optimistic that it need not be long. New Zealand is now part of our Empire, Her Majesty is still my Queen although I will be so far away, and it seems clear to me that life will be full of chance and adventure.' His round face was lit up with enthusiasm and who among his listeners could weep after all when such hope shone, that night?

The servants ran about with hot water long before dawn but Lucretia had already risen: in the night she had realised that her son would need a medicine box, the main ingredient of which should be of course Morison's Vegetable Universal. To this cure-all she added castor oil, camphorated oil, black pepper, liquorish pills and Quinine Dentifrice in case of toothache. Finally, from a bottom drawer, she took her precious Allingham's Rotterdam Corn and Bunion Solvent. William, waking from uneasy dreams, saw his wife in her voluminous nightdress bent over a small box in the candlelight and, enquiring what she was doing, made the suggestion that some of her laudanum might be added. He himself pulled on his boots and could have been seen, a strange figure in his nightgown, making a further, final collection of horseshoes from the stables: 'I can after all obtain these more easily,' he said to the groom who was already harnessing the horses, 'than my dear boy might, so far away.'

By six o'clock Alice and her husband had arrived in their carriage into which Augusta, Harriet and Asobel were ordered. The Squire's carriage and the cart of luggage travelling behind it were ready. Horses snorted, ladies gathered their petticoats about them. John and Edward and their father and Donald and the groom all checked ropes again anxiously in the half-light. The cook and the maid waved tearfully as first the carriages and then the heavily loaded cart rattled away down the gravel drive past the blackcurrant bushes and the green and overgrown grass, past the familiar fields of the old farm, finally turning, as the dawn light showed on the horizon, towards the road to London.

Along the Thames huge chimneys spewed out black smoke; along the docks drains ran into the river; on the river coal was unloaded from the sailing colliers by lightermen on to the small boats and the barges that were ferried ashore. Yellow fog entwined itself with the smoke from the big chimneys of the tanneries and the factories and the new steamboats and the chemical works and the loud, bustling railways. And as the black grime covered the buildings and the population of the city, people said to each other: *how beautiful London is, look at our beautiful gaslight, look at our wonderful railways.*

The yellow-black fog rolled along the river and into the city, insinuated itself into the houses of the rich and of the poor indiscriminately; into the churchyards where so many bodies had been piled; into the hospitals, where doctors breathed, *hardly daring*, a sigh of relief. That week the cholera deaths had declined to thirty-one. The General Board of Health was still not able to pinpoint the cause of the epidemic but they pointed to its passing and gave again advice: the public should avoid over-exertion, late hours and excitement; they should take meals at regular intervals and preserve a quiet frame of mind. The General Board of Health had also issued orders to the Metropolitan Burial Grounds: graveyards must be covered in quicklime and burials in the city churchyards were to end forthwith. There was much talk of further baths and wash houses for the poor like the one already opened in St Pancras, and the Prime Minister fervently hoped that the frequent, unwelcome visits from health officials to his chambers would now cease.

The composer Chopin, who had played in London, had died in France, to much regret. Books such as 'Jane Eyre' by the mysterious author Mr Currer Bell were described as 'anatomies of the female heart' to much outrage, and The Hungarian Vocalists were touring the country. Cart-boys whistled 'Yes! I Have Dared to Love Thee' through the murky air, trundling with their vegetables and their bread and their parcels through the sawdust and the rotten fish and the vegetable peelings; trudging over the mud and the horse excrement and the human excrement all turned to slush; and ignoring the continual, all-embracing smell of that which most people didn't mention, and which the lower orders called piss.

It was already night when the carriages, followed doggedly by the packed cart, rolled into Bryanston Square. In the foggy darkness, with the street gas lamps shining through as best they might, Mary waited at the door, her face wreathed in happiness, her two brothers dutifully standing in as hosts while Sir Charles was still at the Palace of Westminster. Lucretia Cooper was almost overcome as she climbed heavily down, overcome by London, asking for her laudanum. She spoke like one possessed of the crowds, of the dazzling carriages they had passed coming in to London, of seeing bejewelled ladies, of thinking their coach should crash. Asobel was also overcome because before it got dark she had seen a balloon in the sky with people in it. Now she hopped up and down clutching her globe, staring with open mouth at the streetlights; had never used a water closet, was taken hurriedly there by a maid instructed by Mary. Edward and John with their cousins and the grooms at once attended to the ropes of the cart; Uncle William could hardly manage to climb down after such a long journey; the footmen bowed stiffly at all the commotion. Immediately Harriet got out of the carriage, running towards Mary, the smell of the cesspits of Bryanston Square hit her so that she gasped even as she ran. She had forgotten, at Rusholme. The exhausted horses snorted and whinnied and were led round to the mews. Harriet and Mary at last held each other tightly and walked up the steps.

The country Coopers were, as always, overpowered by the oppression of the house; once inside they spoke more quietly, aware of the servants everywhere. Asobel bounced on the bed in the room she was to share with Augusta: pronounced it horrible and hard, but she only whispered it very quietly and she kept looking at the flaring gas lamps, listening to the hiss they made.

And Harriet sat for a moment in her room.

She heard the grooms and the horses in the mews, and the dull sound of all the carriages in the distance. The smell of meat and cabbage and old cigars wafted up the stairs as if she had never been away. There was a knock at the door: she tensed at once. A maid entered and gave a small nervous curtsey.

'Is there anything you want, Miss Harriet? Shall I assist you to dress for dinner?'

'No thank you.' Harriet looked at the girl in puzzlement.

'I'm your new maid, I'm called Lucy. I began work here the day you left so you probably don't remember me, I forgot the milk on the first day but I'm a quick learner and I hope I please you,' and she bobbed again. She looked about twelve, and anxious, and Harriet remembered: Lucy was the maid who sang to Quintus.

'Has my sister asked you to be my new maid?' Mary had not said.

'No, ma'am. Sir Charles, ma'am.'

'I see.' (She looked so young to be one of her father's sentinels.) 'Well, Lucy, I imagine I shall not be here for some weeks yet.'

Now the maid looked puzzled, but knew better than to speak. 'Very well, Miss Harriet.'

And Harriet was alone again, listening to the sounds, and smelling the smells, of the city.

An hour later the Right Honourable Sir Charles Cooper, MP, arrived home; everybody had dressed and the evening meal was immediately served. Quintus the dog and Harriet had just discovered each other; Quintus became deeply over-excited, and had to be removed. Sir Charles said a long grace and then began to carve, footmen bent over wine glasses, food was served by an array of maids. Although Mary spoke warmly to her cousins and her aunt, the Cooper women (even Lucretia) only murmured politely, the conversation was dominated by men's voices. Sir Charles's voice dominated most of all; every now and then his hooded eyes took in his younger daughter, who was home again. And who would not be leaving.

Before dessert, his face flushed, he stood in his place at the end of the table, pouring more wine before he spoke. 'Well, Edward,' he began. Everybody was silent and attentive. There was something about Sir Charles Cooper that made people pay attention: the leonine face, the hooded, blank eyes, the mane of silver hair; and something else: an air of barely concealed danger, or violence, or rage. The dining room was very quiet.

'Her Majesty's government, if I may say so, has not had much interest in this "emigration" business. Therefore I think we have not been careful enough about the type of person we are allowing to leave the country; I fear they have not, in some cases, given a good impression of the British. And it seems to be costing us a great deal of money, sending troops to far-flung places that we have decided to interest ourselves in, to quell the natives. However. We cannot, of course, stand by – indeed it is totally out of the question that we should allow ourselves to be humbled by savages. And we are now taking some steps to regulate the whole business of emigration. I am glad that people of Edward's calibre are grasping the nettle: who knows what treasures, what gold, what raw materials men like him may still find! You, Edward, must remember that we, the British people, are the guardians of civilisation – our spirit and our influence is felt all over the world and when I say our spirit, I mean our spirit of adventure, and of moral excellence, and of endeavour, and enterprise, and refinement. We are the greatest race on earth, and the proudest; our influence stretches to every part of the globe and you must never forget that you are crossing the oceans in that magnificent tradition.' Sir Charles raised his glass. 'Under the influence of Edward, and British men like him, lesser races of savage or alien men will see that the British Empire which embraces them is wise, strong, industrious and benign. God save Her Majesty.'

Under the gas chandelier that seemed to Asobel to hold hundreds of soft dancing lights the assembled company rose and drank to Queen Victoria. Sweetmeats were then served, the ladies retired while the gentlemen drank port, and when they joined the ladies Sir Charles commanded his younger daughter to play 'Lo, the Beams of Early Morning', followed by 'Yes! I Have Dared to Love Thee', on the piano in the drawing room where, although the fire had been burning all day, the ladies pulled their shawls about them, feeling the chill in the air.

TWELVE

November in London. Rain overnight had turned the roads and
pavements to slush; by dawn a dark, dank, unpleasant cloud had
settled over everything and the streetlights could hardly be seen.
They had to leave before dawn: the vehicles came round to the
front of the Bryanston Square house like shadows; petticoats disappeared into carriages and horses stumbled through the fog,
sending up great spurts of mud and excrement in their wake as
they turned towards Blackfriars.

There the women huddled nervously under umbrellas, eyed the
crowded and jostling early-morning river. They boarded one of the
new steamboats to Gravesend: people crowded on to the deck to
say goodbye to Saint Paul's Cathedral, the ladies were then handed
into the saloon; all the luggage was loaded on to colliers and small
boats behind them. Edward anxiously watched his worldly goods
sinking low into the water. Inside in the saloon cabin Lucretia discreetly swallowed heroic amounts of laudanum, Asobel insisted
on looking intently at her globe for most of the journey and refused
to speak, refused to be roused by views of London from the river.
There was a great deal of weeping as people who were to sail away
said goodbye to London, not knowing if they were to see it ever
again, not that they could see so much of it now as the fog would

not lift and their own boat added to the smoke and the smell. Harriet, sitting next to Mary on a wooden seat, watched all the leaving people carefully, wondered (as she had wondered about Edward) how they *felt*. She stared out through the fog; she could not imagine how the river traffic: the passenger boats, the barges, the colliers, the small vehicles rowed by men from one side of the river to the other, did not all collide in the yellow odorous mist that engulfed them all. On the deck Edward stood with his father and his uncle and his cousins, all men together: the stink of the Thames came up to meet them as they were stopped for a moment near Deptford; Edward looked at the river in disgust. Through the fog and the rain boats passed, unspeakable things floated on the water, the smell rose, their boat floated among everything as it slowed for some reason, then moved forward once more.

'Surely, sir,' said Edward suddenly to his uncle, 'the Thames should be cleaned.'

'The tide cleans it,' said Sir Charles shortly.

'But the drains, the sewers, look, you can *see* the stuff flowing out when the tide is low like this. There, from that tannery. People drink this water.'

'You don't understand nature,' said Sir Charles. 'The water is cleaned by the tide,' and he turned away from his nephew to his sons and lit a cigar, shielding his flame from the rain as the river slowly widened before them on their journey.

Gravesend, when they arrived at last, was like a circus. People and sailors and belongings were everywhere, tents and traders crowded together. Somehow Edward was found and embraced by his two travelling companions, Chambers and Lyle, and they excitedly followed the progress of their luggage: some for storage but as many pieces as possible to be squeezed into their cabin. Much luggage had been taken aboard nearer London; Edward briefly could not identify his own among all the boxes and furniture lying everywhere; his friends and some of the servants hurried about, tripping over ropes, dodging sailors. The rest of the family stared at the *Miranda* with various degrees of enthusiasm. The rain had stopped at last and sailors were unfurling ropes, and a very tall man, pointed out as the pilot, was preparing to come aboard to lead the *Miranda* downriver and out to the channel. The men and the younger women climbed aboard; Mary and Lucretia were among the group of women winched aboard on chairs: it had been suggested Lucretia stay on shore but she wished to see where her son would spend the next months and endured the winching bravely. They had to pass surly sailors swinging up rope ladders and swarms of poor-looking people carrying bundles of clothes who were travelling below, in steerage. At one point two pigs got loose from a pigpen on the main deck, and, perhaps having some idea of their fate when the ship was out at sea and fresh meat was called for (for the cabin passengers), they ran squealing loudly all over the ship, eluding the grabbing hands of sailors and passengers alike for quite some time. And Mary, staring below quickly and carefully as they passed, looked shocked and quite pale, murmured to Harriet that there must be almost no air for those people who were travelling steerage, *there are no windows down there at all*, she whispered.

They found the impossibly small cabin where the young men were to be ensconced but now the usually placid Edward was shouting and servants were carrying a trunk and trying to get it in through the door and Chambers was looking worried because his bed seemed to have disappeared. Things had to be nailed or screwed to the floor so that they would not move about the small space during the voyage, carpenters were called for everywhere but Edward had his own supply of nails and screws and hammers. Both Chambers' and Lyle's families were also trying to say goodbye, women clutching at arms, men trying to help with the luggage, upwards of twenty people trying impossibly to get inside the cabin and bumping in to others along the narrow corridor.

'We must go to the dining saloon,' said Sir Charles authoritatively. 'The travellers can join us when their luggage is safely stowed.'

The dining saloon was as wide as the ship itself, but nevertheless seemed narrow and dark, the only light coming from small round windows. It was decorated for cabin passengers in the style to which they were accustomed: Greek arches, cornices, carpets, and high-backed, damask-covered chairs, cupids dallied with bows and arrows and primroses in each corner of the ceiling, but everything in miniature, as befitting the space. It was crowded with milling people; Lucretia, suddenly aware of the ship moving slightly beneath her, looked around wildly, said very, very nervously to her husband, 'It is very *small* after all, to go on large oceans. Will Edward be *safe*, William, do you think?'

'My dear Lucretia,' said Sir Charles, 'of course he will be safe. This is a British ship. After some earlier disasters all ships have to be surveyed and found seaworthy and certificated. And should something untoward happen to him let me assure you there is a surgeon on board. I have already spoken to the Captain and made him aware that Edward is a nephew of mine. He will be in good hands. These ships were once disease-infected hellholes, but that was long ago. We learnt a great deal from the early ships that went to Canada and the Government has made a great deal of difference now.'

'What about the people below, Father?' asked Mary. Harriet thought: *How pale she looks. She really does care what happens to those people she does not even know.*

'What about them?' Through a tiny window Harriet saw a woman in a thin shawl clutching, with the rest of her bundles, some buddleia she had picked from a ragged bush at the dock's edge, as if to take a little of England with her.

'It would seem that they will be so crowded, there seem to be a great many of them, and there is no air.'

'Do you realise that many of them are not even paying for their passage?' said her father. 'Or only part of it? They are going out as labourers. The New Zealand Company is wisely sending out a proportion of servants to meet the needs of the better classes who are emigrating, otherwise chaos would ensue of course. So these people have guaranteed employment when they arrive. What are your complaints?'

'Just that it would seem to be a very uncomfortable four months. The *Miranda*, as we can see, is not a large ship. Will they have enough food and water?'

Sir Charles looked at his elder daughter with impatience. 'I think it is not your business, Mary. Edward will be dining at the Captain's table.' As if in gratitude at Edward's good fortune the doors of the dining room were suddenly held open by two liveried servants and to everyone's astonishment Lord Ralph Kingdom and Sir Benjamin Kingdom entered, escorting between them their formidable mother, who was looking rather stunned, presumably from her winching aboard. Nevertheless with a regal air she bowed slightly to the Coopers when she saw them through the crowd that had parted at her majestic entrance, and allowed her sons to escort her onwards. Sir Charles Cooper, stepping forward to bow, did not miss the fact that Ralph Kingdom's eyes immediately sought, and found, Harriet. He missed the fact that Benjamin Kingdom was looking at her also, although the latter might have appeared to be more interested in the construction of the dining saloon.

'Ah, Charles!' said Lady Kingdom. 'We thought we might find you here on this—' she paused for the precise words, '—tremendous emigratory occasion for your family. Where is Edward?'

Edward's absence was explained, Uncle William introduced Mary and her two brothers: but, despite Lady Kingdom's best efforts, and her placing herself firmly upon one of the damask-covered chairs, the formality of the occasion could not be properly adhered to because people kept being propelled into the dining room, by excitement, or by the crush of people. The noise of excited voices rose and rose as sailing time approached.

'What an extraordinary thing, for them to come to say goodbye to Edward!' whispered Lucretia to Augusta and Alice. 'An honour to our family indeed.'

'I think, Mamma,' said Augusta sourly, as Ralph took Mary's hand and then turned to Harriet and bent towards her, 'that Lord Kingdom has developed an interest in Harriet.'

'I am very glad to see you again,' murmured Ralph, holding Harriet's hand for a fraction longer than was necessary.

'Nonsense!' said Lucretia.

Sir Charles Cooper watched Lord Ralph Kingdom impassively.

'My dear Charles,' said Lady Kingdom, 'we just happened to be passing and hoped we might see you. You have not been down to our part of the world since your niece's wedding, I think. My sons have agreed to spend some time with me in the country before Christmas and we have decided to have a Christmas Ball to which we would very much like you and your family, all the Coopers of course (and she smiled imperiously at Lucretia), to attend so that we might see more of you. We have already been delighted by Harriet. An invitation will be delivered.' Nobody ever said no, of course, to Lady Kingdom, but at this moment a bell began ringing over and over: the ship's bell: it was time for visitors to go ashore.

Edward appeared, rushing through the door as if shot out of a catapult. His face was red and pale by turns, red from his exertions, and pale with distress as he began his final goodbyes. He showed surprise to see Lady Kingdom but greeted her pleasantly and shook hands warmly with her sons: 'It was good of you to come, Ralph, Ben, I'll let you know how it all turns out,' and Benjamin said again, 'I shall look for news of you, Eddie,' and Ralph wished him good fortune. Then Edward said goodbye to his London relations, much shaking of hands and back-slapping from the men. Harriet somehow planted a remote, and at the same time intense, kiss on his cheek; Mary smiled at her favourite cousin and put her arms about his shoulders for a moment.

'Please, please write, Edward,' Harriet begged. 'Please share this adventure with us if you can.'

'Edward,' said Mary softly, 'do not have too many wild hopes. It will be a difficult life, I think.' Both Harriet and Edward looked at Mary in surprise.

'Dearest, dearest Mary,' said Edward. 'I am organised. You know that I have looked into this journey carefully and I have no fears. Just *write* to me!' and he kissed her cheek.

And then he turned at last to his family. The unspoken question hung between them: *when would they ever meet again?* Lucretia, when the moment came, perhaps inspired by the presence of Lady Kingdom, behaved with great dignity as she put her arms around her son. Alice and Augusta had tears running down their faces which they endeavoured to wipe away and not make a public spectacle of themselves, even Cousin John looked upset as he said goodbye. William, biting his lip, shook hands with Edward over and over again, saying only 'God bless you, my boy,' but Asobel clung to her brother and wept aloud, sobbed and sobbed as if her heart would break. All around there was a crying sound as families began to disembark. For everybody understood: there was no turning back now. Not only did they not know when they would meet again, but it could be so many months before there was any news at all.

Farewell, the voices cried to their loved ones and the word resonated with meaning: *fare you well on your long and hazardous journey.*

Lady Kingdom and Ralph and Benjamin turned towards their carriage but most of the Coopers, gazing upwards, hardly noticed, so intent were they on seeing Edward still. Ralph's (and Benjamin's) last view of Harriet was of her staring up at the *Miranda*. She was looking intently, unaware that she was being watched, not at her cousin but at the prow of the ship as the sails began to fill. A figurehead had been carved on the prow, long hair streaming as she led the ship towards its destination.

And Lord Ralph Kingdom, as at last he turned away to escort his mother, did not know that Sir Charles Cooper was carefully watching him.

After interminable waiting there was the sound of the anchor being winched upwards, a loud metallic noise that grated on the ear, made everybody feel uneasy. The tall pilot they had seen boarding stood on the deck with the Captain issuing orders to the crew; the smaller sails that had been unfurled swelled, caught the wind suddenly, and then there was the heart-stopping moment when the ship began to move and the gap between the dock and the *Miranda* became wider, and wider, and wider. The families left behind stood staring at the water between, waving to the people they loved who were moving farther and farther away; they heard the harsh calls of the sailors and the sound of the capstan turning; watched the sails taking up and then losing the wind, taking it up and losing it, until the ship had turned away and was properly on its journey to the mouth of the river and the sea.

Farewell, they all called, one more time, to the departing sails.

And then a kind of eerie silence, or so it seemed to the shocked, bereft families left behind, echoed about the dock. There was not a silence at all of course: the cries from the costermongers and the merchants who had been selling items to the passengers right up to the last minute were not muted as they made their way from the dockside, the barges and the small boats noisily crowded the river as always; yet perhaps the people left behind heard nothing for a moment but the beating of their own shocked hearts as they abruptly understood the reality of what had happened.

Then somebody called loudly about boats to London and the spell was broken and the steamboats filled up with passengers as the white sails of the *Miranda* diminished in the distance.

The country Coopers, all their faces pale with sadness on the river boat, were adamant they would return at once to Rusholme no matter how long it would take; Lucretia muttered that Asobel had had far too much excitement. All of them secretly wanted to write to Edward at once, this minute, tonight, to catch the next boat, to send something at least of themselves to the loved one who had gone.

Darkness came inexorably on; they had almost reached Blackfriars Bridge when there was a commotion of boats and people. A woman had jumped off the bridge, her body was being pulled out of the water; her shawl or her dress was entangled in boats or detritus or oars or hooks, it was hard to see exactly as the lanterns moved backwards and forwards in the dark. Lucretia immediately stopped Asobel watching: in horror the others saw the body, arms hanging, dress open, being finally thrown up on to a small barge. It seemed like a bad omen. Their own steamboat rang its bell, little boats flashed across the bow again, they moved towards the pier beside the bridge.

The carriages stood waiting under the gaslights. Sir Charles, who had stood aloof on the small deck as they travelled back on the subdued boat, irritated the whole journey by the fact that his nephew John seemed to be hovering with some question of import, turned abruptly to his brother and sister-in-law.

'I am required to return to Parliament even at this hour. Thank you for your kindness to Harriet. The epidemic is almost over and I see no reason for her to return with you to Rusholme.'

Under the gaslight Mary saw that Harriet stared at her father in startled, then shocked, surprise. She had not brought her belongings with her; her father had said nothing about her returning. Before anyone could speak Asobel, still clutching her globe of the world, exhausted and shocked and grieved by the terrible day, threw herself at Harriet.

'No!' she cried. 'No, Uncle Charles, you cannot take her away too!'

People turned in disapproval at the commotion beside the coaches, at the small, spoilt little girl behaving so improperly. Lucretia was mortified.

'Asobel!' she said sharply.

But Asobel's little arms reached around all the petticoats and the corset and the skirt and the mantle, feeling for some sign of the realness of Harriet somewhere there, after the unreality of the day, reaching for Harriet herself. And the globe of many colours fell from her hands and smashed into a hundred pieces on the cobblestones at Blackfriars Bridge.

Harriet's face, by the side of the River Thames, was as pale and as white as the moon.

THIRTEEN

The yellow, dank fog that had never really lifted from London that day had mixed with the night, making any journey hazardous, but the country Coopers were not to be persuaded and had left for Rusholme, Asobel in tears still, refusing to kiss Harriet and Mary. She huddled, weeping, into her mother's skirts as the coach rolled away from Bryanston Square. Sir Charles and his sons had gone about their business and Mary and Harriet were left in the empty house. They drank tea in the drawing room where the fire was lit as usual but where, as usual, the chill of the house was never quite removed. Harriet stared into the flames.

'What would make someone jump off a bridge into the Thames?' said Mary suddenly, violently.

'Mary?' Harriet looked up, alarmed, and saw her sister pull herself together at once.

'It's all right, darling. I'm all right.' And Mary smiled.

Again Harriet looked into the flames, and saw, not the woman in the water, but the woman with the streaming hair on the prow of the *Miranda*, leading all the passengers to a new world.

'It is hard to understand that Edward has already gone, already begun his fantastic adventure.' Harriet spoke slowly. 'I love you, Mary, and I wished we two were going on the *Miranda* also.'

Mary only smiled again, stared too into the fire. For some time the sisters sat in silence.

'I have another new maid,' said Harriet.

'Father chose her, of course. But she is the one I spoke to you about, Lucy. I saw her doubly polishing all your furniture again, and telling Quintus you were returning.'

Harriet nodded. 'The one who sings, and reads stories to Quintus, *to be continued next week*.' And she gave a small smile. But both women knew that in this house servants were a drifting, uncertain presence: sentinels. Spies.

Another maid came in to ask Mary something about a lack of sugar. Somebody (said the maid) had been stealing it again. Harriet watched her sister as she dealt with the matter calmly; when the maid had gone she said: 'Oh Mary, I have missed you so much. I only feel half myself when you are not there. But you look – pale somehow, and you have been very quiet. Have you been working too hard?'

'Working? I don't *work*. If only I did. If only I could do something useful. I—' To Harriet's immense surprise Mary's voice broke slightly. 'I feel as if I am wasted. I am trained for nothing. I want, so much, to do something, make something of my life before it is too late. My friends and I have still been going into St Giles even though the epidemic seems almost to be over, but I cannot get away every day if Father wants something and I feel—' she searched for a word, '—stupid, as if I am not to be taken seriously. I want to – I want to . . .' Mary's face looked angry, an expression Harriet had almost never seen there. 'I am thirty years old. I expect half my life is already over and I have done nothing. I think I am – Mother always insisted I was – an intelligent woman and I feel that intelligence shrivelling and wasted. For I may only use it in *ordering sugar*!'

Harriet could hardly comprehend this sudden change in her sister. She looked at Mary, confused. 'But, darling, this isn't like you at all.' She racked her brain for comfort for her sister, so unusually needed. 'There is still the Ladies' College perhaps?'

'I told you: I may not have my money.'

Harriet moved to her sister, sat beside her. 'Mary.' And she took her sister's hand. 'Whatever you feel, it must not be that you waste your intelligence. You taught me. Everything I know, I know from you, I've learnt from you. I am a product of you. How can you be wasted?'

And then Mary became herself again, as if a storm had passed by. 'I know,' she said, and she kissed Harriet briefly. 'I don't know what has made me speak like this. I am just tired. Everyone will be tired after such a day. It was sad saying goodbye to Edward, not knowing what will happen to him. And I so hated seeing that woman being – fished – from the water. It was somehow like a portent. I wish the others had waited till tomorrow to return to Rusholme.'

'It was Asobel. She will be ill if she does not get back to normal. Poor child.'

Mary said quietly after a moment, 'Lord Kingdom seemed much interested in you. That would be considered a triumph indeed.'

Harriet's manner changed at once. 'I certainly don't see why he should be in the least interested. In fact Cousin John told me – warned me! – that he is engaged with one of the *corps de ballet* of Taglione or some other dancer! so I do not think you need to worry. We have hardly exchanged a dozen words. The other one, Benjamin, is more – more interesting. He said it was possible there is no God.'

Mary looked at Harriet strangely. 'My darling. My darling sister. You cannot doubt, no matter what happens, that there is a God who created us, who sees us, who watches over us. How, otherwise, could we be here? Who would be watching over Edward on his long journey? How could there be music and paintings and all the beauty of the world? I believe there is a God, and he is the reason we exist in this beautiful world. Nothing I have read has persuaded me otherwise.'

'I know,' said Harriet humbly. 'I know, Mary.'

The fire spat.

'Nevertheless it is true that Lord Ralph seemed interested in you. I am not sure why else they were there. One might have hoped that Father would have been pleased at such elevated attention. But – he did not like it.'

There was another silence. Harriet said at last, 'Is that why he made me stay?'

'Perhaps. And Cousin John is obviously looking for the moment to press his suit.' But seeing her sister's face, Mary changed the subject. 'I hope Edward will be careful.'

'When you said goodbye, you seemed to be warning him. That was unlike you. I thought you were pleased for him.'

'I had some – some other information.'

'What do you mean?'

'I read as much as I could of all the literature Eddie received from the New Zealand Company when he was in London—'

'So did I. It sounded very sensible and exciting, all at the same time. And the people who wrote those handbooks had been there. They would know.'

'My friend of the second-hand bookshop, Mr Dawson, knew I was interested, because of Edward, and one day recently when I went in he'd found me something else.' Mary sighed. 'I could not decide,' she continued slowly, 'whether to give the book to Edward or not. It was too late of course, and I wanted his long journey to be happy and full of anticipation. But – listen.' And Mary limped to a shelf and took down a small volume and brought it back to the fire. 'This is written by someone who, like Edward, bought land in London, without seeing it, from the New Zealand Company. I comforted myself with the knowledge that it was written six years ago, and so may be out of date. She began to read to her sister.

> With New Zealand we have been partially disappointed; by the New Zealand Company not a little deceived. Their glowing one-sided representations of the 'Land of Promise' induced respectable families to forego the substantial comforts of a home for the dream of independence abroad. Ship them off! Ship them off! is the cry, careless of what fate awaits the emigrant on reaching his destination.

'This must be some disgruntled person, surely,' said Harriet in puzzlement, 'and six years ago. Things will have changed, surely?'

'That is what I have told myself. Yet the book implies more serious things: that roads and bridges have not been built; most importantly that the land they are offering people has not been properly purchased by the New Zealand Company from the natives.'

'Would the natives understand "purchase", do you think?'

'I don't see why they would not. And listen.' And Mary commenced reading again.

> The climate of Wellington is boisterous rather than agreeable. The winds are its scourge. Whaleboats are staked down to the beach to prevent their being blown away. A house upon our own town acre had its verandah torn off by the wind; the poles were dragged out of the ground, and the entire fabric, composed of one-inch plank and heavy rafters, lifted clear over the tops of trees and carried to another acre some distance beyond the dwelling.

Harriet began to look a little alarmed.

'But it does say,' Mary went on quickly, 'that because of the wind it is a very healthy place and there is no disease found there at all.'

'But then imagine such a thing!' cried Harriet at once. 'No disease at all. Then I am still glad he went. He will not be put off by a little wind. I would not be. I love the wind. And for the rest, in six years they will have improved things. You were right not to give this to Edward.'

Mary did not reply. She sat so still for such a long time that Harriet said at last, 'Mary?'

Her sister smiled. 'I think I'll rest now,' she said. 'I am so glad you are home, my darling. I hope Lucy will prove to be a good maid for you.' And kissing her sister she limped out of the room. She spoke back over her shoulder, but very quietly. 'I will be awake of course, till Father comes.' And then Harriet heard her very slowly ascending the stairs.

Then there was just the faint hiss of the lamps in the drawing room. Harriet walked to the window, pulled aside the heavy curtains for a moment and looked out over the Square. Two carriages rolled along past the door, the horses' hooves echoing on the cobblestones, and some young street boys argued about something in high, sharp voices and laughed. Even though every window was closed she could hear, as she always could, the roar of the traffic from Oxford Street and Park Lane. One of the gaslights in the street flared in the darkness, and the smell of old cooking wafted up from the kitchens. Harriet suddenly understood that she was back in Bryanston Square and the life that came with it. She called several times for Quintus, but her voice echoed around the silent house and Quintus did not come. Shivering, she pulled a shawl about her shoulders and then she too slowly made her way upstairs to her room.

She was sitting by her window when she thought she heard an odd sound. She walked quickly along the dim passage to her sister's room.

'Mary?' she said, partly opening the door.

Mary, her hair falling over her face, was half on and half off her bed, vomiting uncontrollably into a basin.

'My darling, I must have eaten something,' she managed to say and then she gave an almost animal-like cry of pain and vomited again. Harriet tried to loosen her sister's corset as Mary's body retched and heaved; terrified, she called to the servants, her frightened voice went echoing down and down the stairs. The doctor was sent for; servants ran with soiled petticoats and clean sheets, the new maid Lucy ran up and down with basins of hot water from the basement. By the time the doctor arrived Mary was almost unconscious and the bedclothes had been soiled again and changed again. At first Mary had cried out with that animal cry over and over, now she lay still and Harriet felt her cold clammy skin as she knelt beside the bed, clutching her sister's hand in a frenzied desperation.

'She must have eaten something that disagreed with her,' said Harriet wildly to the doctor, 'she must have. We have been to Gravesend, she must have eaten something. Or she is just overtired.' The doctor looked at Harriet but saw her pain, said nothing, felt again and again for Mary's pulse.

There was the sound of heavy footsteps running up the stairs. A voice called out, uncontrolled: *Harriet!* The door burst open. Sir Charles Cooper was breathless, his hair dishevelled, he saw Harriet kneeling, he saw Mary on the bed. He paused in the doorway.

'I had a message that my daughter was ill.'

'I must speak to you, Sir Charles,' said the doctor, and he took him by the arm, led him outside into the passage. In the shortest moment they were back.

'Leave immediately!' Sir Charles addressed the servants first, and with a backward, fearful glance at their mistress lying on the bed they obeyed him quickly.

'Harriet, you must go to your room at once.' The urgency of his tone that had frightened the servants seemed not to affect Harriet. She did not move.

'It is the cholera,' Sir Charles whispered to her, 'you must not stay here.'

'It cannot be the cholera.' She did not even look at him, still held her sister's hand. 'The cholera is with poor people. The cholera is over. You said yourself it was over. I cannot leave my sister. She will never leave me.'

'The cholera has never been a respecter of boundaries,' said the doctor. 'And it is not over. This is the cholera, my dear. I am certain. I think – there is nothing to be done.'

Still Harriet held Mary's hand. 'We were talking together only a few hours ago. We were in the drawing room, by the fire. If you check you will see the fire, I am sure it is still burning. She could not get ill so soon.' Then she bent to her sister and whispered something: *we will go to New Zealand as soon as you are better for we have heard there is no disease there. Because of the wind.* The father and the doctor did not hear the words: but they looked at each other.

'You must go to your room, Harriet. I am ordering you to go to your room. It is not safe for you here.'

But if Harriet heard her father, her father's anguished voice, she gave no sign. Still she stayed kneeling by the bed, holding and feverishly stroking her sister's hand and arm. Little gasps kept coming from her, little puffs of pain in the room, over and over.

'Get her out of here.' Sir Charles's voice was twisted and hoarse with fear and he moved towards his daughter.

The doctor moved towards her even more quickly. 'Harriet, my dear. When cholera strikes it moves faster than any disease I have ever seen. You can see your sister's face. See how something has happened to it. She appears older. That is one of the signs.'

'She is still alive,' said Harriet, not looking at him, only looking at Mary. 'I feel that she is breathing.' Then she looked up uncertainly for a moment and the odd little gasps came faster. 'She is alive, isn't she?'

'She is breathing faintly,' said the doctor, and he held Mary's pulse. 'Yes, she is still alive.'

He was rewarded with the oddest flash of a smile. Then it was gone again. 'I knew she could not leave me,' said Harriet, 'I cannot

live without her,' and she bent over her sister and bathed the somehow wizened face, but the face she loved, with a cloth.

'She must be moved,' said Sir Charles impatiently, 'she must not
sit in this room,' and he made at last as if to force Harriet to her feet.
The doctor somehow stopped him with his arm.

'Sir Charles,' he muttered, still holding Mary's wrist, 'it is almost
over. Leave her. She is blue now. It will be over immediately.'

'No,' said Harriet. *Not blue*. And she put her arms around her
sister.

There was a kind of silence in the room of gasps and breathing
and anger and fear and pain. And then the doctor let go of Mary's
wrist and straightened up and nodded at Sir Charles. 'I am so
sorry,' he said. 'Your daughter is dead.'

'No,' said Harriet.

Still she held her sister. *No.*

'No,' said Harriet.

She stroked the face of Mary, the shrivelled face of the cholera.

Then she took the cloth and dipped it into the warm water that
had become cold. She wiped her sister's face, wiped the blue-
tinged lips of the cholera.

'No,' said Harriet.

There was no old retainer, no loved servant from childhood to
put her arms around the girl and help her to cry and lead her away.
Mary had been the one who comforted Harriet.

So the last sound of that long, long day was an eerie kind of
keening, low at first, then rising higher and higher like a wild
scream, a sound of grief which the doctor, so used to sounds of
grief, had not heard in all his life. And the doctor saw that Sir
Charles stood, impotent, staring not at his dead daughter, but at the
one who was alive. At last the doctor somehow forced Harriet to
drink something from his bag and finally led her away from the
bed where Mary lay.

Sometime in the night Harriet started awake from her heavily
drugged sleep. She saw her father sitting beside her bed. She tried
to scream for Mary but no sound would come.

FOURTEEN

First the high hats of the undertakers festooned in black appeared over the hill as they walked before the horses; then the black plumes attached to the heads of the funeral horses waved in the air as the animals trotted into view with funeral bells ringing, pulling the funeral carriage towards Highgate Cemetery. In the glass hearse the closed coffin of Mary Cooper, daughter of the Right Honourable Sir Charles Cooper, MP, lay covered in white wax lilies. As Sir Charles was a large shareholder in the suburban Highgate Cemetery, having been persuaded some years ago that death could be profitable, there was no question of the burial being elsewhere.

Sir Charles Cooper, MP, his two sons Richard and Walter, and his remaining daughter Harriet travelled behind the hearse in a closed carriage. The Rusholme Coopers and Aunt Lydia travelled behind them. Members of Parliament and Members of the Chelsea Water Board, businessmen from various enterprises who had connections with Sir Charles (all with their families, all dressed in black) travelled behind the bereaved. It was a large procession, befitting Sir Charles's position. Lord Ralph Kingdom and Sir Benjamin Kingdom and their elderly mother were commented upon. Quietly at the end of the procession came the doctors and the women who had been with Mary in Seven Dials, the man from the second-hand bookshop: Mary's friends.

People noticed, in the chapel, how kindly Sir Charles supported his wraith-like daughter: *she will be a comfort to him*, they told each other, *the poor man is a widower.*

Lord Ralph Kingdom, bending over Harriet's hand once more, saw briefly, as his eyes caught hers, a look of such utter desolation that his heart contracted with a kind of pity. And behind the desolation there was something else, some wild, desperate, unwomanly madness. (That night he felt relieved to be back in the company of his ballet dancer, where he knew where he was. But in the night the eyes of the girl behind her glass wall haunted his dreams.)

Harriet was made to wait in the chapel with two maids while the public burial took place on the hill; she was of course considered too frail to be at the final resting place. The procession went slowly forward; it was Benjamin Kingdom who lingered, looked back through the door into the chapel. The black figure, the small picture of utter desolation, carved into his mind: it was as if, like some mythical creature, she had turned to stone. Again he felt something beating at his heart, like a warning.

Not even Asobel could reach her cousin. As the family spoke in low tones at Bryanston Square, surrounded by servants wearing dark armbands and caps handing funeral meats to industrialists and Members of Parliament, the little girl realised that Harriet hardly saw her. She could not understand. She tried to take Harriet's hand and felt it was cold and unresponsive; *Harriet seemed not to know her*. She whispered to her father, away from the servants and loud men and the black-clad old people who reminded her of eagles, 'Papa, she looks like a ghost.' So that William broached the subject with his brother of taking Harriet back again to Rusholme. 'This has been a terrible, terrible shock for her, Charles. She will need time to recover.'

He saw, and so did their sister Lydia, who had absolutely decided that Harriet should come to Norfolk, the obstinate set of their brother's mouth that they knew from long ago.

'The Doctor has assured me that if she was to have caught the cholera from her sister she would have done so by now. I feel she is best with me, where I will watch her day and night. And when she is recovered she will of course learn to be the mistress of my house.'

'It is ridiculous, Charles.' Lydia spoke briskly. 'You are too busy. Anyone can see she is in a state of shock at Mary's death. Mary was like a mother to her. She needs to get away.'

William looked across at his niece. He could not get out of his mind what Asobel had said: *Papa, she looks like a ghost*. Perhaps it was the way the light shone, as Harriet stood, quite still, by the window. 'She will be a great asset, Charles, of course, in the days to come. But she is not – well.'

'I will make her well. Then she will be the mistress of my house.' And he gave a brief, dismissive smile to his brother and his sister and said, 'It is what I have always wanted.'

FIFTEEN

The moonlight shone across the bare, polished wooden boards; it glimmered in the mirror, caught the edge of the bed where Harriet slept.

Harriet, too, had been given a little 'quietness'; the doctor had prescribed a mixture for her that made it certain she would fall asleep at night and somewhere in her jagged thoughts she sometimes remembered not Aunt Lucretia's laudanum but Seamus's sister Rosie, sleeping under the dirty blanket in the old barn, being given the Godfrey's Cordial. Lucy had been told by Peters that there was no need for her to sleep there, in Harriet's room. Sir Charles would guard his daughter. But sometimes Lucy crept down the servants' staircase to satisfy herself that her beautiful, desperate mistress slept. Just once, on one of those visits, Harriet had started up in something like fear, had clung to her maid in despair: Lucy did not know if Harriet was awake or asleep, only that the tears were real.

Tonight the curtains were not quite closed: perhaps the maid had been careless, perhaps at some hour Harriet had woken, stared at the Square as she so often used to, but now the moonlight did not wake Harriet as it shone across the room.

The sound of the door did not wake Harriet as it opened gently and then closed again. Footsteps walked across the room. Someone was walking quietly but not able to stop the creaking of the polished floorboards near the bed. But Harriet did not wake.

The Right Honourable Sir Charles Cooper, MP, sat down on a chair beside the bed and as his eyes got used to the darkness and the moonlight he made out the body of his daughter as she slept: one hand clenched beside her hair that lay about so wildly as if she had tossed and turned before she slept at last. The other hand lay over her bosom as if to protect it. The hand, and the breast beneath it, moved together as she breathed, very gently, up and down, up and down. The man stared as if mesmerised: the beautiful, sleeping face, the breast rising and falling with the hand upon it; it was the most touching, the most innocent sight he had ever seen. It was the innocence that trapped him: somewhere in his mind he was fevered by what she did not know. A thousand images churned his senses in the quiet, moonlit room; if anybody had been near, had been listening, they would have heard a kind of muffled groan. But there was nobody here near the room, Harriet's room. Night after night since Mary's death two weeks ago he had come in here, hurrying home from parliamentary duties, shouting at the cabmen to hasten the horses along Oxford Street, up towards Bryanston Square, his excitement almost uncontainable. His man Peters would be waiting, the whisky and the fire ready: Peters would disappear into the shadows, the whisky was quickly consumed. Then through the silent house of mourning the master walked.

Sometimes a scurrying maid late from the kitchen (or was it Lucy?) stifled a scream as she saw him walking, stalking, silent on the stairs.

Now, trying to control his breathing, he stood; leaned nearer. First, as always, he loosened the blankets to find the beautiful feet, to gently, gently hold them in his hands, gently, not wanting to wake his sleeping princess. This is what he did, back from the Palace of Westminster, night after night, his daughter never waking, *she need never know*, his tormented mind told him night after night, *she will never know*. (But her dreams: what of them? But he did not know of her dreams.) Then tonight a wilder vision had come upon him: a desolate distortion of the many nights he had paid for, elsewhere; it sprang suddenly into his mind because of the unruly way the body lay, the hand there, the innocent hand across her breast. *I want*: his mind finally articulated what he wanted: *I want her to offer it to me* (offer the breast to its master: he wanted the hand around the naked breast, offering it to him); he wanted her to offer her father her breast. Girls did it in the houses around St Martin's Lane, smiling, to please him, to entice him. He wanted Harriet to please him. And all the time she was to be asleep and not know what she did, how she offered her breast to her father. And then when she looked at him with that blank look, he would *know*: his secret. She would be running his house, she would be there, always. The muffled groan again, he could not wait. *I have waited, all her life.*

Gently, he pulled the quilt down. The moonlight fell across her body. She lay, quite still, in her white nightgown. The hand that had lain across her breast fell back across the bed, he saw the buttons. He was breathing so heavily now that he was more clumsy: he tried, fumbling, to undo the small buttons at the top of the nightdress. One button. Two. Her pale flesh glimmered where the light from the moon caught it. Then the girl stirred quietly, but he could not stop. When the last button was undone he took her hand, tried to place it inside the nightgown, under her breast, and Harriet opened her eyes and out of the mists of the laudanum and whatever else she had been given she *smelt* her father leaning over her: the whisky and the wine and the cigars and the smell of his skin.

Something, something made her close her eyes again as if this was the only way to protect herself. Breathing heavily her father cupped her breast in her own hand with his hand around it, then he ran his hand down her nightdress, down her body, his hand over her body, then suddenly he leaned back, away from her; she heard him doing something to his clothes, breathing faster and faster, making little groans. She did not understand: but, of course, she understood. She struggled violently to come out of her deep, drugged sleep; with all her strength she tried to come up through the mists in her head and her body and just then, was it in her head or was it real? she thought she heard a loud banging on a door somewhere, someone was urgently calling her father's name.

When he had gone, for he had gone, Harriet half-walked, half-crawled across the room where she vomited into the basin on the washstand, over and over and over again. Her hair fell forward, touching the basin, there was vomit on her hair but she did not see that, in the shaft of moonlight that still shone across the room. What she saw, in the moonlight, was the shadow of her own face in the mirror. And what she heard in the silent room was the clock. The measured ticking went on still as though nothing had happened, beating its slow, unchanging time as if to say *Mary is gone, but you are here, and you will always be here, and it will always be this way, on other nights.*

Suddenly Harriet Cooper seized the clock and hurled it wildly at the mirror and a thousand shards of glass glittered in the moonlight as they fell and the sound of the clock parts echoed and twanged as they rearranged themselves, at last, into silence.

Next morning at breakfast, after prayers attended by all the servants that asked for the hastening of Harriet's health and well-being, Sir Charles announced tersely to his sons that he had to go urgently to Norfolk for three or four days.

'Is it Aunt Lydia?' asked Richard, surprised, for their father did not usually show sibling affection. 'Was that what the messenger came for, in the night? A dreadful noise they made, sir, it woke me. I would have flogged the rascal if I hadn't been so tired.'

'He woke even me!' said Walter, notorious in the family for his heavy sleeping.

'No, it is not Lydia,' Sir Charles answered ill-humouredly. 'It is – parliamentary business that I cannot avoid.' Sir Charles had been given an urgent, disturbing message in the night that there were secret plans to unseat him in his constituency: an unheard-of audacity that it was necessary for him to forestall at once; the seat had cost him a great deal of money and belonged to him alone. 'I have instructed the servants to be with Harriet day and night, to give her anything that she may require. I will not be gone long. I expect you both to honour your sister and see her each day. The Doctor says she must get up for short periods every afternoon; he will come today and see that everything is provided for. Where is the *milk*?' A new maid made old mistakes: she scurried now to Sir Charles's aid: all three men would be glad of the time when a woman presided over their table again: when Harriet took her dutiful place.

At last Sir Charles rose and walked slowly up the stairs to the room of his daughter, Harriet's room. He paused for a moment

and his hand trembled as he knocked, but if any memory stayed
with him of his moments in this room in the darkness nothing of
this showed in his inscrutable face. Harriet's new maid, Lucy,
opened the door; he brushed past her unseeing into the bedroom.

Harriet looked somehow different in the dull, grey daylight that
came in from the curtains that had now been opened. She was not
in bed where she had been for so long: she was sitting in a chair in
the corner of the room. He noticed at once that she was wearing a
different nightdress under a dark shawl. (But he did not notice that
the clock was gone, and the mirror from the wall.)

His heart beat to see her, his princess of the night, but his face
did not change.

'Harriet.'

She waited.

'I must go to Norfolk for several days,' and he saw her eyes
widen as she looked up at him.

'There is some urgent constituency business that must be
attended to. It cannot be avoided, but I am most sorry to leave you
when you are not yet well. The servants have full instructions to
attend to anything you require and the Doctor will be here later this
morning. Anything you want will be brought to you.'

She had spoken almost nothing since Mary's death. Now she
said, in a voice cracked from little use, 'How long will you be away,
Father?'

'Try not to worry, my dear Harriet. It will only be three or four
days. I will send a message. Everything, everything you want will
be given to you. And the Doctor will give you more medicine so
that your nights at least will be tranquil.'

Perhaps he should not have mentioned nights. It seemed to
Lucy, sitting unnoticed with her sewing, that the girl's hand caught
upon the chair in a kind of wild blow, an extraordinary gesture.
And then Harriet looked up at her father. He (nor Lucy) never
forgot the look she gave him then: something so turbulent, so
almost *savage* that his breath caught at his throat; he turned away at
once, then, reminding himself that she was still ill, turned back. By
the time he turned back her face was blank. He for the first time
flicked a glance across at the maid but she was bent over her
sewing. He shook his head a little, almost like an animal trying to
free itself from something. Then he walked towards his daughter

and bent and kissed her cheek the way he always did. And then he left the room.

Lucy saw that Harriet listened to the sound of his receding footsteps. And then she said quite matter-of-factly, as if she had not been so ill and so quiet and shed so many tears, 'What day is today, Lucy?'

'It is Tuesday, Miss Harriet.'

Harriet stood. Shaking off the proffered help she walked across to the window that looked over the Square. There she stayed motionless, waiting. Finally the sound of the larger carriage coming round from the mews was heard, the four horses stepping and jingling in the cold morning. Sir Charles Cooper was seen getting into his carriage; quickly the horses were on their way to Norfolk.

First Harriet asked for the bath to be brought up, and hot water.

Then Harriet asked for Quintus. The poor bereft dog, who thought he had lost both of his beloved mistresses, lay at her feet, not taking his eyes from her.

When the doctor arrived Harriet was dressed in a plain black crêpe dress and sitting beside the fire with the dog. Lucy had noticed, when she helped Harriet into her corset, that no matter how tightly she pulled the corset was of no use, so thin was Harriet now. The doctor too was surprised to see the figure by the fire, so thin and pale and black.

'My dear. Are you feeling better at last?'

Harriet's manner to him was impersonal and precise. He thought of her kneeling by the bed, the day of Mary's death: the passion and the pain, and the fleeting smile when Mary at that last moment was still alive. There was something wayward about this girl, he had always recognised it, but he felt very sorry for her, he had known her all her life and thought the household sad, some element missing; he had attended her birth and remembered the laughing mother.

'I do not need to see you again, Doctor.'

'As you wish.' He would come anyway, he was very used to dealing with hysteria.

'But I would like some more laudanum, or whatever it is that you give me.' He had given her opium as well but she did not need to know that: in some cases it was prudent.

He looked at the brown bottle beside the bed. 'There is enough there, for the moment.'

'I wake in the night. It needs to be stronger.'

'I will give you a little more, and then we shall see.' He fumbled in his bag for a moment, brought out another bottle.

'But you must eat, my dear. I know you have not been eating. If I am not to call every day you must promise me, for this—' he weighed the bottle in his hand, 'is not – useful – unless you have eaten also.' He did not think she would do anything foolish, she had more grace than that. But with hysterics you could never be certain.

Harriet stood up and held out her hand for the bottle. *Laudanum would be her last resort*. Quintus stood uncertainly, never taking his eyes from Harriet. His tail wagged slightly.

'I will eat, Doctor Adams. Lucy, please bring me something now.' The maid curtseyed and was gone. When the door closed behind her Harriet said abruptly, without any preamble or social niceties: 'You knew my mother.'

'Why yes, of course.'

Harriet's whole manner changed, she moved towards him. 'Doctor Adams, please. Tell me something about her. I keep thinking that now I have lost her too. My – sister was my only link and . . .' She made a small, hopeless gesture with her hand and he saw that her eyes filled with tears at once and that she bit her lip with the effort of not breaking down.

He turned and looked out of the window into the greyness of the sky and the bareness of the trees. He spoke gruffly and did not turn back to look at her. 'I liked your mother very much. She was very pretty, she had a low and pleasing voice and there was something about her that made everyone around her want to smile. Charming.'

How bare the trees were. How grey the day.

'If I am to be truthful about her I would add that I always felt that her ideas for the education of your sister were a mistake. But of course she always made your father's happiness her first priority, of that I can assure you. She was a wonderful wife to him. One can understand, in a way, why he has not married again. Your father's happiness and comfort were always her prime concern, nothing got in the way of that, which is as it should be, of course.' Harriet made no sound, no answer. After a moment's silence the doctor continued, still looking out across the Square.

'I always felt that your mother, too, read rather too much than was good for her, though no doubt you will find me old-fashioned for thinking so. I am old-fashioned, I expect. But I have seen many things in my profession as a doctor and nothing I have learnt has made me wish to be more modern.'

Still Harriet made no sound. The doctor sighed and turned back towards the room, although not exactly looking at her. 'I would very much like to say something to you, my dear, if you will allow me. The reason I am against too many books is that I do feel that young ladies have a duty to be satisfied with the limitations that their sex has put upon them, otherwise they will be unhappy – and perhaps make others unhappy too. There is too much human misery in the world, Harriet, for us to add to it with our small dissatisfactions.' He knew he was lecturing Harriet but felt it was his duty, he thought only of her happiness of course. And then the doctor seemed suddenly to sigh and his voice sounded quite different.

'Ah, I do remember how your mother laughed, her gift of laughter. Your house in Clapham was full of laughter, a most pleasant place to visit. And most of all I remember—' and he turned and looked at Harriet at last, 'how much she wanted another daughter. She told me that if God gave her another daughter as beautiful as Mary, she would thank him for it, for the rest of her life. She knew you were a girl before she died, she smiled at me when I told her.' And he turned back to the grey morning square.

He thought perhaps he heard her crying.

Then there was a tap at the door.

The doctor turned then and saw Harriet standing in the middle of the room with the damned dog right beside her, looking up at her face. If she had been crying she had stopped now. He thought for a moment that she was going to say something to him: she seemed to flutter; it was as if she were a bird, waiting to – *fly* – it was the only thing he could think of. She stood facing him, unstill, holding the bottle of laudanum, he was sure she would speak. And then Lucy entered and said, placing a tray on a small table, 'Your breakfast, Miss Harriet,' and the moment was gone.

'Thank you, Doctor Adams,' said Harriet, and although he saw from her face that she *was* thanking him, not for the medicine but for the words, nevertheless he also felt himself dismissed in some way, as if she had made up her mind about something.

He went down the stairs of the dark, silent house and allowed the footman to fuss with his coat, for he was thinking of Harriet, wished he had seen the smile again, the one that lit up her face, just the way her mother's had.

Lucy saw Harriet eat the food: silently, neatly, disinterestedly, as Quintus looked on enthusiastically. But she ate it nevertheless, the first time Lucy had seen her eat anything.

'Would you like to go down to the drawing room, miss? There is a fire there, it would be a change for you.' Harriet looked at the maid. *The drawing room? Where she and Mary had had their last conversation? About the Ladies' College. And the wind.*

'No. I would like the carriage brought round, please.'

Lucy looked deeply alarmed. It had been her job of course to empty the bowls from the wash stand, full of vomit. And sweep up the broken mirror. And the clock. She had seen the look on Harriet's face as she stared at her father. 'The carriage, Miss Harriet? Do you mean to go out?'

'Yes, I am going out. Please tell them I want the carriage here.' Then, quite harshly, seeing Lucy's face, 'My father said I was to have anything I want.'

'Yes, miss. I will get my shawl, miss.'

'I wish to go alone, thank you, Lucy.'

'Yes, Miss Harriet.' Lucy curtseyed, hurried downstairs, and had the extraordinary thought that Harriet would run away. Lucy's heart began to beat faster: she had to keep this place, she could not lose this place, her mother needed the money, her mother lay in Spitalfields with the inflammation of the lungs that weaver women always got, would die without Lucy's help.

Harriet slowly pinned on her hat, slowly pulled the veil over her face. Her hands shook. There was no mirror. Quintus watched her intently.

Downstairs there was much consternation. Peters, her father's chief manservant, was firm. He was his master's eyes and ears as they all knew. The master's instructions had been quite clear.

Harriet was to be watched over at all times until he could be back to take charge again: no-one had imagined for a moment she would be anywhere but in her room.

'This is ridiculous, she oughtn't to go out at all till Sir Charles comes back.'

'And she don't want me to accompany her,' said Lucy, confused. 'She said she wanted to go alone.'

'She can't go alone and that's that.' Peters was adamant. 'If we can't persuade her she's not to go I shall ride with one of the footmen on the carriage and you, Lucy, will ride inside. She's sick. She's probably got hysteria. It'd be more than our jobs are worth to let her go out alone. Suppose something happened to her, suppose she fainted. He would never forgive us.' *Watch over my daughter* were the last words Sir Charles had said to him.

'Then you tell her,' said Lucy.

'You can't be afraid of a *young girl*!'

'You tell her.' Lucy was afraid for herself: she had to keep this position; a broken mirror meant seven years' bad luck.

Down the stairs, slowly, Harriet walked, the dog just behind her. The servants fell silent at once. Her pale face shone under the black clothes. They saw that she hardly saw them, that she looked at the walls and the doors and the rooms in an odd way as if they, not her, had changed. Servants stood, uneasy in the hallway, nobody spoke. She stared at the door of the drawing room for a long time. And then she said to Peters, 'Is my carriage there?'

'It is called for, my lady. But we feel that you must not go out alone – you have been very ill. Some of us must accompany you.'

'I shall be visiting friends. I shall be quite safe.'

'Young ladies never go out alone, Miss Harriet. The Master left strict instructions with us, that you were to be – looked after.'

His words hung there in the dark hall and to Harriet the servants in their black were like gaolers, an army of gaolers left by her father. She remembered how Mary had described them as chess pieces and she saw it too, standing on the squares in the hall at odd, pointed angles, or was it her? Quickly she put out her hand and steadied herself at a small hall table.

'The last words of my father to me were that every wish of mine was to be attended to. I wish to visit an old friend of—' her voice faltered and then she went on, 'an old friend of my sister, who will be waiting to see me. I shall not be gone for very long. I do not wish to be accompanied by servants.'

Silence in the hall: nothing moved on the chessboard. The will of Peters and the will of the pale, beautiful girl quivered in the gloom. Harriet remained motionless, her hand still on the table. Peters did not falter. That she was her father's treasure was known to everyone: she must be watched over.

They heard the carriage and horses stopping by the door. Quintus barked. Still the footman did not open the door to the dank winter day, waiting for instructions. The other servants stood, waiting also. And then somebody banged on the doorknocker outside.

Immediately the tableau was broken, the door was opened and the illustrious Lady Kingdom could be seen in the grey misty morning, descending from her grand coach with the help of two servants. She swept into the hall and, seeming not to notice that Harriet was dressed for outdoors, was at once escorted into the drawing room; Quintus was removed by Lucy. Harriet slowly took off her hat and her mantle and walked into the drawing room as if in a dream, to preside over her first call. The servants were shut out: reverted to their place in the scheme of things.

Lady Kingdom gave formal condolences for the death of Mary.

Harriet gave a formal, polite reply, in the room where she had last sat with her sister.

Lady Kingdom commented adversely on the weather for some time.

Harriet agreed.

Lady Kingdom asked Harriet if the servants in the house were satisfactory. 'I believe they were chosen by my father, that is what he prefers,' said Harriet, as if all satisfaction was encompassed in that answer, and her guest, acknowledging Sir Charles's odd domestic situation, nodded, satisfied.

If Lady Kingdom noticed that her hostess was deathly pale she gave no indication, for these things were best not mentioned. She enquired after the health of her father. Harriet did not say that her father had gone to Norwich.

'He is well, thank you, Lady Kingdom.' *He undid the buttons on her nightdress he leaned forward.*

'Much exercised still by your sister's funeral, I have no doubt.'

Harriet inclined her head.

'It was a well-attended funeral. Your father had much honour given him.'

In the silence in the drawing room the fire spat *and then he.*

Harriet suddenly spoke, a little fast. 'I was on my way to see my father. He had asked me to visit him. At Westminster.'

'Then when we have had tea, I shall take you there.'

Thus reminded, Harriet rang the bell. Tea appeared at once.

Harriet poured. If her hands shook a little as she passed a small, exquisite cup and saucer to her visitor, again it was not commented upon.

Then Lady Kingdom expressed deep regret that Harriet and her father would in the circumstances be unable to attend her Christmas Ball.

Harriet inclined her head again, from which Lady Kingdom understood that Harriet was also regretful.

Soon afterwards, to the consternation of Peters who was hovering in the hall, the two ladies swept into Lady Kingdom's coach and were gone, along Bryanston Square and down towards Oxford Street. Unbeknown to Peters or to Lady Kingdom, a small hansom cab rattled along behind them, always keeping them in view.

'Lord Ralph is particularly sorry not to see you at Christmas.' Lady Kingdom raised her voice effortlessly against the noise of the carriage wheels rumbling beneath them.

'Your sons are well, Lady Kingdom?'

She nodded. 'Benjamin has come under the influence of that madman Darwin, but Ralph says he will grow out of it. Ralph will call on your father, my dear, he wishes to present his condolences in person.'

'That is kind.' Harriet looked out into the crowded streets, unchanged by Mary's death, wild and noisy and rackety and filthy as ever. All those people hurrying by, laughing, living their lives, knowing nothing of her pain. And bleakly one of the harsh rules of the world came to her: *no-one can ever know another person's sorrow.*

The carriage rolled on towards the Palace of Westminster, delayed partially by a herd of recalcitrant cows and sheep which were being whipped unwillingly towards Smithfields Market. Having seen her charge safely into the hands of the parliamentary footmen who would escort her to her father immediately, Lady Kingdom drove away, contemplating that the girl, though so grieved at present and still not at all what she herself would have chosen, had beauty and grace. But Miss Cooper was *beneath* them; Lady Kingdom shuddered at a marriage into Water Boards and sons of squires. The girl would require much education in what it meant to marry into one of the great families of England (for so Lady Kingdom saw the matter). But Ralph had shown interest and in the circumstances she supposed the match must be pursued. Ralph was a fool, but he must be saved from greater folly.

Inside the Palace of Westminster Harriet waited as if for her father. She could not think of what else to do; servants hurried away: it was recognised at once that she was the other daughter, in mourning of course. *He loosened his clothes little panting sounds came from him.* She sat quite still in the huge hall where workmen still laboured on the new Parliament. She froze as she suddenly thought Sir Charles approached her, but it was another honourable gentleman on another mission. When the servants at last returned with the news that her father was not present, she asked them to hail her a cab although she had never been alone in one in her life. There was a cabman just outside, he was leaning on some railing almost as though he had been waiting for her.

'I know that young lady's family,' he said cheerily, 'I'll take her.' She asked the servants to tell the driver to take her to the Strand and the driver helped her into his hansom cab, the one that had rattled along behind Lady Kingdom's coach. In the privacy of the closed cab Harriet fumblingly took some papers from her reticule. She knew the address off by heart; she had no money with her; young ladies did not handle money. She told the cabman to wait. Then she entered the premises of the New Zealand Company.

Again servants took charge of her, placed her on a high-backed couch in a reception room. Many men in frock coats moved purposefully in and out of the doors. There were two women there with their husbands, there was a group of women in bonnets laughing nervously. At the far end, some obviously poorer people were waiting. And there was Harriet Cooper, tall and still on the high-backed couch, waiting also.

Very soon one of the frock-coated men was at her side, assisting her to rise, escorting her to one of the inner rooms, mannered, careful, particularly noting her mourning attire, wondering why she was not escorted. Two other men were waiting there: noted her youth and her beauty and her black veil; Harriet was settled again, this time in an armchair, and tea was brought. All the gentlemen smiled and bowed and asked what they could do for her.

Harriet began the story she had planned as she watched her father's coach take him away. Everything she had learned, everything she had read, everything she had heard about from Edward had been dredged up out of her numbed, grieving, shocked mind. There was no expression in her voice as she spoke, she could have been making a polite enquiry.

'I believe you have a ship leaving soon for New Zealand.'

'The *Amaryllis*, yes.'

'When does the *Amaryllis* sail?'

'Why, she is loading and boarding already. She is to sail at the end of the week.' Behind her veil which she did not lift they might have seen the glitter of her eyes.

'Is there, by chance, room for me to travel aboard her?' Her voice remained expressionless. It could not have been noted whether she was anxious to travel or not. But the three men looked at each other in surprise, exchanging meaningful glances.

'You would not be travelling alone? We do not encourage young ladies to travel alone, of course.'

'Of course.'

'With whom would you be travelling?'

Harriet's voice remained flat. 'My cousin travelled several weeks ago on the *Miranda*. My sister and I were to have joined him in Wellington. My sister—' her voice faltered, '—my sister – passed away—' and for a moment she stopped speaking completely. One of the men stood but she began again with an immense effort, 'very – very shortly after my cousin's departure. It seems best that I go to New Zealand at once.'

Again the men exchanged glances. It was working women who were required most in New Zealand, there was a shortage of servants. The New Zealand Company wanted the gentry in New Zealand, certainly, but not impoverished and distressed gentlewomen who could get neither a husband nor a position in England. The man who had stood a few moments before now said, 'Would you be so good as to tell me your name? And perhaps your age?'

Harriet's frame suddenly rose before them: she was taller than the speaker.

'I do not see,' she said icily, 'that all these questions are necessary before I have even obtained from you the basic information that I require.' Just for a moment she saw the woman carved on to the prow of the *Miranda*, the way she stretched forward towards her destination, unimpeded. Then she said, as the men remained silent, 'My cousin who is already on his way to New Zealand is Mr Edward Cooper. My father Sir Charles Cooper is a Member of Parliament. My name is Harriet Cooper.' She prepared to lie about her age but she saw that the mention of her father's name had galvanised the men into action: the New Zealand Company was at present engaged in trying to get money from Her Majesty's government to get them out of various financial difficulties.

A bell was immediately rung, some papers were brought in, another man appeared and laid a plan out on the table. All this Harriet observed from beneath her veil; she still stood in front of them, tall and elegant and very young.

'It is such short notice, Miss Cooper, and travelling alone is, as I say, most unusual. And we would worry of course that it would not be possible for you to get your possessions together on board, you would need furniture as well as your personal belongings; it does not seem to us that you could be ready in time. The ship is already loading at the East India docks. Perhaps next year—'

'Is there a place?'

'Well, as it so happens, there is a small cabin, yes.' He ran his finger down the plan. 'A last-minute cancellation. Today is Tuesday, let me see. People are already beginning to board, most of the steerage passengers are got on board earlier so as to be out of the way of the cabin passengers, but cabin passengers themselves would be required to begin boarding on Thursday at the East India dock. Or you would need to be in Gravesend with everything on board early on Friday afternoon at the very latest. The Captain will want to take the *Amaryllis* out to the mouth before dusk. It is surely not possible that you could be prepared in the time?'

'It is possible. My father will assist me of course.' Again the gentlemen exchanged looks.

'We have papers for you to sign – for your father to sign of course. For anyone to go alone on such a long journey with such little notice is out of the ordinary, to say the least. But of course your sad circumstances are out of the ordinary also, and your father will of course know what is best. He is not able to be here with you today?'

'Running the country,' said Harriet (*and she had the oddest feeling that Mary floated somewhere beside her, smiling as Harriet quoted the oft-used words of their father: she was so shocked she looked for a moment round the room*). 'Running the country,' she repeated, pulling herself together, 'is a difficult and time-consuming business.'

The gentlemen thought of the financial assistance they required and nodded, anxiously.

'Give me the papers,' said Harriet.

'Should we charge the fare to your father perhaps?'

He leaned forward, placing her own hand under her breast. 'No!' said Harriet sharply. 'I will bring the money and the signed papers back to you, or send them with a servant.'

'This cabin, which you will not be sharing, will cost forty-one guineas.'

'Thank you,' said Harriet.

'You do understand you must furnish it yourself?'

'Of course I understand that. We have already sent one of our family across the world and we understand how it is. My father will assist me in every way.'

'Of course. We would very much like to see him here.'

'I will tell him that,' she said and the gentlemen looked positively chirpy.

She had to wait while papers were gathered, notes were made, pleasantries were exchanged. Behind her veil she watched the frock-coated men, saw how they mentioned her father importantly to one another several times. Her heart was beating very fast, faster than perhaps it should, she felt so strange, but somehow she could not bring herself to sit down again. So she stood there still, as they bustled about her.

She had to find forty-one guineas and much more beside.

As she came out into the Strand a thin, watery sun was trying to shine and she stopped for a moment on the pavement, steadying herself. *Could she truly have had a vision of Mary? It felt as if she was near.* The cabman was leaning against his vehicle in amongst all the loud, unruly passing traffic, and he was whistling, but such was the roar of the noise that she could not pick up the tune. He saw Harriet, gave a cheery wave, helped her into the cab. She told him to take her to Bryanston Square, and then changed her mind suddenly.

'Where is the Ballet?' she asked the driver.

'Why, Her Majesty's Theatre, ma'am, of course.'

'I wish to go there.'

'The Haymarket.' He nodded, enclosed her in, jumped up to the top of his vehicle, flicked at the horse; the cab with its whistling driver trotted its way through the carriages and the carts and the people. Inside the cab, suddenly alone at last, Harriet crumpled. *What am I thinking of? The Haymarket is where the street women go. And if I see him all I would do would be to ask for the other brother, the one whose eyes seem to smile. But what would I say? However do I ask for a loan of forty-one guineas? And I will need more money than that. How will I get to Gravesend with whatever luggage I can arrange? I have no furniture for a cabin. The servants will be watching me always. Am I mad? It is impossible! O Mary, Mary, my beloved sister, are you really somewhere near? Have I gone mad?*

Almost, she wept.

But then the same distorted vision of Sir Charles Cooper came into her mind and she did not.

The cab stopped outside Her Majesty's Theatre and Harriet stepped out. But the theatre was closed of course: there would be a performance in the evening. In amongst the traffic, people crowded the street talking and smiling and arguing; there were ladies resting their gloved hands on the arms of gentlemen, businessmen with top hats and bundles of papers, young lads hurrying and scurrying, darting through the traffic, laughing and cursing; the ladies of the street were perhaps not yet parading. By the front of the theatre a small dirty boy was waiting with his broom to sweep a path for the ladies and gentlemen: Harriet was near enough to see mud and filth all over his face and clothes, grey-yellow stuff running from his nose, his eyes flicking anxiously from face to face, ready to dash into the roadway. No sign of course of Lord Ralph Kingdom, let alone the grey eyes of Sir Benjamin, *what am I thinking of?* She leant against the side of the hansom cab and closed her eyes. Almost at once the whistling driver was beside her.

'You all right, ma'am? Shall I take you now to Bryanston Square?'

She had no strength left, she felt it draining from her as he began to help her back into the cab.

'I don't know what to do.' He heard her, felt her falter on the carriage step.

'Can I help you, ma'am? Anything I can do?'

'I – I think – I am so sorry, I need some water.'

'Here, I'll take you in the theatre.'

'Into the theatre?' Harriet's voice was faint and confused.

'My sister's the one what makes the tea for the girls and that. Hey!' and he called one of the skylarking lads, tossed him a coin together with some dire threats about holding the horse and somehow quite gently led Harriet through the stage door and down into the basement. She wasn't quite sure what happened then, but later she found she was in an old chair with her hat on her lap and holding a mug of tea given to her by a woman who did indeed look like the cab driver. She remembered the pot of tea Seamus had made for her so proudly in the old falling-down barn full of pigs and people, and how she had refused it.

'Thank you,' she said to the cab driver's sister. 'My name is Harriet.'

'I'm Phyllis,' said the woman, 'and me brother is Cecil but he's gone to check his horse. You had a little faint.'

'Did I?' She looked around, confused, at the armchairs and the fire, not sure why she was here.

'Only a couple of minutes. You ain't missed much of the world I shouldn't think, not in a couple of minutes,' and Phyllis was rewarded by a brief flash of one of Harriet's rare smiles. 'There, the tea's made you much better, sailed all the way from China just to warm your heart on a nasty London day. My girls won't dance without it.'

'Could I . . .' She looked about her, deeply embarrassed. Ladies were never caught like this, it was one of the things she had been taught at the finishing school.

'There, behind the curtain.'

'Thank you.' The skirts and the petticoats were gathered and held as she crouched down to the bucket.

Cecil clomped down the stairs again, they knew it was him by the whistling. Harriet was back in the armchair. 'There you are, ma'am. Right as rain now, I shouldn't wonder. If you stop long enough you could see *Giselle*!'

Then Harriet remembered why she had come to the Haymarket:

she got up at once, her hat fell to the floor, she stooped, confused again, to pick it up; how terrible if Lord Kingdom found her here. 'I am so sorry, I must go, I have many things to do. Thank you so much for your kindness,' and she had gone up the stairs, Cecil whistling after her.

'Piccadilly,' she said to him.

In Piccadilly she bought stout shoes, a warm shawl, underwear and a sunhat, about which the gentleman assisting her made a small joke about hope springing eternal. All the clothes she signed, as she and Mary had always done, to her father, even as he gasped and moaned inside her head.

'Oxford Street,' she said to Cecil, and she tapped on the roof of the cab as she had seen Mary and her father do, to get him to stop outside Mary's favourite bookshop, Dawson's Book Emporium. And Cecil smiled to himself, to see where she had stopped. He was glad she was going there, Symond Dawson would be the man to help her, and he whistled his tuneless song. As Harriet pushed the door she was at once assailed by the smell Mary had so often and so lovingly recalled: the smell of books. All around her, on shelves, in piles, in boxes, on tables, books stood. The bookseller, a man from somewhere in the north of England, came forward at once when he saw her, for all the world as if he had been expecting her.

'Come in, Mary's sister, I'm right glad to see you. Tha sister was a right bonny lass,' he said. 'I shall miss her. I believe she saw life in smiling terms.'

It was such a strange, and such a loving description of Mary, the first real words that anybody had said to her about her sister, that Harriet lifted her veil at once.

'She did,' she said. And she repeated his odd words: *in smiling terms.* He saw, before she was almost aware of them, the tears that suddenly streamed down Harriet's face.

'Nay, lass, nay,' he said. And he helped her to a chair in a small room at the back of the shop.

'I cannot—' the words came out like great, choking cries, 'I do not know how to live without her.' She did not even crumple in the chair, she just stared at the bookseller helplessly as the tears fell down.

'Nay, lass,' he said again, and she saw that he too was making her tea. 'Just wait a minute now.' He walked over to the door of the shop and flipped over a notice that said, in beautiful copperplate handwriting: DAWSON'S BOOK EMPORIUM CLOSED FOR FIVE MINUTES, and pulled down a blind.

'Now,' he said, as he poured the tea, stirred in sugar. 'I think tha must weep as often as tha can, to help the pain of it. But after that tha must take her with thee.'

Harriet was so surprised she actually stopped crying. He handed her the tea.

Thinking of it long afterwards she never knew if he did know she had planned to go away, or if they were talking at cross-purposes, for all he repeated was, 'Tha must take her with thee, wherever tha goes. Talk to her if it helps. But most of all, take her smiling terms with thee.' And after a while he said into the almost companionable silence, 'And her books of course.'

Again she looked at him most curiously. 'I came to ask you if I could sell you her books. I need some money very quickly.'

She was so grateful for the way he asked no questions. 'There's nae money in books. And I think you should keep her books.' He pronounced them *boooks*, which seemed to give them even more weight and value. 'I'll take them of course if tha must sell them, but – have tha no jewellery? Had Mary no jewellery?'

She thought quickly. Her father gave her expensive jewellery every year: she knew it was expensive. He often told her so. 'Yes, I have jewellery. I should have thought of that.' *Of course. She did not need to borrow money. She could sell all her jewellery.* Mary had said: *if anything happens to me, take all the jewellery. It is in the second drawer.* She had forgotten. *My brain isn't working. How could I have forgotten something so important?* 'But – I do not know how to sell it. It has to be at once.'

She understood he was pondering on this as, observing that her tears had stopped, he went across to raise the blind and flip the notice over again so that it read: WELCOME TO DAWSON'S BOOK EMPORIUM.

'It's an odd business, selling jewellery. There are right rogues about.' He picked up a book absent-mindedly. 'Along Oxford Street, by Bond Street, there's a man called Sandford. I'll go and have a word with him this evening. You go tomorrow and tell him I sent thee. And bring me any books tha can do without.'

The door of the shop opened. Harriet quickly put down her cup, pulled her veil over her face as Mr Dawson went to meet the customer, but little notice was taken of her as she came out into the shop: they were discussing the man Darwin.

'Take her with thee, lass,' murmured the bookseller nevertheless as she passed.

'Thank you, Mr Dawson,' said Harriet and through the veil, just for a second, the smile flashed and was gone again.

It was then that the customer recognised her.

'Good afternoon, Miss Cooper,' he said, and his grey eyes observed her gravely.

She was thrown, felt as if she had *conjured* him. She was unable to speak, gave him her gloved hand and for just a moment they stood there, among the books.

'I am so very sorry,' he said. 'I understand that you loved your sister very much.'

She bowed her head so that he would not see tears.

And then Sir Benjamin Kingdom said gently, 'Is there anything at all that I could do for you?'

Harriet kept her head bowed. *What could she tell him, of her life?* She looked up at him and shook her head without speaking. *I can sell the jewellery and pay for my passage.*

He spoke again. 'Will you be – all right?'

It was the strangest question.

I can sell the jewellery and pay for my passage. She answered him truthfully. 'I think – I will be all right,' she said quietly. Only then did he let go of her hand.

She looked just once more at his face: she had for a brief moment the most extraordinary feeling, like an odd recognition, something important about him that she could not quite catch. And then it was gone.

Harriet bowed to the gentlemen and left the bookshop.

The amiable driver waited still as dusk fell over London and the first lights came on all over the city. Cecil, seeing her, climbed down to light his cab lamp. Harriet watched him for a moment. *I can sell my jewellery. I will have money.*

'Cecil,' she said.

'Yes, ma'am.' He was pulling at the wick, trimming it with his fingers.

'I need you to help me,' she said shyly. 'I will pay you of course.'

He waited till he had lighted the lamp at last and then turned towards her. 'On with it, Miss Harriet Cooper,' he said. 'I'll be pleased to be of assistance, payment or no payment,' and she did not notice that he knew her name.

Sometime later Cecil drew up, whistling still, at the house in Bryanston Square.

The front door flew open as the cab stopped outside. Peters and Lucy, both looking deeply relieved after her long absence (yet who could complain of the mistress going off with Lady Kingdom of all people), came quickly down the steps to help her out of the coach, to carry her parcels. ('A *sunbonnet!*' Lucy confided later in the kitchen. 'Death makes people mad.')

'Please pay the driver,' said Harriet and she inclined her head upwards towards Cecil very briefly and then passed into the hall and was overpowered by the smell of meat cooking, and the drains. Behind her Peters was already quizzing the driver about the details of her journey.

She had her dinner in her room with Quintus. She did not want food, her stomach rebelled against food, her heart beat too fast for food, but she knew she must become very strong very quickly. She cut the beef into very small pieces, tried to chew them without being sick. Lucy watched her and Quintus watched her until Harriet could bear it no longer: she pushed the plate away and Quintus barked joyfully at the remains. She could not bear Lucy to brush her hair but she accepted help undressing and putting on a nightdress and a shawl. Again Lucy saw the thin frame, the useless corset. Harriet sat in a chair beside the small fire in her room. Quintus sat beside her. Her legs were weak with exhaustion but there was much more to do. She tried to make her legs and arms less tense. Then there was a tap at her door.

Her younger brother Walter stood there looking embarrassed to see his sister in her night attire. He lingered in the doorway even though Lucy held the door open for him. He pulled at his rather wispy moustache. 'You are better now, Harry, are you?' He'd called her Harry since she was born, but only when their father was not present of course.

She thought about what he could possibly mean: *you are better now, are you?* Remembered just for a moment Benjamin Kingdom's different question: *will you be all right?*

'Yes, Walter, thank you.'

'Richard will not be home until late and I am going out,' he said. 'Just for dinner, and to visit a few friends quietly.' Harriet expected he was still going to play cards for money even though he wore a black band on his sleeve. And she wondered what was all the cooking for, when nobody ate it?

'Is there anything . . .?' Walter floundered.

'Thank you, Walter. I shall go to bed soon.'

But he could not quite leave. 'Peters said you have been out.'

No doubt Peters had. 'Yes.'

'Where did you go?'

She got up from the chair, moved towards him, Quintus followed joyfully. 'I went out with Lady Kingdom. I visited some shops in Piccadilly.'

'Ah.' That was the kind of answer that made him feel secure. Shopping, Lady Kingdom. Good.

'Harry,' he said in a rush suddenly, and the words tumbled out like a prepared speech, 'Harry, why not write your journal again, you know, TO THE DEAR READERS OF MY JOURNAL, like you used to. It – it would be good for you. Look, look, I've got you a notebook.' He stood there in the doorway, holding out a book for her. His sister did not answer. 'Would it be good for you?' he added uncertainly.

'I will try, Walter, if you would like me to, when I am feeling – more like writing.' And she took the notebook from his outstretched hand, turned it over and over, saw its pale cover. 'Thank you, Walter,' she said.

'I always liked them, Harry, your journals. I wanted to encourage you. It would be something for you to do.'

'Thank you, Walter. It is very kind of you to think of it.' And she repeated the word: thank you.

Another pause. She wondered what he thought about Mary, whether he had wept, although men did not weep.

'Have you had a good day, Walter?' How odd it was: they both stood there, embarrassed, yet trying. She thought of the easy manner her cousin Edward had with his sisters.

'Yes, yes. Thank you. Well then . . .' And he prepared to take his leave.

'Walter.'

'Yes?'

'Thank you for the notebook.'

'I am glad you like it. I am really glad, Harry. I liked your journals.'

'Walter.'

He turned back yet again. 'Yes, Harry?'

'Could you – would you be so kind as to inform Peters that – that it is good for me to go and look in the clothes emporiums. That I will be going again tomorrow.'

'Well of course. Yes.'

She was aware that Lucy was listening but it could not be helped. 'He seemed to think – that he had some sort of right to keep me here. I think only you or Richard have that right.'

Walter's immature face took on immediate understanding. Servants must know their place. He would see to it.

'Of course, Harry. You are quite right. Of course you may go tomorrow. I will tell Peters that I allow it.'

'Thank you, Walter.'

'Goodnight then, Harry.'

'Goodnight, Walter.' She saw he was relieved to be gone.

'Now, Lucy,' said Harriet, 'now I would like to be by myself.'

'There is nothing else, miss?' Lucy wished she could tell Harriet how glad she was that she hadn't run away; how much she hated Peters, how he told her she must report everything and how she did not; how he spied on the servants also. But she had to keep this position. One word from Peters and she would be gone, she knew that. She wished that she could say that *she guessed about Sir Charles*. (But of course she would never say that.)

'Nothing, Lucy. Thank you. Take Quintus now.' But before she let him go she suddenly knelt down and just for a moment buried her face in his coat. 'Goodnight, Quintus,' she whispered and he seemed to smile.

'Goodnight, Miss Harriet.'

'Goodnight, Lucy.'

She heard Lucy talking to Quintus as she went down the stairs.

And then, as if she could suddenly hardly walk, she made her way slowly across the room to her bed. Her head swam: she knew if she lay down she would not get up again. So she sat there for a moment, feeling her heart beat fast. Then with a great effort she got up again and walked to her jewellery box. She hardly glanced at the contents, removing only a tiny locket and a ring, both of which had belonged to her mother. Then she simply emptied the contents of the box straight in to the satin interior of a reticule: the bracelets and the necklets and the lockets and the jewelled brooches inlaid with diamonds that her father had begun to give her: was it enough to pay for a cabin? She had no idea.

Back to the bed. This time she did lie down and at once the room spun round and round. She had to close her eyes, *but I must stay well and I must stay awake I have only two more days to change my life.* But weakness and exhaustion overcame her and for the first night since Mary died, without the laudanum that had clamped down on her dreams, Harriet fell asleep.

She woke with a start. The lamp was still burning. *Was someone in the room?* At once her eyes flicked to the doorway and around the room, her heart began the over-fast beating. But the door was closed and the room was empty. And no clock ticked. The house was silent. She remembered all she had to do: she got up quickly. She went to the window and pulled the heavy curtain slightly, looked over the Square. London was in the time of most quietness: the time when it was truly night. The streetlights were burning but they were enclosed in a cold night mist, seemed like a row of ghostly candles. If there were moon and stars tonight they were not appearing, just dull, misty darkness. After a moment she made out the shape of the big oak tree in the Square. A shadowy figure walked beside the Square and disappeared into the distance as she watched. In the distance the traffic still rumbled, but muted now.

She turned from the window abruptly. She had to do this most difficult thing in the night: desperation gave her courage of a kind. She picked up the lamp, opened her door and stepped into the dark, silent passageway. She tried to breathe normally but could not still her heart, it pounded against her chest like a drum as she moved like a shade along the hall. She turned the handle of the door and walked into Mary's room. Closing the door softly behind her, leaning against it with closed eyes, she was aware of little sounds in the room. She opened her eyes, raised the lamp, looked about the room in terror: realised after a long moment that the sounds, the small gasps of pain, came from herself.

The bed had been stripped and Mary's books had been tidied away from the table. That was all. The pictures were still on the walls: the paintings of the English countryside, the copy of the Mona Lisa with her secret smile that her sister had so loved. But the emptiness of the room yawned at her. *Mary was dead.* With a sob Harriet put down the lamp and quickly crossed to the bed and knelt beside it. *O Lord*, she prayed, *take unto thy heart the soul of my beloved sister Mary so that she may be comforted and see thy light.* Even praying she could feel and hear the beating of her heart. *O Lord*, she whispered, *tell Mary I miss her so.*

Perhaps she knelt there for a long time, for her legs were stiff and cold when she at last tried to rise and she had to cling to the bed for a moment.

Then she went to the chest in the corner and opened the second drawer.

Mary's jewellery box had belonged to their mother. It was bigger and older than Harriet's and contained many pieces, much that had belonged to Elizabeth Cooper. Harriet had to walk to the long mahogany wardrobe to find Mary's reticule; opening the wardrobe door she was overcome by the *smell* of her sister, as if, truly, she was there somewhere among the gowns and the bonnets and the shawls. Harriet, shocked, stayed stock-still. Then very slowly she leant her forehead against the clothes. *Darling Mary*, she whispered again, *help me. Give me strength to do this.* The dresses in the big wardrobe did not answer but Harriet breathed in the scent of her sister, who had been her life.

At last, with Mary's reticule in her hand, she walked back to the chest and emptied the jewel box. At the very bottom of the box Harriet knew there was another compartment: it was their secret when Harriet was a little girl. She opened it: there were some papers inside. There was a prospectus for the Ladies' College in Harley Street. There was a letter from their mother to Mary that Harriet had seen before, the long graceful curl of the letters faded now, but still folded there. And there was a letter with Harriet's name on it. Startled, she picked it up, turned it over several times in her hand in the light of the lamp, opened it. There was no date.

My dearest sister Harriet,

If you are reading this it may be because something has happened to me, perhaps something we did not expect. I have worried for some time about what might become of you without me here. I would like to think that God would watch over you and bless you but in my heart I cannot be certain that the person to whom you should be able to turn has (Here some words were heavily scratched out.)

I therefore decided, on my thirtieth birthday, when I understood that Mother's provision for us would perhaps never be available, to begin to try to accumulate a little of the one thing we must never mention or have anything to do with because we are young ladies.

I may not have been able to obtain our mother's legacy but have sold some of her jewellery, and some of mine. I feel I have had every right to act as I have done because I believe it is what our mother would have wanted me to do. Look at the back of the bottom drawer of this chest. Go to Mr Dawson at his Book Emporium. He will help you.

Be strong, my dearest, most beloved sister and always remember you have been greatly loved by me, your sister Mary

Harriet, who had not believed there was room for any more pain, saw her own tears blurring the beloved handwriting. She wiped them away, made herself kneel down and feel at the back of the bottom drawer.

A box was filled to the brim with sovereigns.

She stood at once with the box of money and the letter, picked up the reticule full of jewellery and closed Mary's drawers. She could not carry the lamp as well; she would come back for it: suddenly she felt it was important to get these treasures back to her own room. She felt her way back along the corridor; she had left her own door slightly ajar, now she pushed it open, placed everything in a drawer, then at once felt her way back to Mary's room where she could see the lamp dimly burning on the chest. She was halfway across the room to close the door of the wardrobe when out of the corner of her eye she realised that someone stood in the doorway. Her heart gave a great lurch and she screamed.

'I beg your pardon, Miss Harriet.'

It was Peters, her father's manservant, who stood at the door of

Mary's room. He did not have a light of any kind; he looked like a black shadow, she could not tell how long he had been watching her. With an immense effort, even though her legs felt as if they would give way, she walked to the mahogany wardrobe, closed it, walked back to the chest and picked up the lamp. Then she stood silently in front of him, for he barred the way out of the room.

'Is everything all right, Miss Harriet?'

Still she said nothing. Her heart beat too fast.

'I thought I heard a noise,' said Peters.

'It was me, Peters. I came to say goodnight to my sister.' In the lamplight she saw that her words had disconcerted him; she took the moment to slip past him with the lamp and walked quickly to the door of her own room. At the doorway she looked back. Seeing her watching him he closed the door of Mary's room and turned away into the shadowy corners that led towards the servants' staircase.

On her bed, as the house became silent again, Harriet picked up the coins in a kind of wonder. She had not properly handled money ever before in her life; she counted them several times in disbelief and a kind of elation, feeling them, turning them over and over in her hand, seeing the face of the Queen. There were one hundred and ninety-one sovereigns.

Finally she knelt beside her bed. *Dearest Lord who knows all things, please guide thy servant.* She hesitated and then added uncertainly: *Thank you, Lord, if this has been by thy hand.* Then at last she rose. She could hardly believe what the day had held. Then she lay down, let her head touch the pillow at last. She fell at once into a deep, deep sleep. Underneath the pillow one hundred and ninety-one sovereigns lay.

Quintus barked below, chasing rats.

SIXTEEN

When Lucy appeared at first light, to set the fire, to bring the water, to empty the chamber pot and the washbasin, she found to her surprise that Harriet was already awake, sitting at her table in her nightdress and her shawl. She seemed to be signing a lot of papers, Lucy observed as she knelt beside the dead fire, clearing the ashes.

'Lucy.'

'Yes, Miss Harriet.' Lucy scrambled to her feet, gave a small, nervous curtsey. Was she too late this morning? Yet it was only just after six o'clock and she had already put the water on downstairs.

'I am going to clear my sister's room. There are two large box-chests in the attic. I used them when I went to live in Norfolk. Please tell them to bring them to my room after breakfast.'

'Yes, Miss Harriet. Will you have breakfast in your room?'

'Yes, of course.'

'I'll get it now then, after the water, well, let me just light this fire, you will be cold.' ('Poor thing,' said Lucy in the kitchen, filling a big jug with hot water, 'having to touch her poor dead sister's things in her state.' 'I would have done it this week,' said the housekeeper, vexed, 'it's not a task for her and heaven knows how she has got it in to her head, just now, with her father away. I shall assist her at any rate.')

But when the footmen had delivered the box-chests from the attic, and the housekeeper knocked on her door, Harriet said: 'Thank you, but it will take me some time to sort things. I shall call for you when I require your assistance.'

Sending Lucy to the Pharmacy in Oxford Street, asking her to bring back some Morison's Vegetable Universal Pills, and camphor oil (remembering Edward's medical box), Harriet quickly packed half a dozen of her own gowns into one of the boxes, her new stout boots, some shawls and several bonnets. Then she made herself walk down the passage again to Mary's room. She steeled herself for the remembrance of Mary again: as she walked in she suddenly saw how small Mary's stripped bed looked. She stared at it for a long moment. *But – of course!* Hastily she gathered together some of her sister's dresses and hats and carried them back to her own room; put them in her wardrobe behind one of her gowns, so that it did not look as if her own clothes had been moved in any way. Then quickly went through all the books: she would have liked to take every one, all their favourites, all the books they had read together all their lives, but she knew it was not possible. The ones she did choose she put down the side of the gowns in the chest, putting chemises and petticoats and stockings in the space that was left. This first box was full: she closed the lid and locked it, hiding the key at the back of a drawer with the one hundred and ninety-one sovereigns. The books that were left she piled against the wall.

As she came down the stairs she stopped for a moment below the large painting of her mother that hung in a bend of the stair-case. Sometimes it was said she looked like her mother. Like the painting of Augusta and Alice and Asobel (for family painters had always wanted to please their subjects), Elizabeth Cooper had been painted to look angelic. But from the angel eyes laughter shone.

Never again – and Harriet's mind faltered for a moment – would Mary recall for her the magic picture: the laughter in the rose garden; now only Harriet herself would be able to recall the memory of a memory.

And the memory of a painting.

For some minutes she stared at her mother, taking her into her heart.

Then she walked down the stairs to the hallway.

Peters was ready for her: he was dressed to accompany her. But Harriet was ready too: 'I would like to have Lucy to travel with me,' she said. 'As you have observed, a young lady does not travel alone.'

She had managed to put all the jewellery together in one larger reticule together with the signed papers for the New Zealand Company and some of Mary's sovereigns: this reticule she secreted in a large pocket inside her mantle. Hanging from her gloved hand was another smaller bag, from which a letter showed. Icy wind blew into the hall as the footman opened the door and Harriet and Lucy and Peters and one of the footmen all hurried to the coach, Lucy picking up Harriet's skirts and petticoats and bundling them in behind her mistress before climbing in beside her.

'Tell them Oxford Street,' said Harriet, and named the jeweller that the bookseller had told her of. 'I mean to have something made in memory of my sister,' she said to Lucy. But when the coach stopped and the footman opened the door, Harriet prevented Lucy from leaving the coach. 'Stay here, Lucy, with my reticule. It has a very important letter in it. I am on a sad mission here, I would prefer to do it alone.' As the servant of the jeweller bowed her inside she looked back. Peters had already alighted from his place on the carriage and was watching her, was already questioning Lucy.

Harriet emerged from the jeweller's shop in about fifteen minutes. The large reticule was empty of jewels, and lay once more deep in the pocket of the mantle. But *over two hundred* more sovereigns lay there also, heavy and powerful.

She asked to be taken to the Strand. In the carriage she at once saw that the letter, which she had not sealed, had been moved. Lucy observed her mistress's face.

'It was Peters, Miss Harriet,' she whispered nervously. 'He read the letter.'

'Good heavens,' said Harriet as the carriage rumbled along Oxford Street and down towards Piccadilly, 'what an extraordinary thing for a servant to do. I shall complain to my father.'

'He said, miss,' Lucy faltered, 'that he had your father's permission.'

'To read my mail?'

'Yes, Miss Harriet.'

'How very odd. Then he will know that I am delivering the letter to the New Zealand Company on the Strand. It is to send my cousin Edward in New Zealand the news of my sister's death. That is why we are going there.'

'Yes, Miss Harriet.'

Harriet was silent for a moment. 'And I suppose he asked you what I was doing in the jeweller's?'

'Yes, Miss Harriet. I told him about your sister's memorial piece.'

'Ah.'

'Not that it's his business, miss, if you don't mind me saying so; he's always poking his nose in everyone's affairs, no-one likes Peters, miss. He tells everything to the Master.' And then she stopped at once, fearing she had gone too far.

But Harriet said nothing more, stared out at the carts and the carriages and the omnibuses, held her precious mantle about her. *He leaned towards her, undoing the buttons.*

When the carriage stopped in the Strand Harriet allowed Lucy to come with her. When they got to the reception vestibule they both sat for a moment. Then as the frock-coated men approached them Harriet said, 'I shall deliver my letter, Lucy,' and disappeared inside. The letter she had written for Peters to read she tore into many pieces as she handed them the money, secured her passage and showed the disappointed gentlemen her father's signature, instead of her father himself. 'It was a letter to my cousin about my sister's death,' she explained as the pieces of paper of her torn letter floated down into a receptacle, 'but of course—' as she took the ticket from them, 'I will be there to tell him in person, before any letter.'

'You will be prepared in time? For the sailing on Friday?'

'Of course,' said Harriet. 'My father has done everything he can to make it easy for me, and will be at Gravesend if it is possible,' and they were satisfied.

As she came out of the building with Lucy she caught sight of yesterday's whistling cabman. She thought he did not see her but she gave the smallest of smiles under her veil as she stepped back into Sir Charles Cooper's carriage. Cecil watched her carefully, saw how she was watched also by Peters. Cecil whistled thoughtfully.

*

They saw that she was serious about completely clearing Mary's room: before they were allowed to assist her, chests of drawers had been emptied, books were stacked in a corner, the wardrobe was empty.

'The room is to be cleared completely,' she said to the housekeeper. 'There must be nothing here to remind me of my sister. I have packed her clothes in the two chests and I have arranged for all her furniture also to go to a deserving family in Newman Street who were known to her.'

But then, almost at once, she fainted. In vain she told them she did not need to see the doctor: he was called, came very quickly and insisted she should get into bed again.

'You cannot tell grief to go,' he said to Harriet. 'It takes its own time.'

'I know that,' said Harriet.

'Giving away Mary's things is something you may regret later. And most certainly should not be done without your father's permission.'

'I believe he will understand,' said Harriet.

'You need to eat a little food, and to rest. Wait till your father returns before you arrange these matters of Mary's belongings and whatever else you have got it into your head to do. It is most inappropriate for the servants to see you clearing drawers and wardrobes and goodness knows what else the housekeeper has told me that you have been doing.' Again he thought her hysterical, yet understood that the loss of her sister had been a body blow. 'I would like you to take a little laudanum, Harriet,' he said. 'Just to calm you,' and he reached for the brown bottle.

'*No!*' said Harriet. He looked at her, surprised, and saw that the blood had come to her cheeks.

'I beg your pardon, Doctor Adams. I prefer to keep the laudanum for the nights. It – it makes my thinking muddled.'

'What have you got to bother your pretty little head about?' he said in an effort at joviality, pouring some of the medicine into a small glass.

She looked at him strangely. 'I have to decide what to do with the rest of my life.'

'Harriet, my dear. It is not for you to decide. Your father will make choices and judgements and plans for you that you would not be capable of making, nor would you be expected to make. All you have to do is rest and get well again.' He handed her the glass. 'Now drink this like a good girl.'

Harriet wondered if he would go so far as to open her mouth and pour the medicine in. She placed the glass on the table beside her bed. She saw his lips tighten, but he said nothing more and rose to go. But he looked at her with disapproval, and something else she saw, disappointment, as he left her room.

'Lucy.'

Lucy had been following the conversation avidly, her head bent over her sewing.

'Yes, Miss Harriet?'

'Could you – would you bring me an egg?'

'A cooked egg, miss?'

'Yes.' Somewhere Harriet had heard or read that eggs were given to invalids because they were easy to swallow. Surely she could swallow an egg?

When Lucy returned with the egg, Harriet was dressed and sorting books on the floor. Lucy saw that the small glass lay in the washing bowl, the medicine trickled into the water.

'Here is your egg, Miss Harriet.'

'Thank you. Please tell them to call the carriage round. I wish to take my sister's books to Oxford Street. Then I will go back to bed as Doctor Adams requests.'

'This is not work for you, Miss Harriet,' the housekeeper protested in vain. They talked in the kitchen uneasily about the inappropriateness of her behaviour but she could not be persuaded differently. The carriage was to take a great many books to Oxford Street. When Peters protested also Harriet asked him coldly if he expected her to carry the books herself; she and Lucy went with the books, Peters insisted on accompanying them, the footmen helped carry the books into Mr Dawson's Emporium. Mr Dawson saw that the pale sister of Mary Cooper adopted a very formal manner in front of the servants: when the books had all been brought in and they had gone back to the carriage she stepped towards him quickly.

'Dear Friend, if you will allow me to call you that, I am indebted to you. Now I know why Mary spoke of you so often. Tomorrow I will return and will be grateful for whatever money you can raise for the books, but I have kept some, the most important. I am,' she whispered, 'going away.'

'Did tha call on the jeweller's?'

'It is all done. He was most kind and I thank you again for all you have done for me.' He took the gloved hand she offered him and said no more.

'What is today?' asked Harriet suddenly of Lucy as the carriage turned back to Bryanston Square.

'It is Wednesday, miss,' said Lucy.

'Wednesday,' Harriet repeated after her. Her father must not return early.

She could not sleep. She could not pray: repeated the Lord's Prayer over and over. She had, when Lucy had finally left her alone, packed the second, smaller, chest with books and candles and boots and her writing things and soap and linen and nightdresses and two small cushions from Mary's room, the covers embroidered by Mary long ago. She was ready. But the hugeness of her task kept threatening to overwhelm her, more problems appeared, she did not know if she had the strength for two more days. Tomorrow she had to arrange the most difficult part of all: the removal of Mary's furniture to the *Amaryllis*. She was entrusting this to someone she hardly knew. How poor her life, her friendships, her affections when she had to turn for help to a working man who happened to be passing. She and Mary had been their own whole world, not understanding that it would be shattered. She had read Mary's letter over and over: *be strong, my dearest, most beloved sister, and always remember that you have been greatly loved by me*, and from the words she tried to take one more ounce of strength but over and over in her head other words came *I must sleep I must sleep I will fail if I do not sleep forgive us our trespasses as we forgive them that trespass against us* and at last in desperation she reached for the brown medicine bottle. She tried to be careful, to take less than the doctor had prescribed for her, a little was spilt on the bed linen. Then she lay there stiffly and waited for sleep to come at last. At some time a heaviness did come and the truth and the untruth of the world drifted over her as she watched anxiously for the grey light to appear in the gap in the curtains.

It was so hard to drag herself up but she knew she must: so

much to do and it must be morning already, *everything must be con-cluded today everything quickly quickly*, so she forced herself up out of the mist of the laudanum and the opium and whatever else lay in the brown bottle and, her legs weak beneath her, she half-fell and knocked the contents of the chamber pot across the floor. The smell of the contents immediately permeated the room; in despair she seized a shawl, began ineffectually to mop up all that oozed around her in the cold, still-dark morning. A shocked Lucy (who had come even earlier this morning: it was not yet half past five) found her, tears rolling down her cheeks, pushing the reeking shawl back and forth across the floorboards.

Then Harriet knew she could not, after all, do it. She relin-quished the soiled shawl to Lucy and lay on the bed in silence. Everything smelt of her own disgust. In vain Lucy said there was hot water, she could wash, the mess was cleared, breakfast could be made. Harriet remained unwashed on the bed, her head turned away. She would never escape from the house in Bryanston Square.

From somewhere distant she heard Lucy's voice. 'Please, Miss Harriet, let me wash you at least and change the bed. Please. I will lose my position if anyone sees you like this.' There was some-thing desperate in the girl's voice, perhaps Harriet's own desperation heard it. Without a word she allowed herself to be sponged and changed; the bed was cleaned, Lucy put the quilt over her. She could hear the ashes being taken from the fireplace and someone calling in the street. She fell asleep.

Lucy saw her wake almost five hours later, saw the hands clench and unclench as she returned from sleep. The fire had been lit, it crackled and glowed; the room was clean and warm, the morning light did its best to shine through the half-opened curtains. Lucy saw that Harriet looked about the room, collected her thoughts, then she turned her head slowly and saw the maid who sat, as usual, sewing beside the fire.

'What time is it, Lucy?'

Lucy said nothing about the smashed clock; looked at the pocket watch on Harriet's small table. 'It is almost a quarter after eleven, Miss Harriet.'

Harriet was silent for a moment. 'Quarter past eleven on Thursday morning?'

'Yes, Miss Harriet.'

Harriet sat up at once. 'I would like to get dressed.'

Lucy had hoped that today would be restful, that Harriet would stay in bed. 'I will fetch some more hot water,' she said dubiously.

While she was gone, Harriet took some money from where she had placed her store, counted it. It was the third or fourth time she had counted it: Mary's money and the money from the jeweller. She had paid for her passage on the *Amaryllis* and had money left. It still felt odd, handling money, being in charge of anything but a few coins for church collection: to her it seemed that she now had a great deal of money. She walked in bare feet along the icy hall, to Mary's room. There stood the empty bed and mattress, a small table, an oil lamp, and the chest of drawers where she had found Mary' s letter. That must do. The Mona Lisa smiled down at her, as if she had a secret. Quickly she went back to her own room. When Lucy came with the hot water she found her mistress staring at the two locked box-chests.

'Peters is not here,' volunteered Lucy, pouring the water. 'He has been sent for.'

'Sent for?' Harriet's heart lurched violently.

'A message came this morning while you was sleeping. He was sent for to Norwich.'

'Is my father to return earlier? He is not coming today?' Suddenly her voice was tight and breathless.

'I'm not sure, miss.'

'Find out for me please. Quickly, quickly.' She could not do anything while Lucy was gone, stood transfixed, her heart beating uncontrollably. If her father was to come home earlier she was lost: *he must not come yet. O Lord, as I am thy servant and as you are all-powerful please help me and deliver me from evil as thine is the kingdom, the power and the glory forever and ever amen.*

'He will be back on Friday evening.' Lucy was puffing slightly from running up the stairs.

'I thank God!' breathed Harriet and did not notice that Lucy looked at her curiously.

Soon after midday the servants were again taken aback when Harriet appeared downstairs.

'A man with a cart is coming for all my sister's belongings, and her furniture,' she said. 'To take it to a poor deserving family in

Newman Street. Please have everything that I have marked from my sister's room, and the two chests from mine, carried out to the back.' They did not know whether to obey or disobey, Miss Harriet was obviously not at all well, yet Miss Harriet was obviously to be the new mistress of the house and might have power over their positions. Muttering to themselves that the furniture was much too good for Newman Street they carried it downstairs and out to the mews. And there Harriet saw, whistling in the icy wind, the driver, Cecil: such was Harriet's relief that he was waiting there that it seemed to her as if he had appeared by magic. Today he sat on a cart, chatting to a servant from another house. Servants of Sir Charles Cooper muttered and heaved, coming and going from the house: perhaps they did not see Harriet speak to the driver at some length, give him a paper, give him some money. The furniture was tied on, and the wooden chests, and covered with some canvas; the servants went quickly back inside, out of the cold. Lucy, just at the last, waiting for her mistress who seemed not to notice how cold it was, thought she heard Miss Harriet say to the driver, 'I will see you there,' but she may have been mistaken. Then the driver, seeming not to mind the cold, tipped his hat, called to his horses, and the cart carrying two chests and Mary's furniture trotted away.

Lucy had to bring Harriet in, for she stood at the door in the mews, watching the cart until it disappeared into George Street.

An hour later Harriet had slipped out the back door and into the wintry city by herself. She wore a shawl just as Mary used, walked quickly through to Oxford Street. Mr Dawson in his emporium was waiting for her; counted out for her seven sovereigns. She looked at the precious money shining in her gloved hand and then up at Mr Dawson, wondered if it was too much for books, if he could spare such a sum.

He raised his hand. 'They belonged to my friend Miss Mary Cooper and tha'art her sister. That is enough for me.' Then he looked at her closely. 'Will you be safe, lassie?'

'I think I will be safe, Mr Dawson. God will watch over me.'

'There's some that say perhaps there is no God.'

She saw in her mind the grey eyes of Benjamin Kingdom, quickly pushed them away. 'Mary and I have talked about this,' said Harriet. 'There has been no doubt in our minds. We believe in Him.'

'Then may He take great care of you, Mary's sister.' Once more he took her hand. 'Good luck, lassie.'

'I do not know what I should have done without you.'

'You know where I am. Let me have news of you.'

Out in Oxford Street, she took a few small coins from under her glove. From a flower-seller she bought a bunch of violets. As she gave the coins to the girl, somebody called Harriet's name. Perhaps she did not hear; if she did she did not turn. Holding the violets to her she turned quickly away, hurrying through an alley, back towards Bryanston Square.

Lord Ralph Kingdom, who had halted his cab when he saw her, was shocked. Young ladies did not walk alone in the streets of London, wearing a shawl and carrying violets.

A footman opened the door on her return: the housekeeper in the hall looked most disturbed.

'We did not know you had gone out, Miss Harriet.' The house-keeper observed the violets disapprovingly.

'I just wanted a little air. Please have the carriage brought round for me.'

'You are not going out again? In this terrible weather? I think it may snow.'

For once she did not need to dissemble. 'I am going to Highgate,' she said. 'To see my sister.'

She hardly remembered the earlier journey to Highgate but some-times in her dreams she saw plumed black horses, trotting. Now Sir Charles Cooper's carriage came up the lane to the cemetery again, swept in the gates and came to rest beside the colonnade. The superintendent at once came to the door of the vehicle, raising his top hat, bowing, enquiring how he could be of any assistance to Sir Charles Cooper's daughter.

Harriet told Lucy and the footmen to wait for her and, accompa-nied by the superintendent who gave her his arm in a most dignified manner, walked up the hill. Despite the cold wind gar-deners worked over the immaculate flowerbeds and the tidy graves, they bowed respectfully as they saw her dark clothes. Here on the cemetery hill the air was clear: London could hardly be seen far below them on the dull late afternoon: only a grey-yellow shroud with black smoke rising, seen in the distance. Soon dusk would fall and the lights of the city would flicker beneath them. Other people dressed in black passed by; Harriet did not see them, looked only ahead, to where her sister lay, to where they had kept her from, the day of the funeral. The superintendent, having shown her the way, held back respectfully and turned away: she moved forward and to the side of the path where Mary's new grave, still earth-turned, still with some of the stiff wax lilies from the day of the funeral, suddenly appeared before her. At first she just stared, there among the urns and the angels. Then very gently she moved forward across the grass, knelt beside the earth, to be nearer to her sister. She removed the lilies, placed the violets where she thought her sister's hands might be, crossed in prayer against her body. She stared at the earth for a long time. After a while, somewhere inside her wild, anxious mind, a picture came to her of Mary lying there in the ground. More than two weeks now, waiting for the grave to sink down into the receiving earth. Would worms be crawling all over her sister? *No! That was not what Death was, Death was glory in God.* But still she saw the body, remembered the blue lips, saw worms, crawling over Mary's withered, cholera-ruined face. *O God! No! It is not that! Dear Lord, help me to know that my sister Mary is with thee and that her soul has gone to heaven. Dear Lord, help me.*

There was no answer. The sky faded. A family walked decorously by, staring inquisitively at the kneeling black figure; somewhere at a discreet distance the superintendent thought of his tea while Harriet Cooper wept beside the grave of her sister. At last, with the light dimming, she sat up and began speaking to her sister, softly at first but then, hidden in the dusk, as if Mary was there to hear her, as if she could pour out her heart at last: *Dearest Mary, you must forgive me, for I am going away from you and I have come to say goodbye. We talked of going, you remember. To where the wind is so clean and nobody gets ill, where we would so have wanted to go together. It will be right, Mary, because of you. I found the letter and the money, I will go to New Zealand. To New Zealand, Mary! It is so far away that surely I will be safe at last. I will make a new life but you will always be part of it. But I wanted to tell you that I will not be coming to talk to you here, perhaps for a long time, but I will talk to you always, in my heart.* She stood at last, still staring at the earth where now the violets lay. *Goodbye, my darling.*

She had not heard somebody come up behind her, until he coughed discreetly. Harriet froze. It could not be Peters. But the superintendent was also an employee of her father's. She turned violently to meet her enemy, saw at once, even in the fading light, Lord Ralph Kingdom standing there.

'I beg your pardon,' he said gravely and in some embarrassment. 'I certainly did not mean to frighten you.' *How long had he been there?* 'It is almost dark, I assured your maid I would bring you safely back to the carriage. I spoke just now to the superintendent.'

How long had he been there? Why did he follow her? What right did he have to follow her?

'I came to call on you this afternoon. They said you were here and so I came in the hope, perhaps, that I might find you.'

A bell rang somewhere. The cemetery was closing. A few stragglers lingered still, unable yet to leave so easily the ones they had loved. A cold mist seemed to fall over the perfect lawns and the flowerbeds and the graves.

Still Harriet said nothing, still she stared at him. *Had he been listening?*

'Harriet . . .' He stepped forward. She could not step back, she was right beside her sister's grave. He stood close to her now, the cold air caught his breath, turned it to smoke. *Had he been listening? If he had heard, what would he do – would he help her or hinder her?* Her shoulders drooped. But she suddenly thought of Phyllis in the basement of the theatre, making her tea for the dancers, for Lord Kingdom's dancer. And then of Cecil, whistling with the furniture, nearer and nearer, even as she stood here, to the *Amaryllis.*

And so Harriet Cooper, regaining her balance beside the grave of her sister, stepped past Lord Ralph Kingdom. She did not look back to where her sister lay: she had to believe that Mary's soul had flown upwards, to where God waited in Heaven. Then she began to walk in the half-light along the path and back to the gate. A gardener trudged ahead of her, carrying a rake over his shoulder.

'Harriet – wait.' Ralph came up behind her and this time he laid his hand on her arm to detain her. 'I would not,' he said, 'intrude on your grief. I am very sorry that your sister has been taken from you in this cruel manner.'

'Thank you, Lord Kingdom.' She had stopped in the path because he stood in her way.

He spoke very formally. 'You will recover from this terrible loss.'

She remembered what she had understood in his mother's carriage. 'I think – that no-one can know another person's sorrow, Lord Kingdom,' she said very simply, and she did not so much shake off his arm as just walk away from it. She turned downhill. A light flickered in the chapel by the gate. His stride easily caught her; he did not speak again until her carriage came into view but she could hear his breathing and suddenly the formal tone was gone.

'Are you – going away, Harriet?' he said.

Then she did stop. *He had overheard her then.* He had spoken very quietly yet she could see that he was as greatly agitated as herself. *What had it to do with him?* For a moment she did not speak. The superintendent's bell rang again and again, calling the mourners back to the gate. Her heart beat too fast, she was sure he could hear it. 'Lord Kingdom, I do thank you for your very kind condolences. I would like you to think well of me, and – not to think that my wild words to my sister's grave are more than that. Her death has—' her voice caught for just a moment, 'has wounded me more than it is possible for me to convey to you.' Her heart did not quieten: of course, it would be his duty to tell her father. But the *Amaryllis* would sail tomorrow: he could not conceive of that. By the time he saw her father she would be gone.

Then Ralph Kingdom did an odd thing. From inside his coat – in a mad moment she recoiled, thought it might be a court document or (it flashed wildly into her mind) a *pistol* that he brought forth – he took a small book.

'Please accept this.'

In the darkness she could not even see the title but she took the book from him, turned it over for a moment in her gloved hands and then put it into her reticule. At least he had not questioned her further.

'Thank you, Lord Kingdom,' she said politely. 'You are very kind.'

They walked in silence down to the colonnade and the carriages. Already the drivers had lighted the lamps on their vehicles and the horses snorted and shook their bridles in the freezing air. The superintendent hovered, rubbing his hands together slightly, anxious that his duty had been well done. Ralph bowed low over

Harriet's hand in the way that he had. Then he handed her into her coach where her cold maid waited.

Her brothers would not be back for dinner, the servants said.

In the quiet, uneasy house Harriet ate (carefully, determinedly, eating slowly, swallowing correctly) in her room. Quintus lay at her feet looking at her with devotion. She gave him some meat, hugged him, ruffled his ears: his cup ran over; all seemed almost well again, although one of his mistresses had disappeared. The servants moved about the house on quiet feet as they had been taught.

Harriet dismissed Lucy early, saying she wished to sleep; she hugged Quintus again as he was led protestingly away.

But she knew she must not lie down. As soon as Lucy had gone Harriet forced open the big window on to the Square, breathed in the cold night air to keep herself awake. She felt distinctly strange, odd: as if she watched herself in all she did. She saw clearly that her hands shook in all that she was doing. *It is almost tomorrow. One more day.* Quickly she rearranged her wardrobe: she had decided to wear as much as she could in the morning; the cold weather was her friend. Mary's gowns behind the remnants of her own made her wardrobe look untouched: gently she arranged Mary's linen where her own had once lain on the lemon-scented shelves. From her small reticule Lord Ralph Kingdom's book tumbled: she looked at it hurriedly, a slim volume by the poet Tennyson, something called 'The Princess'. It had fallen open at the front; there he had written *For Thee I Love.* In great embarrassment she pushed it back to the bottom of her reticule. She packed one more small bag: the bag she and Mary used to take with their embroidery if they were to stay overnight at weddings, or at funerals. Here she placed her passage papers, her money (counting it one more time), the few pieces of her mother's jewellery, Walter's pale notebook, all the laudanum the doctor had given her, Mary's last letter. And on top of all these she placed her embroidery, for all the world to see.

She had to leave the house early in the morning, she must be early, to take the small steamboat to Gravesend. She walked up and down her room, making herself move, forcing her mind to think of what she had yet to do when all she wanted was to lie down on her bed. She took up her lamp and walked, one more time, into Mary's room. But Mary was quite gone. The room was

empty not only of its belongings but of its owner. There were some
marks on the floor where the bed had been which the servants,
polishing, had been unable to remove. Only a simple washstand
stood there, alone by the window. And the Mona Lisa with the
smile. She wished she could take that, but there was no more room.
She made a small vow, standing in the empty room, that one
day she would find another copy of the secret smile, and hang it
where she would see it always, and remember her sister. Then
quickly she went back to her own room. She wished she could
strip it bare, leave it in the same state of anonymity as Mary's:
knew she must not. Every hour that they did not know where she
had gone would be precious. The fire had died down, the room was
cold, but she did not notice; somewhere Quintus barked, but she
did not hear.

Finally she sat down at the table beside her bed and picked up
her pen. It took her a long time to write the few words; she seemed
to ponder over every sentence.

> *Dearest Asobel,*
>
> *Perhaps this is the first letter ever to arrive at Rusholme
> addressed to you. I think I did not see you at Mary's funeral, not
> properly. Please forgive me, little Asobel. You will understand one
> day. I hope you are reading your books in the way that I taught
> you and being a good child for your kind parents and brothers and
> sisters.*

Harriet hesitated then, staring at the page in front of her, thinking of Asobel's open, happy face in the summerhouse. She wanted
to write about Edward, but she did not dare.

> *I will write to you again, dear Asobel. I promise.
> I think of you all very often.*
> > *From your affectionate cousin
> > Harriet*

She heard a clock chime midnight from somewhere in the city
outside. Once more she moved to the window and stared at the
shadows of the Square, at the oak tree and the railings and the gas
lamps. A cold mist covered everything. There was the sound, as

always, of distant traffic, wheels rumbling along Oxford Street, down Park Lane. The smell of the drains wafted upwards and Quintus barked again. It was this that was her memory of London.

Then Harriet, quite clearly, saw herself walk out into the dark passage in her nightdress and down the wide staircase, down and down to the bottom. The silent house creaked. One small light burned at the last turn.

From the hall she walked to the back of the house and down the small staircase and into the kitchen where another lantern burned. She did not know the kitchen. She saw the knives hanging. She took a small, sharp knife. She walked back into the hall and up the stairs past the portrait of her mother but she looked straight ahead, glancing neither left nor right. She did not see little Lucy standing at the bottom of the servants' stairs. Harriet came into her room. She placed the knife in her embroidery bag. And then she saw herself walk back at last to the bed and lie down under the quilt.

SEVENTEEN

Walter and Richard were surprised, and alarmed (lounging at the table and yawning, cravats undone, at the damnably early breakfast insisted on by their father), to see their pale sister enter the dining room. Something had made her wish to see them once more, though she was not sure what that feeling was. Her brothers stood up, pulled at their cravats, apologised for not visiting her more often, sat down again, made polite conversation, as the servants bustled about them. She wondered if they would perhaps mention Mary, say something, just something, about their dead sister. But they did not. Harriet was neatly dressed, her hair pulled back from a face that looked as white as parchment; even her brothers could not but notice that her hand shook as she picked up a cup.

'Harriet, should you not perhaps have stayed in your room a little longer?' She looked at her elder brother, Richard, hearing his words. It was the first statement of concern she had heard from him that she could ever remember. She must appear well. She must *smile* at Richard. She must have her brother's permission: one command to the servants from him would overrule any of her own.

'Father will be home tonight,' she said. And she smiled at her brother. It seemed to her that her voice was very loud in the room. 'I am, of course, much better.'

Richard seemed satisfied. But Harriet had not finished.

'I have decided to go to Church this morning,' she said. And she smiled again.

Both brothers looked at her, nonplussed.

'What will you go to Church for today, Harry?' said Walter, and she saw that he was trying to be kind, thought she was muddled. 'It is not Sunday.'

Harriet laughed. It seemed to her that her laugh echoed round the room, on and on, in under the dishes on the long table. She tried to hold to the side of the table, *I must not fail now*.

'People do go to Church on other days, Walter,' she said rather shakily. 'I wish to talk to the Vicar.'

She saw that Richard looked uneasy.

'Father thought it might be – good for me. He spoke to me about it. As soon as I felt well enough, he said.'

'Very well.' Richard gave his permission, nodded to the head footman.

'And then I shall call on Lady Kingdom.'

'You are in mourning. Surely people can come to you.'

'She has already called here. It is proper that I return her call. Father wishes me to do this.'

Neither Richard nor Walter were expert in the exact niceties, shrugged, lost interest. 'But he should have mentioned it,' said Richard. 'We understood you were to stay in your room, or at least the house. He wants you to be well.'

'I am trying, Richard,' said Harriet humbly.

'Shall I come home early this evening and sit with you before Father comes?' Walter asked rather guiltily. 'I don't mind.' He knew, in mourning themselves, they would not be gallivanting around London now that their father was returning.

'Thank you, Walter, but I expect I shall rest. I wish to—' and again she gave the odd laugh, then held again to the side of the table, 'I wish to be prepared for Father's return.'

'We must all be here for Father's return.' Richard, too, knew there would be stricter hours kept from now on.

'Yes. Of course.' And for a moment Harriet contemplated the long nights that might stretch ahead; her brothers would go about their business, and she alone in the house, waiting, and listening, for Father. *Never, never, never.* Suddenly her head cleared and the diverse bits of her joined together again and she reached out a firmer hand for a piece of the thin toast and asked her brothers about their day.

When the brothers got up to leave the house Richard bowed to her and was gone. Harriet's eyes followed him expressionlessly. Walter lingered for a minute.

'You are quite well, are you, Harriet? You look very pale. Can I – do anything for you?'

She looked up at her younger brother, took in his features, his hair, the way he always looked slightly anxious, not as confident as Richard. No doubt the gambling troubles continued. She did not know if he missed Mary. She did not know if she would ever see him again. And she smiled, and put out her hand.

'Thank you, Walter. I think – I think I will be much better after today.'

'Oh well. That's good.'

'And I shall begin my Journal again, as you suggested. In your notebook.'

His face lit up in genuine pleasure. 'Oh that's good, Harry.'

'Yes.' And the brother and sister clasped hands rather self-consciously for a moment and then Walter was gone.

Not once had anyone mentioned Mary.

Harriet at once went to her room, looked carefully around, asked for the carriage to be brought round immediately, to take her to St Paul's Church in Covent Garden.

'Is it not too early, madam?'

'No. The Vicar is always there early.'

Her veil was already down over her face when Lucy came to tell her that the carriage was ready; she had put an extra petticoat under her gown, two extra shawls under her mantle. She gave Lucy the letter for Asobel. The bag, she told Lucy, had a few more of Mary's things, something she had been embroidering, to give to the poor. She would leave it at the church.

She did not look back as she left her room: she knew she could not risk calling Quintus, to say goodbye. Quintus would know.

The footmen climbed up; Lucy assisted Harriet, picked up all the skirts, noting the extra petticoat, before she clambered in beside her mistress. Harriet did not look back as the horses trotted off down the side of Bryanston Square.

Pale yellow light tried to shine from the east and light the grey, cold fog of the city. As they trotted up towards Covent Garden they overtook costermongers and carts. Somehow a herd of sheep had come the wrong way, they skittered in front of the vehicles, slipping on the ordure and the mud, their eyes looking sideways in terror, their bleats mixing with the shouts of drivers and boys with carts.

'It's too early to be out, miss, said Lucy dolefully, 'ladies and gentlemen come later,' but Harriet's face was hidden by her veil and she did not reply.

When the carriage stopped at the front of the church, Harriet said to Lucy: 'I would like to speak to the Vicar alone. He is a busy man, and I may be some time,' and she alighted quickly from the carriage: despite her extra clothing a thin veiled figure in black. She took a few steps and then whirled back, reached inside for the embroidery bag. 'The Vicar will advise me as to where to send these things,' she said to Lucy, and one of the horses jangled at his bridle and its feet moved sharply on the cobblestones as a cabbage rolled under the wheels through the excrement of the sheep. Outside the church a man in a cassock kept the wrong sort of people out; he bowed low to Harriet's veiled figure and she disappeared inside.

She walked quickly down the long, dark aisle, past the pews and the flowers and two gossiping, yawning clerics and the women cleaning. Already she heard the shouts of the sellers, calling their wares. Just before the altar she paused, knelt. She could not think of anything except the Lord's Prayer, began quickly *Our Father who art in heaven hallowed be thy name* as the market men shouted and bargained just outside. Then she slipped out of one of the side doors opposite the altar and into the wild, crowded, jostling, shouting, hectic madness that was Covent Garden. The smell hit her as she came out into the piazza.

Somehow the noise and the energy and the vitality around her gave her energy, and a kind of desperate euphoria spurred her on. This was her only chance to be free and she could not let herself think of what would happen if she failed now. She held her precious bag very tightly, both her gloved hands around the handle, knowing that this, more than anywhere, was where she could lose it; pushed through the noise and the people swirling about her: out of place, observed.

'ORANGES!' called the voices. 'SWEET ORANGES!' 'CAR-
ROTS!' 'POTATERS!' 'VIOLETS!' 'CABBAGES!' 'LILIES!'
'PUMPKINS!' and people pushed past her, other people's servants
and cooks, dog sellers, farmers' lads, pickpockets, fools. Open
drains swirled their contents nearby, horses stood ankle-deep in
dung. In her blind haste Harriet tripped over, but did not even see,
a young girl clutching a baby and some dead bunches of flowers,
who sat in the mud weeping. Her face under its grime was as pale
as Harriet's, looking up with her hopeless bunches; seeing Harriet's
panicky haste, she did not even bother to call out. Harriet saw
nothing but the end of the market. She pushed on, not knowing or
caring that mud and other filth smeared her skirts, that rotten vegetables stuck to her boots, that watching eyes continually swept
over her as her incongruous figure hurried past, a black veiled
figure out of place in the wild chaotic world of the market. At last
she came to the south side. A hansom cab appeared, she called
urgently to the driver to take her to Blackfriars Bridge. Once inside,
hidden from view, she thought her heart might burst, so breathless
and heated and frantic was she; the market and the extra clothing
and the fear of someone calling her name. She took up her veil,
tried to breathe calmly, felt trickles of perspiration running down
her body under her corset. She knew very well she might faint
again but she could not faint now, not now, and even as her head
spun she spoke aloud to herself in the cab, *only a little longer, only a
little longer.* She passed great edifices she might never see again: the
palaces and churches and spires and bridges of her city; she gave
no sign. From building hoardings advertisements shouted to her:
GUINNESS DUBLIN STOUT, CHARRINGTON'S ALE, but Harriet
did not see or hear. The Blackfriars Bridge was the only thing she
was interested in; at last it came into view. She lowered her veil as
she descended from the cab, handed the driver some coins from
under her glove.

At the jetty she understood the crowds and the weeping families;
quickly she made her way through the people to one of the small
steamboats that was going to Gravesend. A man thrust a paper
into her hand, she did not see what it was. She knew she must go
inside the cabin where the women and children gathered; she could
not sit in the air however desperate she was, it would make her too
conspicuous, she was conspicuous enough, travelling alone. Her

lowered veil gave her a kind of protection; she sat alone quietly. In her hand she saw to her horror she was holding a leaflet offering CURES FOR VENEREAL DISEASE, quickly she crumpled it and thrust it behind her seat. At long last a bell rang, the small gangway was removed and in an important and noisy manner the steamboat turned, steaming past St Paul's Cathedral and towards the mouth of the river, pushing its way past the sailboats and the lighters and the barges, belching smoke into the smoky sky. On deck people waved and called, in the cabin they wept and laughed and pushed against the windows; everywhere there was calling and loading and passing and colliding: it all drifted past Harriet as if in a dream; she sat very still, clutching her embroidery bag. Just once she looked back: London was wreathed in fog and smoke and soot, and disappeared.

As the boat steamed past, all the great docks and warehouses bustled about their business: Harriet did not see. All she heard, suddenly, were the screaming gulls, proclaiming that the sea was near. Her eyes hidden under her veil, she willed the boat quickly onwards, she prayed that Cecil had carried out her instructions: yet if he had not she would sleep on the bare boards of her cabin; nothing mattered now but that the *Amaryllis* set sail and was gone. *Lord, help thy servant in this, her affliction, give me strength for just a few more hours so that I may be saved in the name of our Lord Jesus Christ.* Children nudged each other at the lady praying.

Greenwich came into view, the domes of the naval college. Her brother Walter had wanted to join the navy: their father had insisted to Walter that the world of business was the only one to enter; to which he, Sir Charles Cooper, held the key.

The domes were gone. Walter was gone.

The steamboat ploughed on and on through the grey morning, hour after hour, its own black smoke mixing with all the other smoke and fog and grime that rose from the docks and the factories all along the Thames. When at last they arrived at Gravesend, they saw at once that all the boarding and loading of the *Amaryllis* was in full swing. Harriet was helped on to the dock; she quickly raised her veil, stared at the ship that was to save her. She saw at once that it was smaller than the *Miranda* and just for a moment her heart gave a great leap at the thought that this small vessel was to take her across oceans; in this she would traverse the world. Then she saw, at the prow, another figure, a kind of mermaid, hair streaming (red hair, her hair had been painted red and her fins were blue), straining to lead the *Amaryllis* onwards and Harriet Cooper, standing alone on the Gravesend dock, smiled. Then, collecting herself anxiously, clutching her embroidery bag to her, she looked about for Cecil. Huge boxes stood everywhere, beds and bundles, traders were selling their wares, knots of steerage passengers stood anxiously on the deck and on the dock with their small possessions, sailors were hauling ropes and boxes, women were being winched aboard, swinging wildly in their copious skirts.

She saw him. He had seen her already, stood beside his cart with his arm raised. She saw with alarm that his cart was empty, hurried towards him. He grinned. He was wearing the same slightly squashed top hat.

'It's all aboard, miss, I had to leave it at Deptford but I watched it like a hawk, it come aboard about an hour ago from one of the lighters. You must go aboard at once and point it out and sailors will take it to your cabin.'

She and her possessions and the *Amaryllis* were here at Gravesend: Harriet was so relieved that her legs seemed to buckle under her. She put out her hand to steady herself. Cecil understood, gave his arm for a split second. She said, almost weeping with relief, 'I am so pleased to find you,' as if he was a long-lost relation. Then she pulled herself together. 'Cecil.' She swallowed. 'Could I ask you to come aboard with me, to assist me with my belongings. I will pay you, of course.'

'Be glad to, Miss Harriet.' If Cecil thought it was unheard of for a single woman to be trying alone to board herself and some furniture on a ship bound for the other side of the world without a single family member to say goodbye, he gave no sign; the odd couple walked the shaky gangplank to the ship, Cecil whistling some tuneless song of his own, Harriet assuring an official that she had no need of winching.

As soon as they had boarded, Cecil and a sailor almost immediately began – like a lot of other people around them trying to clamber past with boxes and wardrobes – arguing. The voices got louder and louder and the language was words Harriet had never heard before; then just as quickly the two found they knew someone in common, shook hands, enlisted the help of some carpenters, carried – banging and bumping and swearing, kicking at some squawking chickens in a small cage, lunging at dirty excited children who should have been down below in steerage – Harriet's belongings to her cabin. It was so small she could not believe they would get the bed in the door but they laughed, said it was easy when you were used to it, unfitted the legs, pushed and shoved: the small bed, the chest of drawers, the small table, the locked boxes, all piled on top of one another. They quickly put the bed together again, the carpenters then proceeded to nail the furniture to the floor, as they had done in Edward's cabin; all the while joking and laughing with Cecil who seemed to know them all; he persuaded them to nail some hooks into the bulwarks on which Harriet could hang things; Harriet paid them, they departed, shaking hands all round. From above them, on the poop deck, came the sound of people walking and running, outside the cabin people passed to go on deck; she glimpsed an arm, a hat, a waist through the half-open door. Through the small round cabin window she saw the legs of people passing.

'What you got in them boxes?' enquired Cecil politely.

She thought. 'Clothes. Books. Candles, I think. Oh, yes, and a lamp.'

Cecil looked slightly embarrassed. 'I been looking at your belongings,' he said. 'You got no wash things?'

'I—' She blushed brightly, looked around the tiny, now chaotic cabin. She hadn't somehow thought of these essentials. In Mary's empty room, the washstand stood alone by the window. Realising the enormity of her omission she put her hands to her face in mortification.

'Well, they got a water closet on this boat. Nevertheless, for nights and storms and that, when you can't get about.' Her heart suddenly jumped at the idea of the danger. 'You seen them traders,' Cecil went on, 'in the small boats hanging around, and on the dock?'

'Yes.'

'They sell everything. You won't be the first person to come without.'

'I—' She paused, blushed again, quickly got some of her money from her embroidery bag. 'Could you?' She looked at him with such excruciating embarrassment that he laughed as he took the money, although kindly.

'Excuse me, Miss Harriet, but I think you've got a few shocks coming crossing the world, if you don't mind me saying so.'

While he was gone she took off her mantle and her extra petticoats and all but one of the shawls, unpinned her hat, sat for a moment on a small clear space on Mary's bed, which looked so strange and different in its new home. The mattress was wet. All the time a feeling of fear gripped her, that something could yet go wrong. She got up and looked around her tiny, crowded cabin and out of the small window which let in the light and where people's legs passed. She did not know what time it was, but it must be late afternoon and soon, surely, the ship must leave. Before dusk, they had told her. The servants would long ago have come into the church to look for her. What would they do? What would they think? Had they already sent word to her father? She knew she would not feel safe until the shores of England were no longer in view. She had that same feeling, of seeing herself. She was standing in a small box with a small, round window, *I am Harriet Cooper*, she whispered fiercely to herself. *I am Harriet Cooper and I am going to New Zealand where I will find my cousin Edward.* She found two small keys at the bottom of her embroidery bag. She stared at them for a moment: at last she unlocked the box-chests, opened the lids. She thought she saw some insects running away in a corner of the cabin, perhaps she imagined it. There was a knock at her door, she thought it was Cecil returning but a uniformed official stood in the doorway with some papers. 'Miss Cooper?'

Has someone found me already? She held very tightly to the small table. Her face was expressionless. 'Yes?'

'Ah, Miss Cooper, we are glad you have embarked at last, I have been looking for you.' He bowed to her. 'The Captain had been hoping, we were all hoping, that your father was here, to say good-bye.' He looked rather dubiously around the cabin. Usually people were surrounded by family.

'My father and I have already – parted. He is detained on government business but – my brother – my brother was here to see me safely aboard. He has just disembarked.'

The official bowed again. 'I am so sorry not to have met him. There have been some later arrivals among the passengers even than yourself and I was detained earlier. The Captain sends his compliments. He was so hoping to meet your father. We had an embarkation breakfast this morning with many leading dignitaries present; your health and that of your father was drunk in your absence.' Harriet looked at him in horror. 'The Captain would have liked to greet you himself – and your brother of course – in person when you boarded but now the estuary pilot is on board and he is called to his duties. He will of course be looking forward to your eating at his table and all care will be taken of you. For we are not used,' he added confidingly, 'to ladies travelling alone. We understand, of course, about your very sad bereavement – my condolences to you – and have made an exception in this case. Because of your father, of course. And as you are without a natural protector we will, of course, find a suitable married couple to be your guardians.' Somebody called, he looked flurried, and was gone with another bow and many apologies.

Cecil came back stumbling under a small cupboard, disappeared again. She opened the cupboard, found it contained a big chamber pot decorated with rather large, bright crimson roses; she blushed in deep embarrassment. In a few minutes Cecil returned with a bowl, and a jug of the same pattern.

'Have you got curtings?'

She looked at him blankly.

'See this window? Where the people are passing? When it's cold and stormy you'll have it closed but when you go through them tropical oceans you'll want to have it open, for the breeze. So you should put up curtings. There's some of them Indians on the dock, with their stuff, their silks and their cottons, and you could sew it. You could come down and choose the colour and that.'

She nodded, put her hat back on, and lowered the veil, followed him out on to the deck.

'What do I do if I see – bugs?'

'Burn them and chuck them overboard.'

'Thank you,' she said politely. They side-stepped people and boxes and animals and children. There were ropes everywhere, and coils of big chains, and wooden buckets full of water; pigs in cages complained bitterly of their small space, grunting and snorting. Above, a lifeboat hung, suspended over the deck, and far above the lifeboat flags fluttered. 'How do you know so well – how things are arranged, on board the ship?' she asked Cecil.

'I was a sailor, long ago when I was young. I like seeing the boats go, it reminds me; I sailed once, to India, and me daughter's gone to Australia,' and with this surprising cornucopia of information he helped her down the gangplank and on to the part of the pier where people were selling and shouting their wares; shabby steerage passengers bought second-hand saucepans and children tried to steal oranges. Cecil pushed his way through to where brown men in coloured turbans held out rolls of cloth. He began bargaining with the Indian traders at once; he and they seemed to have a fearful argument but when the price was struck everyone bowed, including Cecil; he carried under his arm back on to the ship the material of Harriet's choice, had insisted she buy a big cup and saucer also. 'For drinking water, the water will be rationed of course, you need to have your own cup.'

'I know,' she suddenly said eagerly, putting up her veil, remembering Edward's manuals, 'to catch the rainwater.' Cecil smiled, pleased, and Harriet smiled back at him.

So that was how Lord Ralph Kingdom saw her coming towards him, as he looked for her in vain about the ship: she was smiling on the deck of the *Amaryllis*, holding a cup and saucer.

When Harriet turned, and then saw him, she dropped the cup and saucer at once. They did not break on the wooden deck but bounced down the deck towards Cecil, who picked them up.

'I wondered if I might find you here,' said Ralph, very gravely.

She looked as if he had struck her. This time her legs did give way and if he hadn't stepped forward and quickly caught her arm she would have fallen to the deck.

'No. *No!*' was all she whispered.

Cecil, behind her, looked on with interest. He was familiar enough with the ballet dancers at Her Majesty's Theatre, and their teatime stories, to know much about Lord Ralph Kingdom.

Ralph, so tense himself, was nevertheless appalled by Harriet's reaction. One moment she was smiling, next moment she looked at him as if he were the very devil himself. *Good God, did she not realise yet that he loved her!* He led her, his arm half around her, to the ship's rail, where for a moment she stood, her head bowed. Below on the shore people scurried about, calling, waving, directing luggage angrily, buying last-minute supplies, but Harriet saw none of this: only understood that somehow, at the last minute, she had been discovered. Tears of shock burst from her eyes, she was not protected by her veil, she put her hands up to her face and the embroidery bag bumped against the rail.

'Why should you stop me!' she exclaimed wildly.

He looked bewildered. 'What are you doing here on your own? Who are you travelling with? Where is your family?'

Cecil stood at a respectful distance but near enough to hear most of their conversation. Gulls screamed past now, diving towards the ship and then flying upwards again.

'Who are you travelling with?' Lord Kingdom's voice was low and urgent.

'I am travelling alone.'

'You are travelling alone to New Zealand?' His voice was disbelieving. 'What of your father?' He was still holding her arm and she felt his fingers tighten. 'He would not allow you to do this, of that I am certain.'

'Please. You are hurting me.' Cecil tensed slightly, but Lord Ralph let go of Harriet's arm at once and in some confusion.

'I am so sorry. I did not mean to hurt you.'

He had become acutely aware of people pushing past, passengers calling, sailors and carpenters passing with boxes and furniture, and of Cecil, standing there behind Harriet with his squashed top hat and his waistcoat, holding some material and a cup and saucer.

'Who is this?' said Ralph to Harriet, indicating Cecil.

Cecil bowed slightly: 'Cecil Forsythe, at your service, sir,' he said, and Harriet, not noticing his slightly mocking tone, said weakly, 'Mr Forsythe has been assisting me.'

'I imagine the constabulary would have good reason for arresting him if he has encouraged you in this ridiculous adventure.' Ralph, usually so calm and sardonic whatever the circumstances, would have been mortified to know that his distress had made him pompous and loud. People passing stared at him. The German band below broke into 'Home, Sweet Home' with enthusiasm, as if it was an appropriate item.

'Excuse me, sir,' said Cecil, above the band and the cacophony of noise, 'I believe it would be better to conduct this conversation in more privacy,' and it was Cecil who led the way back, past all the ropes and the people, to Harriet's cabin.

Ralph looked in total disbelief at the small space, at the boxes and the bed and the vulgar red wash bowl. For a moment words deserted him. Never in his life, not even with the ballet dancers and their wild and bohemian ways, had he felt as shocked as he did now: to find that a young lady of his acquaintance, who he cared so much about, had somehow got herself, unknown to her family, into this situation; ready it seemed to travel twenty thousand miles and never tell a soul. Cecil stood just outside the partly closed small doorway like a centurion guard. He had his back to them: Ralph presumed that despite his rascally appearance he was some old family retainer, knew that it would be most improper that the door be closed properly and he and Harriet left alone together in the small space.

'How did you find me?' said Harriet in almost a whisper.

He turned back to her, spoke in a low, urgent voice. 'I – quite by chance as you know – overheard you talking to – that is to say – talking to your sister's grave. There was something – that is to say – I understood you were desperate about something. I dreamed of you last night, Harriet, for – oh, Harriet,' and his voice, too, lowered to a whisper, 'I love you.'

He did not see that she looked at him in fear, hearing these words; that she had placed herself in the far corner away from him, holding her hands in front as if to ward him off.

'You must forgive my impertinence, these are words that I would not have pressed upon you so soon in our acquaintance, and certainly not in a situation like this.' He looked back at the door, but only Cecil's shoulder could be seen, he was almost absent. 'But I dreamed last night that I had lost you and I cannot bear to lose you because I believe you are the woman who can make me happy. Such was my despair at even a dream that something made me send to the Strand this morning to find out when next a ship was leaving. When I heard it was today I went to Bryanston Square at once and was told that you had gone to St Paul's Church and had not yet returned, although they had been expecting the carriage for some time. I know your father is in Norwich on parliamentary business and somehow it seemed to me that my worst nightmares were confirmed, that for some reason that I do not understand you were doing something extraordinarily foolish. And so, even knowing I was foolish too – thinking one day we might laugh at my folly – I rode here, hoping that I was wrong. I arrived not half an hour ago and have been looking everywhere and could not find you and thought perhaps I had been mistaken; I was about to speak to the Captain. Thank God I have found you in time.'

She looked at him in total despair, said nothing.

'Does your father know you are here?' She shook her head.

'Does anybody know you are here, your brothers, anyone but this servant?' He indicated the door. Again she shook her head.

He, finally, asked the question that was uppermost in his mind. 'Is it Edward?'

She looked at him blankly.

'Are you in love with your cousin? With Edward?'

Her pale, pale face looked so puzzled, so incredulous through her tears that he understood at once that this was not so and something in his grim look relaxed. He took one of her hands.

'Dearest Harriet.' He looked at her for a long moment, at her pale, tear-stained face. How full of sorrow she seemed. But he had to have her for his own, there was no denying such feelings, even now her beauty almost overpowered him. He vowed to himself that he would make her happy. 'Now let us go back to London at once. If you wish, I will keep this story to myself. I do think that is best, for it is such an incredible story, it would start a scandal; think what that would do to your father.' He did not mention his mother. 'I feel that the death of your sister has perhaps unbalanced your judgement, but I will look after you, and you will become yourself again.'

'I will not go back with you. I cannot go back.' She spoke low, but with such intensity that Cecil easily heard her words. 'Please, I beg you, if you have any feelings for me at all, go at once, and leave me here.'

He looked at her, unbelieving. 'Harriet, I do not think you understand, I am here to save you. You are not well. We will call for the ship's doctor if you wish who will certainly confirm my diagnosis. But even if you were not ill I could not in all conscience let you go all the way to New Zealand, a country we know nothing of, alone, unaccompanied, without your father's permission. You must know it is quite out of the question and that I cannot possibly let you do it. Apart from any other consideration it would be dangerous for a woman to make the journey alone. I simply cannot consider it for a moment. Try and understand what I am offering you. I love you, Harriet Cooper.'

Cecil, hearing these words and the odd, breathing silence between them, absented himself completely for a moment, to give the girl time to fly into his Lordship's arms and rethink her plans should she so desire (although he could tell her a thing or two). He walked to the rail of the deck, saw ropes already being unwound, loosened, looked down on to the bustling dock. Then he looked up at the sky, wondering if it might rain, if the captain was ready. The bell would go soon. He pursed his lips as if to whistle. Then he walked back to the cabin. Harriet still looked like a trapped animal there in the corner. They were both tall but the man seemed to bear down on her, make her smaller. The man was still speaking, hurriedly, tensely.

'I love you, Harriet. I have spoken to my mother and told her I want to marry you, and I believe I have obtained her agreement. I intend speaking to your father on his return. Of course if this – if this incident became public knowledge my mother would be greatly shocked, you can imagine the consequences. So you have my word, as well as my heart. I will tell no-one. We will forget this day and I promise you that when we are married I will take you to New Zealand, if you so desire. But you cannot go on this ship without your family's knowledge.'

'If I go back to London, I will surely kill myself.'

Ralph looked alarmed. 'Harriet, I want you to come off this ship quietly. I want your reputation to be saved. But you are being hysterical.'

'Ralph.' It was the first time she had ever called him Ralph. 'I beg you to believe me. I am not ill, and I am not hysterical. And I must travel on the *Amaryllis* as I have planned, or I will die.' Something, something desolate in her face caught him, pulled at his heart.

'Tell me why you are doing this,' he said quietly.

'I cannot. I cannot tell you.' Again, something in her face touched him deeply, some bleakness in her dark eyes full of pain where he could not – would not wish even – to go. He remembered how he had first seen her: the girl with the invisible wall between herself and the world. 'Ralph,' and he waited, '*I do not know the words.*'

She saw from his face that he did not know what she was talking about.

For Cecil, however, some of the bits of the jigsaw fell into place. And then the ship's bell began to ring.

At once people shouted, rushed along the passageway outside and out on to the deck; sailors were unfurling the smaller sails, ready to go out into the channel.

Cecil walked inside the cabin and closed the door. Harriet and Ralph were both immediately acutely aware of Cecil's sweaty, unwashed presence in the small space: he may have been aware also, but time was short. He glanced at Harriet carefully out of the corner of his eye for a moment, seeming to inspect the roof of the cabin. *She's lost her stuffing*, he thought to himself. *Not that she had much to begin with.* The man's visit seemed to have made her shorter, more crumpled. Ralph was looking at him in surprise and anger. Again the ship's bell rang.

'Excuse me, Lord Kingdom,' he said. 'I think that if this lass wants to go, is determined to go, you should not stand in her way.'

'How dare you have the impertinence to think anything at all. What has this got to do with you?' He turned away: Lord Ralph Kingdom did not converse with servants.

'Lord Kingdom, there is not much time, so I won't beat about the bush. I by chance took this lady to her home the other day where I was questioned and bullied by one of the servants as to her every movement in a most unpleasant manner. I was not taken with the atmosphere, so to speak. You may perhaps think young ladies should be imprisoned in their own homes, but I do not.'

The ship's bell rang on continuously, jangling into the cabin. Lord Ralph Kingdom did not converse with servants but this one seemed determined to be conversed with. 'Of course not,' said Ralph haughtily, 'but that was only a servant, like you. Her father is away.'

'This "servant" told me that the Right Honourable Sir Charles Cooper, MP (for he gave me the whole title), had given strict instructions that Miss Cooper was never to be alone, and if possible kept in the house.'

'I expect he has been worried about her great grief at her sister's death, as have I.'

'All I'm saying, Lord Ralph, is that perhaps she should be allowed to deal with her grief her own way and if travelling the world is her decision, I say you should leave her to make it.'

'Miss Cooper is only seventeen!'

'Old enough to marry you but not old enough to know her own mind, is that it?'

'That is completely different. She would come into my care.' They had begun to speak as if she was not there.

'My daughter was fifteen when she emigrated to Australia. She wanted to better her life and I said good luck to her.'

'She was a working girl! It is quite different.'

'I would think educated girls would be even more equipped myself. They got money. They got cabins. My girl travelled steerage. However, the fact is I think Miss Harriet should be allowed to decide and for all we know she has her reasons.' Some legs ran past the window, someone was shouting, the bell was continually ringing.

'Harriet.' Ralph dismissed Cecil from his mind and turned back to her. 'I have told you over and over, I simply cannot let you do this. I insist, come with me now, quickly, and I will take you back to London and your father's house and we will forget this terrible day ever dawned.' And he took her arm.

'Different rules, eh, Lord Kingdom? But I tell you this, I'd never imprison my daughter in my house, because I think of my daughter as a person. You people don't let your women into the real world, you know that? Why should Miss Harriet be imprisoned just because she is unhappy? By her father or by the servants or by you or by anyone else. And different rules for little ballet dancers, of course, their fathers don't imprison them in their houses. Or where would you be, Lord Kingdom?' Ralph's face blanched in shock: he wheeled round to Cecil again and it seemed as if he would hit him. Cecil was ready, balanced, waiting. 'Does she know about your little ballet dancer, Lord Kingdom?' Harriet saw that there was violence now in the air: yet the cabin was far too small and crowded for all this drama and ringing bells: in a mad moment Harriet saw Mary, hovering and *laughing*.

'Different rules again, Lord Kingdom, different rules for Lords. You toffs and Lords, you make me sick. Drag her off this boat big and strong, go on, why don't you? But she'll always know you're a hypocrite. Tell her about your little place in Park Lane.' But Harriet saw that for some reason Cecil too was now really angry in a different way, as if the argument was suddenly about something else. 'And just maybe her father's a hypocrite too. And both of you running the country, isn't that just dandy? There are changes coming, Lord Kingdom, one day in the not too distant future England will be ruled by men who *deserve* to rule, who'll be chosen by people like me. The world's filling up with people like me, and people like you don't realise it. You're a hypocrite, Lord Kingdom, and you've come in here and told this girl what she must do as if you own her. I hear you – "I can't possibly allow it" – you make me sick, you hear that?' And Cecil, breathing heavily, nodded to Harriet. 'I'll be on deck if you need me, the ship will go shortly.' And he turned and left the small cabin. The smell of his sweat remained behind.

The ship's bell was now ringing continuously, and they heard feet above them, hurrying from side to side, things being dragged across the deck.

Lord Ralph Kingdom was literally speechless. So Harriet spoke.

'Please, Ralph, leave me now. If you have any feelings in the world for me, leave me now.'

'That man should be horsewhipped. How dare he speak that way in front of a lady.' As Harriet said nothing he went on, with difficulty, 'He should not have – the ballet dancer . . .'

She wanted to say she did not care about the ballet dancer. But some instinct made her understand that mention of the ballet dancer had undermined his position of authority with Harriet, and that he cared more about that than anything else Cecil had said.

'Of course,' he continued stiffly, but honourably, 'I will leave. I have no wish to force my attentions upon you.' He picked up his hat. 'But quite apart from my feelings for you I will feel it my duty to tell your father that I have seen you. He can easily board the ship from a pilot boat off Falmouth, you must realise that.'

'What do you mean?' She looked at him in terror.

'The ship must wait for tides and winds once it has gone down the channel. It could be a week or more before you finally say goodbye to the English coast.'

'Ralph. I fear my father. It is because of him that I am leaving.' If he could have, just then, only looked at her carefully, listened to her properly, he would have understood there was something beneath her words. But he was not looking at her, he was not listening to her: he was thinking of his own position, of what he should do.

'You love him, I am certain, all girls love their fathers. And he will want, as I do, only what is best for you.'

Now they called from the deck, LAST VISITORS ASHORE. LAST VISITORS ASHORE.

So Harriet gathered up her final remaining strength, and crossed a line she had never crossed before. 'In that case, Lord Kingdom, you leave me no option. If my father boards this ship I will feel it my duty to inform both my father and your mother that I know about – about your ballet dancer. It is common knowledge and my family at Rusholme will confirm that I have known about it for some time. I have your gift of Tennyson to me with the inscription and it will be understood that I took this ship because you broke my heart.'

Ralph looked at her in utter disbelief. Then he turned and left the cabin.

Cecil found her there; she had fainted yet again. Caution made him not call for a steward but lift her himself. Before she opened her eyes she smelt the sweat and the clothes.

'I have to leave you, Miss Harriet,' he said hurriedly. 'They're just going to take up the plank. I don't even have water for you but I daresn't wait any longer or I'll be coming with you and my family would have something to say about that. Are you well enough for this adventure? Do you want to disembark? I could still get you off.' She shook her head weakly, fumbled in her embroidery bag to give him money, half of which he laid discreetly back on the small table on top of a letter that he had placed there.

'Is it true we shall take a week to leave the English coast?'

'Depends on the weather. This time of year, anything could happen.'

'Then Lord Ralph could stop me still.'

'Do you think that is his intention?' Cecil was trying to get out of the door, looking anxiously upwards.

'I – I'm not sure. I said I would inform his mother and my father about his ballet dancer, and tell them that I had left—' she gave an odd half laugh, 'because he had broken my heart.'

'Good girl. That's the spirit. I'll tell the servants I put you on a train. That'll confuse them for a while!' Just then there was a harsh cranking noise: the capstan starting to drag the chains and very slowly pull at the anchor. Sailors shouted, footsteps ran across the deck and then the sailors started singing.

'Good luck, Miss Harriet,' but she followed him, calling to him as he was disappearing down the gangplank.

'Cecil!' He turned. Two spots of colour had returned to her face. She had to lean towards him to speak above the noise of the cap-stan turning. 'In my life I never heard a man talk as you did. You sounded like John Stuart Mill himself! How I wish you had known my sister Mary.'

'I did,' he said, and he was gone.

The harsh cranking noise got louder as the anchor was raised: finally there was a juddering at the stern as it was pulled aboard by the sailors. Harriet walked slowly, as if in a dream, along the deck which was overflowing with waving, weeping people. The German band below was playing a last hymn. On the deck children ran everywhere, trying to get a better view, adults pushed past her, waving and calling. She was knocked and buffeted but did not seem to notice. Then she heard the wind catch at the sails; looked upwards, saw the Captain and the pilot and the officers shouting instructions, saw the sailors pulling on the ropes, singing, saw the sails billow noisily outward and then flap loudly against the masts as the ship began to move. Away from the shore. As the stretch of water widened the sailors relaxed for a moment, stood watching the sails and the ropes for the next command: briefly the sound of the sails and the sound of the water was all that could be heard. Harriet suddenly saw that people had stopped calling and waving, stared back at the disappearing land with taut, terrible faces.

On the shore a man with a battered hat standing beside a cart raised his hand in farewell as the *Amaryllis* got smaller and smaller.

EIGHTEEN

In London the consternation was much, much worse than Harriet had anticipated. She had thought of herself and her disappearance as the object of the consternation: for everyone else the object of consternation was her father.

When she had not come back to the carriage outside St Paul's Church; when first Lucy and at last the head footman had gone into the church, found the vicar and ascertained that Harriet had not spoken to him, the immediate assumption was that she had been kidnapped in Covent Garden, the daughter of a Member of Parliament, perhaps held to ransom. The servants were terrified for their very lives. Messages were sent to the brothers, Richard and Walter, who in turn sent a messenger to Sir Charles in Norwich: not only the police but the Prime Minister had soon been alerted; over and over Lucy wept that she would be dismissed.

Sir Charles (disdaining the London and North Eastern Railway even though he was a shareholder) arrived, incandescent with rage and fear, on horseback. He had ridden, whipping his horses to the point of collapse, leaving even Peters, who was usually a galloping match for his master, struggling to catch him. Sir Charles marched into his house, striking the footman who opened the door across the face; the servants were assembled and the police inspector was waiting. Each servant went over the events, Sir Charles shouted, the police took notes (Peters smugly thought to himself that this would never have happened if he had stayed in London). The cook and one of the butlers confirmed that a hansom cab driver, the same one who had taken the furniture away in a cart, had come to the door in the mews, anxious to volunteer that he'd taken the young lady to Fenchurch Street Station, but could say nothing about her further whereabouts; he had come, he said, because he felt uneasy about dropping off a young lady at a railway station on her own: when the police tried to find this cabman to ascertain whence he had collected her, he was nowhere to be found. Lucy was instantly dismissed, Sir Charles unmoved by her weeping: she was the personal maid, she should have known where Harriet was at all times.

Mary's stripped room was observed in incomprehension; Harriet's own room was studied, but not by Lucy, who would have recognised that Mary's gowns and hats swelled Harriet's wardrobe: Lucy was now trudging to Spitalfields. Sir Charles and Richard and Walter and the police saw Harriet's clothes untouched, it seemed: how could they have been expected to know that it was Mary's linen that lay on the lemon-scented shelves?

A heavy police-presence was seen in Covent Garden and at Fenchurch Street Station: if anyone had seen Harriet quickly making her way through the cabbages and the chickens in one, or the new railway trains in the other, or the rats in both – would they tell the bobbies and get into trouble themselves? In Covent Garden the pale girl with the baby and the violets remembered Harriet: nobody asked her. Although the police inspector assured Sir Charles that they would find the culprit, that no young girl – he corrected himself, no young *lady* – could simply disappear, by Sunday evening they had drawn a blank. No ransom note had been received. No matter that Sir Charles Cooper lashed at his sons and his servants with his anger, no-one could throw any further light on Harriet's disappearance.

Messages were sent to Aunt Lydia in Norfolk, and the Coopers in Kent; nobody at Rusholme of course took any notice of Asobel, who had received Harriet's letter, her first letter.

'She has gone to New Zealand,' said Asobel.

Lord Ralph Kingdom, who was, in his way, an honourable man, wrestled with his duty and his conscience and his heart and his reputation, undecided. Finally he confided fully in his brother, Benjamin. Benjamin listened intently, then remained silent and thoughtful for so long that Ralph thought he was not going to speak. Then at last Ben's grey eyes regarded his brother ruefully. 'You're a fool, Ralph. There must have been some terrible reason for her to act as she did. You should have gone with Harriet if you love her. For I would have done if I were you,' said the younger brother, 'without so much as a change of linen.'

Sir Charles made things more difficult by at first refusing to let the matter be mentioned in *The Times*, abhorring publicity of any kind, as any gentleman would.

For of course, on Wednesday, when he finally agreed that a very small paragraph should be inserted about his daughter's mysterious disappearance, half-mad by then with grief and rage, he found that any number of people knew where Harriet had gone. There were for instance all the dignitaries from the embarkation breakfast on board the *Amaryllis* who had drunk her and her father's health. And most importantly, of course, and to their horror, there were the officials of the New Zealand Company who were hoping for government preferment through Sir Charles Cooper himself.

And most of all there was Lucy. Back, without a reference, into the horror of the dark, deadly weaving rooms of Spitalfields and her mother's illness and no money, she sat for several days going over and over her mistress's movements, what she could have missed. And a clue somehow floated above her head. Something to do with the furniture: always, the furniture had reminded her of something. And at last, the night before Harriet's disappearance was made public, she remembered, and then at once she understood what Harriet had done. She put on her shawl and ran back all the way from Spitalfields to Bryanston Square. She hoped upon hope that Harriet was long gone. Lucy knew why she had gone. But Lucy was desperate. She had to have a reference or she would never get another position. She had to work. Her mother would die without Lucy to somehow support her. When Peters awoke next morning he found Lucy crouched in the kitchen with the cook.

'I want to see the Master. I know where Miss Harriet went. I've been up to her room. I got to have a reference.'

Peters tried to turn her out of doors, Cook refused to let him. 'Tell the Master at least,' she said, 'or we'll all be without places.'

'What are you bothering him for? Tell me what you know.'

'I want a reference,' said Lucy. 'I'll only tell him.' There she sat, trying to warm her blistered feet by the fire, saying nothing more.

At last she was sent for. Sir Charles stood in the cheerless drawing room. She was horrified at how he looked, old suddenly, and something else she could not describe in her head, a sort of madness in his eyes, and she thought again that if her own situation wasn't so desperate she would never tell him anything.

'Well,' he said coldly.

'I got to have a reference. I know where Miss Harriet has gone.' These were unwise words: Sir Charles grabbed her and literally hurled her on to the floor.

'*Where is she?*'

'I went to look. Her clothes are gone.'

'Her clothes are in her room, we have seen them.'

'They're not her clothes, they're Miss Mary's clothes. Miss Harriet said she had given them to the poor.'

'*What?*'

He stared at Lucy for a moment and then ran upstairs, Peters and Lucy behind him. Sir Charles flung open the mahogany wardrobe, Lucy pushed back Harriet's remaining gowns and showed the dresses behind. 'These are not Miss Harriet's dresses. Look how short they are.'

'Where has she gone?' It was almost a whisper.

'It was the furniture, sir. There wasn't so much but it was packed up just like Mr Edward's furniture when he left. And we spent all that time in the Strand and I think she meant Peters to see her letter.'

Sir Charles looked wildly at Peters who answered very quickly, nervously, seeing the look in his master's eye. 'It was a letter to Mr Edward, Sir Charles, which I happened to oversee. She took it to the New Zealand Company for delivery. To tell him of Miss Mary's passing – I read it, it said nothing more.'

'She meant you to read it,' repeated Lucy, 'else why weren't it sealed? She took it in to them offices, Sir Charles, and I went too, but she went into another room with the gentlemen. And she was there for such a long time, over an hour, and I did think it was a long time, for a letter. I think that furniture was to go on a boat and I think she's done like Mr Edward and gone to New Zealand! But now I got to have a reference.'

And, like fate, as Sir Charles stared in disbelief at the stupid girl from Spitalfields, there was a loud banging on the door below and the footman admitted the *Times*-reading Chairman of the New Zealand Company.

By the time Lord Ralph Kingdom, struggling with his duty, arrived at Bryanston Square determined to save Harriet even if it damaged his own reputation with Sir Charles, Sir Charles had already received all the information he needed and was on his way south.

They rode wildly, changing horses when they could. It began to rain and darkness fell but nothing could stop Sir Charles, he rode like a man possessed, and the New Zealand Company Chairman kept sending urgent messages to God, asking him to delay the *Amaryllis*'s departure from the Cornish coast. The Chairman had been advised that the estuary pilot had already come ashore at Deal; another pilot was escorting the ship down the English Channel: it was now Falmouth or nothing.

The weather got worse, they could hardly see where they rode; the Chairman had done this dash more than once for various reasons to catch one of his ships: this was the worst and wildest journey he had ever been forced to make. He kept assuring Sir Charles that the weather was in their favour, that the Captain would not depart into a storm. Trees fell across their path, they could hardly keep their way in the darkness, their clothes and their horses were soaked in rain and mud and sweat, still Sir Charles would not stop. Finally dawn broke, the storm eased, and Falmouth was still an hour away. The horses were whipped onward and Sir Charles Cooper never spoke.

At last Falmouth came into view, they saw the sea in the distance; the rain had stopped but the waves were still crashing up along the shore. They galloped down towards the pier. Small fishing boats rocked on the waves and were thrown sometimes against the jetty. But there was no big ship berthed, and the horizon had disappeared. There was nothing but mist and fog and cloud as far as the eye could see.

'I believe – they are sheltering somewhere, Sir Charles, further back along the coast.' The Chairman was so exhausted he thought he would vomit. 'They are probably – probably still carrying the

Channel pilot. Yes, look! look, there is the pilot boat, tied up and waiting.' The Chairman stood, bending over, trying to breathe.

Two men were sitting trying to fish, right on one corner of the wooden wharf, their thin collars turned up against the weather. They watched the sweating visitors carefully, feigning disinterest. Sir Charles raced towards them, took hold of one of them roughly by the shoulder, pulled him to his feet.

'How long have you been here?'

The man quite insolently pulled himself away from Sir Charles, saying nothing.

'How long have you been here, man?'

The fisherman stared at Sir Charles in his wet city clothes and spat. 'We been here all night, have we. Waiting for the weather.'

'We are waiting for a ship.'

'Oh aye.' He was pulling in his line.

'We are waiting for the *Amaryllis*.'

The fisherman laughed. 'Oh aye.' He threw the line out again with a flourish, regarded Sir Charles shrewdly, and the other one, standing by the horses, being sick over his trousers. 'That'll be a long wait then.'

'What do you mean?'

'The *Amaryllis* is long gone, sir, that's what I mean. Never came near Falmouth, though we seen her riding, way, way in the distance. The pilot was disembarked here yesterday. Said the Captain thought that storm'd blow itself out if he could get well ahead of it. Gone to New Zealand, the pilot said. Why, they'll be halfway to Africa by now, them will.' The fisherman grinned to himself again and then looked up. For the life of him he couldn't understand why he suddenly felt a pinch of sorrow for the arrogant gentleman who had arrived so wildly. His face had crumpled and his body seemed to go small as he stared outwards. The fisherman watched the man for a moment, curious, and then went back to his fishing.

The man stared at the wild, green, changing sea.

It reached outwards, on and on forever, to the other side of the world.

NINETEEN

On the second day out from the English coast, as the *Amaryllis* sailed into the notorious Bay of Biscay, the Captain himself (not unaccompanied of course) went to Harriet Cooper's cabin under the poop deck. Behind the Captain hovered Mr and Mrs Burlington Brown, cabin passengers, who had agreed (after much discussion about the importance of Harriet's parentage) to become the guardians of Miss Cooper for the duration of the journey: that it was their Christian duty to do so.

The door was quietly but firmly knocked upon, the presence of visitors was announced, and then the cabin door opened by the Captain himself, majestic in his uniform and braid. The visitors, having received several earlier reports from the doctor of a silent woman with her face turned to the wall, something more perhaps than the seasickness from which everybody suffered, were surprised to see Harriet dressed in her neat black dress, and sewing a curtain.

There was not room for three visitors in the cabin: as Miss Cooper was decorously dressed the Captain felt it was therefore perfectly respectable for him to be the person to move inwards and initiate the conversation.

'Good morning, Miss Cooper. I am Captain Stark. The *Amaryllis* sails under my command.' He was immediately startled by her appearance: they had not warned him that she was beautiful.

'Good morning, Captain Stark.'

'We have been anticipating your presence in the dining room, and on deck, my dear young lady. You have not been seen anywhere since the ship left Gravesend. Miss Harriet Cooper, we thought, was only a ghost.'

Harriet smiled and the Captain saw that the face lit up astonishingly for a moment. 'I believe I am real, Captain Stark. I expect you have many passengers who, like me, have taken a short while to find their – I was going to say "balance" but I believe the correct term is "sea-legs".'

'But my dear Miss Cooper, we did not even see you farewelling the English coast off Falmouth, which is most people's last memory of their country!' Harriet regarded him steadily and silently.

'But perhaps you were too sad to say goodbye? As for "sea-legs", we have only just begun our journey and the *Amaryllis*'s passage towards Spain has been unseasonably calm.' Trousers walked past the small uncurtained window and footsteps sounded on the deck above. Harriet recalled all her lessons in etiquette.

'How lucky we are, Captain Stark, to be in your experienced hands.'

'I hope you will still say that in weeks to come. The Bay of Biscay is only the first of the seas on our journey not known for its charity towards us but at the moment the wind speeds us well. We are in God's hands.' And Harriet nodded gravely.

'Now,' and he turned to the business in hand, 'we have been most concerned that you, as a young lady travelling alone, should be properly chaperoned. Mr and Mrs Burlington Brown – Mr Burlington Brown is travelling to New Zealand as the Chairman of the Starlight Gas Lighting Company – have agreed to spend time with you as your guardians, which is only right and proper for a young lady like yourself. I would have arranged this with your father, had he come aboard with you, and I was most sorry not to meet your brother, who I understand farewelled you at Gravesend.'

Harriet inclined her head gracefully.

'I will leave you with the Burlington Browns then, and will expect to see you at my table for dinner. We dine at three.' And the

Captain bowed and was gone, leaving her other visitors to fill the space.

The voice of Mr Burlington Brown of Starlight Gas Lighting boomed, 'My dear Miss Cooper.' His eyes flickered over the small, feminine things in the cabin, settled somewhere near the ceiling. 'Perhaps a prayer.'

'Perhaps a prayer,' echoed his wife.

Harriet looked at him uncomprehendingly for a moment. 'Here?'

'God,' said Mr Burlington Brown, 'cares not whence our devotions rise upwards,' and his wife nodded several times. 'You have not been present at our evening prayers in the dining saloon. The Captain of course will have Sunday services on deck as we near the Equator. But let us pray now, in anticipation of our well-spent time together on the *Amaryllis*. Your father, I am sure, will be glad of our presence.'

There was the sound of the wind filling and stretching the sails above them, and of the rush of the sea as it carried them along. Mr Brown and his wife knelt together suddenly beside the bed where Harriet was sitting, taking up most of the floor space of the cabin; she heard their knees crack. She saw that Mr Burlington Brown had made notes on a large piece of paper; she herself slipped to the floor also but not before a vision of Mary's quizzical face seemed to flash before her.

Almighty and everlasting God *(he began)*,

and Harriet closed her eyes, trying to draw comfort from the familiar words,

have compassion on thy daughter Harriet who travels alone on this long journey. Save her from the follies and dangers of youth and make her obedient to thy will in all things.

Their bodies swayed with the movement of the *Amaryllis*, paper rattled as Mr Burlington Brown strove to see, in the dim light from the window, what else he had written. Below them the sea churned; they felt the ship's speed under their knees.

Prepare thy daughter Harriet for whatever future thou hast planned for her. And may we all live together on our journey to the other side of the world in Christian peace and harmony and love; endeavouring to administer to each other comfort and friendship, and above all, dear Lord, keep us safe on our journey. We pray for thy blessing on our dear Queen, and our dear country; on our friends and relations and family. We pray for thy blessing on the soul of Harriet's dear departed sister (*he had been apprised of her circumstances: he thought he heard a sharp intake of breath*) and on Harriet's father, the Right Honourable Sir Charles Cooper, MP, until he is happily reunited with his daughter. We pray for all who are afflicted in mind, body, or estate. We ask these things in the name of Jesus Christ.

Amen.

'Amen,' said Mrs Burlington Brown.

'Amen,' said Harriet.

She opened her eyes, saw Mr Brown already helping his wife to her feet; Harriet rose also.

'Now, my dear Miss Cooper,' said Mrs Burlington Brown, 'it is a little blustery, to put it mildly, but we walk on the poop deck once in the morning and once in the evening, with my husband's sister, Miss Eunice Burlington Brown, who is travelling with us. At first the steerage passengers thought they too could wander on any part of the ship but the Captain soon put a stop to that and our walks now are brisk and pleasant, if somewhat overly invigorating. I and Miss Burlington Brown will call for you each time we set out that you may walk with us, as it would not of course be proper for you to walk alone. Then perhaps we could do some reading together.'

'I should like that very much,' said Harriet, 'I have some of my books with me. It will be a pleasure to read in the fresh air, think of a poem by Wordsworth on the open sea, I shall very much look forward to that.'

Mrs Brown demurred. 'I meant Bible readings, Miss Cooper,' she said firmly, 'or other books of moral merit. We are most exercised with the importance of moral merit on a ship, on a journey. We shall read perhaps in the dining saloon, or our cabins. The weather is not at all suitable for spending long periods in the open air.'

'However,' said her husband, who was beginning to feel uneasy again in the small, feminine room (a hairbrush, a small piece of jewellery, the smell of something like lemons), 'these matters we will discuss when six bells rings. Come, my dear.'

And then they were gone, and Harriet was alone again in her cabin, quite still. She heard again the wind in the sails and the sea rushing by. There was a creaking of timbers everywhere about her as the ship strained forwards, which might have been alarming but was yet somehow rhythmic and comforting to listen to. Last night she had understood that they had truly left England. That she was safe at last. Last night she had at last opened the surprising letter that Cecil had left for her. His handwriting was large and child-like.

> Dear Miss Harriet,
>
> I met Miss Mary at Mr Symond Dawson's Book Emporium in Oxford Street, Mr Dawson was my tutor at the Working Men's Club she was a good woman was Miss Mary. One night she said to us both if anything happens to me please take care of my sister Harriet, it sounded odd to us as if you did not have a family. Mr Dawson and me was at the funeral but you did not see us. That is why I was waiting for you outside the Parliament, hoping to be of assistance, I had followed you when you went in that lady's carriage.
>
> If you come back to London I will always serve, my sister Phyllis will find me.
>
> > Yr true friend
> > Cecil Forsythe (esq.)

Mary's care had still lived on.

Last night also Harriet had heard one of the sailors singing *fare you well, my lovely girl* from somewhere in the darkness. And the words had echoed on and on in her dreams, *fare you well, my lovely girl, my lovely girl*. And then this morning she knew it was time at last to look forwards, not back.

She gathered a shawl about her and for the first time since the ship had sailed away she went outside and up on to the deck. Strong winds blew about her at once and she clung to the rail.

Her first reaction as she looked upwards was one of amazement. The white sails full of the wild Biscay winds were so beautiful. She had never seen a ship in full sail before, how the sails reached out towards their destination like a myriad of white birds, how the ropes pulled taut and strained against the spars and the masts. As she walked further on to the main deck the wind whipped at her too, tried to fill the shawl as if it was a sail also, pulled at her skirt and her hair and her face, brought tears to her eyes. She turned away from the wind, saw the lifeboats swinging above. Right at the back of the poop deck, a lone sailor stood, holding the wheel.

Harriet stood at the ship's rail, time forgotten. In every direction, the sky disappeared into the horizon, grey and lowering, only the brave little *Amaryllis*, scudding onwards, nothing else as far as the eye could see. She looked over the side of the deck. Grey-green water slipped by, white waves curling and churning and disappearing beneath them. As she looked back she thought perhaps she saw suddenly a flock of birds in the far distance but the vision disappeared into the greyness of the sky and she wondered if she had imagined it.

Further down the ship, by the steerage hatch, a group of young women stood close together talking, holding their shawls tightly, nodding, blown about the deck, coming together again. Two sailors walked past: she saw the sailors and the women stare openly at each other. And then they all laughed – even from where she was standing Harriet caught bursts of laughter that carried to her on the wind. Then one of the ship's mates called to the sailors and they were away at once, up to the front of the ship, pulling at ropes, winding chains.

Harriet stared again at the sea below, seeing shadows and journeys in the foaming waves' white curves and falls. And everywhere the smell of salt and air and rope and tar caught at her, pulled at her, and the sound of the sea over and over again declared to her that she was free.

'Ah there you are, Miss Cooper, I have been looking everywhere. Really it is most unsuitable that you walk alone on the main deck, the sailors are everywhere, my dear, and there are lots of unscrupulous men in the steerage compartment who think nothing of the

Captain's ruling, and wander very much in this direction. I think it will be best if you walk only with me. And although the niceties of fashion are not my field exactly – rather my wife's or my sister's – a hat, I think, Miss Cooper, rather than a shawl. We of all people must keep up appearances so that standards are maintained aboard ship. With so many of the lower classes travelling with us it is up to us to at all times preserve the rules of etiquette and propriety against the vulgarity and impertinence that could easily overrun us. I think you will find the Captain feels the same.'

Harriet had turned and regarded the long nose and piercing eye of Mr Burlington Brown of Starlight Gas Lighting. From his nose droplets of water hung and the wind stung his eyes as it did hers, pulled at his frock coat.

'I am most grateful for your attention,' said Harriet, 'but I do not wish to trouble you and your family unduly—'

'No, no, no,' protested the Chairman, endeavouring to pat her shoulder.

'And sometimes, the – the seasickness, you know, I needed to hurry here, there was no time to call for you.'

'Ah, ah, quite, quite, but look at the time, my dear Harriet (if I might call you that),' and indeed as he spoke the ship's bell rang. 'Time to dress for dinner; the Captain appreciates this also, even though, of course, we understand that you are still – as it were – in mourning.' And he ventured a further fatherly hand upon her shoulder and then ventured it down to her arm, and propelled her back towards her cabin.

She looked back, at the sea and the sky and the echo of birds.

A shipboard dinner, Harriet saw, was a large affair. Onion and pork broth; roasted fresh pork (one of the travelling pigs had already been slaughtered, the Captain proudly told her, because last night it had broken its leg, that's how fresh it was) served together with roasted onions and parsnips and much prune and plum compote and many potatoes, plus cold mutton and cabbage and large bowls of gravy. There were several extremely elaborate fruit pies decorated with iced pastries, and jugs of custard, and a big cheeseboard. There was glacéed fruit, and wine and beer, and port for the gentlemen. Although it was mid-afternoon lamps had been lit, as only dim light came in from the small windows.

Harriet was given pride of place at the Captain's side and made a great fuss of now that she had appeared at last. As there were only fifteen cabin passengers she met them all: smiled and bowed; saw gentlemen and ladies; saw a cross-looking girl of about twelve kick her younger brother when she thought nobody was looking; met Miss Eunice, the rather pinched sister of Mr Burlington Brown; admired a baby belonging to a magistrate's wife which was displayed just before prayers. Stewards bowed and removed plates for all the world as if they were dining in London (but the sound of the wind in the sails above them, and the occasional sliding of cutlery, and the way liquid moved in the glasses reminded them they were not). The Captain spoke of the joys of their destination: this was his fifth journey; of the chance of making many fortunes; of the necessity of keeping a tight rein on the natives. A bridge school was suggested for the long days ahead, and the possibility of a few amateur dramatics; Harriet was asked if she would honour them with something on the ship's piano this evening after tea had been served.

She enquired how many other passengers were aboard the *Amaryllis*; found that over one hundred men and women and children were in the steerage quarters; that they had different food ('A lot better than they had in their previous lives, I'll be bound,' said Mr Burlington Brown knowledgeably). She was told that single men and women (with married couples and children between) were housed at either end of the steerage space at the bottom of the ship, with a matron in charge of the single women; how they must all be in bed by ten o'clock when the ship's bell rang. ('Otherwise they'd be careering around the ship in the darkness getting up to no good, I'll be bound,' Mr Burlington Brown contributed.) And they told Harriet how water everywhere must be treasured.

'Even you, my dear Miss Cooper, must learn to catch the rainwater: water shortage is the most vexatious problem, salt baths are the rule rather than the exception, and water with meals is a luxury.' Harriet stared at the odd-coloured water in carafes on the table which she had declined to drink.

'Much safer to catch rainwater,' said a young man whose name was Mr Aloysius Porter, 'for I expect the water we took on board comes from the Thames.'

His friend Mr Nicholas Tennyson ('no relation to the poet I'm afraid') agreed: 'It would seem foolish to bring our London bacteria to the South Pacific.' But the gentlemen were turning to the port and the ladies were retiring to one end of the dining saloon, only Miss Eunice Burlington Brown hung on Mr Porter's every word and nodded. Harriet, as she moved with the ladies, said to Mr Porter and Mr Tennyson that she was looking forward to catching water out of the sky.

'I say, Captain Stark,' said the doctor in the evening after tea, 'the Bay of Biscay is treating us kindly, I've heard a story or two about its treacherous gales.'

'Indeed,' said the Captain, and he turned courteously to the ladies to explain. 'The Bay of Biscay has a fearsome reputation, especially at this time of year. Ships on their way to the Antipodes have been wrecked before even they sighted Spain, but we seem, so far, to be having a brisk but extraordinarily smooth passage, all things considered. We have been running before the wind and have covered many miles today. Perhaps your presence, my dear Miss Cooper, is bringing us luck, and all such journeys as ours need luck.' Stewards had lighted more lamps; outside the sun had set on the horizon.

'Miss Cooper.' The Captain spoke again. 'Perhaps you will play something for us now as this evening is your first excursion among us, even though we left Gravesend a week ago.' The rebuke was soft, the request was firm: it was Harriet's duty to entertain them prettily. Dutifully, Harriet went to the piano. A little sigh seemed to go round the dining saloon: so beautiful, so pale, so dressed in black.

For a moment Harriet sat quite still before the small upright instrument. She had not touched a piano for so long, it seemed: it was another life when she lived at Rusholme and played in the evenings before Eddie and Augusta branched out into 'When Other Lips'. When Mary was alive. And she quickly bowed her head and played one of Chopin's études. The piano did not move with the roll of the ship, it was nailed to the floor, but no doubt dampness got in to the strings inside and it was perhaps not quite in tune. But there was something about the way the pale young woman played: the dining saloon was silent and the notes hung in the air although all the time the wind in the sails was there above them in the Bay of

Biscay and the *Amaryllis* ploughed through the waves. The last notes died away and Harriet stood abruptly.

'Goodnight,' she said.

And like Cinderella she was suddenly gone, even before the gentlemen could rise and accompany her with one of the swinging lanterns that hung over the round wooden table.

Later the murmur of voices outside her window mixed with the rushing sound of the sea as some of the gentlemen endeavoured to take a somewhat blustery evening stroll with their cigars. For a long time she heard the other cabin doors opening and closing, people using buckets or chamber pots or walking to the water closet beside the cabins, walking back again, coughing, settling. She sat motionless on her thin bed, her candle burnt down. She counted again the sovereigns and placed them carefully in one of the boxes, remembering how she had seen her Uncle William and Cousin John and Edward shut themselves in the study and speak about finance, a subject never discussed with women: she could only hope that English money was currency at her destination. She had over three hundred sovereigns: she believed it was a great deal of money. Finally she took out her pen and her ink and Walter's pale cream notebook and put them on Mary's little table by the cabin window. She sat on the end of the bed for a seat and picked up the pen.

Very slowly, by the light of the candle, she wrote:

TO THE DEAR

She stopped. She could not imagine who her dear readers were to be. But then she thought of her mother whom she had never known, writing all those years ago and leaving a message for Harriet. And then she wrote firmly, holding on to the ink bottle that was sliding from one end of the table to the other in an alarming manner:

TO THE DEAR READERS OF MY JOURNAL
30 November 1849

I am, on this day of my life, sailing to New Zealand.

TWENTY

The Right Honourable Sir Charles Cooper, MP, persuaded himself
that he was travelling to New Zealand on government business.
The activities of the New Zealand Company had been troubling
Her Majesty's Government for some time: they now troubled Sir
Charles Cooper exceedingly: almost he could say they had kidnapped his daughter. His rage was monumental, and frightening
(he seemed sometimes almost to have taken leave of his senses
although nobody voiced such an unthinkable sentiment): he
blamed everyone in Bryanston Square as well as the New Zealand
Company, he also blamed all his relations in Kent for putting
ridiculous ideas into his daughter's head. It could not be kept
from the Prime Minister and others that Miss Harriet Cooper had
not been kidnapped but had run away; or at the very least had
travelled without her father's knowledge or permission and if
that wasn't running away what was it exactly? Quite simply it
was unheard of. So Sir Charles Cooper told everyone (and came to
believe it himself) that his daughter's mind had been temporarily
unhinged by the death of her beloved sister: people remembered
her, that pale ghost, at the funeral on the hill, nodded, felt much
pity for the poor, wifeless father. An even smaller paragraph in
The Times pronounced that the MP's daughter (her name was not

actually given), much distressed by the death of her sister, had nevertheless been found safe and well.

His younger son, Walter, offered to go and find Harriet. Sir Charles laughed shortly. 'You would drown on the first week out,' he said, 'in a poker school held in steerage.' His older son, Richard, laughed also. His laugh was like his father's in the cold, formal dining room, where now only three of them sat for breakfast. Nobody noticed or cared that Quintus no longer appeared.

Walter could not tell his father how frightened he had been, a man of twenty, to have twice now woken in the night, weeping. Harriet's terrible disappearance had suddenly shown Walter how much he missed Mary, how he had not grieved for the death of the sister who had mothered him. And now it seemed both sisters were lost to him and he was marooned in this world of indecipherable businessmen. How could he explain these things to this suddenly wilder, older man that was his father?

'I wish you would let me go, sir,' he repeated doggedly. 'I should like to find Harriet. I should like to look after her, so far away from home. I don't like to think of her alone.'

Sir Charles strode without answering from the dining room and into the privacy of his study. It was *he* who would find Harriet. *He* who would look after her. *And when he found her he would punish her*: there was no question that she must be punished; he had lost face and she would be punished for it. He would beat her. Alone in his study he held his head in his hands and went over it again. *He would take her perfect feet in his hands. And then he would beat her. He could see her. He alone would administer the punishment, a special kind of punishment, and she would beg him to stop, and beg him for more, and he would tame her at last and she would offer him her breast as she had once before.* Every time he conjured her beautiful, closed face he almost groaned aloud. Every time he remembered the night she had held her breast for him his heart, his head, all his being gave a wild, wild leap. When he found her – and he never for a moment doubted that he would find her – he would never let her out of his sight again: he could not live without her. She was his daughter: she belonged to him.

The Prime Minister agreed: a reliable person should look at New Zealand. It was arranged that Sir Charles would leave as soon as a passage could be arranged. All information that the New Zealand Company held on his nephew Edward Cooper's land purchases and his daughter Harriet's travel arrangements was of course made over to him. He puzzled over how she had paid for her fare, and how she was planning to live: he did not believe she was in love with her short, fat cousin, he had observed her so carefully and the only person he had ever worried about was Lord Ralph Kingdom who was obviously a problem no longer since he remained in England; the servants said he had called. Sir Charles hoped he would not call again. He acquired some immediate facts about New Zealand. He enquired as to the number of people in the whole country: it was infinitesimal. He enquired as to the number of people in Wellington where Edward had bought his land: they told him 4,381 at the last census and he laughed. She would no doubt try to find Edward; Sir Charles himself would be able to find Edward within an hour of disembarkation.

He would punish her (again the visions came) and then he would bring her home. But one thing she had forfeited: her right to freedom. He alone, from the moment he found her, would hold the key. Peters would accompany him: between the two of them she need never be alone again. From Doctor Adams he obtained, without question, a large amount of laudanum. She may need to be calmed. They would be back with Harriet by the end of the summer.

There would not be an election until the winter at least and the Right Honourable Sir Charles Cooper, MP, leaving Peters to deal with the final arrangements, went back to Norfolk with various inducements that would make sure that his seat was absolutely safe. All was under control.

Only in his deepest, unconscious dreams did Charles Cooper recall how Harriet had looked at him the morning he left for Norfolk: that last wild look. And then all at Bryanston Square in the watches of the night heard a terrible cry, as if a man visited hell and could not forget what was shown to him there.

Lucy the maid stole Quintus the dog.

She did not mean to; she didn't want a dog, she couldn't feed herself, let alone a dog. Once again she had been forcibly removed from Bryanston Square, without a position, without the wages due to her, without a reference, with blisters on her heels from hurrying from Spitalfields just to apprise Sir Charles Cooper of the whereabouts of his daughter.

She sat on the steps in the mews behind Bryanston Square on the grey, cold November day. She had managed to sleep in the kitchen for three nights in all the turmoil of the household; had heard with relief that Harriet had got away, felt shame at her own perfidy. But Peters had found she was still there. Cook had quickly given her a small parcel of food and some stockings: she knew Lucy had been badly treated, but there was nothing to be done; all their places were uncertain now. Peters rampaged about the house in a rage mimicking his master's: Peters was to go on a long sea journey, and Peters was afraid of the sea.

'Get out! Get out!' he shouted to Lucy. 'And never come back. You're an Anathema in this house.' Lucy presumed that was a new swearword.

In the mews she did not cry (Lucy never cried). Instead she fumed and fulminated at the unfairness of life and ate a cold chop. She licked her fingers, getting the last traces of meat, not knowing when she might see meat again. That position in Bryanston Square had been meant to change her life.

Although Lucy looked so young she had actually turned fourteen. Lucy's eldest sister had disappeared when she was fourteen. They heard she'd been seen parading in the Haymarket where some of the young girls had luck: Lucy's sister had not had luck. She had come back to Spitalfields with big scabs and a big belly: her father had kicked her in the belly. Lucy never forgot that day. The vicar's wife had spoken to Lucy at her sister's pathetic funeral, Lucy had thereafter, aged twelve, trained in the vicar's house and a girl never tried so hard: she was the best, hardest-working maid the vicar's wife had ever had, and the vicar's wife had taught her to read. At last, like a gift from the Lord, she had been chosen for Bryanston Square, chosen by Sir Charles Cooper on the recommendation of the vicar. What would Sir Charles say to the vicar now?

It was starting to rain. She supposed she must go back to Spitalfields. Lucy was otherwise on the streets. Like her sister.

She got up and started walking. It was then that she saw Quintus. He lay mournfully beside the stables, his face on his paws.

He raised his eyes to Lucy, recognised her, the one who sang to him; he gave an almost imperceptible wag of his tail to show Lucy that he remembered.

'Hello, Quintus,' said Lucy, equally mournful, and she stopped for a moment in the rain and threw him her chop bone. He tried to be pleased but his eyes stared at hers, great pools of unhappiness: his owners had gone away and left him and he did not know what he had done.

Lucy talked to him. 'Well you might feel cheated, but not as cheated as me. I did my work best as I could, but I lost my position. I suppose I should blame Miss Harriet but she was just a sad thing, wasn't she, dog? In all the time I worked for her I never saw her smile, that's a funny way to live your life for a start. And in a way she should blame me because I told her father she'd run away. But I need a reference that bad, 'cos I've got to work. And she got away. And I'm glad, because—' and here Lucy cast a glance back at the door of the house but it was deserted. 'Because—' but then a groom came out of the stables. He saw Lucy but hardly saluted her: since Sir Charles had ridden so wildly off to Falmouth nobody's position was safe; he walked with hunched, angry shoulders to the servants' entrance.

'Because—' Lucy was absolutely determined to finish her sentence so she found herself crouching down beside Quintus in the rain. 'I think—' (and she whispered her suspicions about Sir Charles Cooper into Quintus's ear). And then having unburdened herself of unpleasant thoughts she patted him in a desultory manner before she got up again.

So that when she started off on her long journey home Quintus stirred himself and followed her. She was the first person to talk to him since Harriet had gone. Perhaps she would know something.

At first Lucy, so deep in her own problems, didn't notice; then she told Quintus to go back; then she thought, *why should I care?* and talked to him all the way down Oxford Street about the unfairness of life: a short fourteen-year-old girl with only a thin shawl, limping from her blisters and talking to a dog.

The girl and the dog wandered through Covent Garden ignoring the harsh cries of the costermongers and the sad faces of the flower-sellers; Quintus snuffed at old vegetables and fish bones, someone kicked him and Quintus yelped and Lucy shouted in high dudgeon.

She stared again at St Paul's Church, thought again of her mistress planning her escape. *I'd like her to know how her scheming fell back on me*, but try as she would she couldn't really work up an anger towards Miss Harriet, she would just like her to know the trouble she had caused. *She could've taken me*, thought Lucy wistfully, *I would have helped her, and not told a soul. Fancy crossing the world and getting away from here,* and she kicked in despair at the cobblestones.

And then, just off Trafalgar Square, a notice caught her eye on the door of a house; slowly and carefully she read it aloud.

FEMALES IN SERVICE
REQUIRED FOR EMIGRATION.
ENQUIRE WITHIN.

'Wait there,' said Lucy to Quintus.

Lord Ralph Kingdom became moody and distant, his dark eyes smouldered. He had even taken to occasionally haunting cab ranks near Bryanston Square in the hope of seeing Cecil, but the rascally-looking driver in the waistcoat and the squashed top hat was nowhere to be seen.

Sir Benjamin Kingdom became very silent and thoughtful also, spent a great deal of his time alone in his house or walking around the Regent's Park. For he clearly understood at last, without knowing why, that a plan was forming in his mind; that this was what the knocking at his heart had been saying, *this* was the decision he must make: it was the action he had somehow foreseen. He tried to laugh at himself again: this was indeed an extreme excuse to see again a beautiful woman! this was indeed an extreme justification to travel the world! At last he went back to Kent to visit the man he admired most in the world, Charles Darwin, who was ill in bed but who seemed pleased to see him.

Sir Benjamin Kingdom had been one of a group of privileged men who had been made privy, at a private meeting, to Charles Darwin's explosive thoughts on the origins of the human species: the devastating, painfully correlated information that Darwin was still working on was to be presented finally in a book; the lives of all who had listened to him and knew what the book would contain were subtly changed.

Benjamin enquired concernedly about the other man's well-being. Charles Darwin was often ill: it was thought by doctors that he had perhaps contracted some tropical ailment while on his long voyage on the *Beagle*. It occurred to Benjamin, not for the first time, that somewhere in this extraordinary man's being was an understanding that the place his meticulous studies was leading him to would bring the world crashing about him; that sometimes his spirit crumbled under the weight of what he was going to say about the world, for it could only lead to one conclusion: that religion was a fraud.

Benjamin engaged Darwin's interest with his talk of the fabulous flightless bird, the New Zealand *moa*; both men knew of the large, shambling extraordinary bird, maybe ten foot high, that was said to have looked a little like an enormous ostrich. It was said that it could not fly but it could run like the wind. And it had been found nowhere else in the world.

'They say it is long extinct,' said Ben expressionlessly.

'Some most interesting specimens of the enormous bones have been sent to England,' said Darwin, 'and it is very likely long, long extinct, young Benjamin, but I am presuming you have been listening to rumours!'

'I have,' Benjamin admitted, laughing. 'Apparently there has been talk of a sighting. As it turns out, it is possible that family business may send me to New Zealand: at least I could test the air!'

'Bring back a skull at least!' said Darwin.

Outside, some of his children were playing with a dog in the cold December afternoon, their cries and laughter and the barking of the dog rang out over the garden. In the distance thunder was rumbling ominously; a woman's voice called the children indoors and their voices and the laughter faded. Somehow Benjamin managed to turn the conversation to the subject of forebodings and premonitions.

'They cannot exist, surely, in our new world,' he said dubiously.

Darwin listened, looked at Benjamin shrewdly.

'There are some things that are becoming clearer and clearer to me, Ben, and nothing I shall present is not explained by meticulous scientific proof. But I nevertheless understand that there is something more to the human heart than science, all the same.'

'But – premonitions?'

Darwin looked out across his winter garden. 'My father taught me many important things that have nothing to do with science,' he said. 'And nothing I have studied has led me to negate the indomitable complexity of the human spirit.'

He was tiring now, Benjamin knew he must go.

'*Intuition*,' said Darwin, watching Benjamin Kingdom.

Finally Benjamin asked his brother to dine with him at his club.

He had persuaded Ralph to forgo the ballet one night and to come instead to a meeting of the Royal Geographic Society in which the African interior had once again been discussed; they had met there Lieutenant Richard Burton fresh from adventures in India where he had travelled disguised as an Arab trader, and their relation Isambard Kingdom Brunel, full of more plans for bridges.

'By God!' said Benjamin afterwards, over the port, in what seemed to be a burst of uncharacteristic garrulity. 'It is a grand, grand time to be an Englishman. I tell you, Ralph, I would not have been born at any other time. Whatever other changes are to be made in this world till the end of time, *this*, this time of discovery will never be matched, never, and it seems to me a trip to New Zealand would not go amiss.'

Ralph's cigar was halfway to his mouth – and it stayed suspended for a moment in surprise, neither advancing or retreating.

'New Zealand?'

Ben busied himself with cutting the end of his own cigar. 'There is, perhaps, a most fabulous bird still in existence there. The *moa*. I would very much like to search for it.'

Slowly Ralph's cigar found its place. A waiter brought more port. Benjamin continued, still seemingly intent on the tobacco. 'I think,' he said, 'to literally cross the world at this time in our country's history should be part of the experience of any man.' Then after another pause he added, 'I wondered if you felt Miss Harriet Cooper might be worth pursuing, Ralphie?'

Ralph gave his brother a long look and then stared at the white tablecloth moodily.

Since his younger brother had told him he should have stayed on the *Amaryllis*, Lord Ralph Kingdom, so elegant, so cool, so man-about-town, had been made thoroughly uncomfortable by his own thoughts. He thought he might have behaved in an ungentlemanly way towards Harriet. Fencing, drinking, shooting, riding, nor Mimi Oliver could shake him out of the conjecture that haunted him: Harriet Cooper had been trying to tell him something and he had not listened. Over and over again he had told himself he had had her best interests at heart when he ordered her ashore, he was thinking of her reputation as much as her welfare: yet the more he thought about the thin, pale, desperate and utterly determined girl crossing the oceans of the world alone on a small ship, the more he wondered what might have driven her to such reckless action. Benjamin knew nothing about women, yet Benjamin, Ralph knew, would not have grabbed Miss Cooper by the arm and tried to force her off the ship.

'I love her, Ben,' he said now to Benjamin, 'and she was trying to tell me something. And I did not listen.' He stared at his brother a little longer, and then excitement began to burn in his wild dark eyes. 'If I went to New Zealand I could of course express my remorse. She will then, I am certain, listen to reason and become my wife. Besides,' he said, suddenly feeling more cheerful than he'd felt in weeks, understanding that Ben was suggesting a wonderful idea and offering to come with him, 'it would be, as you say, a marvellously interesting adventure to travel across the whole world and back. By God, Ben, it's a splendid plan. I should have thought of it myself. We can do it in less than a year and then we too shall have something to say at the Royal Geographic Society!' and the brothers leaned across the tablecloth to each other and shook hands on their plan in great delight.

'This will not be quite like our jaunts to Paris and Hamburg and Spain,' said Benjamin carefully. 'There is the business of telling Mamma.'

'Indeed.' And the brothers fell silent then, and thought of Lady Kingdom sitting alone in the high, chilly drawing room waiting for the infrequent visits of her sons with only the painting of their dead father, the interminable long-windedness of the oleaginous Reverend Cornelius Boothby, and the monotonous ticking of the huge old clock for company.

'YOU CANNOT POSSIBLY GO!'

Lady Kingdom sat in the drawing room, upright in her accustomed chair. Icy tentacles of fear clutched at her stomach. The word 'stomach' never passed Lady Kingdom's lips of course; nevertheless that part of her anatomy contracted with terror. *What would befall the House of Kingdom if both her sons made such a reckless, dangerous journey?* Her world was the Kingdom estate and the Kingdom family.

'You cannot do this!'

Her voice shook in a most unaccustomed manner.

'I completely forbid such an extraordinarily ill-conceived plan! You cannot go gallivanting around the world over a foolish and ill-behaved young woman. Sir Charles Cooper's reputation cannot but be damaged by the fact that his daughter has seemed to *run away*! No young girl of class would ever do such a thing, I was foolish to think Miss Cooper could be in the least suitable. I will not have the reputation of the Kingdom family besmirched and it is clear that if people heard you were chasing after her we would be the laughing stock of London!'

And all the time she spoke the terror moved through her, numbing her legs (that often ached with pain in the night, telling her she was old); making her cold hands colder. She was a woman, and she knew that her real power over the Kingdom name was illusory.

Desperately she reminded herself that she nevertheless had power; she had emotional power over her sons, if they stayed in her orbit she could manipulate many things. Ralph must not go. He was wild and reckless: only his mother could save him from himself. She reminded herself that her instincts had been right. Miss Cooper's extraordinary actions had betrayed her origins: Charles Cooper was only the son of a country squire after all, whatever his pretensions now, and some of his business dealings were, she was sure, no better than *trade*. She would never, never agree to such a conjoining now: the girl was talked of in morning rooms and *her name had more or less been in the newspapers.*

A wild rage shook her and mixed with her fear. 'I will not agree, Ralph!' and, despite herself, she almost shouted. 'You must put Miss Cooper from your thoughts!'

Ralph, standing beside the fireplace where a puny fire made no assault on the chill of the room, glanced at the painting of his father. The eyes twinkled as they always had, as Ben's did, but apart from that there was no answer. His mother saw and was enraged still further.

'You cannot possibly image that your father would *agree* to this? Your father was a great believer in *breeding*, Ralph. Miss Cooper has been shown to be sadly lacking in such an important attribute, let alone good manners and good sense. A young lady who has *run away* is not a consort for Lord Kingdom!'

Benjamin cleared his throat mildly to speak but Lady Kingdom was now in full flow and was so angry that the lace on her cap actually shook. 'And what, pray, is New Zealand? No more than a native colony where working men buy land for baubles. I heard from Lady Butler that one of her grooms went there, set up business as a blacksmith and now, she is reliably informed, he *owns a house*! And he cannot even *read*! Next I suppose we will hear he is taking tea with Lord Russell. Surely you understand that the real world, our power, is here, in England! The rest of the world is merely something we own; Her Majesty does not see any reason to visit her primitive dominions and no more should you!'

The head footman bowed discreetly at the door of the cold room. Dinner was served.

Lady Kingdom struggled to become calm: a lady never, never lost control of herself. She motioned to the footman to leave and then she rose slowly and majestically. 'You, Benjamin, go if you must, bring back wild stories for your brother of the savage world around us. But, Ralph, you must stay. Your duties are to the business of the Kingdom estate, and to the Kingdom family and lineage, and to Her Majesty, and to the House of Lords where it is high time you took your rightful place, and I absolutely refuse to agree to any other course of action!'

By a sign as she sailed to the dining room on the arm of her elder son, where they were joined by the Reverend Boothby, Lady Kingdom forbade further discussion: over dinner mutual acquaintances, the opera, and the weather were spoken of. But there were stiff and terrible silences and Lady Kingdom's plates remained untouched; only the Reverend Boothby's appetite was completely unaffected.

The brothers did not discuss the matter over the port with the Reverend Boothby either. He began a long rambling monologue on church windows. But at last even he began to understand from their demeanour that there was something in the air and as always he at once began to worry how matters would affect him, the poor relation. Being so reliant on others for his existence was a situation continually fraught with difficulty. He must not offend. His rambling petered out. He had perhaps one more glass of port than was absolutely necessary and so did not see that it might have been better that he retire to his room. On their return to the drawing room, where Lady Kingdom was waiting to pour the tea into exquisite small cups, the gentlemen noticed two high, bright spots of colour on her usually pale cheeks. She seemed to tremble as she passed the cups. Ralph and Benjamin glanced anxiously at one another – was their strong-willed mother about to swoon? The Reverend Boothby became most uneasy. The reliable thing about his relation was that she never lost control. But there was the ominous sound of a china cup tinkling louder than usual against the saucer as tea was passed. The Reverend Boothby coughed tensely, wished the port bottle was still accessible. He offered a small private prayer to the Lord that nothing would imperil him personally.

The clock ticked loudly. Minutes passed. Lady Kingdom maintained a dignified, ominous silence. She had said all there was to be said. The Reverend Boothby burped discreetly.

At last Ralph spoke. The vision of the beautiful Harriet Cooper, pale and alone on the high seas, gave him courage. 'I will go, Mother,' he said firmly, 'I have made up my mind. I wish to put my suit and I am deeply sorry if that is distressing to you, because I believed you had assented to my hopes for myself in regard to Miss Cooper. Perhaps she will not accept me but—'

'Not accept Lord Ralph Kingdom? Have you gone mad? A cheap and common daughter of a tradesman?'

Benjamin spoke suddenly. 'Please, Mother, do not talk of Miss Cooper in terms she does not deserve. We do not know what has made her do something so – unusual.'

The Reverend Boothby looked from one to the other, mesmerised. This family did not ever confront each other in this manner. He felt himself perspiring in embarrassment.

'We shall not be gone for so very many months.' Benjamin addressed his mother gently.

Ralph pushed on. 'It shall remain a confidential matter among us, Mother, if you so desire. I say again, I am determined to put my suit. For Benjamin there will no doubt be uncharted mountains and unbridged rivers and most of all birds. But we will in any case, as Ben says, be back within a year and I do not think it is necessary for anybody in London to find our journey strange in the least. Englishmen are travelling all over the world these days – India, Africa, Australia – and we shall merely be two of many.'

Any colour in Lady Kingdom's face drained away.

Her son had spoken.

With every vestige of control she possessed she seemed to remain calm. She simply bowed her head so that they would not see her face. She closed her eyes and prayed that Miss Harriet Cooper would drown in the Indian Ocean.

And then wildly it came to her, unbidden, with the force of an earthquake, that the exact same fate could befall the sons of the House of Kingdom. In terror she saw before her high seas and violent storms and uncharted waters. She saw the small, crowded ship that Edward Cooper had sailed on. She felt pain that she had forgotten, and loss, and love. *Do not leave me, my darling boys*, she wanted to cry out, *do not leave me*. The delicate handle of her china teacup snapped in her hand.

The clock ticked loudly in the silent room.

Then with the iron control for which she was famous Lady Kingdom raised her head high, regarded her sons, and gave them a small, wintry smile.

'It is to me, then, that the maintenance of the dignity of the House of Kingdom falls.' She was silent for a moment and then she spoke again and her eyes betrayed nothing. 'You, Benjamin, although I had hoped for more wisdom from you, may do as you please: that is the fate of a younger son. I hope however that you, my dear Ralph, and I, do not live to regret this day. Of course I cannot prevent your going. But my cousin' – she gave an imperceptible nod at the Reverend Boothby who was suddenly looking at her in terror – 'will at least accompany you both. He will go as my moral representative, and your moral judge. May God watch over you.'

Holding her head still very high, Lady Kingdom left the room. Her stern, straight back spoke clearly to her elder son of his enormous folly.

TWENTY-ONE

The luck of the weather continued to follow the *Amaryllis*, although the cabin passengers who regurgitated their large dinners more than once might not have called it luck. What the steerage passengers were feeling nobody asked, although should you happen to pass the hatches on the main deck leading downwards a terrible smell of bodies and unmentionable things assailed the nostrils: cabin passengers' daily walks therefore were kept, on the whole, to the back of the ship. But the Captain assured everybody that even at this worst time of year the winds were with them, not against them, and they made tremendous, rollicking time right through the Bay of Biscay. Always, day and night, a helmsman stood at the back of the poop deck, guiding them forwards; sometimes the Captain could be seen beside him. In less than ten days away from Gravesend, the coast of Spain was glimpsed far in the distance, and at last a thin sun tried to shine. Less than a week later they caught a glimpse of the Madeira island and the sea was calmer and the sun shone brighter and brighter. As Harriet walked dutifully with Mr and Mrs Burlington Brown and Miss Eunice, steerage passengers could be seen on the deck below, bringing what seemed to be hundreds of thin mattresses on deck, shaking them, washing them with sea water, drying them, airing them; men smoked their pipes and one of them soled a boot; thin, worried-looking women shouted at children; laughing young women pretended not to see the sailors. (Miss Eunice, whom Harriet judged to be perhaps in her middle twenties, seemed very exercised by the sailors, said she thought it was important they kept to their place on the ship.) The hold was opened so that people could take out their necessaries from their stored luggage (but all Harriet's belongings were stowed with her in her small cabin). She watched the cabin families unpack lighter gowns and frock coats and boots and soap and candles into the sunshine, and a young man from steerage scrabbled to find his concertina.

On the third Sunday out everybody dressed in their best and a service for all the passengers was held by the Captain on the main deck: the crew had stretched a tarpaulin across to protect them from the now fiercely shining sun. The steerage passengers sang:

> Amazing Grace, how sweet the sound
> That saved a wretch like me!
> I once was lost, but now am found,
> Was blind, but now I see

accompanied by the man with the concertina, and the cabin passengers were very touched (for indeed it sounded beautiful as the *Amaryllis* sailed on, alone on the open sea) and forgot that the steerage passengers smelled.

That afternoon a school of porpoises followed the *Amaryllis*, dancing and playing in the water beside the ship, graceful Sunday companions, disappearing again before somebody suddenly thought of shooting them and brought out a gun. Some goats, perhaps thinking the sun augured well for them, escaped from the goat pens; great sport was had trying to catch them. One of the cabin passengers, Mr Aloysius Porter, fell flat on his face reaching for a skittering goat, tripping his friend Mr Nicholas Tennyson as he did so. The crew laughed derisively.

A wind suddenly got up, Harriet's hat blew off, it bowled down the deck and one of the young girls in steerage caught it and came laughing and running towards Harriet as Harriet ran towards her.

'There you are, miss.' She had bold, laughing dark eyes.

'Thank you so much. I thought I was going to lose it overboard!'

'Oh well, Mrs Moore makes hats – there – her,' and the girl pointed to a stout woman who was holding a little boy by the hand.

'Oh,' said Harriet. 'Well, I will remember that.' She smiled shyly at the girl who seemed to be her own age. All her curves seemed to fill her blue dress and she looked so healthy and strong that Harriet was suddenly aware of how thin she herself was. 'What is your name?'

'Hetty Green.'

'Then thank you, Hetty Green, for saving my only black hat. I am Harriet. Harriet Cooper.' In silence the two stared at each other curiously. Then Harriet spoke again shyly. 'What – what are you going to do in New Zealand?'

'I'll be a maid first. That is, I'm going to learn to be a maid. Maids is well-paid, better than England because there's not enough of us for the gentry. Then maybe I'll have me own shop.' Hetty squinted up at the sky where a curious white light was forming. 'Then I'll have me own house. Then I'll have me own children.' And her eyes sparkled at Harriet. 'And in that order, miss. I've got me head screwed on.'

'I can see that,' said Harriet. And she cast a glance at the mysterious steerage quarters. 'Is it – forgive me, I sound very curious – I suppose it is very crowded down there?'

'Is it *crowded*! Ain't you ever seen steerage?'

'No – of course not.'

'You want to come down?'

Harriet looked discomposed. 'It might seem – rude. To the people who live there.'

'Nah, look – they're mostly on deck now that it's fine at last, there'll be hardly anybody there. Come on.'

Harriet looked about her, embarrassed. But there seemed nobody, no Burlington Browns, to prevent her, and she had not heard that it was not allowed. 'May I?'

Hetty grinned. 'Only if you show me yours after?'

'Of course.'

'Come on then.'

Taking her cue from Hetty, Harriet lifted up her skirts and climbed backwards down the laddered stairs. The smell, already obvious from the deck, was overpowering. Then at the bottom, turning, she gasped. There were two long rows of small, narrow beds, one above the other, all around the bulwarks: hundreds of beds. A long thin table ran down the middle. People's belongings were stacked, hung, piled, thrown, dropped, everywhere. There were no windows – the only light came in from the open hatch – and although several women were cleaning and sweeping in the half-light a strong, fetid stench filled the dark space.

'We have to take turns cooking as well as cleaning, I can't cook so I do the washing. Terrible food, ain't it, all them ship's biscuits and potaters and salted pork?' Then Hetty pointed to a curtain across one end of the space.

'We sleep behind that curtain, the single women,' and she laughed, 'so that the single men can't see us. But we're smart – some of the girls even got up to the crew's quarters but the matron found them and they was punished, locked in with bread and water. Catch them locking me in here, though it's a long time without a man.' She caught Harriet's shocked look. 'Sorry, Miss Harriet.'

'What do you mean exactly, it's a long time without a man?' said Harriet shyly, but in puzzlement. 'There are men absolutely everywhere, it seems to me.'

Hetty looked at her in equal puzzlement and for a moment said nothing. 'Don't you know what I mean?' And then after another odd silence in the dark space she said quietly, 'Ain't you done it? Don't you miss it?'

Harriet shook her head, unable to speak. Hetty looked as if she was considering how to proceed with the conversation. She chose her words carefully.

'Ain't you ever been in love?'

'Of course not.'

'Well.' Hetty considered again. 'How old are you?'

'Almost eighteen.' Harriet suddenly wished she could get up on deck, wished she could get away, was aware of the smell and the darkness around her.

'Me too, I'm eighteen,' said Hetty. 'That's why I've got my head screwed on. I'm careful now.' And there was something about the way she said it, *I'm careful now*, that spoke of untold things. Harriet should have gone then, up the wooden ladder, but instead, unable to stop herself, she said nervously but intently, 'What did you mean?'

Hetty looked genuinely puzzled. 'You're different, ain't you,

you're a lady. I suppose you ain't been with a man so you don't even know what I'm talking about.'

'What do you mean?' (But Harriet thought of her Aunt Lucretia talking about Alice's 'dark duties'.)

Hetty began to look exasperated. She too would have liked to go back on deck. 'Well I don't know how to say it to a lady,' she said, losing patience, 'all I'm saying is – when you do get it, you'll miss it after.'

Harriet looked as if Hetty had hit her. This was not what she understood.

Three young children came tumbling down the ladder followed by a shrieking woman. 'You bastard little bastards. I'll throw you overboards if you don't bloody behave.' Neither the woman nor the children saw Harriet in the dim light; careered around the big long table, the children screaming, the mother yelling, someone else complaining from one of the beds in the distance.

'Oh come on,' said Hetty. 'It's like this all the time down here,' and she led the way upwards to the fresh air. The brightness seemed to have disappeared, the sky had become even more oddly white, and the wind was much stronger.

'Now you show me yours,' said Hetty and Harriet, still shocked into silence, walked dutifully back to the end of the ship.

'Oh look,' cried Hetty, 'look!' A large ungainly bird flew low across the strange white sky, over the *Amaryllis*.

'Oh!' Harriet gasped, looking upwards.

'What is it?' cried Hetty. With both her arms she reached upwards as if to catch the bird. Her blue dress stretched tightly across her bosom.

'I think – I think it might be an albatross,' said Harriet in amazement. She stared, one hand shading her eyes from the odd light. 'Yet I don't think we're far enough south for such birds. Perhaps it's something else.' She stared, confounded, as her skirt whipped about her. 'I never, never expected I'd actually see an *albatross* with my own eyes, I thought one only read about such a thing in books.' The bird seemed uncertain, rested on the wind it seemed for a moment, flew over the boat several times and then appeared to want to return to shore, wherever its invisible shore might be, Africa perhaps. Both women watched, mesmerised by its curious, gangling movement, until it had disappeared.

'My dear Miss Cooper, there you are. Oh.' Mr Burlington Brown had caught sight of Hetty. 'I don't believe you are permitted on this part of the ship, young lady,' he said sharply.

'This is Hetty,' said Harriet. 'She kindly saved my hat.'

'Ah. Well thank you, Hetty, that will be all, off you go,' and the Chairman of the Starlight Gas Lighting Company shooed Hetty with his hands, as if she was a chicken. Harriet protested but Hetty gave a little curtsey, her dark eyes laughed at Harriet, and then she was gone, swinging along beside the rail on the lower deck, her blue skirts billowing.

'Now my dear Miss Cooper—' Mr Brown began, most disapprovingly.

'I saw an albatross,' said Harriet.

During dinner a joint of pork went tumbling from the table and a jug of gravy spilled on to the floor, narrowly missing the newly unpacked summery gown of the magistrate's wife. People in the dining saloon went on trying to eat as if nothing was happening and polite conversation was kept up grimly. Miss Eunice maintained a gay conversation with Mr Aloysius Porter until suddenly she was forced to leave the dining saloon in a hurry, her hand to her mouth. Harriet saw that the sea reared right up outside the small windows and the angels cavorting with the primroses on the ceiling seemed to change places in a most odd manner. The Captain, who had been seen earlier observing the odd white light suspiciously, had excused himself from the dining table, was already on deck. Bells called all the crew, sails were being pulled in, foreshortened. And then suddenly, at a spectacular jolt, the ship's bell rang by itself, and echoed on across the deck and it became very dark.

'To one's cabin now, I think, everyone,' said Mr Burlington Brown rather shakily, when the ghostly bell clanged again. 'Quickly, Harriet,' and he watched her to her door as he assisted his wife to their own cabin.

On deck, lightning lit up the sky, rolls of thunder followed, and then it began to rain. Not London rain, not Kent rain, but Atlantic Ocean rain, wild, and heavy like lead, and whipped by the wind. Harriet heard the rain, remembered about catching fresh water, and so, *it will only take a moment*, grabbing the big cup Cecil had helped her buy at Gravesend and her water jug, she opened the cabin door again and pushed her way against the squalls that blew into the passageway as she made her way on to the main deck. Rain soaked her at once, she didn't care; she stood there, holding out her cup to the elements, placing her jug beside her, holding her face upwards and licking at the rain as it fell down on to her face and into her mouth, the most extraordinary sensation. But the next roll of the boat sent the jug flying across the deck, she ran after it still holding the big cup, slipped, slid, fell against one side of the deck and then found herself flung in the other direction in the half-darkness. The sails of the ship were down, pulled down by the sailors, and one of the masts had been smashed down by the gale; Harriet did not know all this but could hear frenzied voices and banging and hammering and then a sheet of lightning showed her the empty rigging, and the lifeboats above her, swinging madly.

For the first time Harriet was frightened and she cried out. She needed to catch hold of a rope, a rail, but could not see properly to do so. She could hear the terrified cries of the chickens and the pigs and the goats above the wind, she realised she must be some-where near their cages; then some big object came bowling down the deck towards her, a barrel? a cage? she could not be sure; it just missed her as she reached out, trying to find something to hold on to; she scrabbled convulsively at the deck, trying to stop herself being thrown about.

'Oh dear God!' she cried aloud as she felt the boat rise up again and then something large fell against her face as the boat ploughed downwards, she thought it was the hen coop, heard the high terri-fied screeching, could not stop it, could not hold it, could not save it, sheets of water poured over her, took her to the other side of the deck again. *I must hold on to something.*

Above the wind as the *Amaryllis* coasted before the next wave threw it forward she thought she heard someone calling: 'Miss Cooper! Miss Cooper!'

'I'm here!' she called as loudly as she could. 'I'm here! Here! Here!'

A figure with a guttering lantern seemed suddenly to appear near her, struggling, holding the ship's rail. She wondered if she was hallucinating as she drowned, yet the brave lamp gave a small, real flutter before it disappeared altogether.

'Hello!' she called again desperately. 'I'm here!' as she began once more to slide back. Then a figure loomed in front of her, she saw a hand, grabbed it, held with all her strength, felt herself pulled until her hip and her leg hit the side of the deck.

'Stand if you can and grab the rail,' called the voice through the raging wind. The hand pulled her, somehow she came upright, felt the rail, clung to it.

'Quickly now, hold my coat with one hand and the rail with the other, we're walking back to the cabin passageway.' The lantern had indeed died but Harriet followed with her hands, feeling the coat and the rail as the wind and the rain smashed across her body, tried to tear her away. They fell forwards with the boat, then picked themselves up and continued onwards, clinging to the rail as the *Amaryllis* was pitched backwards and sideways into the heaving waves. Somehow her rescuer got her to the door of the cabin passageway which was shut tight, he banged on the door and then turned and put his arm around Harriet. From the inside someone else opened the door and the two of them were pulled inside and guided into the first cabin, where Harriet was at once thrown against a wall and on to a bed. A lamp glowed inside the cabin, its light moving up and down with the movement of the ship.

'Oh my God, my God,' she whispered, 'dear God, thank you.'

'It's all right, Miss Cooper.'

Holding on to the bed as it plunged upwards and downwards Harriet at last saw that she was in the cabin of Mr Aloysius Porter, and his friend Mr Tennyson. And she saw at once, as he tried to take off his wet and torn coat, that it was Mr Nicholas Tennyson, who had talked about the infected water of the Thames, who had saved her.

Every single thing in the cabin had been nailed down or put away. The three of them tried to wedge themselves on the beds as they were buffeted from side to side.

'Mr Tennyson, *this* water will be clean,' said Harriet, half-laughing, half-crying, 'and I believe you have just saved my life.'

He still battled with his coat, gave up, sat wedged in a corner of the cabin beside the window, and they had to raise their voices above the noise of the storm. 'I saw you go past the window,' he said. 'We are in the cabin next to yours and I saw you going out with a jug.'

'It was to collect the clean water.'

'And the storm suddenly got so much worse, it seemed, and it was suddenly so dark so I thought I had better come after you.'

'It must have been the albatross.'

He knew at once.

> And I had done a hellish thing
> And it would work 'em woe
> For all averred, I had killed the bird
> That made the breeze to blow

and just as he finished the words the ship gave a particular crash and the light of the swinging lantern glistened on water as it poured in under the cabin door, swirled about their feet.

'Hold on to me, Miss Cooper,' called Aloysius Porter and she saw he had managed to wedge himself into the opposite corner from Mr Tennyson on one of the beds and had wrapped his arms about a bend in the bulkhead, was able to hold on to an iron ring. Harriet was thrown against him, put her arms about his waist as the ship plunged upwards again and more water surged about the floor of the cabin.

'Think of those poor devils in steerage,' shouted Mr Tennyson, 'I heard them battening down the hatches as I came looking for you.'

'What do you mean, battening down?' said Harriet, thinking of the crowded dark space.

'They nail them down. To try to keep the water out of the lower part of the ship.'

'And nail the passengers in?' She could hardly conceive of such a terrible thing.

'And the passengers in, I'm afraid, yes.'

'But – but there's no windows, there's no air.'

'That's why I was thinking of them,' said Mr Tennyson. 'There's a hundred and seven people down there.'

Dear God, prayed Harriet, seeing the dark space again, *please have mercy on us all in these terrible hours and the people in steerage, help them to bear it. Lord see us safely through this storm if it be thy will for the sake of our Lord Jesus Christ, Amen.*

And then there was a silence in the small cabin; a silence of voices at least, for the sound of the sea and the sound of the wind and the crashing of things as the ship rolled onwards, or backwards, was deafening. Improbably the small lantern still shone.

Harriet wondered why in all this wildness she was suddenly reminded of long-ago days when she was a little girl, and she and Mary had read 'Frankenstein' together, excited beyond measure that it was written by the daughter of Mary Wollstonecraft; how they had got more and more frightened in a thrilling kind of way in the upstairs drawing room. How in the night, when monsters walked in her dreams, she had crept into Mary's bed and held her warm back and fallen at last to sleep, safe and comforted.

Up on deck other masts snapped, spars broke, the sailors battled to bind the sails. The Captain himself had taken the wheel, judging the wind and the waves and the sky; other, younger, stronger men physically helped him as they tried to keep the *Amaryllis* on an even keel against the power of the sea. Water poured over the decks, smashed now the skylight in the passage to the cabins, ran into the galley, under the closed hatches into the steerage area. There were cries coming from all directions but they could not be heard: nothing could be heard but the sea and the storm.

In the small cabin Harriet clung to Aloysius's back. The three of them began to sing in a kind of desperation

> Amazing Grace, how sweet the sound
> That saved a wretch like me!
> I once was lost, but now am found,
> Was blind, but now I see

almost unable to comprehend that it was only today, at the church service in the sunshine, that they had listened to the steerage passengers singing to the accompaniment of the man with the concertina.

As the ship rose so high they felt it would overturn, and then shuddered back down with a crash into the water, Aloysius began to sing 'Home, Sweet Home', then Harriet started 'I Dreamt that I Dwelt in Marble Halls', and Nicholas Tennyson sang 'Cherry Ripe', and each time the others joined in and sang as loudly as they could above the storm and the little lantern burned bravely on. Sometimes they were silent, then one or other would start talking again, or singing, or would quote poetry.

Harriet, clinging to the back of Aloysius, thought of how small the *Amaryllis* had seemed to her as she had arrived at Gravesend; tried to picture the red-headed mermaid now, ploughing through the waves, rising and falling, her expression unchanging. For a moment she was consumed with a terrible anxiety that the mermaid might be damaged in this storm. She vowed to herself that, if she lived, she would describe this storm to Asobel, greater, she believed, than the storm of Robinson Crusoe himself, and her mind almost cracked on itself in the small water-filled cabin when she pictured herself sitting in the summerhouse with Asobel. When Mary was alive.

And all of a sudden, in this wild storm, clinging to the back of Aloysius and knowing it was *that* (the warm back, the comfort of Mary's warm back, of Aloysius Porter's warm back) that had reminded her of reading 'Frankenstein' with Mary, Harriet began to weep.

Aloysius felt her crying beside him.

'Oh please don't cry, Miss Cooper. We will surely survive. This is a brave little ship, I can feel it.'

'Don't cry, Miss Cooper,' said Mr Tennyson. 'You have been so courageous even though I feel you have hurt yourself in the storm. The Captain has done this trip before, he will know these waters well. And like Aloysius I feel the brave *Amaryllis* will get us through.'

'No!' cried Harriet, between convulsive sobs. 'It is not the storm. It is my sister Mary. She died, and I loved her so. And suddenly I am thinking of her and it makes my heart break '

'Tell us something of her,' said Mr Tennyson.

'What do you mean?' Harriet could only see him vaguely in the light from the lantern as the ship moved upwards and sideways: he seemed to be looking at her thoughtfully from his wedged corner.

'Tell us about her.'

For a time all they could hear was the sea and the wind and the creaking, straining timbers, and Harriet's occasional swallowed sob. And then she began to speak.

'My sister Mary was the person I loved most in the whole world. Without her I cannot feel the ground beneath me properly. She educated me. She taught me to laugh and I have forgotten how. She loved me and – protected me, and taught me everything I know.'

The sea smashed suddenly against the small window, Mr Tennyson held his hand against it, as if to protect the glass.

'Was she beautiful?'

'Oh yes. Yes. She was the most beautiful person I have ever seen. You know when people laugh, how it makes them beautiful?'

'Of course.'

'Sometimes still, I actually see her, I see her face. Do you think I'm mad?'

Nicholas Tennyson's face flickered in the swaying lamplight. 'I heard you praying earlier,' he said, not answering her directly. 'Do you believe in God?'

'Of course.' Again the sea smashed against the glass. Again Mr Tennyson held his hand to it, trying to protect it. Water had seeped in this time down one of the sides, running down the wall of the cabin.

'I am not so sure as you are,' said Mr Tennyson, 'which is my misfortune,' (and for a split second Harriet saw the grey, thoughtful eyes of Benjamin Kingdom, in another life.) 'But I believe a person's everlasting life is in the people that remember. Of course you are not mad.'

The ship lurched upwards. Then Harriet suddenly felt Aloysius moving beneath her arms and her body, that rested against his back. At first she thought he was laughing. But as the next crash came she understood, because she could smell it, that he was quietly vomiting on to the churning, eddying water of the cabin floor.

Above them the Captain stared into the distance for the first light. His hair was wild, his clothes were torn and drenched. They could do nothing more in the darkness but try to keep upright. He loved the *Amaryllis* and trusted his life to her, but the unexpected violence of this storm out of clear weather had stunned him. It was not the first time this had happened as they moved into the tropics, but it was the worst time, and he was not certain how badly his ship had been damaged or where exactly it had been blown to.

And then, not all at once, but gradually over some time, his experience told him: the worst was over. He waited until he was sure before he spoke. And then he gave the briefest of touches to the shoulders of the helmsmen beside him.

'Well done,' he said, and as he looked again far away to the horizon in the distance the first light shone, very faintly.

When they finally unlocked the hatches by order of the Captain as morning came and the wind lowered, a terrible sight confronted the crew, who had seen many terrible sights. Water lay up to two feet deep all over the steerage area. The slats of the bed-spaces had disintegrated, most of the hundred or so mattresses were waterlogged, the long table, even though it had been nailed down, had been smashed. Belongings floated everywhere: food tins and pots, sad small shoes, vomit, faeces, hats. Some of the passengers from the cabins, although in various states of shock themselves, came to help: Mr Nicholas Tennyson and Mr Aloysius Porter and Miss Harriet Cooper were amongst them. Mr Burlington Brown, dressed in his best, although wet, frock coat, was ashen-faced; he nevertheless sent his be-hatted wife forward to reprimand Harriet whose hair was wild, whose dress was torn; when Harriet turned to Mrs Brown, her bruised and blood-encrusted face and her wild eyes stopped the rebuke on the good lady's lips: she could not speak.

Word quickly went around that a small girl had died: she was three years old. She was handed up to the waiting crew, to the doctor, but one look at the tiny body told everything. People had broken bones, ripped clothing, bloodied faces and limbs. One by one they came up the ladder from below in a terrible silence, like people who had seen hell. Hetty, who had laughingly saved Harriet's hat not twenty-four hours earlier, had a badly broken arm; it hung, obviously painful, and unusable. The doctor was overwhelmed with work; Harriet ran to her flooded, chaotic cabin, found a towel, ran back, tried somehow to tie up Hetty's broken bone. In the absence of the Captain at his duties, Mr Burlington Brown thanked God for their deliverance, but not a soul sang. And all the time the crippled *Amaryllis* sailed on and sailors hammered at masts and tried to mend sails and ropes.

And then there was a sound from beneath them. It began low and got louder and louder and then a woman appeared at the top of the hatch. People looked on, appalled: it seemed as if half of her hair had been torn from her head. Her mouth was open very wide as if it was jammed, as if it would not close, and from that open mouth came the sound. She was screaming on and on and on, a terrible terrible sound: she stood on the deck and screamed and not a soul spoke, or could think of any comfort. Harriet stared transfixed: the woman stood beside the deck rail, behind her the sea still rose and fell in an echo of what had been. One of her hands was raised to her mouth as if to pull the nightmare out of her, and still the noise came, on and on. At last the doctor appeared beside her and somehow the woman's mouth was literally jammed closed and then the doctor somehow forced her to drink something and finally there was just the sound of the wind again and the torn sails flapping and the great wide sea all around them. And this small group of people, all alone in the wide empty Atlantic Ocean.

A Union Jack and some canvas was made ready by one of the crew as the passengers stood there. The small body of the little girl, so tiny and unprotected in the same summer dress she had worn to the church service in the sunshine, was wrapped in the canvas and laid on the flag. The Captain himself, impeccable in his formal uniform and his hat (even though the clothes were wet), stood in the white morning light and commended the soul of one of God's children unto His care. The mother stood, shocked and dry-eyed, staring at the small bundle; her husband had tears running down his pale and bloodied cheeks but he made no sound. As the Captain began the Lord's Prayer voices joined in, reluctantly at first, unevenly, then becoming stronger as the familiar words took hold,

thy will be done on earth as it is in heaven.

Very slowly and with great dignity, two exhausted-looking sailors dropped part of the deck rail and gently consigned the little canvas parcel to its vast, wild grave.

TWENTY-TWO

It is interesting to speculate what would have happened had the Right Honourable Sir Charles Cooper, MP, found Lady Kingdom's two sons sitting across from him at the Captain's table as the *Lord Fyne* disappeared from sight of Falmouth on 16 December 1849, but fate (in the shape of Lady Kingdom who absolutely insisted that her sons spend Christmas Day with her) had decreed that Lord Ralph and Sir Benjamin leave ten days later. The fishermen on the Falmouth pier raised their heads and pondered on the madness of humankind as departing ships got smaller and smaller and the wintry seas churned. In Falmouth they lived on the gossip of the seas: who was travelling, who drowned, which ships (of which there were a fair number) foundered in the Bay of Biscay and never even made it past the Spanish coast.

Sir Charles did not farewell the land; he sat at the Captain's table drinking heavily; Peters lay in steerage, seasick and deeply fearful and full of vengeful thoughts about Harriet Cooper, whom he blamed for his fate.

If Lucy's mother hadn't finally died (her lungs full of cotton threads finally refusing to take in one more breath of air) Lucy might have had the dubious pleasure of living with Peters again, part of the small group of single female emigrants (clutching letters of good character signed by vicars) who were herded from their hostel by the matron on to the *Lord Fyne* and into the Unmarried Women's Quarters in steerage. As it was Lucy was given permission to delay her departure briefly and did not travel on the *Lord Fyne* either.

And so it was that Lucy recognised, with a frisson of excitement, the two young gentlemen on the *Cloudlight* which sailed from Gravesend for New Zealand the day after Christmas Day. To his surprise Quintus found himself on board the *Cloudlight* also. All Quintus knew was that Lucy had secreted him under her thin coat and somehow got him aboard (where he was strictly forbidden); by the time he was discovered Lucy was (luckily for her and for Quintus) a favourite of the Captain (who had an eye for young girls) because she often sang on deck in the evenings even if the sea was wild. Her clear voice echoed over the ship with great sweetness, the winds snatching at her tune and throwing it up into the sky and then bringing it back again.

> Cherry ripe, cherry ripe
> Ripe I cry

she sang, and so Quintus's presence was tolerated as long as he did not chase the hens and the pigs and the goats. At first he was seasick. Lucy thought he might die (for a ship was surely not a place for a dog) but she nursed him and whispered in his ear that she was taking him to see Miss Harriet and what would he bet that Lord Ralph Kingdom and Sir Benjamin Kingdom were going to be looking for Harriet also? At last Quintus found his sea-legs like any sailor and was, the sailors found, good company in the long watches of the night, sitting up with great alertness, staring keenly towards their destination with his ears cocked upwards. He also caught rats that ran about the ship, and quickly learned to find a safe corner to brace himself when the ship rolled. But Lucy continued to believe that dogs were not really made for ships: she persuaded one of the sailors to make a small wooden cage which he then nailed to the foot of her small space in steerage. If the steerage passengers had to suffer the battening down of hatches, so did Quintus.

It was not a good time to be leaving England: the weather was at its most treacherous as ships came out through the English Channel and, although the *Lord Fyne* had left earlier than the *Cloudlight*, both ships were extremely battered in the Bay of Biscay, could have been seen out from the same coast at the same time with fishing boats and small trading vessels all fighting for survival; the *Lord Fyne* in particular lost many days and then, limping southwards, finally had to call at the port of Lisbon for repairs.

The *Cloudlight*, which had left England later, therefore overtook the *Lord Fyne*; sailed bravely down towards the tropics. Several of the women who were cabin passengers on board the *Cloudlight* (some of whom had already swooned at the sight of Lord Ralph Kingdom) remarked together that although, indeed, they could not find fault with the way their Captain handled his ship, it was quite clear that he, when not sailing his ship, *drank*, and in the important areas of class and breeding he was sadly lacking. They spoke to one another in low voices, serving tea in their immaculate gowns, remaining polite to the Captain of course, and smiling at their husbands. And although Lord Ralph Kingdom and his wonderful brother bowed to them dazzlingly it was clear that their minds were elsewhere. As the journey progressed, the ladies dressed less exquisitely; sometimes, suffering from *ennui*, they did not dress at all.

On the *Cloudlight* Lucy observed that the two heroic young men (for so she liked to think of them after all the romantic stories she used to read to Quintus: heroes sailing across the world to save the princess) were followed about by a large clerical gentleman who smiled all the time but somehow looked rather sad. Once too she saw Lord Ralph Kingdom looking at her curiously, as if he had seen her somewhere before. But it had been dusk when he found Harriet in the Highgate Cemetery and Lucy was only a maid, after all.

Sir Benjamin Kingdom stood often on the deck and watched the changing sea. He had done what his mind, and possibly his heart, had insisted upon. They were travelling towards something important, that was all he understood, and the great, exciting world lay before them, to be unravelled.

TWENTY-THREE

On the *Amaryllis* it took days for the cabins, let alone the steerage area, to be cleaned and dried and restored to some sort of order after the storm. Almost every single item of clothing of every person on board had been soaked as the water seeped into cabins and trunks. When she was alone Harriet rolled up her sleeves and scrubbed her own cabin inexpertly but readily; for just a moment she saw herself in Bryanston Square trying to clean up her own excreta, the day she nearly gave in: remembering that terrible dawn, she scrubbed her cabin with a kind of joy.

Mr and Mrs Burlington Brown were rendered speechless by Harriet's account of the storm. Miss Eunice Burlington Brown could not believe that Harriet had done such a thing. At first she thought they were disturbed at the danger she had been in on deck: soon she understood that it was the danger she had been in while remaining in the cabin of Mr Aloysius Porter and Mr Nicholas Tennyson that concerned them so fearfully.

'You mean, my dear Miss Cooper, that you were alone with two men for a whole night?' Eunice Burlington Brown had become quite pale.

'I think I have not properly explained. Mr Nicholas Tennyson saved my life.'

'Then why, having saved it, did he not escort you to your cabin?' Mr Burlington Brown's face loomed in front of her.

'I truly think it was not possible, or even thought of. The danger was too great. I had nearly been swept off the *Amaryllis*.' Harriet was puzzled by their shock and anger. The bruises and cuts on her face had not yet disappeared, nor the big bruises on her body. She had been hit, it was presumed, by the cage of chickens, which was never seen again after that dreadful night.

'Nothing, Miss Cooper, can be as dangerous as spending a night alone in a confined space with two young men. No wonder young girls are not allowed to make this journey alone if the rudimentaries of good breeding are so easily thrown away. Surely you see that your reputation is ruined, completely ruined! What would your father say?'

'I imagine anyone who cared for my safety might thank Mr Tennyson for his bravery.'

'His "bravery" as you call it did not go so far as escorting you to your own cabin,' retorted Mr Burlington Brown, 'which any gentleman would have done immediately. I am afraid I am going to have to speak to Captain Stark. We explained to you when we first agreed to take on the responsibilities as your guardians that etiquette and social mores must at all times be adhered to, that it was up to us to keep standards high and never allow vulgarity or impropriety. We simply cannot allow such breaches of propriety.'

The Captain, in this instance at least, was more sanguine. He observed Harriet's injuries and spoke to her kindly, understanding how terrified she had been. To the young men he was more admonitory: a young lady should always be delivered to the safety of her own cabin, he said to them curtly, her honour is paramount: their behaviour had not been that of gentlemen.

Passengers were taught how to tie themselves to their beds for future reference.

Miss Eunice Burlington Brown, be-hatted, insisted on sitting with Harriet in her cabin and reading from 'The Women of England: Their Social Duties & Domestic Habits'.

'I think this will assist you, my dear Harriet,' and she cleared her throat. 'I will read the important bits.'

> The women of England are deteriorating in their
> moral character . . . When the cultivation of the

mental faculties had so far advanced as to take
precedence over the moral, leaving no time for
domestic usefulness ... the character of the
women of England assumed a different aspect.

'I have read this book,' said Harriet, 'my father gave it to me.'
Miss Burlington Brown was delighted, and she fanned herself
with her glove in the small room. 'I shall read on a little,' she
said.

Women of England, you have deep responsibilities, you have urgent claims; a nation's moral
wealth is in your keeping ... In her intercourse
with man, it is impossible but that woman
should feel her own inferiority; and it is right
that it should be so. She does not meet him upon
equal terms. Her part is to make sacrifices in
order that his enjoyment may be enhanced.

'I am hoping to be domestically useful,' said Harriet humbly.
'For my cousin Edward has bought a farm in New Zealand.'
Miss Eunice pricked up her ears at once. 'He has a farm?'
'If he has already arrived,' said Harriet. 'I see now that the jour-
neys are haphazard and uncertain. We may arrive before him.'
Miss Eunice suddenly saw herself married to a farmer perhaps.
She had had hopes of Mr Aloysius Porter: his behaviour might yet
prove him not to be the one; it was important to keep all one's
options open.
'Are you fond of your cousin, Harriet dear?'
'He is my favourite cousin,' answered Harriet. 'He is the kindest
man I know.'
'Does he—' Miss Eunice could not help herself, 'does he have a –
that is, an intended?'
'I do not believe so,' said Harriet.
'Is he – handsome?' *Somewhere in the cabin Mary gazed down, her
quizzical eyes dancing.*
'To my eyes he is handsome,' smiled Harriet. 'Although I may be
biased. Miss Eunice, do you think that perhaps we could walk
together on deck now?'

'Of course, dearest Harriet.' Miss Eunice's eyes shone with unexpressed hopes for the future, with one man or another.

*

In steerage, although the *Amaryllis* had now crossed into the calm of the tropics, people screamed in the night, dreaming.

*

TO THE DEAR READERS OF MY JOURNAL
3 January 1850

4.30 am On this third day of this new year we are becalmed! It is our thirty-eighth day at sea. We crossed the Equator some days ago and now we are in the Southern Hemisphere. I believe – although it is so long since we caught sight of any land – that we are travelling parallel to the bottom half of the coast of Africa, all that wild, undiscovered land of which we know almost nothing. I think often of Asobel's globe and the route she had drawn for Edward, travelling near land so that he would always be safe. But Captain Stark has told me that often we must avoid land, not cling to it. He expects soon to pick up the trade winds which will help us to travel on southwards and round the Cape of Good Hope, and so eastwards towards our destination.

I have never been so hot in my life, which is why I get up at first light and come and sit here on the poop deck to write to my dear readers. It does not matter that it is so early – time has no meaning at all (except at the Captain's table of course, where etiquettes are most strictly observed). I have seen sunrises that I could never have imagined in a thousand years: how the sun appears, just a strand of light at first, and then more strands, forming a glorious flaming whole that fans out across the still, calm sea, which changes colour every day. How could I have even imagined that this is how the sun rises, looking out sometimes from my bedroom window over the rooftops of Bryanston Square?

But now – such sights I have seen! I have seen fish that fly into the air, they fly upwards and then twist again down into the water and their shining scales catch the sun. And I have seen the friendly porpoises, they play around the bows of the Amaryllis to the delight of all the children on board; they seem to nudge each other and then they too leap into the air, and in the air they seem to shake themselves for joy before they dive back into the water. Of course some of the men try to shoot them: when they succeed the children weep.

The crew have rigged tarpaulins over both decks and it has been explained to Miss Eunice and to me by Mr Aloysius Porter that tarpaulin is canvas treated with tar so that it is waterproof – a most necessary accoutrement in New Zealand. Most people spend much time on the deck underneath these canvases but it is sometimes too hot to do even that. In the cabin area we have a salt-water bath that we can use for cooling ourselves: the salt sticks to the skin in an odd, scratchy manner. The girl Hetty who saved my hat still has her arm bandaged from the storm; I do hope it will mend satisfactorily. She told me it 'makes her that mad' because it is so painful and she cannot do everything she wants to do, and I do not enquire what those wants are for fear of not quite understanding her answer. I do, of course. I . . .

Here Harriet stopped writing for a moment. This was a journal for her dear readers, whoever they might be one day (and always she thought of Walter since he had presented her with the journal, and Asobel perhaps), not for herself. The sun was rising now, soon it would be too hot to sit even here. Harriet looked about her: at the still sea, at the drooping sails of the *Amaryllis*. There was nobody much about, only the helmsman at the wheel at the back of the poop deck, and at the front of the main deck trying to catch any hint of wind a group of steerage passengers sat together talking; perhaps they had been there all night. With her pen she crossed out the last five words. An odd idea had come to her: that she might keep a more private diary where she could talk to herself more freely, which she could keep locked in one of her boxes in her cabin.

Slowly she took a fresh piece of paper from her folder. And then she began writing again.

Without Mary, who understood, it was as if I was in an inferno.

What the girl in steerage, Hetty, speaks of so fondly and freely, what Aunt Lucretia spoke of as Alice's dark duties, are the same thing, although I cannot quite understand how that can be. My father has done great wrong, and great damage. I would rather die than go back to that. I will die rather than go back to that.

She folded the sheet of paper carefully and put it in her folder and for a long time she stayed motionless, staring at the furthest horizon. Then she seemed to shake herself slightly and began writing again in her main journal.

Soon now Mr or Mrs Burlington Brown or Miss Eunice Burlington Brown – or all! – will come and admonish me that I should not be sitting here alone, with a man (they will mean the helmsman who stands by the big wheel at the back of the ship and steers us onwards). They will also say that my cheeks have caught some sun, unheard of for a young English lady, and most inappropriate, not to say deeply unfashionable. Then the Burlington Browns will watch over me at breakfast and dinner and tea. At each meal there will be complaints about the food – there is only one more pig to be killed for fresh pork because some of them, and of course all the chickens, were lost in the storm; the last goat died; and we are reduced to eating salted meat and food from tins a great deal of the time and we are not even halfway. I never thought I would think longingly of a fresh cabbage! The men will fish, but so far nothing edible has been caught: the other day they brought up an octopus and all the ladies (including me) screamed at the writhing arms. How the steerage passengers are coping is not to be thought of: imagine how hot it must be down there! We are not encouraged to have anything to do with those people – Captain Stark is very strict on this point: that order, and therefore social rank, must at all costs be upheld. He makes it clear that an ordered ship is a safe ship and that he must be obeyed at all times. And indeed we know only too well that our very lives are in his hands. He is a kind man and a fine Captain of our ship. I have been told that not all captains are so reliable, and that it is the Captain that gives the tenor of the ship. I spend much of my time reading, a pastime I will never grow tired of; I read Mary's books, books we shared. But many of the cabin passengers are showing signs of boredom and discontent and there are small quarrels daily that may grow to larger ones: Mrs Burlington Brown and the magistrate's wife are hardly speaking – something to do with who should pour the tea.

Miss Eunice Burlington Brown, while escorting me, will continue to question me about my cousin Edward, she has got it into her head that he is an eligible gentleman farmer. Then there

*will be a continuation of a chess tournament this afternoon: there
was some surprise when I asked to compete; it was expected to be
only men but I explained that my sister was a chess player par
excellence and had taught me. I then beat the magistrate, which
was I think considered ill-mannered. This afternoon I am to play
Mr Nicholas Tennyson – the Burlington Browns will disapprove
and think I somehow engineered to play him deliberately, that he
has taken my heart since he saved my life.*

How little they know of me and my heart.

*I like Mr Tennyson very much all the same, and he and I will
again discuss Coleridge. As far as we both know he did not make a
long sea journey like ours – yet we note the power and knowledge
of 'The Ancient Mariner' again and again; how on these still,
tropical days the Amaryllis is*

> *like a painted ship
> upon a painted ocean.*

*I think often of Mary and myself, poring over our books in the
upstairs drawing room, trying to make some sort of intelligent
sense of the world. And all the time the world was here: the sea
and the stars and the sky stretching outwards and upwards and
onwards – I have the strangest feeling that I am in eternity, that I
am in the world as a whole, that is the only way I can describe
what I am feeling. When the Bible spoke of eternity I didn't
understand – now I feel I do – that this is God's world and we are
infinitesimal creatures in it. And I know that somewhere in this
vastness Mary is here too.*

That evening the cabin passengers, including the ladies, sat on the
deck to try to catch a breeze. The men, with the ladies' permission,
smoked their cigars and the smoke drifted upwards. The sound of
the sea was like a soft whisper. The Captain explained again how
sailors had learnt to take what wind they could in these latitudes,
tacking east and west, until, in two days or twenty days, they
caught the soft trade winds which would fill their sails and take
them southwards.

Although night had fallen the sky seemed to shine with light.

The Captain pointed out to his passengers the stars, allowing them to understand that so far had they sailed already, that the stars too had changed. From the main deck came the sound of the concertina, and voices singing.

> When other lips and other hearts
> Their tales of love shall tell,
> In language whose excess imparts
> The pow'r they feel so well,
> There may perhaps in such a scene,
> Some recollection be,
> Of days that have as happy been,
> And you'll remember me . . .

Miss Eunice Burlington Brown cast a glance at Mr Aloysius Porter: her sister-in law had pointed out, and she had noticed herself, that he smiled a great deal, which perhaps was not a good sign: much smiling made a man a little frivolous perhaps. Mr Nicholas Tennyson cast a glance at the beautiful Miss Harriet Cooper who sat so quietly, but in the light of the stars he saw that her thoughts were far, far away.

Sometimes something flashed in the distance: lightning or a comet or a shooting star falling towards the sea. Sometimes phosphorescence danced along the top of the water, silver in the darkness, glittering beside the bows. And on the horizon the gentle trade winds sighed, waiting for the *Amaryllis*.

*

TO THE DEAR READERS OF MY JOURNAL
25 January 1850

Today is the sxtieth day since we left Gravesend and on this day the Captain has informed us that the trade winds have taken us, at last, far enough south: we are approaching the Cape of Good Hope and will be turning eastwards. The weather, which has been so balmy in those warm winds, and so beautiful, has changed yet again: almost a week ago the barometer fell and it has been raining for two days. Nobody cares about the rain – when he made this announcement everybody rushed to the railing to peer

into the horizon. Just to see land would be enough, just to know
we are not alone in the wide world we are traversing. But stare as
we would no land materialised – we are too far from the African
coast and anyway the grey rain clouds hang heavy over us and we
can see nothing. The Amaryllis is our world and there is nothing
else.

The passengers on the *Amaryllis* did however see something
unexpected on the sixtieth day: another ship. They could not
believe their eyes and there were great cries of excitement. At first
they thought it was a ship returning to England: people rushed to
write letters, or seal up written ones in the hope that mail could be
exchanged. Miss Eunice Burlington Brown was dismayed to see Mr
Aloysius Porter writing at length and feared it was to another
woman. Mr Nicholas Tennyson noted that Harriet did not write
anything.

But as the ships came closer together, close enough to see tiny
stick people moving about, flags were run up and messages were
exchanged. And it was found that the vessel was a Portuguese ship
which had recently been damaged in a storm, sailing home from
Africa. The disappointment on the *Amaryllis* at not meeting some
other human beings was extraordinary, and people offered to speak
to the Portuguese with sign language. But Captain Stark, looking at
the way the clouds formed menacingly over his ship, sailed
onwards.

Captain Stark had reason to be anxious. The weather was dete-
riorating badly, especially to the eastwards: was his poor sturdy
ship to be caught in another bad storm? He made a decision not to
travel east but to venture further south, perhaps as far as the island
of Tristan da Cunha where there was a tiny settlement and where
whaleboats stopped for water. At dusk the first iceberg reared out
of the mist: this now was another danger in the South Atlantic
Ocean. Low over the *Amaryllis* an albatross flew: here was its lati-
tude rather than further north where Harriet and Hetty had stared
in amazement. Winds roared about the ship, ropes flew outwards,
torn from the sails, mountainous waves again appeared.

Night followed day and the Captain seldom left the helm; he
and his men watched for icebergs, sailing with only the rigging,
tossing and rolling with the ocean. The cabin passengers tied them-

selves in their beds; the steerage passengers pleaded with the crew not to nail them down, at least not till the last possible moment, knowing many of the people below could hardly bear another lock-up; the Captain did not heed them: the *Amaryllis* must not founder. Terrified screams were caught on the wind, but nobody heard. Every night Harriet tied herself to Mary's thin bed the way she had been taught; in a strange way she knew no fear: she told herself over and over as the *Amaryllis* flew forward and then smashed downwards, *I would rather die than go back.* On one such night she realised she had turned eighteen.

Finally, but without anyone catching even the smallest glimpse of the wild barren cliffs or the whaling station of Tristan da Cunha, the *Amaryllis* managed to tack eastwards and the wind began to take the ship with it. Suddenly, for some days, the ship made extra-ordinary progress with the wind – in two days and nights they travelled nearly five hundred miles. And then another contrary gale would catch them and all the effort of the crew was simply to stay afloat and not hit the white ice that would appear so un-expectedly.

The winds subsided a little.

Once again wild faces appeared on deck from steerage; once again there was a funeral. A pregnant woman had died trying to give birth in the worst of the gales, the baby had never breathed. As the winds still blew they buried them together in one canvas shroud, the baby in the mother's arms. Harriet wept as they laid the shroud on the flapping Union Jack, at the useless, terrifying death of a woman, at the birth of a dead child. *Thy will be done on earth as it is in heaven*, the passengers prayed.

One day the Captain appeared in the dining saloon in his uni-form as if he had not been standing at the wheel in oilskins for days and nights. He told Harriet, who was clutching the table and trying to eat some cold beans as water eddied about her feet, that if she could see into the distance due northward she would see the con-tinent of India: nothing lay between the *Amaryllis* and the beautiful flowers and the spices and the coloured birds and the sunshine. And Harriet smiled at him, and at the imagined scent of tropical flowers instead of cold beans and the smell of rancid fat.

The winds subsided further and they felt a warmth in the air.

And now the passengers knew that they had come much more

than halfway. It was already February. By midway through March they might reach their destination. For the first time Harriet began to think properly about her cousin Edward Cooper, about when he might have arrived; about what she herself would do in this new land with her new life. She tried to imagine the surprise on his dear, round face when one day she came into his view. And she felt a great, great surge of relief, that soon now she would be with someone who knew her. With all the other passengers she laid clothes and blankets in the warmer air. She helped Hetty, whose arm seemed not be healing, whose natural high spirits seemed now so subdued, to dry her few belongings from her tiny space in steerage. Harriet was careful not to offend the Captain's proprieties, but nevertheless insisted on working with Hetty in the sunshine, helping her because she could not do it herself, to lay out blankets, to tie a thin dress to the ship's railing so that the winds would dry it. They sang 'Home, Sweet Home' as they worked, singing always cheered Hetty a little, but Harriet thought how she disliked the song; at least until home meant something other than Bryanston Square. She asked the doctor to look at Hetty's arm: he said he was too busy, the arm would knit if Hetty kept still.

'I have to be able to work!' said Hetty. 'It must heal. My life depends on me being able to work!' Harriet talked to the doctor again; impatiently he rebound the thin arm tightly, causing Hetty to scream in pain.

'I have much more important matters to attend to,' he said.

Mr Burlington Brown challenged the magistrate to a duel for some slight no-one else could ascertain: *I will be answered*, he shouted over and over again, *I am a gentleman*. Captain Stark finally managed to dissuade them, but their wives were found screaming at each other on the poop deck for all the world as if they were women from the steerage area, and Miss Eunice Burlington Brown wept when it finally became clear that Mr Aloysius Porter had a fiancée.

Harriet wrote of such events for her dear readers in the early mornings. She stared at the horizon lost in thought. She had studied an iceberg at close range. She had seen an albatross. She had turned eighteen. She had been in a storm on the deck of the *Amaryllis*. She had scrubbed her flooded cabin again. She had seen the sky change completely: instead of the Plough she had often seen from Rusholme, and even occasionally from Bryanston Square, there was the Southern Cross, a new constellation. She felt – it was a new feeling – strength. She was no longer afraid. And one night she took the secret white piece of paper from inside her folder and wrote: *I understand that my father crossed a terrible line and it has damaged me. He invaded me. I believe it will be a long time before I can properly heal. But I will put the past, and the memories of that pain, away now.* Then she tore the paper, over and over, dropped the tiny pieces overboard, into the waters of the Indian Ocean. The laudanum bottles followed: *the last resort*, as she had told herself.

She knew she would never need laudanum again.

TWENTY-FOUR

The island of Tristan da Cunha is known as the loneliest place in the world.

Sir Benjamin Kingdom knew something of Tristan da Cunha, it had been spoken of at evenings he had attended not only at the Royal Geographical Society but at the Royal Geological Society. So when the Captain of the *Cloudlight* said it was imperative they put in to the island for water Benjamin was even more delighted than the other passengers (for of course all were delighted at the thought of seeing land). Benjamin spoke to his brother and the Reverend Boothby as they perambulated the deck, of this tiny isolated spot in the South Atlantic in which England's only, and brief, interest was entirely due to Napoleon's enforced residency at the next, nearest island of St Helena, over a thousand miles away.

'They thought he might try to escape to Tristan da Cunha,' said Benjamin, 'and so they sent a garrison. But it was soon considered too expensive for so unlikely an event and they closed the garrison down again. But I believe several of the men asked for permission to stay on, and may still be there. Perhaps—' and his face lit up, 'we may even have a chance to make their acquaintance.'

The Reverend Boothby stared moodily at the sea, keeping to

himself his less than favourable reaction to meeting rejects from Her Majesty's garrisons in whatever circumstances. He would put it in his daily report to Lady Kingdom, he thought, though when she would receive such missives he could not imagine. The Reverend Boothby sighed heavily, huddling into his coat for warmth. The two young men had gone to lean on the deck rail; the Reverend Boothby stood alone (or as alone as it was possible to be on a small ship carrying one hundred and sixty-two passengers) beside the entrance to the cabin area.

All he had ever wanted from life was a tiny country parish with roses growing over the rectory front door: here he was in the middle of the South Atlantic Ocean. He (who made his living by smiling, it might be said, and remaining cheerful) felt God had not been watching over him. He had never wanted a wife, although he was very fond of children. He didn't even want parishioners, with their problems. He saw the small church, and himself leading little country boys by the hand, to paradise.

There had been, in his youth, some – he always explained it to himself thus – minor transgression; Lady Kingdom's elder sister had extricated him because he was the son of a distant cousin and because his name was, as theirs had once unfortunately been, Boothby. The 'trouble' had disappeared into the mists of time past, for years he had been no trouble at all. He still always wore his clerical garb and he was useful when a sudden prayer was required. He was useful too, he knew, as a fourth at bridge, or as an escort to ladies at functions which must be attended. He was always available, smiled a great deal, and never offended. His only weakness was a perhaps over-enthusiastic consumption of alcoholic beverages: even regarding that small frailty he had become, over the years, extremely cunning at secluding himself, during moments of extreme inebriation, at the bottom of Lady Kingdom's huge grounds. If he was occasionally found talking to trees it was averred that he was really talking to God. When Lady Kingdom's sister died many years ago it was only natural that Lady Kingdom herself inherit the Reverend Boothby, along with the family silver. For years he had smiled and smiled and never offended anybody, yet here he was, being tossed about upon raging salt water and having to walk round and round the deck of the *Cloudlight* in the freezing wind, like a punishment. (Whether Ralph and Benjamin felt it was a punishment to have to walk round and round the deck of the *Cloudlight* in the freezing wind with the Reverend Boothby it did not occur to him to consider.) The Reverend Boothby sighed heavily again at the unkindness of fate, hoped the Captain would invite him to join him for a tot later this evening, put a smile on his face, and rejoined his charges.

There was a small scrawny boy (the son of a coffin-maker from Bow travelling to New Zealand where he hoped his trade might prosper), who perambulated the deck of the *Cloudlight* also. The boy had taken to following Ralph and Benjamin and the Reverend Boothby wherever they went. Something about the trio fascinated him, the fat man in his clerical collar and the thin men in their beautiful clothes. Although his parents rebuked him continually, threatened him with hellfire or at least the back of their hand, the small boy always somehow evaded them, was always at the corner of the main deck when the gentlemen appeared, waiting for them. He would hop and skip along beside them and offer over and over again like a parrot the words 'hello, hello' always given in an enquiring tone, as if one day he expected an answer.

'Hello, hello?' he said, as they continued their discussion about Tristan da Cunha. Benjamin explained to his companions that it was actually three islands with the largest known as Tristan; explained that the islands lay, one of the most southern outposts before the Antarctic, between southern America and southern Africa. They discussed together whether the place was of any strategic importance.

'If Tristan da Cunha is on the route between two great continents,' said Ralph, 'it would seem madness not to make sure the Union Jack is safely flying there.'

'Hello, hello?' said the small boy, walking just behind them.

'Surely the climate is not conducive to any sort of constructive life,' smiled the Reverend Boothby, hearing the rigging rattling in the wind and fixing the grey-green rolling sea with a stern eye.

'It is indeed prone to the sudden, violent storms of this part of the world,' Benjamin agreed. 'Yet I understand that for a great deal of the year the climate is relatively mild – bracing if not exactly temperate – and much can be grown there successfully. The largest island is, I am informed, an extinct volcano and this I do long to see.'

'Hello, hello?' came the small voice from behind them. 'I'm George.'

Ralph, slightly irritated by the incessant voice, stopped and rather impatiently gave the boy a penny and told him to go away. Instead of taking the penny the boy George gravely indicated that Ralph should keep it.

'You don't want the penny?' said Ralph, somewhat surprised.

'I want you for my good friend,' said the little boy.

Ralph couldn't help being amused by the first urchin who had ever given a penny back. He went down on his haunches so that he was nearly (but not quite) level with the boy.

'And what would you like your good friend to do for you, George, if you do not want my money?'

'In them stories,' said George, 'the gentlemen swear about being good friends.'

Ralph laughed, rose, and gave the boy his hand to shake.

'I swear,' he said, 'but you must not interrupt adults again when they are talking. Do you swear?'

'I swear,' said the boy. 'I'll fight in your army.'

'You may fight in my army too,' said the Reverend Boothby, his voice booming with jollity.

This interesting conversation was terminated by the wife of the coffin-maker who, mortified to see her son with the gentry, grabbed George and took him away, apologising and curtseying and nodding shamefacedly to Lord Kingdom as she did so.

Lucy had found a friend on board the *Cloudlight*. She had found Annie. Annie was from Holborn and like Lucy had come upon the FEMALES IN SERVICE REQUIRED FOR EMIGRATION notice. She was fifteen, prettier than Lucy but not as smart and she couldn't sing, and so they complemented each other, admired and encouraged each other's talents. They talked about men a lot. They both knew what men did: you couldn't come from Spitalfields or Holborn without knowing a great deal about what men did. They decided to get kind, hard-working husbands, even if they weren't handsome; day after day and night after night they planned their lives. And their friendship was set forever when one night Annie held Lucy tightly as Lucy (the girl who never cried) wept at last: bitter angry tears for the terrible death of her mother with the cotton threads in her lungs. *I will never go back to that, never.* Lucy and Annie became inseparable.

'The men say,' said Annie breathlessly, running along the deck to Lucy, 'I just been hearing them talking, that they can earn one pound a week and get ten pounds of meat provided to them. Ten pounds of meat *a week*, do they mean? I ain't seen ten pounds of meat in my life. A week? *A week?*' And they would literally dance around the deck together in a kind of mad, disbelieving joy.

They planned their new and different lives: how they would save money and how – they had heard that this impossible dream was possible – they would have a *house of their own.* Their husbands, they planned, could be mostly in the back room with their pipes and their dirty clothes. They, Lucy and Annie, would sit in the parlour and sew for their children and sip tea from china cups with saucers.

'And eat chocolate,' said Annie and they giggled along the deck, passing the Kingdom brothers and the Reverend Boothby, still perambulating.

Next day the Captain announced they would reach Tristan da Cunha in forty-eight hours, weather permitting. Excitement rippled through the *Cloudlight.* Land. *Land.*

'I imagine,' said Ralph, 'that apart from being an expensive business, so far from home and so remote even from our garrisons in Africa, it might have been hard to persuade many men to live for any length of time so cut off from any contact with the outside world.' He could not conceive of such a life.

'Hello, hello?' came the usual voice behind them.

'The whalers who put in there for provisions have a worse time of it, poor devils,' said Benjamin. 'To them, I imagine, Tristan da Cunha represents civilisation.'

'It is to be regretted,' said the Reverend Boothby crossly, in one of his very few lapses from polite acquiescence (but he had slept badly after an evening spent with the Captain and his rum bottle), 'that the young woman who has caused us to embark upon this journey did not choose Tristan da Cunha for her destination. We could almost, now, be arranging our return home.'

'Everyone! Look, *look!*' George screamed in such terror that all three men stopped walking and turned to him and saw that he was pointing to a huge iceberg that loomed up to their right out of the sea fog. To see a huge island of ice rising from the sea was indeed an awesome sight, particularly if you had grown up in the back streets of Bow, and George threw himself in fright at his good friend, winding his arms round his good friend's legs. Ralph looked down on him in some amazement, patted the boy's head, put a comforting hand on his shoulder.

'By Jove, that is a sight,' said Ben. He meant the iceberg of course, but he observed with interest the sight of the little boy clinging tightly to his elder brother.

George raised his head gingerly and looked again. 'It looks like a monster,' he said in a small voice.

'Look again, George,' said Benjamin. 'It looks like an elephant.'

George looked. 'I ain't never seen a hele – one of them,' said George.

'Elephant.'

'Elephant,' copied George carefully. He stared again at the ice. 'Is a elephant a monster?'

'No,' answered Benjamin in a considered tone, 'an elephant is a very big animal but I don't believe anyone would call it a monster. I think I have a book with a picture of an elephant in it that I could show you.'

George was now holding the hand of Lord Ralph Kingdom. 'Have you got books?' he said to Ralph.

'My brother and I have very many books,' answered Ralph gravely.

George turned to the Reverend Boothby. 'Have you got books, Mister Church?' he asked.

In the ensuing frosty silence Ralph and Benjamin heard the sea, and the sound of the wind in the sails as the *Cloudlight* sped along safely past the iceberg towards the loneliest place in the world.

'My name is the Reverend Boothby,' said that good man, 'and I have lots of books to show you.'

'Off you go now, young George,' said Ralph firmly, 'and play with your other friends,' and although he looked for a moment downcast George remembered their pact, saluted Ralph and was gone.

'Those people smell,' murmured the Reverend Boothby, nevertheless looking after George rather wistfully.

'I think there is nowhere to wash, you know, in the steerage quarters,' said Benjamin.

'There is no need, even for the lower classes, to behave like animals,' smiled the Reverend Boothby. 'Surely even those people could keep up some sort of standards.'

Benjamin stared back at the iceberg, his eyes thoughtful. He privately thought a great deal about the steerage passengers and their lot though he would never have dreamed of saying so to the Reverend Boothby. Even Ralph would probably not feel the same as Benjamin. 'I think,' he said, 'that many of the people in steerage are hoping to better their standards by making this journey to a new country. They would have to be quite desperate, it seems to me, to travel so far, for so long, in these conditions. They get nailed down in the worst of the storms to try and keep the sea water out – now *that* I could not endure: I am sure they are thinking only of survival, not of cleanliness.'

Ralph nodded in a vaguely agreeing way, but he was thinking, once more, of Harriet.

'It shows they are not educated,' said the Reverend Boothby, feeling he was speaking for Lady Kingdom on this point. 'Cleanliness is next to Godliness, as the Bishop rightly says,' but he had followed George with his eyes until he had disappeared, with his once-more scolding mother, to his proper place below.

On a clear March morning Tristan da Cunha rose before them like a mirage. The largest island stood straight upwards from the sea like a cone, stark and beautiful. It was a cold, clear morning: the sun caught the white of the snow on the highest peak and they saw the sea breaking gently in the distance on the black shore. The cliffs were dark, and stark, and high, and every now and then a waterfall, the object of their visit, flashed as it fell to the sea below. Smoke seemed to rise from the shore.

'Well, here we are arriving at the bottom of the world almost,' said Lucy to Annie (and to Quintus the dog who she was holding to her, to try and keep him, and herself, warm). 'Who would've thought that we should ever see such a strange place.'

The Captain would have preferred not to stop at the bottom of the world: he had not been here before and had heard many stories of the treachery of the weather in the area. But the *Cloudlight*, so badly storm-tossed in the Bay of Biscay where much water was lost, and then becalmed in the tropics where there was no rain at all, was dangerously short of water: he had no choice. Besides, the weather was calm.

'We will not stay long,' he said.

It was necessary to anchor a fair way from the shore, for Tristan da Cunha was known to be surrounded by reefs. And although it was clear where the landing place was, it would obviously only be possible in a small boat. As the sails were being lowered a whaleboat was suddenly seen coming towards them: Queen Victoria herself could not have caused more enthusiasm. Steerage and cabin passengers tried to get a better view: the deck of the ship swarmed with eager people, small boys including the boy George shouted with excitement, pushed through anyone who got in their way, not minding their manners at all. Four strapping young men, islanders, were rowing towards them; waved; hove to and called up that they would take some of them back through the dangerous rocks to the shore, would be able to provide them with fresh provisions as well as water if they so desired; told the Captain to keep an eye out for the north wind; announced that their leader would come aboard later in the day. *We saw you from the island last night, did you see we lit fires? we've been waiting for you, welcome! welcome!*

The passengers were overcome with quite wild excitement at seeing other human beings, they waved and called back and laughed and threw their hats into the air: *hello, hello*, they called again and again, one hundred and sixty-two voices, *hello there!* Here were other people, here was land, the world existed, and the sea before them was as calm as glass. Everybody hung over the rail to look, at the islanders with their great beards, at the strange high shape of the whaleboat; declared to each other they would like to jump into the sea however cold and swim ashore, stay for a few days. The Captain, his ship safely at anchor, poured himself some rum and looked at the clear sky, but repeated that he would leave before nightfall.

Ralph and Benjamin eagerly asked to go with some of the crew, even to row the high-ended whaleboat (they were both considered expert rowers from their university days); their offer was politely refused, but they were instead afforded seats in the stern with the water containers. Quintus, frantic with excitement, evaded Lucy's arms and jumped in after them. The islanders raced off again, showing off their prowess, crested the inner waves with style and great care, skirted past the scarcely concealed rocks of a long reef as they made for land. Ralph saw that his brother's face was wreathed in eager anticipation and sheer joy as the dark cliffs of the island came nearer and nearer.

'By Jove, Ralphie,' cried Benjamin and his blond curls danced in the breeze the whaleboat made, 'look at the sea birds, look at their size! Look at the lava cliffs from the time the island was a volcano, look how black it shines, I wouldn't have missed this for the world!'

Ralph laughed aloud in his own enthusiasm as he too looked with delight on the land ahead. 'Look, look, there's quite a little crowd waiting for us on shore,' and Ralph waved his hand in a pleased salute. And then a thought struck him. 'Perhaps she too has been here!' The further he got from England the more his admiration and love for the enigmatic Miss Harriet Cooper had grown: she too had experienced this journey, and without him to protect her. Over and over he replayed the last scene with her on the deck of the *Amaryllis* and his own role in it: he had lost her instead of going with her; next time he found her he was determined that he would never, never let her go. She could not possibly refuse him: he thought of her every hour of every day. He had crossed the world to marry her, and he would do so.

'Perhaps indeed she came this way,' agreed Benjamin. From day after day after day of thoughtful contemplation at sea he had come to accept that, whatever the meaning of his own strange premonition – intuition, love for that beautiful girl, whatever it had been – it was his brother of course who was to find Miss Harriet Cooper again, to see that she was safe and to seek her hand in marriage: Benjamin had merely set that chain of events in motion and now he must pursue his own life. He must not keep thinking of her. 'Listen, Ralphie,' he said now, 'this wonderful journey is not going to end for me. I have decided I will not return home at once, there is too much for me to see and learn. When you return with Miss Cooper, if that is what transpires, I shall travel further. I am not needed at home as you are and there is so much of the world to see. Look, just look at this dark island!' and he stared ahead in amazement.

Ralph regarded his brother again, smiled, said nothing. Let time show what the future held for Ben: his own future held Harriet.

'But I say, Ben,' he cried suddenly, joyful. (But then he remembered that voices carried clearly across the water and lowered his voice.) 'What a relief to be away from the Reverend!' And the two brothers whooped in delight like small boys, and then grinned at each other, as the islanders rowed for the shore.

The *Cloudlight*, anchored, rocked gently. The passengers left behind watched the progress of the whaleboat enviously, but feasted their eyes on a sight of land: the snow-topped mountain, the dark cliffs, the dull green of small bush-like trees, the sight of other, actual, human beings. They saw seals, and sea-elephants, and big, wild birds: felt, even in this loneliest of places, that they were part of the human race again. The Captain, from the poop deck, stretched, winked down at Lucy, his favourite (thought nothing of a gentle north-west wind that ruffled his hair as he poured his rum): Lucy gave him a grin, she knew he was a rogue but she had known many rogues and was ever grateful for his acceptance of Quintus. Little, scrawny George stood with his mother, shivering slightly in the cold but staring at the beautiful island in fascination. The Reverend Boothby in a black greatcoat sauntered to George's side: began to point out things for him to notice. Occasionally George pointed out things for the Reverend Boothby to notice: all the monsters for instance that he assured the minister lay hidden in the sea below them.

The whaleboat came up to the black sand, Ralph and Benjamin leapt ashore followed by Quintus, the sailors approached the waterfall. The air was so still and bright that the passengers on the *Cloudlight* could clearly see the tiny shape of Quintus racing up and down the shore in a kind of demented, delirious excitement to be on land again at last: barking at men, barking at sea-elephants, barking at birds. Lucy, longing to be with him, laughed to watch.

'From here he looks like a mad flea!' she said to Annie. They stood arm in arm on the deck, friends forever.

Lord Ralph and Sir Benjamin Kingdom stood on the shore talking with great interest to their hosts, other men had appeared, and children, who hung back shyly. Benjamin picked up small black pebbles, let the cold, dark sand fall through his fingers, watched the big sea birds as they circled and dived. The sailors filled the water carriers, arranged to collect provisions on their second trip, were rowed back past the rocks and delivered precious water to the *Cloudlight*, then returned for more. Quintus chased birds bigger than himself. Some of the islanders chewed on pipes that were empty of tobacco; Benjamin noted this, decided tobacco must be sent back from the ship to these lonely men before they sailed away again. One of the sturdy young islanders, who introduced himself as William, showed them the steep path to where their small village lay on a plane above them; they saw the carefully built small houses; they were invited to climb up if they had the time and the inclination. Benjamin looked upwards in anticipation.

'Will the volcano ever erupt again?' he asked as he stared further and further upwards in awe.

'That is in God's hands,' said William.

Once or twice as they were talking an old man looked at the sky. Then suddenly (his experienced eyes seeing something in the sea, or the sky, that others could not) he excused himself to shout across to the young islanders who were helping the sailors, to hurry with the second lot of water. On the shore the waves changed their sound just a little, seemed to become a little louder, yet nothing appeared different exactly, the *Cloudlight* still rode at her anchor: perhaps the sea swell was slightly more. Ralph and Benjamin looked a little uneasily at the cliffs behind them and then back at the *Cloudlight*. There was no problem, surely?

The old islander came back. 'We are worried about your ship. Has your captain been in these waters before?'

'He has not,' said Ralph.

'Then he may be unaware of the danger of this nor-westerly. They come, literally, out of nowhere. He should make for shelter at one of the smaller islands, not stay at anchor here, surely he would have been informed of this, all captains know of the dangers here. If the swell takes hold he could be dashed against the rocks,' and he pointed to the jagged line near the shore that the whaleboat had negotiated earlier.

They stared out to sea. There was no sign of the *Cloudlight* raising anchor.

The sailors left the waterfall, came to where the others stood on the dark shore. They all looked out to sea: there seemed now to be much bigger swells between the ship and the shore and the *Cloudlight* seemed to be coming closer.

'Why doesn't he go?' muttered one of the men with the empty pipes incredulously. 'He must see what is happening.'

Ralph and Benjamin exchanged apprehensive glances. Were they to remain on Tristan da Cunha while their ship made for safety? The islanders made no move now, to row back to the ship.

'He will go, surely,' said William.

The men on shore stared outwards. At a frightening speed the waves between the ship and the shore grew bigger and bigger: sometimes now the *Cloudlight* was hidden from sight by the mounting walls of water. Now the surf crashed more and more violently on the black shore with a sound like thunder: at last Ralph and Benjamin understood the danger that surrounded the ship: she was dragging her anchor, *she was getting bigger*, she was moving inexorably towards the submerged rocks, her anchor no longer holding her as she was driven towards them by the wind.

Ralph and Benjamin suddenly turned with one accord to the whaleboat, meaning to row towards the ship to give warning, were restrained by their own sailors and by the islanders.

'We cannot row out now,' said William, 'we would not get through that sea out past the rocks. We can only pray for the wind to die, it does sometimes, just as suddenly.'

'But we know the people on board!' cried Ralph. 'And our mother's cousin is there. We cannot let them drown!'

'We must wait now,' said William firmly and the wind whipped the words from him and the sea crashed wildly towards them, bringing the *Cloudlight* closer and closer, hidden from them by the waves and then appearing again, helpless, dangerously nearer. Quintus stood on the shore quite still, his ears standing upwards, hearing perhaps what the others could not.

Sir Benjamin Kingdom may have counted himself a friend of Charles Darwin. Nevertheless he put his face in his hands for a moment. *Spare them, dear God*, he prayed.

God did not hear, it seemed.

Within less than sixty terrible minutes from the time it lay unsuspecting on a calm sea the helpless, drifting *Cloudlight* smashed against the out-shore rocks of Tristan da Cunha that it perhaps did not even see, blown there by the dreaded north-wester that came from nowhere. Ralph and Benjamin stood transfixed in horror and disbelief at a sight that would haunt them for the rest of their lives, the *Cloudlight* rising, falling, smashing. Only the realisation that the islanders and two of the sailors were now frantically launching the whaleboat brought them to their senses. Both young men ran out into the churning water.

'Only one of you!' shouted William, who stood as helmsman.

Ralph did not even wait to consider: he was the elder. He ran forwards into the sea up to his waist, heaved himself aboard, took an extra oar at the stern as ordered, did not hear himself yelling at the top of his lungs *Hurry!* did not hear William's words: *thank God it is daylight.* The others were left, impotent and transfixed, on the black shore.

The whaling boat made slow, wild, dangerous progress towards the rocks, guided by the young man William who used a long oar to steer from the high prow; taking the waves in a way only the most experienced of seamen would have dared, even so the wild water whipped and smashed the bodies of his crew; sometimes they thought they heard terrible screams above the crashing of the sea and the roaring of the gale; sometimes only a few hundred yards away the *Cloudlight* – the wrecked *Cloudlight* – could be seen, sideways, smashing against the rocks again and again with the force of the water, breaking into pieces. And then the crashing waves would take her from view again. The first thing that came careering past them was a ship's lifeboat. It was empty. Somehow William managed to catch it as it passed, lashed it somehow to the whaleboat; even in his terror, rowing wildly, then stopping as he was directed, Ralph saw the skill.

And then, among the spars and the timber hurtling dangerously towards them, they saw bodies in the water, they could not tell if they were dead or alive as they were thrown upwards and sideways by the sea: just crowded black shapes at first, sinking, rising; then the shapes began to take form, a woman trying desperately to hold a child above her, a sailor pulling a man behind him, an old man sinking, dead bodies floating, catching on masts, on torn pieces of timber, all of the bodies and the bits of wreck smashed forwards by the waves, some towards the shore, some against the rocks. All the time William, shouting to his men above the sea, manoeuvred the boat as near as he dared, somehow keeping it far enough away from the rocks and the wreck and their own almost certain death. Ralph suddenly saw red staining the foaming water, looked frantically, wildly for the people he knew, the Reverend Boothby whom they had laughed at unkindly so often, the boy George who had sworn to be his friend. He managed to pull a man aboard the whaleboat, who then, unbelievably, was still strong enough to help him pull in the woman with the child: they pulled another and another, a fat woman whom they could hardly heave aboard, then the surveyor who had been Ralph's chess opponent from the cabin passengers: spewing, screaming, silent. Then several of the shapes caught at the empty, ricocheting lifeboat, tried to pull themselves aboard it, some helped others, some pushed others away, some were caught on pieces of wood: indelibly etched on Ralph's mind was a young woman, drowning before he could reach her hand, hit by a lunging foot through the thrashing water: he saw her eyes before she was gone. And all the time the wind roaring in their ears like thunder mixed with the crashing sound of the waves and the screaming picked up by the wind and thrown away again. Again and again the remains of the ship crashed and smashed against the reef, thrown by the crazed, violent waves until the *Cloudlight* was no longer a ship but a thousand pieces of splintered timber, and at moments fantastical shapes of twisted iron reached upwards towards the heavens in manic supplication. And still the whaleboat somehow stayed upright, guided by the islanders. Ralph saw William pulling at something that seemed to be caught on their boat: it was a woman's skirt; William shouted something to his companion and then leant far overboard wielding a knife. Ralph saw that William was tied to the whaleboat by a rope, that he was half over the side slashing at the front of the whaleboat; a woman's body careered past and then Ralph saw that something white and small was being half-thrown on board and almost in slow motion he saw that the thing being thrown was the boy George. Ralph lunged forward, fell, could not get nearer, someone shouted to him to mind his oar, Ralph caught a glimpse of the boy's still, white face. William half-disappeared again, trying again to cut something loose, the whaleboat lurched dangerously; William fell backwards on to the bottom of the boat, vomiting sea water.

'Go back,' he shouted hoarsely, 'we can take no more on this trip, we will lose them if we don't go back now.'

Ralph did not feel his shoulders or his back: rowed as the others rowed, caught now dangerously on the swell, then crashing forwards at terrible speed, seemingly out of control, towards the shore, Ralph soaked through to his bones and further though he felt nothing at all, all the time guided by William with infinite, infinite knowledge and skill, calling to the men, guiding and manoeuvring while two of them, leaving the others to row, held on to the lifeboat that battled behind them to try to keep it afloat, the desperate survivors clinging to the sides for their lives, knowing even now they could be lost. And all the time Ralph was aware of the little white body lying with all the others they had rescued at the bottom of the whaling boat, and the eyes closed in the small white face.

Others were waiting on the sand to pull them in, the rope tying the lifeboat was cut; as the survivors were dragged ashore the whaleboat was already turning to go back again. Ralph thought he saw island women as he called hoarsely to Benjamin: that he had not seen the Reverend Boothby, that George was here in the boat. Kind hands began to drag the wild, shocked people as far from the raging sea as was possible: the ones who were alive. Ralph tried to reach the boy: as Benjamin, struggling in deep water, lifted him from the whaling boat, Ralph saw the boy's head fall forward. He seemed to be dead. *I swear*, Ralph had said to George. He saw Benjamin turn for the shore, holding the boy in his arms, he seemed to be talking to him. The whaleboat shot back out to sea, turning to the rocks at once; Quintus stood quite still by the shore: he hardly looked at the boats, pointed his nose to the wrecked *Cloudlight*, waiting.

Ralph hardly knew any longer what he was doing, only that he kept on rowing to the call of the voices, on and on. Once again they approached the wreck under William's orders, once again the whaleboat pitched and heaved.

But now there were no heads bobbing.

Dead bodies were whirled past them among spars and hats and broken planks and pots and boxes and chairs and shoes. Then something else rushed past Ralph, a larger body that he thought he recognised that seemed to be caught in a piece of sail; Ralph reached for the body then a wave dashed it away again. When the sea fell back for that split second before the next wave, Ralph saw quite clearly that the stout body belonged to the bald head of the Reverend Boothby. He had lost his clerical garments, his very large underclothes were so full of water that the body seemed to float as it lay face down, not struggling at all, as if, before the next wave dashed his worldly form against the rocks, the Lord had finally heard his prayers and whisked his spirit away to the rose-covered vicarage down an English country lane in the sunshine.

A faint cry reached them: all the men heard it and turned: there clinging desperately to the rocks were Lucy and Annie, who had hidden in a lifeboat when the hatches to steerage were battened down and so had not been locked below. William turned the boat sideways to the rocks but could not approach nearer.

'You must leap!' called William.

They saw that one of the girls was too frightened to move, that the other tried to persuade her even as waves washed over their heads. Then using all her last strength to haul herself upwards Lucy called, above the wind and the sea the men heard her call, *do what I do, Annie*, and Lucy leapt outwards, a leap of wild faith, hit the churning water slightly away from the rocks, struggled frenziedly out towards the boat, a sudden swell threw her nearer and miraculously William was able to lean out from the whaleboat, the rope again holding him, and catch at her hair that tangled in pieces of the wrecked ship.

Leaning on the side of the boat, vomiting, hardly able to breathe, Lucy nevertheless somehow called: *jump, Annie, jump now.*

Annie jumped but she did not jump far enough. They saw, all of them, how her body hit another rock below and then disappeared almost at once into the wild waves.

Of the one hundred and sixty-two passengers and crew who were travelling to New Zealand on the sailing ship *Cloudlight* to make a new life, one hundred and twenty-five lost their lives in the treacherous waters of Tristan da Cunha, the loneliest place on earth. Most of them were trapped in the steerage area where the Captain had ordered the hatches to be battened as the ship under his command took in wave after wild wave as it was swept by the wind, sail-less and anchorless, towards the fatal shore.

TWENTY-FIVE

The *Lord Fyne*, having had to call in at the port of Lisbon for repairs, then delayed for many weeks in the tropics, made good time in the South Atlantic Ocean.

On the deck of the *Lord Fyne* the lowering, impatient figure of the Right Honourable Sir Charles Cooper, MP, was often to be seen. Whatever the weather he walked the decks over and over, like a caged animal. He seldom spoke. He drank heavily. He had forgotten Harriet's terrible last look; even his unconscious seemed to forget, for his unconscious fed his dreams with such visions of his daughter that he would cry out in the night. His obsession grew until it almost overpowered him.

Perhaps he became mad, there in the South Atlantic Ocean as the *Lord Fyne* sailed past the islands of Tristan da Cunha in the far distance.

The islanders saw the ship, lit fires, raised flags.

Perhaps the Captain of the *Lord Fyne* saw the smoke from the island, perhaps he did not, but the *Lord Fyne* did not stop, sailed onwards to the end of the world.

TWENTY-SIX

On the *Amaryllis*, on the one hundred and fourteenth day, in the late afternoon while Harriet was reading Mary's copy of 'Vanity Fair' in her cabin, a woman who had been wringing out a large cloth over the side of the deck suddenly dropped the cloth into the sea and screamed.

'Land!' she cried. 'I can see land!' and she burst into tears.

The cry was taken up by everybody on board. Not one person was left below, they crowded the rail, pointing, crying out, weeping in relief, straining forwards for the sight of land that would mean the ordeal was over. And there, at last, like a long low cloud on the horizon, hazy at first and then darker and darker, more and more substantial as they approached, was New Zealand.

Land. At dawn next morning most people were still on deck, their eyes never moving from the dark shadow. Who would have thought that land, the very land itself, the long coastline of the southern island, could inspire so many feelings of relief and nervousness and wonderment and anxiety and joy. They were making for Wellington, at the bottom of the northern island: this meant, the Captain informed them, negotiating the narrow and treacherous passage between the two main islands of New

Zealand. It was autumn here now, he told them, and the winds were often wild.

'Let the winds be wild!' cried Mrs Burlington Brown. 'I have lived to see land again, nothing else matters in this world,' and Mr Burlington Brown looked at his wife a trifle worriedly: she had been behaving strangely lately, he hoped the journey had not done her any permanent damage.

All day the passengers stared at the coastline as it came nearer. They could not yet see details as the winds took them northwards. But they imagined trees and rivers and mountains and Englishmen.

On the second day of traversing the coast the land suddenly came much nearer: first snow-capped mountain tops could be discerned, then swathes of dark green bush reaching right down to the sea. And then a canoe suddenly appeared. Nothing could have been more strange to the passengers hanging over the rail of the *Amaryllis* than the sight – their first sight of other human beings apart from the Portuguese stick figures – of scantily clad natives paddling towards them shouting and laughing, some of them women. As it got nearer the passengers of the *Amaryllis* could see that the canoe was laden down with vegetables and fruit, and then they saw there were pigs in the canoe as well as people. An apparent leader and several others climbed aboard with great agility and said good morning. Many of the ladies turned away, deeply shocked by the sight of so much flesh (brown flesh at that) while the crew negotiated to buy the fresh food. Harriet observed that some of the sailors seemed to know a few words of the native language, and that the price of all the produce brought on board was a roll of brightly coloured fabric, which had obviously been carried from England for this purpose.

When the natives – the Maoris as they were properly called – paddled away back to land they began to sing in a strange language and their voices echoed back to the *Amaryllis*. To the passengers' enormous surprise, for of course they did not understand the words, the tune was very familiar. The Maoris were, quite clearly, singing 'Home, Sweet Home'.

And Harriet Cooper began to laugh. On the long days on the *Amaryllis* no-one had ever seen Harriet laugh. They had seen the smile that lit up her face in such an extraordinary manner, Mr Nicholas Tennyson knew he would never forget that smile. But

Harriet was leaning on the ship's rail and laughing. It crossed Mr Burlington Brown's mind that ladies should not really laugh – there was something (he could hardly articulate the word even to himself) *abandoned* in laughter – but he could not stop himself from watching. Her head was back and her hair was caught by the wind and her long, slim hand lay at her throat as 'Home, Sweet Home' still drifted across the water. And then, infected, other passengers began to laugh too: laughter rippled from the poop deck and down on to the main deck; small boys ran joyously over the ship's ropes, thin weary women felt the journey dropping from their shoulders and men smiled. The sound rippled away at last and the fresh food was taken below and people moved, still smiling, from one part of the ship to another, and the timbers of the *Amaryllis* sighed and settled and the ship moved onwards, nearer and nearer to its destination.

Colours appeared as well as the bright, dark green bush: yellow flowers, dark red trees in bloom. Coloured birds that looked like strange parrots flashed inquisitively by. At dusk the *Amaryllis* cast anchor for the first time. They were near the top of the southern island and there they would wait till morning: the straits between the two islands were too dangerous to navigate in the darkness.

Even the steerage passengers were given a pig to roast; at the Captain's table fresh meat and vegetables were savoured, healths were drunk, speeches were made and everyone was aware of the odd silence: there were no sails and the sea was calm. Mrs Burlington Brown and the magistrate's wife had made their peace and vowed eternal friendship. (Again Mr Burlington Brown thought that the sooner he got his wife off the ship the better: she was becoming effusive, that was the only word for it, and she had spoken to him most sharply when he had mentioned the dreadful state of the feathers on her hat.)

There was speculation about friends and relations, about Mr Nicholas Tennyson's older brother who had come here a year ago, about Miss Harriet Cooper's cousin, Edward, the gentleman farmer. Miss Eunice Burlington Brown asked Harriet more questions about her cousin, her recovered heart beat in anticipation.

'There is no way of knowing of course,' said Captain Stark, 'when the *Miranda* might have arrived – she left three weeks before us and for all we know she could have arrived many days ago. But you have seen what the weather can do. The *Miranda* could even be behind us. We made record time through the Bay of Biscay but then we were becalmed. The whole journey has occasionally been done in under ninety days – and over two hundred with the worst of luck. We have had a lonely run with no news of anyone, but sometimes three or four ships are long delayed in the Bay, and I have seen a dozen vessels becalmed together in the tropics for weeks on end. You will have to wait a little longer, Miss Cooper, for news of the *Miranda*.'

Mr Nicholas Tennyson and Mr Aloysius Porter had been told of hotels in Wellington where passengers could stay. Captain Stark advised Harriet of very respectable lodgings for young gentlewomen. 'Those hotels along the waterfront,' he said, 'are no place for an unchaperoned young woman.' Mr Burlington Brown seemed disinclined to give up his role of guardian, made suggestions that Harriet should stay with him and his wife and Miss Eunice. Harriet smiled her beautiful smile at everyone and thanked them for their advice.

The Captain wanted Harriet to sing, as she had so often on the long journey, but the piano had become so damp and so out of tune that such a final performance was not possible. Miss Eunice Burlington Brown surprised everyone, especially her brother, by offering to recite a dramatic poem *Casablanca* 'written by the late lamented poetess Mrs Felicia Henman', and immediately launched into

> The boy stood on the burning deck
>   Whence all but he had fled;
> The flame that lit the battle's wreck
>   Shone round him o'er the dead.

She recited all ten verses and was applauded resolutely.

*

Such was the feeling that they had already landed, that their journey was at last over, that the passengers were extremely surprised and not a little put out to find themselves spending the next night strapped to their beds once more. The straits between the two islands were indeed treacherous. Again and again the Captain had tried to make for Wellington with only the foreshortened mainsail, again and again the ship was turned about by the wild winds. Finally, at dawn on the second day, the winds died down and a cold sea fog came down over the *Amaryllis* so that she might have been in the South Atlantic still. But the fog lifted and the sun began to shine and Captain Stark was able at last to sail his brave and stalwart *Amaryllis* through the heads and into the port of Wellington town.

Harriet, at the rail as soon as she felt the winds subside at first light, gasped.

For there was the magical harbour she had first seen in the drawing in Edward's book, only now she could see it in truth: the small wooden dwellings, the enclosed blue bay, the green tree-covered hills, the sea. But as they came closer she saw that it was different from the picture: there were many more small dwellings, they had spread upwards on to the foothills, the sun caught their roofs. There were fewer green trees. And the hills rose up so high: where would the farms be? There were murmurs of anxiety amongst the passengers. But the calm waters of the harbour sparkled in the morning sunshine and the sky was as she remembered seeing it, leading upwards forever and giving the feeling of infinite space. And there was no wind at all.

She breathed in the fresh, calm air and thought she could smell grass. Smoke rose straight upwards from the chimneys of the little houses. A crowd of tiny birds flew over the *Amaryllis* as if in welcome. Somewhere there on the shore, surely, was her favourite cousin, the kind, rotund and smiling Edward Cooper.

In this place she would make her life. She had no fear at all.

This would be her Home. Sweet Home.

TWENTY-SEVEN

Edward Cooper dreamed night after night of wild, tangled, vicious native bush.

It was trying to destroy him.

He had good reason to recall his father's words: *never buy land without seeing it*. What, on the survey maps of the New Zealand Company, had looked like prime farming acres ready for cultivation had turned out to be unsurveyed, bush-covered hillside stretching up to the sky and down to the sea, only reachable from Wellington town by boat; or by a day and a half's trek, first along fair roads (by the standards of the town) but later through bush and trees along muddy overgrown tracks full of treacherous roots and stumps, then along rocky tidal beaches that tore at horses' shoes on every journey. The 'choice' they were promised was between one section and the one next to it, or the one next to that, all in the same place. Even his 'town half-acre' was over two hours' march on half-roads. Edward, who was as optimistic and positive as an immigrant could hope to be, had found his cheerful manner sorely tried.

His friends Chapman and Lyle quickly made their choice: angrily they tried to sell their land back to the New Zealand Company; when this failed they advertised the sections in the *Wellington Independent* and *The New Zealand Spectator and Cook's*

Strait Guardian and decided to venture up the coast where they had heard the opportunities for good land were much better: flat land (they were told), rivers, roads of a kind. They would not be able to afford to buy unless their initial capital was realised, but they could rent or lease, even (it was said) from the natives. Sheep-farming was the answer (they were advised); it wasn't what the New Zealand Company had planned for farmers but it was turning out to be the most profitable way of using much of this new country. All three of them bought horses: the friends prepared to part. Edward told them he would begin clearing land for his house – not on his town section but on his hillside, a day and a half from town.

'If I am to work the land,' said Edward, 'I must live on the land. I am a farmer.'

'That is a ludicrous plan,' said Chapman. 'That land is absolutely hopeless. Come with us.'

'No,' said Edward.

'Eddie, you're a farmer. What you have been given is not farming land, it is wild bush-covered mountains. Come with us.'

'No,' said Edward.

Chapman and Lyle looked at each other: both had the same thought. They could not leave Edward without helping him: he was intractable, but he was their friend. They went back around the coast with half of Edward's belongings, wondering if a second look would somehow prove the land better than they had thought. But nothing had changed: still the high, bush-covered hills stretched upwards. There had to be somewhere for Edward to live: the three men worked from dawn until dusk in sunshine and rain and the Wellington wind; no-one had warned them of the wind. It was unfamiliar, back-breaking, harsh physical work. They chopped down some of the smaller trees; hacked at tangled, springing native bush; tried to burn a clearing but had much difficulty with damp undergrowth; finally cleared with their axes the best flat space near the sea. In the evenings, exhausted, they sat beside a fire, tearing at old bread and salted pork. They talked of sheep-farming; talked of England. They wondered if gold would be found in New Zealand as it had been in America, Canada, Australia: surely there will be gold here, they said, as they stared at the malign forest. They talked of the disaffected natives who, they had been warned, still stalked the land: always made sure their guns were near when they slept at night. They talked of the women in Wellington town who were obviously looking for husbands: they knew it would be years before they could afford the luxury of a wife and they turned, unsettled, on their lonely mattresses.

Once they had a cleared a place for Edward's house they then completely cleared a small part of the hillside and turned the earth for planting because Edward insisted, and cleared some land around the fresh spring, the one asset on the hillside. Once they heard a strange rumbling sound and felt the ground shake beneath them: they waited almost mesmerised for the land to open, this was one of the famous earthquakes, but the rumbling disappeared into nothing and they felt almost cheated. Once they caught sight briefly of an animal, a large pig or a large dog, reached for their guns, but the animal disappeared back into the bush. They caught their first fish, burnt it over their fire and drank the fresh pure water from the spring and talked of the London cholera. So often the wind blew, but on the calm nights under the stars, eating fresh fish as strange birds and insects called and the sea lapped below them, all three of them – despite their anger and disappointment and sheer physical exhaustion – declared that it was perhaps, after all, an adventure worth having, for England.

When enough land had been cleared for Edward to at least start, when enough good logs for building had been piled high, Chapman and Lyle – assured by their friend that he could build a shelter by himself, that he was a fine builder with long experience of such work on his father's farm – made their decision to press northwards to try and settle somewhere before winter came. Edward rode back into the town with them, spent the night before they went at one of the waterfront hotels. Accordions played, men's voices sang of the girls they left behind them, other girls called in the dark from along the quay. Natives sat in little groups where their canoes lay on the shore, talking long into the night in their strange, soft language.

The three men drank ale from England, hoped to meet again, Edward clasped their hands in farewell and thanked them for their friendship.

He bought a small cart, hitched it to his horse, engaged three natives to help him carry everything round the coast, through the bush and on to his land. They transported the rest of his belongings from England; he bought wooden planks and wooden roof tiles from the Kai Warra Warra mill; he bought better axes, bags of potatoes and flour and pork and other supplies from the stores on the waterfront. Edward had never cooked: Chapman and Lyle had taught him that something at least edible could be obtained if you threw everything into one pot, filled it with water, and left it on the fire. On the journey back to his property the natives entertained him, in quaint English, with fantastical stories of their ancestors, and gossip about other settlers. They taught him to make a bed of the springy bracken that grew everywhere about them; he was surprised at the comfort and smiled at the stars in the middle of the night. They also taught Edward to greet them in their own language: *tena koutou*, he would say to them each morning of their travels. On the morning of the second day it rained. He gathered from the Maoris' demeanour that they would not be moving any further that day. He put up his tarpaulin again. The natives sat under a tree smoking the new tobacco the English had brought, talking and laughing: Edward presumed they were talking about him. When the rain at last stopped the following morning his employees lifted their sacks and walked cheerfully on through the mud.

When they arrived the Maoris stared at the land, at the place that had been cleared for a dwelling. After talking together in their own language they started jumping on the cleared land in a rather alarming manner, then one of them lay down with his eye at the level of the cleared ground, gave orders to the other two: it took Edward a little time to realise that they were levelling his floor. Then they cut stout branches and tamped at the earth: hitting it, flattening it, compacting it, then sprinkling water on it, until a hard base settled.

'Thank you,' said Edward humbly, and understood from them that he must put his tarpaulin over the floor until the house was built above it, that the now firm, level floor must not get wet. Still they had not finished: they looked at the hills behind and dug ditches beside the floor; again Edward understood: they were making him *drains*. They caught a fat bird with a strange snare net, and cooked it on a fire, sharing it with Edward and eating some of his bread. Unasked they nailed the wooden roof tiles together. After several days, in their own time, leaving Edward surrounded by his boxes and his timber and his horse and giving many assurances of friendship, the natives left: so, Edward found later, had many of his precious nails and horseshoes and his best hat.

When darkness fell that night Edward had no idea where the nearest other human being might be and felt the silence of a loneliness he had never known.

In twenty-seven days Edward Cooper, working from first light till darkness, had built himself a rough shack not unlike the one he had practised on at Rusholme, only bigger.

On the sixteenth day when his precarious tarpaulin that was substituting as a roof was taken off in a gale and his beautiful firm floor got wet, he allowed himself, thousands of miles from his loved ones, the luxury of a few angry, disappointed, self-pitying, exhausted swallows of emotion – but understood that an English gentleman never gave way to foolish thoughts and tamped the earth down again, as the natives had done. On the nineteenth day a small party came past in a horse and buggy and he found he had, only an hour away on horseback, neighbours. A whole family who had been here almost a year, with daughters aged fifteen, seventeen and eighteen. To Edward the sight of other human beings – and, what is more, sun-kissed young ladies in pretty gowns and bonnets approaching him smiling and saying he must visit them on Sunday – was more thrilling than had been any other social occasion of his life.

He washed himself all over in his spring for his first social call: he visited the McClellans, the neighbours, for Sunday dinner in the house they had built further round the coast, a house that had perhaps started, once, like his. There was a small community near the McClellans where the land was slightly flatter: some settlers had built houses, found enough flat land to plant crops; sheep grazed above. He saw abandoned dreams also – bush growing back over half-cleared land, signs of a struggle that had been lost.

Mr McClellan said grace and Edward found himself absurdly moved; when Mrs McClellan herself poured hot gravy over his roast mutton he swallowed several times, feeling himself in danger of choking with emotion. The McClellan girls smiled at Edward and cleared the polished mahogany table that had come with them from Scotland; Edward and Mr McClellan sat on the wooden verandah and smoked their pipes. Mr McClellan told Edward of his own bitter disappointments but also of his success with fruit trees and vegetables, how the work was hard but some things could grow on the hillside (though perhaps not Edward's hillside). However, he gave Edward plants and seedlings and instructions. He advised Edward to hire labour. He spoke of the land problems everywhere, of the recalcitrance of the natives, of England's less-than-enthusiastic support for the settlers' arguments with the Maoris. Mrs McClellan served tea. There was no piano but the three daughters sang, very slightly out of tune but with great enthusiasm. Edward could not help seeing that the hands which they held before them as they sang were rough and chapped.

> When other lips and other hearts (*they sang*)
> Their tales of love shall tell
> In language whose excess imparts
> The pow'r they feel so well,
> There may perhaps in such a scene,
> Some recollection be,
> Of days that have as happy been,
> And you'll remember me . . .

Edward applauded most keenly. 'By Jove,' he said, 'you take me back to my own sisters singing in my father's house. I am so very, very happy to be here.'

He reluctantly saddled up his horse just after the autumn sun set on the horizon. Down the hill and along the coast where his route lay the sea was still and he rode under the stars with his lantern, hearing only the sound of the sea and the steady rhythm of his horse's footsteps. He felt peculiarly unsettled. The rustle of gowns so far from home had affected him greatly, the chapped hands also; he tossed and turned on his bed in his half-finished house. Occasionally a night bird called out in the darkness; perhaps Edward called out too.

Early next morning he began building again.

He became, at last, inordinately proud of his rough dwelling. It was just one room and the walls were logs, but they were good stout dry logs lined inside with timber planks and firmly put together; sometimes he would stand outside and run his hands over the logs with almost sensual pleasure. The roof tiles that the natives had nailed together fitted over the walls, more or less. He covered the hardened earth floor with rugs that his mother and sisters had packed, shaking his head as their shocked faces appeared to him. He planned to make a timber floor in time; in the meantime this was curiously satisfactory and curiously clean. The table and the bed from Kent were firm on the level floor and outside, beside the fresh cans of water from his spring, his fire was neat, and safe, surrounded by big stones he had carried upwards from the beach. It was not a house such as his family would expect to come to (he could imagine Augusta's horrified face) but it was a start: one day perhaps (he dreamed) a big house could stand here in the sunshine close to the sea, and the hills would rise softly (covered in fruit trees of every variety), and wheat too would somehow miraculously grow on the hillside and wave gently in soft breezes. The McClellans had done it: he could do it too. His shack would become an outhouse or a stable of course and he would laugh at his youthful efforts. And yet he wondered as he stroked the logs again if anything would give him as much pleasure as this original building, built with his heart.

When on the twenty-seventh day Edward's odd little house was finished, and huge stacks of firewood were piled up by the door and all his trunks and boxes were safely under cover, he lovingly unpacked the painting of his sisters and hung it on one of his planked walls, moving it slightly over and over again, until it hung almost straight. Augusta and Alice and Asobel smiled at him, like angels. Asobel's doll, Lizzie, he sat on the end of the table. Outside the wind blew across the harbour.

And then he opened the bottle of whisky his father had given him and, all alone in his little house, toasted his future. He found himself addressing Lizzie, more than once.

On that twenty-seventh day he was cheerful enough after several glasses and toasts to hammer a small sign into the ground. It said WELCOME TO RUSHOLME SOUTH.

It rained and the ground became softer; he worked even harder, trying to clear more land around the spring, cutting into the hillside; back-breaking work that made him cry aloud in frustration. Sometimes the wind was so strong it would whip the tree branches across his face and bend the low fern and bush to the north as if to say: *get away from here*. Then the wind would die and the bright clear sky would cheer him again. He knew he needed at the very least ploughs and huge saws and the help of others. But the land – in his heart he knew this – was the *wrong kind of land for farming*: it was not land for anything but reaching upwards to the sky declaring that man came and went, and the land did not. Still he worked on, morning till night. The trees mocked him with their strange foreign names the natives had told: *rimu, kahikatea, hinau*. He slashed at them with his knife. Sometimes he talked to himself, sometimes he sang: hymns, popular songs, thought of his sisters sitting in their pretty dresses in the drawing room singing 'Then You'll Remember Me'. Perhaps by now Augusta had found a suitor and was happier. He felt a pang in his heart as he thought of his father: how much he missed his wise advice. And smiled to remember the constant chattering of his youngest sister Asobel whom he loved so dearly. Often his thoughts would turn to his cousin Mary, how he wished he could see her dear, loving face, take her wise advice also: to no other woman had he spoken so freely of what was in his mind; he hoped he would find letters from her in the first mail. Their faces, all the faces of his loved ones, crowded into his mind as he struck and pounded at the terrible, stubborn land. This was worse than building a house because he could see so little for his labours. Five square feet of cleared land was a Herculean task: there were a hundred acres. Even though he knew it was almost hopeless he desperately wanted to plant just a little token of his wheat before winter came, to see if it would grow in this alien, rising ground. As he planted the wheat he remembered how his father and his brother had helped him to pack the precious seed, thousands of miles away, and his heart ached to think of his naïve enthusiasm for his new life. He planted the fruit trees and the vegetables that Mr McClellan had given him but the ground had set hard again and several times he almost gave up. His hands grew tougher, his back ached and he fell instantly asleep each night to the sound of night owls and crickets, calling in the trees.

And then he dreamed and often his dreams were nightmares: all the different ferns and bushes and brackens and wild native trees were one big green tentacled monster, bent on his destruction.

Mr McClellan rode over to tell Edward that a small schooner had brought some sheep and chickens across and would be going back to the town in the morning. Edward was relieved: the boat could do the journey in a few hours. He needed to buy supplies, and also needed to satisfy a deep desire to go to a real church on a Sunday and hear hymns sung. He needed to go to a barber. He needed to talk to other settlers. He needed to consider if he was being foolish staying on his harsh land and, if he was to stay, he needed to hire men to help him. He needed to find out if he could sell the timber from his hills anywhere. He needed to consider whether even the farming of sheep would be possible on his high, tree-covered land. He needed to buy a dog, to feel that he was not so totally alone.

And most of all he needed to search – just in case a ship had arrived – for mail from home.

Wellington was awash with gossip: Edward walked along the paths and the streets slowly, glad of the company of fellow settlers, greeting several people he knew, being introduced to others. It was a sunny afternoon: the weather was warm enough for ladies to be walking in cotton gowns, holding parasols, wearing gloves; the sight gladdened Edward's lonely heart. As usual the main topic of conversation among settlers was land: complaints about the New Zealand Company; rumours about more trouble with Maoris and new rumours that the British government had decided that the New Zealand Company should be wound up. There was talk of the British government being too soft on the natives, there was talk of self-government for the new colony: *no-one but us here understands the problems; we should be in charge.* He was warned once again always to keep his gun near him. He heard news that a ship had arrived from England and mail was at the Post Office, he determined he must not be disappointed if there was nothing for him. He heard much satisfaction that all sorts of goods had arrived from Home: Souchong Anjou tea, turpentine, shot, parasols, tar, violin strings, brandy, corsets. He heard salacious stories of the behaviour of one of the ladies of the town; he heard intrigue concerning settlers who had 'lowered their standards'.

Edward drank in all the signs of civilisation and just walked about the streets, immensely glad to be among people. He was surprised yet again at how Wellington – despite the Maori villages situated at each end of the harbour – was already an English town with all the accoutrements of such a place: houses, shops, offices, banks. He saw a notice in a window:

ASSORTMENT OF HAIR JUST RECEIVED:
ORDERS TAKEN FOR WIGS, RINGLETS,
FRONTS AND PLAITS.

He passed the office of the *Wellington Independent*; saw several advertisements for a theatrical evening. He passed churches and shops and boys flying kites on a village green for all the world as if they were at home in England. A few soldiers from the barracks walked leisurely past: rumours about recalcitrant natives were probably grossly exaggerated: there had been war round Wellington but the war was clearly over. The soldiers widened roads and gave concerts on Wednesdays in their splendid red jackets.

Some of the larger houses on the hill behind the harbour would have been quite at home in England except that they were built of wood because of earthquakes: from one the sound of a piano wafted out into the colonial afternoon; he thought he caught a few bars, *I dreamt that I dwelt in marble halls with vassals and serfs at my side*, slowed to listen to the remembered music. He walked past rows of small neat houses (wryly thinking of his shack), down again to the main street along the harbour. Here there were more neat houses, and other slightly more imposing buildings. In the Mechanics Institute a notice offered lectures:

PHRENOLOGY
ASTRONOMY,
TERRESTRIAL MAGNETISM,
ZOOLOGY

and then right at the bottom of the list in smaller writing, as if added as an afterthought, someone had written: *and the Immortality of the Soul*.

Slowly he walked past warehouses and stores and hotels. The

autumn dusk was falling now. Out in the harbour sailing barques stood at anchor among the schooners and the cutters: from Australia, from Africa, from England. Edward's heart beat at the thought that one of them might at last have brought news of his family.

He took a room at the hotel he knew and then, trying, as he had been all afternoon, to prepare himself for disappointment should there be no letters, he at last set out along the quay towards the Post Office. The hotels were getting fuller and louder, horses were tied at wooden fences; Edward saw with a mixture of embarrassment and excitement that here women offered invitations, that accordion music blared out from the seedier hotels and men spilled outside shouting: whalers in long boots, forestmen with axes; and all the time the girls called and laughed and offered paradise, and lights began to come on all along the quay. People were selling things along the foreshore, shouting and laughing and fighting; natives with meat and vegetables, stockmen with cows and sheep, stalls selling hats, hammers, honey. Carts rolled past, one piled high with furniture, one with big cans of fresh milk. Groups of people stood talking on corners, the men wearing top hats. Natives sat on the shore in groups, wrapped in brightly coloured blankets: one of them sported a top hat also. Along the beach the whale-boats and the native canoes had been pulled up on to the shore for the night. The sun was going down behind the Wellington hills, he saw his own breath like smoke in the darkening, frosty air.

And then he had a hallucination and feared for a moment that solitude and disappointment and nightmares of the wild tangled bush had turned his mind: he thought he saw walking towards him in the dusk his cousin Harriet Cooper, dressed in black.

TWENTY-EIGHT

So great was the shock to Edward: to see Harriet standing before him in Wellington town and then to hear almost at once of his beloved cousin Mary's death, that for some time he was simply unable to rise from the harbour wall where he had sat suddenly, stunned.

Finally, recollecting himself partly – but forgetting that he was to go to the barber, to bathe, to be presentable – he took Harriet to a small back parlour on the ground floor of his hotel where they could obtain tea in a cavalier sort of way, away from the shouts and the music. There he said over and over, incredulously, *on the day I sailed away?* Harriet told him of the events of that terrible night when Mary died of the cholera with lips turned blue, and, recounting for the first time to another person, lived it again, wept. People came in from the darkening streets, and although curious to see two young people so engaged were, in a disapproving way, used to this: news as well as people came sailing from thousands of miles away into the harbour, random, unpredictable. It was not considered polite, however, to show emotions, and the new arrival was carefully perused. Within fifteen minutes Harriet's antecedents were known and passed on: her sister had died, her father was a member of Queen Victoria's government.

At last Edward raised his head from his hands and looked at

Harriet, so pleased and yet so shocked to see her. He was still struggling to take in everything but other cogs in his mind began to turn.

'You came from England *alone*?' he said in a low, disbelieving voice.

Harriet nodded and he saw that she was proud; that some change of confidence had been wrought in her. He had forgotten how beautiful she was: he always took her for granted because she was his cousin, but he saw that there was something else now in her face, some new strength, some loss of softness. He was not certain that it suited her.

'How did you persuade Sir Charles to allow you to do that, to travel alone?' Still he could not take it in. 'I simply cannot imagine him agreeing, especially after Mary's death. I cannot see how you persuaded him – I know how fond he is of you.'

Harriet had known that the question would come. She had rehearsed answers. But finally knew she could not speak of her father even to Edward, her dearest cousin: *even had she wanted to she did not have the words.*

'I did not want to stay in Bryanston Square without Mary,' she said carefully in the small parlour of the wooden hotel in the lamplight, holding her teacup delicately, sitting very straight. And she smiled at Edward through her tears, but her cousin saw a mask come down.

'But Harriet—' Edward tried again but they were interrupted.

'Miss Cooper! Miss Cooper!' Mr and Mrs Burlington Brown and Miss Eunice Burlington Brown, learning that their erstwhile ward was sitting alone with a man in a public place and weeping, bustled into the public place disapprovingly, requiring introductions immediately. If Miss Eunice Burlington Brown was in any way disappointed in Mr Edward Cooper who had a round face and a rather straggling beard and callused hands (not quite the picture of the gentleman farmer she had been led, she felt, to expect), she nevertheless gave no sign. After the introductions were effected, Edward made shamefacedly for the barber's shop, in vain Harriet protested that she wished to accompany him. It was arranged by the Burlington Browns that Edward and Harriet (together with the Burlington Browns) would meet at church the next day, Sunday. Harriet was escorted back to the Gentlewomen's Private Hotel.

Despite his physical exhaustion Edward lay awake in his small hotel almost all of the night: reading over and over again his treasured letters from England written just after he had departed and telling of the terrible death; puzzling over the enigma of Harriet's sudden appearance; but most of all remembering his dearly beloved cousin Mary. Her face seemed to hover beside him in the small room as if she wanted to speak to him: *why does nobody do anything about the cholera?* she had cried, that afternoon in Bryanston Square; his beloved cousin, Mary Cooper, whom he had known always: limping and stoic and wise. His father's dear, remembered handwriting lay on the table beside the bed. Men's drunken voices floated up to his room, and occasionally the laugh of a woman. Grief and shock and loss and distance tugged at Edward's heart. Finally he turned his face into his pillow and for the first time since he was a boy at school, wept.

The next day, Sunday, they all met at the new Anglican church. The Wellington winds had got up at dawn: nevertheless ladies in hats sat at the front of the church: the hats would not have disgraced St Paul's Church, Covent Garden (or indeed St Paul's Cathedral, Blackfriars). Several of the ladies in hats addressed the Burlington Browns and Harriet graciously. A dignified native with a strange, marked face came in halfway through the service, sat at the back, upright as a pillar. Wind blew in under the door and along the aisle, they heard it rattling at the windows and through the pipes of the small organ, sounding an eerie half-note when none had been played. The minister spoke of the new and exciting and difficult life that affected them all, while Miss Eunice Burlington Brown eyed the recently shaven and bathed Edward Cooper with new enthusiasm. The minister's voice rose and thundered as he instructed that they must not give in to loneliness (loneliness being impossible when God was nigh); nor lawlessness (and he gave an eloquent flash of the eyes to the streets outside). And they must never, he reminded them (his voice reaching a climax), most especially in a new land, forget the teachings of their Lord Jesus Christ. They all lifted their voices to God:

> Praise, my soul, the King of Heaven
> To His feet thy tribute bring

and Edward with his head bowed prayed for Mary's soul, and for her life everlasting.

Praise him, praise him
Praise him, praise him

sang the congregation. Edward, singing, hoped he might arrange some time alone with his cousin, to somehow understand how she had suddenly appeared, like a dark angel.

Outside the church Harriet caught sight of Hetty Green, the girl who had broken her arm on board the *Amaryllis*. Her arm was tied in a sling made of a skirt, she looked pale and depressed and would have passed by had Harriet not prevented her.

'Hetty!'

Reluctantly Hetty stopped by the group of ladies and gentlemen, eyeing the Burlington Browns with less than enthusiasm.

'Hello, Miss Harriet.'

'Has your arm not healed?'

'No,' said Hetty shortly, 'it is worse than before. It hurts and it ain't healing.' Harriet explained to Edward about the storm. She (and Miss Eunice Burlington Brown) could not help but see Edward looking at the girl and the arm in the sling with interest.

'Forgive me,' said Edward to Hetty, 'I cannot help but notice. Your arm needs to be re-set, it has not knitted properly. Look how the bone protrudes oddly, and it should not move this way.' Hetty cried out instinctively as he touched the arm, then bit her lip and moved away from him.

'Shall you be able to work?' asked Harriet.

'All the girls have got work, they're queuing for us. But who would employ me?' said Hetty.

'But what will you do?'

'I dunno what will happen.' Hetty shrugged and turned away.

'Mr Cooper,' said Miss Eunice Burlington Brown prettily, 'we would very, *very* much like you to take tea with us and tell us about your farm. We have heard so much of you from your cousin Harriet on the journey out.'

'Indeed,' boomed her brother. A gentleman farmer would be a good catch and take his sister off his hands at last.

'I am afraid,' said Edward rather gloomily, 'that there is not much to tell. The land I have obtained from the New Zealand Company leaves a great deal to be desired. The contrast between the description of the land I was given in London and the land itself does, I am afraid, call into question the integrity of the Company.'

Harriet who had as yet heard none of Edward's news looked shocked, remembered Mary's cautionary words; Mr Burlington Brown looked shocked for different reasons.

'But I am intimately acquainted with several of the Directors. They are most honourable men, I can vouch for that.'

'Perhaps then they have not yet visited New Zealand,' said Edward politely, 'and know nothing of that which they speak of, in London, so engagingly.'

Mr Burlington Brown looked at Edward sharply. Was Mr Cooper being vaguely impolite? He did not want his sister involved with somebody vaguely impolite. However, he took his sister's wishes into consideration and ushered his little party to the Mechanics Institute where tea, he knew, was being served to new settlers. Edward again saw the offer of lectures in PHRENOLOGY and TERRESTRIAL MAGNETISM.

As soon as they were settled Harriet turned to her cousin. 'It took me longer than I'd hoped to find you, Eddie, they told me you had gone north with your friends. Now I should like to visit your farm. I should like to go back with you.'

Mr and Mrs Burlington Brown bristled with disapproval. 'You cannot just take off into the New Zealand wilds,' they said to Harriet. 'What would your father say?' Then they turned to Edward. 'What servants do you have?' they asked. 'What travelling arrangements?'

'I am afraid,' said Edward, 'that there is only me. My companions have gone north, I am still deciding what plans my future will take. My land is over a day's trek from Wellington, or some hours by boat. I have built myself a small one-roomed house on my land: that is all.'

'A house!' said Harriet joyfully. 'You did it, as you said you would.'

'Well then of course it is impossible.' Mr Burlington Brown spoke decisively. 'Harriet cannot go and visit you, it would not be proper.'

'I think you will perhaps find when you have been here just a little longer that what constitutes things being proper is of necessity a little different here,' began Edward mildly but Mr Burlington Brown interrupted him.

'Mr Cooper, I have been here for some days and I have visited India and I think I can say that I understand very clearly what needs to be done in a colonial settlement of this kind. I am not just here on behalf of the Starlight Gas Company. People like my wife and myself are here to make sure that what is proper at home is also proper here, that standards are maintained at all times. I am sure you will agree that it is quite out of the question for your cousin to visit you anywhere without a chaperone of some kind, particularly in a one-roomed house.'

Somehow the picture of a chaperone in his one-roomed shack made Edward laugh and just as he did so Harriet said: 'I intend to take Hetty Green with me as my maid,' and at exactly the same moment Miss Eunice Burlington Brown said, 'I, of course, will chaperone Harriet. It is right that she would want to see her cousin's farm, her father would expect it of her.'

Thus it was that somehow (he still wasn't quite sure how) a bemused Edward Cooper who had been so alone, who had longed one night for the rustle of petticoats, was to be visited by three rustling-skirted ladies at once. In vain he tried to explain the difficulties they would face: Miss Eunice and Harriet packed small valises with enthusiasm. (Harriet, alight with excitement, informed a storage house that she would collect her meagre furniture very soon.) Hetty Green's belongings were in a small bundle. Edward bought a cow for twelve guineas, an expensive but necessary addition to his belongings; and six hens, and a dog as he had planned, but finally decided he would leave his decisions about sheep-farming or labour-hiring or timber-selling for his next town visit. He was sure the ladies would not stay long.

As they prepared to leave the town, intelligence from the natives spread around Wellington that the new, fast sailing ship the *Seagull*, sailed from the coast of Africa and carrying incense and myrrh (the natives got much of their information from the Bible), was not far out at sea. Edward paused, undecided, but then judged that it might take days or even weeks for the vessel to drop anchor in

Wellington harbour and that a cargo ship from Africa was not likely to have more mail from England; Harriet encouraged him to leave at once, herself wanting no news at all. Nobody knew that the cargo ship had a special consignment: some of the shipwrecked passengers of the *Cloudlight* who had been picked up from Tristan da Cunha. And nobody in the small colonial town knew yet that the *Lord Fyne* had been buffeted in a storm on to the Tasmanian Coast and had yet again had to undergo repairs. Now the *Lord Fyne* was crossing the Tasman Sea also; could almost see the long low New Zealand coastline that the natives when they first saw it in the distance had named the land of the long white cloud. Sir Charles Cooper stood on deck straining his eyes, as if his daughter might be standing, miraculously, at the jetty, waiting for her father. And Peters lay still vomiting below, having been terrified almost to death by the journey, planning revenge on Miss Harriet Cooper who had brought him to this.

None of Edward's lady visitors wanted to get on another boat of any description; in vain Edward told them it would only take hours rather than days; the winds had not subsided and his guests were adamant: they wanted to see something of the environs, not toss about on a small boat. He found that they, including the cow, could ride in a miller's cart round the harbour as far as the river.

'But we will still need another horse,' said Edward. Harriet accompanied him, greatly interested, as he walked to the end of the foreshore into a Maori village where for some time he exchanged pleasantries with several natives, some discussion about a floor ensuing. 'They helped me take my belongings round the road and start my house,' he explained to his cousin. And then, bargaining and with some laughter, he acquired a brown mare with dark liquid eyes which gazed at Harriet in her mourning clothes with much the same interest as the natives did. The Maoris did not have a saddle for sale; they walked back, Edward leading the mare, to a store on the waterfront. He insisted on hiring a lady's side-saddle: 'I can ride without a saddle if needs be,' he said, 'but I cannot imagine Mr Burlington Brown agreeing to your journey under any circumstances if we do not have the correct saddle for young ladies! And I can easily sell the horse again, next time I come to town.'

Mr and Mrs Burlington Brown waved them off in the miller's

cart with the greatest disapproval; only the prospect of getting their sister married prevented them from withholding their permission (though it was given much against their better judgement) for this ludicrous journey.

They travelled on the coast road around the harbour. After reaching the river in the cart they embarked on the difficult journey into the wild bush tracks and along the coast with less complaint than Edward had anticipated: Harriet with a sense of joy and adventure and freedom, Miss Eunice with absolute steely determination and carrying a rubber mattress, and Hetty Green with extreme stoicism, in great pain, grateful that somebody was paying her wages. Harriet rejoiced in riding again. Miss Eunice sat respectably side-saddled and upright when it was her turn but often had to dismount to disappear mysteriously into the bushes. Hetty Green had never ridden a horse in her life but the horse could not do much more than walk through the tortuous paths and the trees and pain made her brave; she sat holding on for grim death with one arm, her face as white as chalk, and said not a word. Sometimes as they travelled Harriet and Edward had some privacy to talk further. She gave him a brief account of her leaving; to Edward it was clear although she did not say it in so many words: she had done a thing unheard of amongst the people that they knew – *she had run away.* Edward was much more shocked than Harriet had anticipated. They travelled on, Edward hoped for enlightenment. But Harriet did not elaborate, stared at the dark green bush-covered hills in amazement, washed her face in the river where they slept the night under trees – as if sleeping under tarpaulin and disappearing quietly into the bush if she needed to were matters she had been trained for. Miss Eunice did her best also, determined not to complain, but her face was extremely pale and it was clear – not of course that anyone would have dreamt of mentioning the subject – that she was having some trouble with her bowels and that the beauty of the green hills was not a consolation. Hetty Green lay on the bush mattress Edward had made. She did not sleep, tried not to cry out with the pain of her arm, stared at the hills with wild eyes, wondering if she was to die in a foreign land.

It was almost dusk next day when they finally arrived at Rusholme South. There was only time before night fell for Edward to show them his house, and the spring of fresh water up on the hillside. Miss Eunice and Hetty nodded politely at Edward's building skills but Harriet looked with joy at the name of the house and the painting of her cousins hanging on the wall.

'And here is Lizzie!' she said, holding Asobel's battered doll. 'Oh Eddie, if we could just *see* them,' and in a gesture most unlike her she instinctively hugged her cousin.

Edward gave a sudden huge sigh of nostalgia and relief and patted Harriet's arm; what a difference it made that she stood here and understood what Rusholme South stood for without any explanation. And his mind filled with somewhat incoherent thoughts about families and family ties. But he remained anxious. All the time they had travelled he had waited for her to say something more about her journey, about her father. But she did not.

The first discovery they all made was that, as well as Edward, none of the women could actually cook.

It was a great blow to them all. Hetty was particularly mortified: the specific duties of a lady's maid had been made clear to her in England by a cousin who worked for a lady in Richmond: sewing, washing, hairbrushing, carrying, cleaning. But cooking was not one of the skills required, cooks and housemaids did the cooking.

'I think it is going to be rather different in New Zealand,' said Edward dryly.

'I thought you might be able to advise me, Hetty,' said Harriet dubiously, looking at a big parcel of raw meat unloaded from the pack bags on the horse.

'I'm really sorry, Miss Harriet, but I ain't a cook,' wailed Hetty again, clutching her broken arm. 'I was only in the glue factory, Mum done the cooking when she got in from the early shift. But I'll teach myself as soon as my arm gets better, see if I won't!'

'But I've never been in a kitchen,' said Harriet, 'how do I start?' (*And was jolted by a memory of a dark night, looking for a knife. She had been in a kitchen.*) She would have killed herself with that knife if she hadn't escaped. How far away that terror seemed.

'We didn't *have* no kitchen!' said Hetty. 'We lived in a room, eight of us, that's why I came! Mind you, Mr Edward, it was a little bit bigger than this room,' but she said it kindly and despite the pain she was in she grinned at him and Harriet saw something of her old spirit aboard the *Amaryllis* before she broke her arm, and suddenly Hetty's words came back to her, *don't you miss it? ain't you ever done it?* and for some reason Harriet felt her cheeks reddening at the memory.

'And you've got fresh water,' said Hetty. 'Think of water coming out of the ground so clean and all I ever seen was standpipes! I feel like rushing right in it, clothes and all. I think, Mr Edward, that that water up there's one of the most beautiful things I ever seen.'

Miss Eunice had so far remained silent, her bowels still troubling her. The sight of the raw meat did not help. But she wanted to add to the discussion so she offered: 'Perhaps there are recipe books we could obtain, Mr Cooper? My brother of course had servants but I did help in the kitchen, giving orders and ordering stores and such-like, and I feel that, when perhaps I am a little rested, I will very willingly share anything I know that would be of assistance.' She spoke so tremulously, so obviously unwell, yet so anxious to please, that Harriet's heart was touched and she forgave Miss Eunice a hundred crassnesses aboard the *Amaryllis*.

'I have just been putting everything in this,' said Edward, pointing rather shamefacedly to a pot by the fire. Something mouldy stared out of its depths and although Harriet looked at it in distaste she could not hide her smile as she realised their predicament: her cousin Edward, bemusedly surrounded by women untrained in basic domestic skills, and the small, rough room and all of them exhausted from their journey. The light had faded and there was the sound of the sea, shshshing over the sand below them. The new dog barked outside, chasing something up the hill, and strange insects trilled in the trees.

'We can make tea,' said Harriet. 'And we can light the candles and there is bread. Tomorrow we will try to think of cooking. Edward, I believe I see that you are to be temporarily removed from your new house!' Edward himself smiled at last.

'I am a champion in a tent,' he said.

'Miss Eunice must have the bed tonight,' said Harriet. 'And Hetty could sleep on the rubber mattress. And I will make a mattress from the bracken as you taught me, Eddie, and sleep on a rug on the floor.' Nobody argued, Edward himself made the tea, he and Harriet tore at the big loaf of bread, Miss Eunice had a small dry crust, but Hetty, now both pale and flushed, could not eat at all. In half an hour Miss Eunice wished to retire and Hetty asked to lie down also.

Edward and Harriet sat quietly at last outside the little house beside the fire, both wrapped in blankets that Harriet recognised from Rusholme, tin mugs of tea on the ground beside them. The night was calm, the moon shone down on the quiet, black sea. Occasionally one of the horses snorted. Edward asked if he might smoke his pipe. The new dog sat between them, looking slightly lost, and for just a moment Harriet thought of Quintus, her dear dog Quintus, in another, different life.

'That young girl is not at all well,' said Edward. 'Her arm has not knitted properly after all that time, I can see the bone move. She is very lucky it has not become poisoned, she could have lost the arm, or even died.'

'What can we do?'

'I could try to straighten it, set it again properly.'

'You are not a doctor!'

'I am a farmer! But – she looks like a strong girl.' And Edward stared with an unreadable expression into the darkness and they said nothing more about Hetty Green.

'It's lovely here, Edward. It's beautiful.'

'But not for a farmer,' he said gloomily and his cousin remained silent: she had seen it was not a farm.

'Harriet.'

She saw his earnest, anxious face in the firelight, got up at once to wash the mugs in the water that was warm from the fire.

'But Harriet, we must talk about this.' And Edward gave a small inward sigh. He was a practical person, and a kind person, and he did not relish the role that was being forced upon him, but he was Harriet's only relative here, and he was a man, and he must look after her, he must take a firm stand. 'I have been thinking about your situation. Have you considered that the next ship might even bring your father here?'

She was caught in the light of the fire as she stood there; the look on her face as she stared back at him was one of such shock that he saw that *she had not considered any such thing*.

'But Harriet, *of course* he will try to find you. Surely you realise that? Whatever did you think would happen? He would have looked for you. He would soon have found out what had become of you, surely, a man with his contacts and influence! And then at the very least he will send messages to the New Zealand Company, they will easily find me, looking for you, and you will be sent back to England. Did you not see everybody take in your arrival? In a small settlement like this everybody soon knows everybody else. And as you have heard, standards must be maintained, even your conduct on the journey out will, I assure you, have been already discussed by people you have not yet had the pleasure of meeting, and certainly they will know you have come here to visit my land across the harbour. Should your father have decided to make the journey himself, I expect it would take him, with his particular contacts, fifteen minutes from stepping ashore to ascertain your whereabouts. Surely you must have realised that!' He saw that Harriet had not, she stood as if carved from stone, still holding the mugs and staring at him in horror.

'But, Harriet, whatever did you think would happen? That your father would just forget about you? What would my own father do if Augusta or Alice – or more likely Asobel,' and he permitted himself a small smile, 'had for some unthinkable reason done what you had done? My father would go to the ends of the earth to find them again, because he loves them and is responsible for them, and because it would be his duty to do so.' Still Harriet said nothing.

'And dearest Harriet, just at this moment I have to be responsible for you. As I would be for my sisters if they were here. It is my duty to be so. I cannot tell you how good it is to actually see you here, sitting in front of me – it's almost like a dream, you and I sitting here in front of this fire so far from home. It would be wonderful if you were here *safely*, by that I suppose I mean perhaps with your father rather than without him. But—' and Edward sighed (perhaps he was glad that he was not a young woman to whom these things must be said), 'I think the freedom of your long journey on the ship has turned your mind. You are not thinking clearly. The journey on the ship is just a hiatus, nothing more: when I was sailing here I often thought of that. Such a long journey is something like a pause in one's life and everything hangs in abeyance. But journeys end, and you have to pick up the threads of your life again eventually, you cannot sail on and on forever like the Flying Dutchman! Your father is your legal guardian and what you have done you seem to have done without his permission. Wellington may be thousands and thousands of miles away and seem nothing but a frontier town but we live here under English law, we have a governor and courts and magistrates, and I imagine one of the very next ships will bring your father's instructions.' (*Harriet saw in her mind Peters, her father's servant, shadowy in the darkness at the door of Mary's room; felt suddenly something she thought she had forgotten: the suffocating silence of the house in Bryanston Square and her own terror as she listened for footsteps.*)

She stood up quickly. 'I will just walk down to the sea and back,' she said, 'the moon is as bright as a lantern.' Edward listened to her footsteps, heard her boots crunching on the pebbles and then there was silence. He stood and stared down into the darkness below, then saw her dark figure, ghostly by the sea, quite still. He thought of how she'd struck him when he first saw her: a dark angel. He watched her carefully, puffing on his pipe, the dog alert now, beside him. An owl, or perhaps a strange native bird, called somewhere nearby. It was not so long ago that his cousins and his sisters had screamed at the sight of a fieldmouse: here Harriet could be confronted by a huge rat in the dark, or a wild pig, or one of the mad Maori hunting dogs that they'd heard lurked in the bush. He had not yet had time to warn her of these things, or to tell her that he always kept his gun near, to tell her that there were rumours about disaffected natives coming back to claim their land they said they had not sold: land that they said had been stolen.

At last Harriet came back: Edward made it clear that she must sit down again and Harriet, slowly, obeyed him. Edward spoke again.

'What did you think, Harriet – just suppose you had your father's permission and assistance – that you would do in New Zealand?' By the firelight her face seemed even paler than he ever remembered it and there was something in her eyes he could not fathom.

'At least at first, I thought I could help you.'

'You can see that I am in trouble here. And even should I stay and employ men to help me, it is a man's work that is needed, you surely understand that.'

'I am strong.'

'You are a woman. And you can see the situation, I can hardly help myself. And winter is coming. Ah – I remember how hopeful and confident I was, reading the books at Rusholme. I am afraid the reality is a little different.'

'But, Eddie.' Harriet's beautiful face, all shadows, showed great astonishment. 'It is beautiful! It is free! It is a new chance!'

Her cousin gave her a very old-fashioned look. 'It is not free, Harriet, believe me. All my money is tied up in this useless, beautiful, unfarmable land.'

'I have money, Edward. You can have it. I shall give it all to you, I don't know how to manage it anyway. And I could at least be your housekeeper.' Both the cousins involuntarily looked at the tin mugs that had held the tea Edward had been forced to make for them and both of them, just as involuntarily, even in the middle of the serious conversation, laughed.

'Well, I can learn, Eddie,' said Harriet, still smiling slightly, moving closer to the fire. 'I *will* learn. There are books about cooking, I know there are. Mary always told me she and our mother had for years a book called "New Systems of Domestic Cookery Formed Upon Principles of Economy and Adapted For the Use of Private Families", but try as we would in all the bookcases we could never find it. I've never forgotten the title because it made us laugh. Now Mary should see me being punished for my frivolity! But I will find such a book. I will be glad to learn to cook. It will make me feel useful. Also, I would like to teach young children, I enjoyed teaching Asobel.'

But Edward's face became serious and he shook his head. 'And your father I remember would not even consent to you teaching *her*.' He had to look away for a moment from the intensity of his cousin's expression. 'Harriet, dear Harriet, just suppose you may stay. You must be realistic about the life here. There are many what they call Distressed Gentlewomen in Wellington. There is nothing so sad, truly. I think—' and he lowered his voice, 'forgive me, Harriet, but if I am not mistaken your friend Miss Eunice Burlington Brown seems to be one of those women. They do not have money of their own and were trained for nothing in England except to hope to be wives of gentlemen and that is why many of them came here, I believe, hoping to find a husband – for there are twice as many men as women here. But those unattached men are mostly men like me who simply cannot yet think of the luxury of a wife unless we are prepared to marry below our station – and indeed I have heard that some men have done so and damned the social consequences. They have chosen as a bride someone who can work, rather than someone who cannot and who would expect to have servants as they would at home. So there are dozens of so-called governesses, or music teachers, hoping for the kind of marriage they were reared to in England, in the meantime advertising for work in a discreet and respectable manner, thinking that they can teach young girls to be "ladies". Their position is sad enough in England, but it is clear that girls here are going to have to learn much more practical things than just being ladies. To cook, for a start.' Regarding his cousin carefully Edward saw that her eyes glittered: it could have been unshed tears, or it could have been anger that made them shine.

'I am not a distressed gentlewoman. I have money, as I told you. And I am certainly not looking for a husband.'

'Not you, Harriet. I did not mean you.'

'But it is true I have been trained for *nothing*. Nothing at all. I will have to learn.' And she got up from the fire.

'Goodnight, dear Edward,' she said. 'I am so glad to have found you.'

Outside his house he heard her rustling and moving quietly. Edward sighed. He was, of course, responsible for her. They seemed not to have got very far, but at least they had spoken of her situation. Slowly he doused the fire and made his way to where the small tent and his bracken bed and his gun waited for him. The new dog curled up and sighed outside and at once they were both asleep.

Inside the house Hetty and Miss Eunice slept uneasily in their new surroundings: both of them made little restless noises of agitation; several times Hetty cried out in pain and then was quiet again. Both of them had removed their corsets which hung, ghostly shapes, over Edward's only chair, their laces touching the floor. Harriet realised, touched, that Miss Eunice must have helped the servant girl to undress. She added her own corset to the pile, then lay very still until she heard Edward settle inside his tent. It was cold now, she pulled her blanket tighter round her shoulders.

She had almost fallen asleep when Edward's unthinkable words suddenly shouted in her head, *he could be on the next ship*, and she sat bolt upright. Suddenly the little house seemed so full of hauntings and terror that she gasped aloud, buried her face in a cushion so that the others would not hear. It was so long since she had felt that terror: she had thought it was over but suddenly they were back, the old panic and the fear and the secret disgust that made the blood drain from her face, *ain't you done it, don't you miss it*, these things that she had thought, on board the *Amaryllis*, that she had defeated. Then the unpleasant vision of the soft-footed Peters flashed again into her mind, like a punishment and a warning: for it was Peters that her father would send. She could not imagine, could not conceive that Sir Charles Cooper would sail across the sea, *she simply could not think it*. She did not know how long she lay there, almost paralysed with panic and fear and the terrible loud beating of her heart: *I will have to go away from here; I must not be found; Peters must not find me, I will have to go away tomorrow*. And suddenly into her mind came the oak tree, the one oak tree in Bryanston Square. Some time towards morning, she slept.

Next morning they found clear cold blue skies and the sun coming up from behind the high hills. Edward had already gone up the hill with his axes and his dog: they could hear the echo of the axe falling against wood as they performed their ablutions; they could hear it still as the three of them contemplated again the raw meat. All three of them looked at their surroundings with some suspicion: in daylight it clearly was not a farm, and who knew what lurked in the bushes. Miss Eunice seemed much recovered but at a loss as to how to proceed; Hetty's face was haggard with pain but still she said: 'I think we should wash Mr Edward's biggest pan and put that meat stuff in and put water in it and put it on the fire. It will cook that way. That's how people cook. That's how me mum cooked potaters.' She tried to help to lift the big, dirty pot, her face twisted with pain. 'Oh God, I'm sorry, Miss Harriet, as soon as me arm recovers I'll do it all.'

Nobody had a better plan: Miss Eunice and Harriet between them, with much distaste but much determination, scrubbed at the pot. *I must go. I must go today.*

Hetty would have laughed at the gentlewomen working if she had not been in such pain; suddenly, they swam before her eyes as they filled the pot with bones and flesh of they knew not what animal and put it on to the fire that Edward had lit again when he woke. When Harriet looked round for further instructions from Hetty, Hetty had fainted. In alarm, they lifted her on to the bed, she cried out over and over again with pain but saying also, 'I'm sorry, Miss Harriet, I knocked it again when I tried to lift the pot, I'm sorry for this trouble.'

'Run for Edward,' Harriet instructed Miss Eunice, and then could not help smiling at the sight of the sober brown dress hurrying upwards with ungainly steps and falling often into the green bushes, calling, 'Mr Cooper! Mr Cooper!' She bathed Hetty's face, trying to calm her, told her, not meaning it unkindly, that Miss Eunice looked like a sprightly mountain goat.

'That Miss Eunice,' said Hetty weakly, tears of pain still running down her face, 'would turn herself into a sprightly mountain tiger python if anyone got in the way of her plans for Mr Edward.'

Harriet laughed. 'Mr Edward,' she said, 'is quite able to look after himself. He is a very stubborn man.'

Edward came back with Miss Eunice; they were both carrying water from the spring. Miss Eunice was carrying almost as much as Edward: once again Harriet felt her original opinion of the older woman alter. Edward looked at Hetty's face, rummaged in one of his boxes from England, came back to where she was lying on his bed. He was carrying his old school cricket bat, a child's cricket bat. Despite her protests he gently took her arm; it moved and crunched to his probing and Hetty gave a scream which she tried to contain.

'Hetty,' said Edward firmly, 'it will only get worse if we leave it. The arm absolutely must be re-set. I am so afraid it is poisoned inside. I know—' as she protested, 'I am not a doctor, but something must be done, otherwise we need to take you back to Wellington and I think the journey would be very difficult for you. It can only get worse if we leave it. I've done things like this on the farm if you will trust me.'

'I ain't a cow,' said Hetty faintly.

'We could use the cricket bat as a splint,' he continued. 'The arm must be pulled out and set correctly for you to be able to use it again. And then I could put the whole thing, your arm and the cricket bat, into a big sling in one of my shirts. And my father gave me his best whisky, look! That would help.'

Hetty looked at the cricket bat, at Edward, at the whisky. The other two women looked troubled at Edward's bizarre plan: neither of them thought it wise for Hetty to agree. The sun shone in through the door and they could hear birds, and the gentle sea below. Hetty made a sudden lunge for the whisky, gulped down enough to have made the strongest English gentleman buckle.

'Do it,' she said, 'quick!' and then screamed and screamed as Edward did: pulled it and heard a sound of bone, straightened it and tied it to the cricket bat, remembering how he'd saved his dog.

Harriet, staring at the sea, frightened that they may have damaged Hetty further, told herself she could not think about leaving until Hetty improved; she must take Hetty with her. Miss Eunice, taking her turn at bathing Hetty's face, thought she had never seen such a heroic man as Edward in her life and almost wished it was her own arm that had been broken. Edward looked very pale at his temerity and he stared at Hetty, seemed not to be able to take his eyes off her as she lay, so *unlikely*, on his bed. 'Perhaps I shouldn't have tried,' he said several times. 'We should have taken her back to Wellington.'

Then Hetty slept deeply at last, slept and slept and slept. Once she opened her eyes and said, 'I think I'm making up for all the sleep I never had, all me life at the glue factory,' and fell immediately asleep again. Later she opened her eyes again. 'I just worked out that my arm's been hurting for more than sixty-five days,' she said. And she smiled at Edward and fell asleep again.

More hopeful now, the others took turns to endeavour to eat some rather strange boiled mutton; it was not properly cooked, and yet they agreed some progress had been made, decided to put it back in the pan and cook it again for next day: they were tired now of stale bread, carrots and cheese.

'Throw the carrots in,' instructed Edward but his mind was elsewhere, he must have lost his sense of proportion to go round breaking pretty servant girls' arms.

On the evening of the second day Hetty suddenly sat up. 'It's not hurting the same,' she announced. 'I'm hungry.' The others looked at each other in delight and relief. Miss Eunice had ascertained that Edward had some rather good silver in one of his boxes and a damask tablecloth. She laid the tablecloth and then set the table from Kent with knives and forks that would not have disgraced Windsor Castle. They sat on boxes, and they all ate mutton stew and carrots. And although the water was fatty and the meat was now tough and overcooked and the carrots had turned to an orange scum, they pronounced themselves extremely satisfied in the circumstances.

'I owe you one, Mr Edward. I won't forget,' said Hetty and she laughed. And there was something about the way she said the words, and the way she laughed, that meant something else, that meant she was her own cheeky, charming self again. And because she had colour in her cheeks and was obviously going to get better Harriet and Edward laughed with Hetty in relief, and nobody noticed Miss Eunice's sudden, quick intake of breath.

Then the weather turned suddenly much colder, and a gale blew over from the town. The sea stirred up and then crashed not so far from them. Rain was coming: they could see it across the harbour. Edward at first thought of putting up some sort of curtain inside the shack, hanging it from his rafters to give the women privacy but himself at least some shelter. But he imagined the odd intimacy of noise: all the rustling skirts removed, Hetty's skirt removed, the women turning in their sleep, his own night sounds. So as the storm approached he tied more split logs together to make a rough lean-to against an outside wall of the shack, Harriet and Miss Eunice held the logs as he nailed them and bound them, with his tarpaulin as roof for some shelter that also covered the fireplace. Next time he was in town he would buy more wooden tiles for a permanent roof: there was a kind of satisfaction in his shack getting bigger. He cleared the slanting drains that the natives had laid for him. Hetty wandering about in the wind gave a scream: the cow was bellowing because she hadn't been milked and the hens had laid seven eggs underneath the cart.

The storm came, rain lashing the hillside. The human beings played chess and whist while the rain poured and the sea crashed on the shore just below them. The horses sheltered behind the lean-to as best they could, the dog lay miserably under the cart with the hens. The cow remained stoical at the front of the house while the inhabitants drank her milk. Edward and Harriet read and re-read the letters from Rusholme that had travelled with Harriet on the *Amaryllis*, telling of Mary, the death of Mary. Once Harriet went and stood outside and her tears and the rain mingled and she wondered to herself if anyone really recovered, from grief. Hetty wiped up with her good arm water that drifted under Edward's door and entertained them with stories of the glue factory; the little house was filled with her indignant laughter, the others could not believe her life had been so harsh.

'That's why I came,' she kept saying, 'and look at me now, living like a lady,' but she was careful to watch for the water all the time, and to sweep round the fire and fold up the blankets. It was Hetty too, who cheerfully with her good arm and with total lack of embarrassment emptied the contents of the chamber pots the ladies used in the night, into the bushes.

Miss Eunice read to them from the latest copy of *The New Zealand Spectator and Cook's Strait Guardian.*

> Queen Victoria went to the Annual Highland fete
> in September.

(It did strike Harriet that the news was so old that they had all been in Great Britain when this event occurred.)

> Her appearance was hailed by deafening cheers
> which the distant echoes caught and reverberated
> far up among the hills.
> Her Majesty looked exceedingly well though
> much exposure to the sun's influence had some-
> what embrowned her complexion.

'Oh look, Mr Cooper, thirty tons of salt has arrived in the harbour, and twenty barrels of cement and four bales of grey calico. Well. And gentlemen's white long cloth shirts, Mr Cooper, with Irish linen fronts and wrists.' Miss Eunice read to him as if she was his wife. And she sighed. 'I would give anything,' she said, 'for the *Illustrated London News.*'

As night fell they lit candles. Harriet and Edward allowed themselves sometimes to speak of Mary. Miss Eunice enquired whether Mary had been named after the blessed Virgin; Harriet explained that on the contrary she had been named after Mary Wollstonecraft of whom the others had not heard.

'She believed in the rights of women,' said Harriet.

A long silence followed her remark, Edward cleared his throat in embarrassment and Miss Eunice's lips were slightly pursed. Hetty looked uninterested. They heard the rain drumming on the roof, and in several places drips fell downwards into the house but Hetty, understanding that the earth floor must be kept dry, put tins underneath the drips and wiped the wet floor with rags, and with the newspapers when Miss Eunice had finished with them.

Then Hetty, working on the success of her first cooking idea, went and put the newly laid eggs in a pan of water on the partially covered fire; she came back rather wet and dried her hair with one hand while another game of whist was played by the others. She had never known that people lived like this, *playing cards all day long, as if life allowed that.*

Miss Eunice took little glances at Hetty, a servant drying her hair so casually in front of a gentleman, she could hardly believe her eyes. If she told her brother this he would not believe it either. Somehow although she was fully clothed, Hetty looked *undressed* in some odd way that Miss Eunice could not articulate in her mind. Something about the way, in the confines of the small room, she *moved*, even though one arm was tied to a cricket bat. Miss Eunice wondered if she could suggest that Hetty went back to Wellington town. She cheered herself with observing that Edward seemed sunk in his own thoughts; perhaps he was not noticing Hetty and her long wet hair. Eunice Burlington Brown had invented desperate little pictures of herself and men on the long journey from England on the *Amaryllis:* of Mr Aloysius Porter, of Mr Edward Cooper, seeing herself married, being someone's wife. But when Edward had mended Hetty's arm he had suddenly become real. For such a caring man she would carry water for the rest of her life: no man of her acquaintance would have done what Edward Cooper did, for a woman.

Edward was very quiet, well aware of Hetty with her hair half-dry. The storm only confirmed that the land was unusable. He did not discuss it with the women but he had gone up earlier to look at his newly planted fruit trees. They had been battered to the ground by the ferocity of the wind. He felt his shoulders sink. He would have to go. He had a sudden bleak vision of the native bush triumphantly growing over the house he had built. What had happened to his future? And of course there was the problem of Harriet. Edward was absolutely certain Sir Charles Cooper's powerful hand would soon stretch out, to this small bay round the coast from Wellington if necessary. He presumed that some official from the New Zealand Company would arrive any day now with letters and Harriet would be taken on board a boat bound for England. She would, of course, and this preyed heavily on his mind, have to tell his family of his failure.

Harriet was quiet also. The weather was her friend. Nobody could bring unwelcome messages in a storm. But as soon as the storm was over she would have to go, to find somewhere else to be safe. It meant, and she had never thought of this, never, that she could not stay with Edward. *It would take your father, with his contacts, fifteen minutes from stepping ashore to ascertain your whereabouts,* Edward had said. She did not know where to go.

Hetty's eggs burnt dry. She was mortified. But they were eaten with bread that had become very hard, and pronounced a moderate success. They ate some apples from Wellington. The rain came further under the door and pounded on the roof tiles but the wind did not blow the roof away. Everybody went to bed early and kept dry as best they could: Miss Eunice dreamed of a white wedding in which she was the heroine: yet try as she would, she could not quite see whom she was marrying.

The storm passed in the night: the next morning was bright and clear. Edward had made himself a big tin of tea and was gone up the hill to the spring with his axes and his scythes and his water carriers and his dog before the others were to be seen. But he saw again the destruction of his trees and his wheat: of course nothing had had a firm enough hold in the hillside.

He looked down towards the house and saw that Harriet and Miss Eunice had somehow taken the tarpaulin roof off his lean-to and were laying it out on the bushes to dry. Hetty was stoking up the fire with her good arm and they seemed to have washed some clothes, some womanly things he noted with slight embarrassment, and hung them on the bushes also. The smoke rising straight upwards beside the shack sent signals to him of habitation and a kind of domesticity that warmed his heart after the lonely days before Harriet's unexpected arrival. A house with women. A strange brightly coloured bird suddenly flew out of the bush. In one of the native trees another bird sang on and on, a clear bell-like sound that suddenly caught at his throat, and the sound of a cry seemed to come from somewhere and he realised it was from himself. He bent to his work angrily: he was getting soft. He had heard a hundred birds at home without such sentiment. As he wielded his axe again his dog barked somewhere just out of sight. Just for a moment Edward thought he heard a neighbouring bark far in the distance but he listened again and heard nothing. Perhaps it was an echo.

Miss Eunice swept the earth floor with an English broom, scrubbed and hung out the mats on bushes; it was heavy work and it was not what she was used to doing but she worked hard with intense concentration, pleased with the floor, pleased with the clean mats. *If this is to be my life I will thank Heaven for it. As long as I can share my life with Mr Edward Cooper. I am not so very much older than he, and I will make myself indispensable. Dear Lord, I beg you to let Mr Edward Cooper notice me and learn to love me.*

Harriet scrubbed at the big pot, wondered if she could stay one more day, wondered how she could broach with Edward her return to Wellington, and her moving on to somewhere else. Sometimes she thought of all the servants in her father's house: the cook and the maids and the footmen who kept everything so clean. And so silent. She was very careful not to waste water: she had never realised water was so heavy. Sometimes now she thought of her last maid, the girl with the watchful eyes, Lucy: every morning Lucy had carried water up to Harriet's room from the basement, cleaning the floor and the bowls after Harriet had vomited (she scrubbed the pot harder, pushing away the memory, all the memories that had surfaced in the last few days). *I must go.*

Hetty had decided their clothes must be cleaned. With her one good arm, she was preparing for washing. There was no hiding the fact that Miss Eunice and particularly Miss Harriet no longer looked quite like ladies: their gowns were filthy from travelling, from the mud. But the sun was shining; there was water, there was a fire for hot water; there was soap. She could sponge them and scrub at the worst parts at least. The others would have to carry the water but Hetty could scrub with one hand, see if she couldn't.

'Miss Harriet,' called Hetty.

Harriet looked up from her scrubbing and her thoughts.

'We should try and clean your black dress. Have you another?'

'My boxes are still at the Gentlewomen's Hotel.'

'Well,' said Hetty, 'if you wouldn't mind, just while I worked at the black one, I have my other dress, my blue dress, my luggage is all here because I ain't got much and I had nowhere to leave things, look!' She pulled a blue servant's dress out of her small bundle. 'It is not a lady's garment, of course, and you are not as fat as me, but I do not think that Mr Edward will mind. And you should not wear the black one any longer until I have tried to clean it a little. I tried to brush the mud off yesterday, but it is not just mud, it is everything!' With her good hand she helped Harriet take off the black skirt and bodice and put on the blue one. *Hetty is well enough now. I will decide today. When I have talked to Edward. I will walk up to the spring.*

Just for a moment both the young women were conscious – not just that Harriet was wearing servant's clothes – but that she was not wearing black. Hetty had never seen her not wearing black. Harriet caught her thought. 'I think Mary would not mind,' she said. 'She would be so interested in my life here, she would not mind what I was wearing.' And Harriet, going back to the recalcitrant stew pot, smiled: at Hetty, at the thought of telling Mary about her adventures, at herself dressed in servant's clothes and scrubbing a pot. She must go. But – just one more day at this beautiful spot? She would, definitely, go tomorrow.

At last she stopped her work, stretched her back. And despite the forebodings that had returned to her so cruelly and so clearly she could not help looking about her in a kind of joy. She loved the sounds: the sound of the sea there below her, calm; the birds and the insects in the wild bush. The birds sang and called to each other but did not come near the shack; their colours flashed between branches as they flew above her. The bush-covered hillside stretched upwards, dark green between the blue of the sea and the blue of the sky: who would not feel joy at this and the fresh fragrance of the clear autumn air? Eddie's dog barked up on the side of the hill by the spring where Eddie was working and she remembered Quintus again, chasing the rats in the cesspits under Bryanston Square. Cesspits. How far she felt from the sight and the smells of London cesspits. Here Eddie made holes in the ground, they filled them in again and laid sweet-smelling leaves and branches across so that none of them would forget where the holes had been made. Oh, the things she could tell Mary of, in her blue servant's dress the colour of the sea! And it was then that Harriet turned and looked out across the blue sea where the morning mist had cleared.

A small boat was coming towards her.

It was still too far away for figures to be clear. She stared out to sea as if rooted to the spot. She heard Eddie's dog bark. She saw the sun catch the sails of the boat. The boat came inexorably nearer and figures began to emerge and clarify: men, at least four men. Hetty ran from the fire towards the shore to get a clearer view; she called excitedly to the others. At first the boat seemed to be going further to the west. Then it seemed to see the clearing, or the shack, or the figures on the shore, and changed direction slightly and came straight towards them. And then there was the sound of oars, coming across the water.

'Why, I believe it is my brother,' said Miss Eunice, moving down to the shore also. And then Edward called, his voice nearer and nearer as he came down the hill, but Harriet Cooper had turned to stone in her blue dress. Now Edward's dog was barking excitedly, running down towards the shore and then back to his new master: tail wagging, ears back. No dog answered: there was no dog on the little boat. Edward, who had brought water down as he always did when he made the journey, put the pails on the ground with a grunt, then stared intently at the approaching boat. And then looked at the pale, expressionless face of his cousin.

'I believe it is your father, Harriet,' he said.

She stared not at Edward but at the sea.

She had not believed that it could happen. And she had stayed too long.

I could run, I could take the horse, I could ride away through the bush. But of course, the meeting with her father would thus only be postponed, not cancelled. Another thought clarified coldly: *It cannot begin again. I would rather die.*

Edward, in politeness and with the deference due to his uncle (but somehow uneasy), left his cousin and walked towards the shore as the boat came nearer and nearer. First Mr Burlington Brown was observed, his black cape billowing slightly in the wind as the boat came towards the shore. Then a stranger none of them recognised. Then Edward and Harriet clearly saw Peters, Sir Charles's manservant, dressed in black as he always was. And at the back of the boat, very still but staring forward intently, stood the Right Honourable Sir Charles Cooper, MP.

When the crewman jumped into the shallow water to pull the boat up on to the pebbles, although Mr Burlington Brown was standing at the front of the boat it was Sir Charles who leapt ashore first. Both Miss Eunice and Hetty looked in amazement at his fine clothes and his long boots. Edward said, 'Welcome, sir.' But Sir Charles strode upwards as if he did not notice them, strode upwards to the motionless blue figure by the little shack. Peters climbed rather than leapt ashore; the stranger who turned out to be an official of the New Zealand Company got his feet rather wet; the crewman helped Mr Burlington Brown, who greeted his sister but looked disgruntled. Out of respect for family feelings they all stayed by the boat so no-one but Harriet heard Sir Charles Cooper's words as he engulfed her in his arms, no-one heard what he whispered into her ear, or saw his hands upon her breasts.

There was little delay. Sir Charles made it clear that Harriet would come back on the boat to Wellington town where he had taken rooms in the largest hotel and where they were expected to dine today with the Lieutenant-Governor. He said little else except to order Harriet to put on her mourning dress, smoking a cigar impatiently in the small clearing by the house while Harriet got ready with Hetty's help. He gave short answers to Edward's questions about his family in England; took in without comment the rough dwelling, the washing on the bushes, the servant with the cricket bat tied to her arm, the unwelcoming aspect of the land. The whole thing was a farce, his posture said, and nothing to do with him. Mr Burlington Brown, staring in disbelief at Edward's house, said at once that he did not wish his sister to stay any longer. Peters stood by the boat, did not even come as far as the house.

Miss Eunice, who would not of course for a moment have thought of disobeying her brother, nevertheless did not wish to leave Edward, especially not in the company of Hetty. But when she tentatively mentioned to the general company Hetty's health and the uncertainty of Hetty's fate none of the men even bothered to answer her.

Finally Sir Charles addressed the official from the New Zealand Company. 'If this is the land you were offering to farmers unseen,

Thompson, then my nephew Edward Cooper has been made a fool of.'

The official had been prepared for this, had had conversations with other company officials before he embarked on the boat journey across the harbour, had made plans for this. Sir Charles Cooper was a member of Her Majesty's Government after all and the New Zealand Company needed all the help it could get. He inhaled rapidly and began talking fast.

'Sir Charles,' he said, 'there has been a terrible mistake. Mr Edward Cooper's land is not *here*, it is further northwards, through the hills at a place the natives call Wairarapa – and there is more land up at Wanganui by the river, we have much good land there. He of course has a *choice*, Sir Charles, a choice of a fine agricultural acquirement, we were just, as it happens, in the process of informing him of our regrettable mistake when you arrived on the *Lord Fyne* yesterday. My deepest apologies, Mr Edward, I will take you north tomorrow or whenever suits you and indeed, Sir Charles, we would like you to see the flat, fertile land we have in store for him, to take the good news homewards, as it were.' He looked at Sir Charles anxiously but Sir Charles merely pulled on his cigar and said nothing.

'I am heartened to learn of your mistake, Mr Thompson,' said Edward, expressionless. 'If there should be room on the boat for me to return with you now I certainly will not let you out of my sight.'

'There is not room on the boat,' said Sir Charles, 'for either you or Mr Thompson if the two ladies are to return.' Mr Thompson's look of horrified protest was ignored. 'It will do you good,' said Sir Charles, 'to live on the land you so easily dispense to others. I understand that the journey is rather tedious by road. I will, of course, although I hope to return to England in two days' time with my daughter on the *White Princess*, keep a close eye on the progress of the farm of my nephew, and thus of the progress of the New Zealand Company. I am sure the Prime Minister will be interested in my report. There has been much talk of your activities in the House.'

'But what about Hetty?' said Miss Eunice quickly. 'She cannot stay here.'

Harriet appeared at the door, dressed in black, her face so pale that Edward moved uneasily, watching her. 'Hetty is my maid,' said Harriet quietly but urgently, 'she will of course come with me.' It was the first time she had spoken since her father had arrived.

'I have my own arrangements for your well-being,' said Sir Charles sharply. 'I do not wish you to bring a crippled maid to—' and he paused for an infinitesimal moment before he added, 'interfere with my plans.' And there was something in the way he said *crippled* and *interfere*, so that Harriet understood he spoke of Mary and that he was repeating what he had said to her when he embraced her. *You will be punished*, he had whispered to her, *tonight you will be punished*.

And so, less than an hour after they had arrived, those who were travelling boarded the small sailing boat back to Wellington. From the shore Edward called to Harriet, said he would set off for Wellington very early in the morning with Mr Thompson and bring letters for her to take back to his family in England which he would write today. And he waved in his usual cheerful manner, yet felt ill at ease at the sight of his cousin's face. Hetty said nothing, knowing that now that her arm was healing she would somehow survive. She noted Harriet's white face, expected her father had a husband arranged for her in London, was sorry to see her go who had been so kind but knew that the gentry's lives were a hundred miles removed from her own.

And around Wellington town the news spread like wildfire: a Member of Parliament from Home had come: with them at last was someone who would make a difference, who could take their case back to the Mother of Parliaments and pave the way for the dissolution of the New Zealand Company and to self-government for the colony. So that the natives at last would learn what it was to not co-operate with Men of England.

TWENTY-NINE

From the moment he saw her again in the blue dress against the horizon, Sir Charles Cooper did not let his daughter out of his sight: there were introductions and smiles and bows and arrangements but she was at no time alone until later that afternoon when she was locked (by Peters) in the room Sir Charles had arranged for her at Barratt's Hotel. She was to dress. They were to dine with the Lieutenant-Governor: various important officials were to dine with them. Sir Charles Cooper in person was like gold in the new colony in these tempestuous times: a Member of the British Parliament with the British Prime Minister's ear: people fought to meet him, to give him their point of view. There was to be a large public meeting later that evening that Sir Charles could not avoid addressing: settlers hearing of his presence had begun arriving in the town.

At last Sir Charles insisted on a moment alone with his daughter whom he had not seen for so long: the officials who wished to speak to him nodded understandingly. (Something *odd* about the daughter, they whispered to each other: so pale and silent and beautiful.) Sir Charles placed Peters outside the door of Harriet's room with strict instructions that he was not to be disturbed. There was fresh fruit on a small table by the window, a waiter brought whisky for Sir Charles.

'That will be all.' The waiter was dismissed. With his glass in his hand Sir Charles came to sit on a chair beside his still, pale daughter dressed in fresh black mourning clothes. (But there was no mention, at all, of Mary.) Someone had unpacked Harriet's luggage from the Gentlewomen's Private Hotel and prepared the clothes, a servant had earlier brought in a tin bath and hot water.

For a time Sir Charles sat in ominous silence, unnaturally close to her beside the small table so that she was almost jammed between the window and her father; his leg was against hers, red apples rested on a blue plate, and yellow peaches, and she did not know how to slow the beating of her heart and he did not speak. Outside the wind had come up again, rattled the wooden windows of the hotel. Voices passed by on the quay below them, words and phrases drifted up to the room . . . *the natives say the* Seagull *from Africa is in the straits: it will bring spices tonight, pepper and myrrh . . . what is myrrh? . . . there is a meeting tonight, someone from the Queen . . . there will be mail at the Post Office.*

'Harriet.'

She raised her eyes quickly. Her father's face was unnaturally calm but something in his eyes glittered wildly and her heart contracted yet again in fear. He was so near that she smelled the whisky.

'Harriet.'

She quickly stared down again at the fruit plate.

'You have, by your very foolish actions, forced me to leave my business, and my country, at great inconvenience, to come to this godforsaken place to find you and bring you home again. I have wasted months of my life sailing oceans, because of you.' His voice was calm and tight. 'There is a price to be paid for this.'

The plate had a willow pattern on it: a Japanese figure ran, forever frozen as Keats had said.

'Harriet, I wish you to run my household in Bryanston Square. That is the future that I have planned for you. Richard and Walter will no doubt leave eventually but we shall remain, you and I. It is what I have always wanted. You will meet many people, and your life need not be unpleasant.'

Under the soft, furry skin of the peaches blue trees reached outwards to the plate's rim. *She saw the cold dark house in Bryanston Square, the watching servants, she heard Quintus barking, chasing rats.*

And then suddenly her father reared up and began to shout and move about the room and if the whole of Wellington could hear he seemed not to care.

'You have nothing to say? No apology to give me? How dare you! How dare you shame me so publicly! You are my daughter. You are *my daughter*. You may do nothing without me, nothing without my permission, nothing without my financial support. This—' he pulled suddenly, crudely, at her black dress so that one small button flew off and bounced across the floorboards, 'this was paid for by me, belongs to me. You belong to me. And I wish to know how you arranged to get here, how you paid for your passage, how you were able to obtain money without my permission!'

She saw Mary's treasure at the back of the drawer, Mary's letter.

'How did you find money to pay the New Zealand Company?' he shouted.

'I sold my jewellery.' Her voice was flat.

'I gave you that jewellery.'

'My mother's jewels.'

'Everything of your mother's belongs to me. Therefore you have stolen from me and you are a common *thief*! Everything you say is yours belongs to me, is provided by me, everything, every breath that you take belongs to me. *I am your father*. And as you well know you owe me absolute obedience.'

He controlled himself at last, breathing heavily, drinking whisky.

The peaches were yellow; the apples were red; the plate was blue.

At last he sat again beside her, even closer, leant across the table and took her hand in his.

'Harriet,' he said.

She felt again his leg pressing against her; slowly his hand moved to her face, her neck. But now he was breathing heavily again and suddenly it was the other kind of breathing, the kind that she had almost made herself forget, and now remembered. As if they had not travelled thousands and thousands of miles across oceans, as if they were back in her room in Bryanston Square.

Shouts from the harbour floated through the window, and laughter, a boat being re-moored; again the wind rattled the wooden window-frames. *Edward and Hetty will be safe in the little house though the wind may blow.*

'Harriet.' And his voice became almost a whisper. 'Harriet—' and his voice seemed to catch as the wind blew around the hotel and along the shore. 'I will come to you tonight, in this room. Tonight, after the meeting. For you must be punished.' His hand again stretched across to her, and his hand brushed her breast. The smell of the whisky and no other sound but their breathing in the room, but outside, among the voices, marching feet could be heard approaching as if they were changing the guard. As if they were in England.

She could not move, her legs felt like lead. But at last she forced herself to raise her eyes to her father and with an immense effort of will she said: 'Father.'

'What is it, Harriet?' His hand moved slowly down her arm.

'Father, I beg you.'

'You will beg me, my darling.' And she thought he smiled.

'I beg you to let me go, to let me go and live my own life. Away from you.'

He sat back very slowly. 'What do you mean?'

'Father.' The wind blew, on and on. 'This would be for – for your own sake, as well as for mine.'

As she spoke the Wellington afternoon light slanted across the table and just for a moment as the light caught the side of her face she suddenly looked like her mother. He stared, incredulous, sat back; Harriet saw his wild, confused eyes.

Perhaps he is mad? The thought flashed across her consciousness.

And then Sir Charles Cooper rose and hit Harriet across the face. He knocked the table, an apple rolled on to the floor and then a peach. She did not cry but tears spilled out of her eyes: her father reached again for his whisky.

'You have dragged me here, Harriet, and you have angered me greatly. You do not apologise, you do not look at me, you do not answer. You somehow seem to think that you are superior to me, to your father, and yet without me you are nothing. Without my jewellery you could not have got here, without my name the New Zealand Company would never have allowed you to travel. All the respect in the world that you receive, *you receive because you are my daughter!*' And even as her face throbbed with pain Harriet knew that this was true.

'Without me, you are nothing, and I intend to teach you that lesson. Indeed,' and his voice became quieter, 'I intend to teach you things, Harriet, that you have never imagined.' And he suddenly smiled again. 'I intend to teach you to beg.'

Harriet thought at once of her precious sovereigns that lay hidden in the embroidery bag that she had thrust under the bed. He must not find the sovereigns: they were her key to freedom, he must not find them, he must not know that she still had money. Her heart began to beat even more rapidly.

He stood before her, still smiling slightly. 'Did you know that women beg, my darling girl? They cry out, and beg for more. That is what I will teach you.'

And there was something in his voice, something in the way that he spoke to her that made her understand he was not, after all, speaking of sovereigns. And then suddenly Hetty's words tumbled around her head: *ain't you done it don't you miss it?* 'I intend to make use of the time,' his voice went on, 'that it will take us to get back to England again. By the time a hundred days have passed and I have had the hours and the days to teach you, then, I do assure you, Harriet Cooper will have changed.'

Slowly, in a kind of horror, Harriet looked up at her father.

'She will have learnt to be pleased to obey her father,' he said. And he smiled once more.

He is mad, she thought again. *He is mad*.

'Harriet, my darling, darling girl.' He moved to her and began fumblingly to undo her hair, pulled her head to his body, winding her long, dark hair around his hands.

The marching feet got nearer. They stopped outside the window, a military voice called commands.

'Escort for Sir Charles Cooper!'

Sir Charles did not let Harriet go. 'I am not ready,' he called sharply, her hair still in his hands.

There was a sound of urgent voices and then Peters' voice came gabbling through the door. 'Soldiers have come for you, sir. There seems to be some trouble with the settlers arriving, wanting to speak to you, so the Lieutenant-Governor has sent an escort for you to come to Government House.'

'*Damn you!*'

'I am sorry, Sir Charles. The Lieutenant-Governor's officer is here with me. He is asking for you.'

For a moment there was silence on either side of the door. Sir Charles pulled, but more gently, at Harriet's dark hair, stared at his daughter's ashen face, and the red mark where he had hit her. 'You had better not come,' he said in a completely normal voice, 'there may be trouble. You will be safer here.' Then he pulled her to her feet and very deliberately, his eyes holding her eyes because he had her hair in his hands, he let one hand run down her body; even through her clothes, her petticoats and her corset, she felt his hand *ain't you done it don't you miss it?* on parts of her body she did not even know how to name, as Hetty's words flew wildly.

'Wait for me,' said her father.

Then he leaned close and kissed her lips. 'I have been waiting,' he whispered hoarsely, 'all your life.'

Then he marched to the door and flung it open and she heard him say to Peters, 'Stay here.' She heard him striding towards the front door of the hotel, soldiers giving orders as he went outside into the windy, dangerous late afternoon where the small boats pulled at their moorings on the shore.

As if she could still not move Harriet vomited on to the small table.

The door opened. Peters came right into the room where she stood so white-faced and seemed not to even notice. He put his mouth close to her ear, she could smell his breath. 'I will never, never forgive you,' and his voice hissed through the room and a hanging lantern moved in the wind from the draught from the open door. 'I have travelled through hell because of you. I nearly drowned near Tasmania because of you. Don't try anything clever because this time I will be watching your every move. You will never, never escape again.' And then she heard the door being locked behind her.

Harriet took one deep, shuddering breath, only one. And then, very quickly, she got up and went to the washstand in the corner. She wasted no time at all: it was her life and her sanity and she knew it.

First she quickly washed her face, scrubbed at it, rinsed her mouth, spat him away. Then she took a towel and wiped up her own vomit from the table. *So clearly she saw the maid Lucy, cleaning up after her, in another life.* She looked about her again, as she had when she was first locked in. The room was square, with one window that looked out on to the harbour and a smaller one on to a side alley; there was no other door than the one Peters was guarding. Her room was visible to anyone passing in the street but in the alley, in the dark, she might be invisible. She stared out. What else could she do but jump out on to the road below when night came? While her father was addressing the meeting of the settlers. Through the window and along the busy, bustling waterfront, the sun was low on the horizon. *How could she have let her guard down, waited too long at Edward's house? How could she have persuaded herself that distance would keep her father away?* People walked along the road as if this was an ordinary day, she saw a man calling and a young boy bowling a hoop along; the hoop was light and got lifted by the wind and the boy ran after it, laughing with delight. Soldiers marched by again in their red coats. Small boats lay tied to posts on the shore: whaleboats, small rowing boats, native canoes; the wind was making the water rougher now, the small boats moved and jostled, bumping drunkenly. Out in the harbour, the *Lord Fyne* lay at anchor near the *White Princess* which her father said was to take her with him to Sydney on their journey back to England. Far, far out she thought she saw a sail. She remembered the voices: *the natives say the* Seagull *from Africa will land tonight, it will bring spices, pepper and myrrh.* Beside the hotel people were selling potatoes and honey. She would have to wait for the darkness. Few people noticed a lady in a black dress staring intently out of the hotel window, with her hair undone.

Suddenly the door opened again. Harriet turned quickly.

'Your father has sent for you,' said Peters. 'There are soldiers here again. You also are to be escorted to Government House, your father has decided you should dine there, with him, before he addresses the meeting.'

Harriet's heart skipped a beat.

But she could do nothing before dark. And she would meet other people. Perhaps somebody would see that her father was mad, and she would be saved.

THIRTY

The new, fast sailing ship the *Seagull*, with its cargo of spices and special passengers, finally crossed the straits in the late afternoon, the Wellington winds waiting. Lucy, having sung the boy George to sleep: having sung *I dreamt that I dwelt in marble halls with vassals and serfs by my side* as the ship heaved and rolled (for some reason the song that soothed him most); having waited, holding his hand, until sleep came at last, now stood on deck with Quintus. They had buffeted past the dark coastline for several hours, what they were searching for was a sight of their final destination and Lucy discussed with Quintus the coming reunion with Miss Harriet. Benjamin, who had been standing alone at one end of the ship, joined them as they approached the heads where the pilot boat was already waiting. Quintus stood with his ears up and his nose forward.

'He understands, you know,' said Lucy to Sir Benjamin Kingdom, 'he knows he's going to see Miss Harriet soon.'

'I believe he does,' said Benjamin, watching Quintus. *Why should he believe his own instinctive feelings and not those of Quintus?* He stared ahead, watching the pilot boat and several small schooners fussing around the new sleek ship that had come into their care. Benjamin was perplexed beyond reason. Here they were, arrived safely at last after all that had happened to them – and here it was again, that odd, unexplained uneasiness, beating its wings against his heart. He ran his hands through his unruly curls that were lifted and tangled by the wind, decided he had done far too much thinking at sea: he would leave everything to Ralph, which was as it should be, and would set off as soon as possible on his search for the *moa*.

He smiled at Lucy. 'Quintus probably knows more than the rest of us put together,' he said, only partly joking, and he craned down to see what the pilot did, did not see that Lucy stared at him, something on her mind.

Lucy had become indispensable to the Kingdom brothers.

On Tristan da Cunha the survivors of the wreck of the *Cloudlight*, although so kindly looked after by the islanders, had huddled together, reliving their nightmare: waiting for rescue. Most of them just wanted to go home. George's mother and father had been drowned like most of the steerage passengers, George had miraculously lived and the Kingdom brothers had taken him under their wing. The boy had survived, but spoke very little. He still saluted Ralph, his friend forever, but in a stoical way, as if not wishing to disappoint. He held Lucy's hand a great deal and sat a great deal with Quintus the dog, not speaking. The brothers would have given much to hear the chirpy voice say 'hello, hello?' again.

When Lord Ralph understood at last that the dog Quintus was Harriet's dog, that the young girl he thought he had seen before had been Harriet's maid (had been there on the very evening at the Highgate Cemetery that had changed all their lives), he almost considered it a sign from heaven (although he considered Lucy's determination to bring Harriet's dog across the world somewhat foolish). He had offered her more money than she had ever been paid in her life to come onwards to New Zealand with them and look after George and then return to England with them all when they had found Harriet. But she had curtseyed and said that although she would be very glad, with them, to find Miss Harriet, she didn't want to go back to England. Lucy had many bad memories of her life in Spitalfields, but the terrible, unforgettable vision of her friend Annie trying to jump from the wild rocks of Tristan da Cunha would be part of her forever. And she had decided, as the terror came back to her over and over, that the dream she and Annie had dreamed to themselves – a new and different life in a new and different place – must somehow be realised, for Annie's sake also. She could not articulate this to the Kingdom brothers of course, who would not anyway have delved into the mind of a servant, but Ralph had seen the girl jump into the raging waters and had respect for her courage, and on the journey from Africa with few passengers and mostly cargo Benjamin had enjoyed her company and her view of the world. She looked after the boy and the brothers, was forever grateful that the bottom of the *Seagull* carried cargo not passengers, and was paid most generously. She carefully put away every penny for her new life.

As the *Seagull* had sailed with its small ragbag of unexpected passengers through the Indian Ocean in record time; as the few survivors spoke less of the *Cloudlight*, or the drunken Captain, or of Tristan da Cunha, or of the terrible day, Benjamin had patiently taught George to read and to tell the time and George's eyes had widened in amazement at these new things that he had somehow learned and he became engrossed in any books he could get his hands on. He also became fascinated by the brothers' pocket watches, would plead to be allowed to hold them against his ear and listen to the ticking. But he would seldom come up on deck, could not bear to stand on deck and look at the sea. (Perhaps standing on the deck brought back to his small mind another time, the time he had stood on deck with his mother and the Reverend Boothby and warned him of monsters. As it was decided best never to speak to George of the shipwreck or his lost parents, George's exact frame of mind was not known.) Lord Ralph would have forced him on deck daily, wanted to make a man of him. But Benjamin and Lucy prevailed upon Ralph to let the boy get safely to New Zealand first before he considered manhood. Ralph reluctantly complied but spoke severely to George most days now.

'You must take your fate like a man, George, if you are to be a man!' And George saluted stoically but did not speak.

Only Lucy knew the depths of George's terror, sleeping in the same small cabin, waking over and over again in the night to comfort the unspeakable horrors of his dreams. Night after night he would cling to her and she would sing to him. Slowly her high, clear voice would calm his small heart and his wild eyes would close again. But she would see expressions of terror cross his face over and over, even as he slept. And perhaps it was George's nightmares that at last penetrated Lucy's own dreams: Harriet had once clung to her too in desperation. Lucy had begun to dream, as they approached New Zealand, not of Annie jumping from the wild rocks, but, night after night, of Harriet. Sometimes she saw the white figure, shadowy on the stairs of the dark London house, carrying a knife.

Now as they approached Wellington and the culmination of all his hopes and plans and desires Lord Ralph Kingdom, his body wild with excitement and anticipation, sat in the saloon calming himself with a large Scottish whisky. His thoughts were full of Harriet and their impending meeting: he must marry her now, marry her *here*, in Wellington, *I cannot wait another day!* He nevertheless was trying to write a letter to his mother to be sent off, he hoped, as soon as they landed, to catch the first ship. She would have had no news of them since they left: she had to be told about the wreck of the *Cloudlight*, the safety of her sons and the death of her cousin, the Reverend Boothby. Ralph sat, dipping his pen into the ink, but he kept thinking of Harriet Cooper.

Benjamin entered the saloon.

'Go up, Ralphie,' he said, 'I will add to the letter and finish it. Wellington is at last in sight and who knows but you may see Miss Cooper, waiting at the quay even now!'

Ralph bounded up the iron steps to the deck, the wind at once catching his hair and his clothes; he was strong and young and his life stood before him: he never remembered feeling so happy. The days in London with ballet dancers and gaming clubs and duels now seemed like a dream. His travels had changed him, strengthened him: his love had made him strong. He would marry Harriet and they would have a large family and live in Kent with his mother who would learn to love Harriet and he would attend the House of Lords as was his duty. Ralph knew that the world belonged to him: knew that after so terrible a journey everything would fall into place when he found again the woman he loved.

'There, Lucy,' he said as he leaned beside her on the deck and the dark hills drew nearer and the choppy sea sent spray to cover their faces and their clothes. 'Quintus knows, look how he stares. After all that has happened, there is our destination.'

Lucy, who had been deep in thought, suddenly looked up. 'Lord Ralph, excuse me,' she said. 'Please keep looking at them hills. I've got to tell you something.'

'What is it, Lucy?' he said, smiling indulgently at her. *(Soon now, perhaps even tonight, he would see Harriet again. He would take her in his arms and never let her go.)* Lucy did not answer at once. He glanced down at her: her little fourteen-year-old face was serious and pale.

'You've got to look at the hills, sir,' she said in a tight, determined voice, 'so's I can tell you.'

Again he indulged her: nothing could dent his happiness and his anticipation. It was just beginning to get dark and the setting sun etched the line of the hills in the distance. The wind blew, but still the harbour was beautiful.

'It's about Miss Harriet.'

He looked at her sharply.

'Look away!' she commanded, almost angrily, and he did so, bemused.

Lucy frowned at the immensity of her task. But she knew she had to speak, for Harriet's sake. 'Lately,' she said at last, 'I been dreaming about Miss Harriet and I started being scared for her again, like I was at Bryanston Square.' Lucy, too, stared at the sunset. 'There's some things,' and then she paused, wondering what words to use. Then she started again. 'Don't look at me when I'm talking or I won't be able to tell you all this. I seen some things in Bryanston Square that – that I think I should tell you but I dunno how to use the words.' She saw that he still looked at the hills but that he was frowning now, that he did not like her talking of his beloved. She took a deep breath. 'Sir Charles didn't think I saw, but I did. He – he done things.' She cast a nervous little glance sideways; he had not turned but he was very still. 'There was plenty of men like that at Spitalfields,' she said in disdain, 'it was nothing new to me. But I thought the gentry was different.' She screwed up her courage.

'He came into her room, in the night.' Her voice was very low: the wind took her words and delivered them to the man standing next to her. *I cannot tell you*, Harriet had said to him.

'She used to vomit, when he was gone. She run away from him.'

He turned to her at last, looking at her with a mixture of horror, anger, disbelief and deep distaste that anyone in the world, let alone a servant, should say to Lord Ralph Kingdom such unspeakable, unsayable things.

'I seen these things in Bryanston Square,' she said doggedly, as canoes appeared with natives on board, calling excitedly to the *Seagull*. Quintus ran up and down the deck, wagging his tail and barking. 'Why else would she run away so desperate? And when I went back to try and get a reference, after Miss Harriet had disappeared, the servants said Sir Charles was planning to come and fetch her back. And the reason I thought I needed to tell you all this is I've been thinking what my dreams might mean. Suppose he's already here? She might need us to rescue her! We wasn't delayed as much as we might have been on the island with the *Seagull* seeing the smoke and coming to get us. But who's to say who passed us? Or maybe he's already taken her back again to her horrible life!'

A Maori canoe came near, the Captain shouted to them to get out of the way, but they only laughed and sped past, brown men using the paddles with strength and grace, shouts of their language echoing upwards, the wind seeming to bother them not at all.

'She took a knife,' said Lucy quietly. 'I seen her take a knife.'

Several more small schooners and even rowing boats appeared out of the setting sun, so that a little flotilla was already accompanying the *Seagull* into the harbour, white-topped waves everywhere, dusk in the dark velvety hills.

'I do not believe you,' said Lord Ralph Kingdom, his face like stone as he answered the servant at last. *I cannot tell you*, Harriet had said to him.

'I think Miss Mary knew.' Lucy went on as if he hadn't spoken as the *Seagull* was escorted into the port. 'God rest her dear, crippled soul, she was waiting – it was like a fluttering hen – for Miss Harriet to return from Kent and I saw, she never stopped watching her, always. Like she was to keep her safe. And so when Miss Mary died Miss Harriet had no one to guard her.'

The Captain called, the sailors pulled at the remaining sails, made the anchor ready.

And the few survivors of the wreck of the *Cloudlight*, those who had chosen to complete their voyage after all, stood on the deck as lights twinkled from the shore and the shadowy Wellington hills pulled them inwards. Some of them wept.

Benjamin suddenly appeared on deck holding a blinking, wary George by the hand.

'There is the land, George,' said Benjamin.

'Look at the lights, George,' said Lucy.

Lord Ralph Kingdom said nothing: his face was a cold mask of granite as he stared, not at the new land, but at the destruction of all his hopes and dreams.

THIRTY-ONE

In the Government House silver gleamed as the lamps were lit. White tablecloths stood on a table that groaned with good food and wine; exquisite china and crystal had been laid for the honoured guests of the Lieutenant-Governor and his wife. The company listened, enraptured, to the opinions of the Right Honourable Sir Charles Cooper, MP. He was in fine, ebullient form and, sitting around the long oak table brought from England, the ladies and gentlemen of the new colony deferred to his different knowledge and his closeness to the Colonial Office and the Prime Minister.

'Earl Grey in the Colonial Office has been quite clear. From the moment that British dominion was proclaimed in New Zealand, all lands not actually occupied by the natives ought to be considered as property of the Crown in its capacity as Trustee for the whole community.'

The Lieutenant-Governor looked uneasy. 'I do not believe the natives see it that way.'

'Is that relevant?' said Sir Charles Cooper.

They toasted Her Majesty. The footmen refilled the glasses. It was as if they were in England.

And all the time his daughter's thoughts whirled and hurtled, as the lights glittered, and the polite conversation murmured on: she saw their faces admiring her father and almost cried out in despair: of course he did not seem mad, of course they would never believe her. *Where can I escape to in this small, gossiping town? – I will kill myself rather than live through this – the small boats drawn up along the shore – could I take one in the darkness? – there are islands in the harbour – do natives live there? – I have never rowed, but I have watched the men doing it often enough, I could do it too – Eddie bought a horse – could I get a horse?*

Outside the wind blew and branches fell across the muddy, rutted roads: inside the chandeliers moved slightly, the footmen bowed, the *décolletage* of the ladies gleamed whitely and their diamonds shone.

I refuse to live through this.

As the ladies were rising in a rustle of silk to take tea in the drawing room the Lieutenant-Governor said, 'I believe you play the piano, Miss Cooper.'

'It is some time, sir, since I have done that.' A tiny button was missing from her dress.

'But your fame has travelled before you. Captain Stark told me of your accomplishment aboard the *Amaryllis*. You will play for us tonight, I hope, in the drawing room.'

'Of course she will play,' said Sir Charles and his eyes glittered like fire. 'She will sing "Yes! I Have Dared to Love Thee".'

The ladies went into the drawing room, port was poured for the gentlemen. The rooms were connected by doors that folded back: Sir Charles sat so that, always, Harriet was in his view in the next room. As he answered the questions that officials put to him about matters in London he observed every movement his beautiful daughter made. There was a mark on the side of her face: nobody was so impolite as to mention it: to Sir Charles it only made her more precious and his legs moved suddenly in his chair and his colour heightened and his eyes shone as he contemplated the beautiful, beautiful girl and the long, long night in front of him. Sometimes he could not make any semblance of keeping still, he rose and strode about the dining room with his port in his hand for some moments and then returned to his seat, never losing sight of his daughter.

In the drawing room the ladies regarded the new arrival with interest and curiosity. She alone was not wearing the low-cut gown so necessary for such dinner engagements: she was in mourning and was excused. Polite inconsequences and local gossip were exchanged at first; Harriet nodded dumbly, politely.

'You came to New Zealand on your own, Miss Cooper?' asked one finally. (Such was the odd story that was doing the rounds in the town about this new and rather mysterious arrival.)

Harriet looked at them: smiling, curious, rustling ladies. What would happen if she told them the truth of the room in the Barratt's Hotel, of the mark on her face; threw herself on their mercy? How would their faces react? *What words can I use?* Yet surely they were kind, had hearts like her own? She took a deep breath.

'I came,' she said, 'because—' She looked again at the smooth faces. One of the ladies leaned forward very slightly in anticipation. And Harriet was at once struck by the absolute impossibility of saying aloud what she wanted to say. *She had not even been able to talk about it openly to her own sister.* What words would she use to describe what was happening to her in a locked room not a mile away? She had seen their faces smiling forwards as they listened to her father and they would not believe her.

'I came because I felt my cousin should know about my sister's death from me. He was very fond of her. It was – it was such a ter- rible sadness.' Her voice shook just a little.

'And your dear father came all the way to accompany you home again!'

And from the rustle of the dresses and the nodding of their ringlets she saw that they admired this picture tremendously: *what a wonderful father*, they said, *what a wonderful man*. The lights gleamed on their white bosoms and they spoke at last of the diffi- culties of getting servants in the new colony, how they were paid outrageous wages. They observed the lights from the *Seagull*, which was anchoring below them in the harbour, the sails were furled, small boats worried around the bigger ship like children, lanterns flickered as night fell. The Lieutenant-Governor's wife informed them that messages had already advised Government House that the *Seagull* was carrying not only spices, but shipwrecked passen- gers from the South Atlantic Ocean. And the well-bred ladies shivered slightly, and pulled their evening mantles about them, for all had made the long journey.

The men entered the drawing room with much energy and intent, speaking of the settlers' meeting that was now to be addressed by both the Lieutenant-Governor and Sir Charles.

'And then I must meet the *Seagull*,' said the Lieutenant-Governor. 'We are not sure who is aboard after the terrible disaster of the *Cloudlight* of which we have had news. I expect they will not come ashore until first light but my men will row me out, it is my duty as Her Majesty's representative here to hear their story most urgently. But first, Miss Cooper, to send us on our way, just one song.'

Harriet dutifully rose and walked to the grand piano in the corner of the room. For a moment, as her hands lay still in her lap, the room was silent; they could hear the wind blowing through the trees outside and voices called somewhere from the muddy roads that were not London. Somewhere in the house a door banged. *But I will not sing.*

Harriet played 'Song Without Words'. The notes filled the big wooden room and drifted out into the night. Perhaps they were heard in the hills behind them, perhaps in the darkness soft-footed, sure-footed natives stopped, just for a moment, as they moved through the bush in total silence.

As the last notes echoed into stillness the Lieutenant-Governor wiped a surreptitious tear from his eye. The music of Mendelssohn reminded him of how much he yearned for civilisation, and for Home, and of how he loved his wife.

He cleared his throat. 'Thank you, my dear Miss Cooper. Captain Stark was not exaggerating your daughter's gift, Sir Charles. You are indeed a fortunate man.' His guest gave a slight bow.

'I am indeed fortunate,' answered Sir Charles Cooper. And he smiled.

'And now,' and the Lieutenant-Governor rose, 'it is time for the gentlemen to attend to business. People have come from miles away. We shall address the settlers from a platform on the quay.'

Harriet was to go back to the hotel, Sir Charles decreed. They were to be escorted down to the harbour by soldiers of Her Majesty's 65th Regiment, and as they were leaving several of the ladies told Harriet about the Wednesday afternoon concerts that the regiment's band performed, and how they hoped to see her there.

'We will be leaving the day after tomorrow,' said Sir Charles, 'on the *White Princess* for Sydney. I must return to London as soon as possible,' and the ladies professed sadness at such a short acquaintance.

Harriet looked back once from the uneven road where her father held her tightly by the arm, held up her black glove for a moment, as a last goodbye to the smiling, waving ladies.

The Lieutenant-Governor may have thought that the passengers aboard the *Seagull* would wait until morning to disembark but he was wrong. As the ship had dropped anchor, as the sails had been furled and the ladies from Government House had looked down, Ralph and Benjamin were huddled together on a far corner of the deck. The Wellington wind whipped their words away almost as soon as they had been spoken, as if to lose them before they did further damage. In shock and anger and horror Ralph imparted to Benjamin what Lucy had told him. Such was their faith in Lucy that neither of them at any point queried the truth of what she had said.

'This changes everything, Ben, *everything*.' And Benjamin saw his brother's closed and desolate face.

For a moment the younger man said nothing at all. So this, this terrible story, was the message, beating at his heart. This was what he had seen on her face when he had so lightly informed her that perhaps a God did not exist to protect her. He stared across the choppy water at the little town of which they had had such high hopes, where small lights glittered and blew. He had not understood that the beautiful adventure would turn out this way. Then he turned to his brother, his face grave.

'Ralph. You cannot – you must not – desert her now. Her flight is at last explained and her need of you may be very great. We must find her and make sure she is safe.'

'But—' and Ralph's voice was low and desperate, all his joy gone, all the vicissitudes of the journey suffered for nothing, 'but I could not, of course, marry her now – *O God I cannot bear to think of it*.' Ralph buried his head into his arms as he leant on the dark deck rail and his muffled voice continued. 'Think of it, Ben, think of it, *Sir Charles Cooper to*—' and a groan of pain seemed to escape from the deck rail, '—I am heir to the Kingdom fortune, my wife must of course be – that is to say – *pure*, pure as driven snow, my children's mother . . . I could not, Ben. Not a woman who has been—' he searched and searched for the word he could not say, 'who has been – no, it is out of the question. I *could not.*' And then he repeated, *I cannot bear to think of it.*

Again Benjamin was silent. He heard the sailors whistling out to the small boats that had already brought traders aboard to meet with the Captain and discuss his cargo. He looked at his brother, partly in pity, partly there was something fiercer in his eyes.

At last, in a dark corner of the deck of the anchored *Seagull*, there in the night harbour so far from home, Benjamin took a deep breath and, because he knew he must, gave Miss Harriet Cooper back to his brother.

'Ralph, listen to me. The world is changing as at no other time in history – you and I have often discussed this, how lucky we are to be alive in such a time of discovery and invention and discourse. We are lucky enough also to be well-educated, well-connected men and I believe we should be in the forefront of those changes and I cannot help but think that our – our attitude towards, our whole way of thinking about, women – is to be one of those changes.'

'What are you talking about?'

'I am talking about Miss Cooper and the misfortune that has come upon her that is surely not her fault.' Benjamin heard the wind blowing through the rigging above them. 'What a terrible – what an *unspeakable* thing to happen to a young girl. No wonder she could not tell you why she was leaving.'

'She is ruined.'

'How many women have you—' Benjamin chose his words carefully, '—known? It has not, I believe, ruined you. It has not, has it, defiled you and made you impure?'

Ralph, who had been staring down at the dark choppy water, looked at his brother first in amazement and then in anger. 'How dare you speak to me like that! That is entirely different!'

'It is only different, Ralph, because we *think of women so differently from ourselves.*'

'Of course.' Ralph's voice was even angrier. 'Women *are* different, quite different beings! They are to comfort and to cleanse us, to give us peace and to bring out the best in us. That is what I believed Miss Cooper would do for me. But women of course can only do that if they—' again he could not find the right words, 'if they are *pure*. That is the most important quality that they must have.'

In the darkness Benjamin shook his head. 'So the other women you have known and expended so much energy not to mention money upon are not, now, worthy of any man? If they were worthy when you met them, worthy enough even for you to set up an establishment with one of them, is it not you that has therefore ruined them?'

'Don't play with words, Ben. There are no words to discuss Miss Cooper now, now that we know this – this unspeakable thing. What you are talking of is different. Entirely different.'

'I wonder if it is. I believe that if women are *good* and intelligent, and care about the world and its many inhabitants as we all must learn to do, then, I think, they are more likely to bring out the best in us. Miss Mary Cooper, the beloved elder sister, died because she was visiting the poor in Seven Dials during the cholera epidemic.'

'How do you know that?'

'I know, that is all. Miss Harriet Cooper loved her sister and must have known what she was doing. It is clear from even the short acquaintance we have had with Harriet that she is an intelligent woman.'

'None of this matters. An impure woman could never be the mother of my children, no matter how intelligent. And impure in such a – no, I cannot think on it – such a terrible way. It is out of the question. The Kingdom bloodline is too important.'

'If she has had the courage to run away from the vile actions of her father, to cross the world alone, then it seems to me she must be a good woman and a very brave woman, as was her sister. Do you not think these would be qualities worth passing on in our family?'

In his mind Ralph could see Benjamin's grey, wise eyes: the eyes of their father. Voices called, small boats nudged against the *Seagull* beside the rope ladder at the other end of the deck. Somewhere a sailor laughed. For a long time the brothers were silent.

At last Ralph said, in a low voice, 'What fools have you been meeting with, to speak to me in this way?'

'Not fools, Ralph. Educated men. And women. There are many people who think as I do.'

'Mother would not agree with you.'

'Mother comes from another time, another world almost.'

Benjamin's voice was very quiet: both of them saw their mother sitting so uncompromisingly in the cold rooms of their world. 'A few women of her generation were lucky enough, or brave enough, to obtain the freedom of thought that can come with true education. Mother was not one of them, as well you know.' They had never spoken in this way of their mother in their lives, it seemed almost inappropriate to do so, even now. 'Yet I cannot but think that her life could have been – happier, if she had been able to think about some things differently.'

Ralph sounded impatient. 'Happiness has nothing whatever to do with it. Mother has always done her duty.' It was true that their mother had always done her duty, never once had her sons seen her less than immaculately prepared for their infrequent visits; never once had she complained of the long, empty days in the cold, high-ceilinged manor where she lived out her life. 'She has always done her duty,' Ralph repeated. 'As women must.'

Benjamin did not answer.

The wind ruffled their hair and their clothes and caught again at the rigging and at the sea below them. The *Seagull* moved and swayed at its anchor.

And then Ralph whispered on to the wind: *Harriet – with her father: it disgusts me.*

'I shall go ashore myself then,' said Benjamin shortly and he quickly went below. Ralph caught the sudden disdain in his younger brother's voice.

Below deck Benjamin knocked quietly at the door of the cabin Lucy shared with George. Lucy answered.

'Is he asleep?'

'No.'

George was reading. Perhaps he was reading. He sat with his back to them holding a book but there was something tense and unnatural about his shoulders.

'I am going ashore.' Lucy wished passionately that she also could go ashore now, tonight, touch the new land at last: was glad that she would have freedom soon to catch at the dreams that would change her life. 'I will arrange accommodation for our embarkation in the morning.' He wanted to say something to Lucy of Harriet, of his brother. But what?

Suddenly George ran and flung himself at Benjamin.

'Take me, take me, I want to come with you because now the storm will come!' The boy was screaming with fright. 'Take me! Take me!'

Benjamin looked distressed, tried to hold the small flailing body still, puzzled. But Lucy understood at once.

'There ain't going to be a storm here, George, I've told you. Don't be such a ninny.' And she took him firmly by both arms, shook him to make him look at her. 'Look at me, George,' she said loudly, and he looked at her. 'This is the peaceful side of the world, like I've told you and told you. Sir Benjamin is going ashore in a rowing boat to make it nice for tomorrow.'

'He went in a rowing boat last time,' said George, and now he was sobbing, burying his head in Lucy's apron, and Benjamin understood at once: in George's experience if a ship dropped anchor it was shipwrecked.

'Here, George,' he said, 'look at this!' and he unclipped his pocket watch from his jacket. George looked up but still the tears ran down his face. 'I wouldn't be leaving you with this, would I? if you were going to be shipwrecked again!'

George took the watch and said no more, but his body shuddered still, from weeping, and his eyes held more pain and fear and memory than a small boy's should.

Benjamin came up on deck and whistled for a boat, the way he saw the sailors do.

'I am going ashore,' he said to Ralph. 'Will you not come with me? We must, at the very least, be assured that she is safe. And we may ascertain also whether Sir Charles Cooper is here.'

His brother's face still held the look of rage and disgust and disappointment and if Benjamin had not known such a thing was totally out of the question he would have sworn his brother had been weeping. 'I could not see him,' said Ralph. 'I would kill him if I saw him. I *cannot* see her. Surely you understand.'

'Very well, Ralph, I will go alone. I will find out what I can.' Again Ralph heard something in his brother's voice, something harder, less respectful. Benjamin whistled again and the sailors threw down a rope ladder and a small boat, bobbing on the choppy water in the wind, was rowed off by two men towards the shore, a lantern at the bow to guide them in.

Ralph Kingdom, illustrious Englishman, man-about-town, heir to an untold fortune, watched the boat getting smaller, saw the dark shapes of his brother and the sailors. He strained to see Ben's little boat land in the darkness, saw lights moving up the sand. Ben was a good man, but he knew nothing about women.

Terrible visions again filled his mind, disturbed his body. *I cannot tell you*, she had said and now he knew; he shook his head from side to side to try to cast out the pictures that came to him: terrible, unthinkable, *exciting* pictures of the woman he had loved.

And then quite unexpectedly Ralph heard himself say: *I will have her*. For just a moment he seemed startled by his own words, and then extraordinarily pleased by them. He suddenly leant over the deck rail and whistled out for one of the small boats. Swiftly he went below to his cabin, moved quietly. In a moment he was back on deck. As he was rowed towards the lights on the shore words went round and round in his head. *I will have her. I love her. I will have her*. And just as the boat touched the shingle on the shore: *I will forgive her*.

But his mind was not able to say: *I will marry her*.

The meeting of the settlers was to be held not far from where Benjamin had been deposited on the shore by the boatman, near one of the wooden jetties. He walked up the beach on to the harbourside, and saw at once hundreds of lanterns, heard the voices. Some were angry, some were excited, some sounded as though they had been drinking. Women stood in bonnets, children played in the crowd, running between people, running down to the water, pulled back every now and then by their mothers. There was to be a meeting soon, people informed him, and rumours flew around him: *any moment*, they said; *in an hour*, they said; *a Member of Parliament from Great Britain*, they said. And someone had the name: *Sir Charles Cooper*, they said, *from England*. So he was here. Benjamin walked quickly along the quay; saw, without seeing, Wellington: the stores and the sheds, the neat houses and the notices advertising wigs and the immortality of the soul. Where then was Harriet? His mind was filled with his brother, with Harriet Cooper, and his heart was weighed down with the pain of understanding at last. But now he must find her: *I know about your father. Are you all right? Are you safe?* Suddenly there was a stir, a commotion further down the quay. Soldiers were already escorting the speakers to the meeting. Benjamin quickly turned back to follow Sir Charles, and so find Harriet.

Harriet had been safely returned to Barratt's Hotel through the throng of people, the settlers and the traders and the sailors; just for a moment Sir Charles had entered her dark room and closed the door. Outside the escorting soldiers and the Lieutenant-Governor waited.

'Get ready, my darling girl,' he said and his words slurred slightly. 'I will not be long.' He pulled her towards him as he stood by the door, ran his hand, again, down her body, and she heard the crowds on the street calling and laughing and voices selling meat and flour and nails. 'I will be back as soon as possible. I will expect you to be ready.' He caught her head to his chest for just a moment, and spoke into her hair. 'Do not think of sleeping, Harriet. I have the laudanum, my darling, and you will sleep when I determine.' And then he kissed her mouth, and then he turned to go but just as he opened the door he turned back.

'This is the punishment,' he said. And she saw that his face held a look of triumph at what had, at long last, been won.

She heard him instructing Peters to lock the door of her bedroom and not move from there. And then she heard the heavy lock being turned.

She was poised like an arrow. She had made her plan. She knew she could not go back to the ladies at Government House, or to the Burlington Browns so concerned to keep up standards. She knew she could not: her powerful father would be informed at once, her word against his would be considered so improper, so unbelievable, that they would say she was mad, not him: her flight from England was proof enough of that. Even Edward could not help her now. Somewhere in the hotel someone was playing the piano in a jaunty out-of-tune kind of way, and voices sang of 'Black-Eyed Susan'.

She quickly crossed to the table and lit the lantern, the apples and the peaches still stood on the table. She held up the lantern and the flame moved in the draught that came in even at the closed window as she looked around her. Every second counted. She pulled her embroidery bag and her cloak from under the bed: she could tell someone had been through her luggage brought from the Gentlewomen's Hotel but these she had hidden under the bed and out of sight when she arrived from Edward's land, and these, she saw, had not been touched. She looked quickly as she always did for her money; and then for something she had almost forgotten: the knife – the knife from the kitchen at Bryanston Square. She might have use for it, after all. She checked candles and matches, her Journal. She put two of the apples in her bag. And then she turned the lantern down low and approached the main window, which she opened very carefully and quietly as the wind caught her dress and her hair. Outside the small boats still bobbed at the shoreline, others were being pulled up on the beach in the darkness, lanterns flickered, voices called, carried on the wind. Horses whinnied, tied to fences. Further along the quay, past the small traders who sold hats and honey, she saw a crowd: men shouting, lanterns waving; this would be her father's meeting. Almost everyone was there, it seemed: the path running along the shore beside the hotel was otherwise almost empty: two drunk fishermen spoke of girls, with their arms about each other's shoulders, then drifted towards the lights and the noise. She craned out and looked down far to the left of the harbour: no shouting or sound of boots on stones, no lanterns; yet as she stared into the night something more silent, more stealthy seemed to move in the darkness. Harriet suddenly shivered.

But the natives were friendly, people said. She had seen Edward buy a horse from the natives: she would buy a horse too and travel north, there was a fair road from here along the coast. From travelling with Edward she understood just a little about traversing the bush, she would ride as far as she could and then she would hide. Perhaps she would die: if animals or snakes or natives or her father found her then she would find Mary: she had her knife and this was her promise to herself. *She would never, never let herself be trapped again.* Very quietly she closed the front window.

Almost as an afterthought, it seemed, as she moved away from the window, she paused for a moment and then knelt quickly beside the bed and closed her eyes. The dim light from the lamp on the table threw long flickering shadows on to the walls of the room as she bowed her head.

Dear Lord, who knows all things. It was a long
and dangerous journey that brought me this far.
Please help me to make my journey now. And if it
is thy will that this journey is to be my final journey, that it is to end with me finding my dear
sister Mary, then I will bow to thy will and be
glad. But you cannot mean me to live this way.

And then she added one more short sentence that shocked her as
she heard herself say it.

If thou art there Lord?

Amen.

She was not sure, for a moment, if she had said that.

Then she moved quickly to the side window, opened it quietly.
Her heart was beating very fast. Into the alley she dropped her
embroidery bag and her cloak. She did not dare jump: if she broke
a leg now she was doomed. The alley seemed dark and quite
empty. But suddenly, even as she prepared to climb down after her
precious belongings, she heard the door of her room being
unlocked. In an instant she closed the window, whirled back to
face the door, her heart pounding, her breathing rapid. Her father
must have returned for something.

At the sight of Peters ushering Lord Ralph Kingdom into the
dimly lit room Harriet supposed her heart might actually stop, so
great was her shock, and then, as clearly as if she was in the room,
she heard Mary's voice: *and then just as darkness fell the Lord of the
Manor appeared before her in the gloom to be continued next week.*

'Do not stay too long, Lord Kingdom,' she heard Peters whisper,
'I do not know how long the settlers' meeting will last,' and the
door was closed behind the new visitor whose dark hair was
almost standing on end from the wind and whose wild, wonderful
eyes stared at her in a kind of exultation.

'Harriet, you are so beautiful!' He had never forgotten, yet it
seemed, staring at her, that he had not remembered well enough.
'You are so beautiful,' he repeated almost wonderingly. And to
himself he said at last, purity of bloodlines banished from his mind:
of course I will marry her.

She shook the extraordinary vision of Mary away and said the first thing that came into her head. 'How did you get Peters to allow you in?'

Lord Ralph laughed before he moved to her. 'You can always buy servants,' he said.

And then he threw off his cloak and crossed the room and Harriet was at once clasped in his arms and he began to speak.

'Harriet, Harriet, Harriet Cooper, you belong to me! I so nearly lost you again, how can I have been such a fool. Ben is right, it is not your fault – oh God, to see you at last.' And for a moment he stood back, held her at arm's length, looked at the beautiful woman he had carried for so long in his head who now stood before him in the dim light looking so beautiful and so totally bewildered that he laughed again, but this time in joy, and pulled her to him again.

'You have grown more beautiful still, Harriet Cooper, and what you have done is a most courageous thing.'

She thought of her precious embroidery bag lying in the darkness, anybody could come upon it. She tried to disentangle herself from his arms.

'Ralph – I don't think you understand.'

'But I *do*, my darling, that is the point, I do understand and I want you *nevertheless* to marry me, we shall get married here in this colonial outpost at the end of the world – tomorrow – tonight I would prefer. My brother Benjamin is here and will act as our witness.'

'Your brother is here – in Wellington?' Harriet felt as if shock after shock rained down on her.

'We are here to take you back to England as part of our family at last. Oh Harriet, Harriet,' and he pulled her strongly to him again and buried his face in her hair. That she stood unmoving, quite still in his arms, he did not seem to notice, but felt at last that she again pulled away. This time she went and sat at the table, the table where she had so lately sat with her father. She turned up the light of the lamp: there he stood, the handsome Lord Ralph Kingdom, in whose wild eyes women drowned.

'Please, Ralph, I need to understand what is happening.'

'No, Harriet, you do not! You do not need to understand anything at all except that I am here to protect you, and to marry you, and to take you home.'

'Does my – does my father know that you are here?'

There was an infinitesimal change in Ralph's manner before he said: 'I believe not. I did not know, either, that he was here until I saw the crowds in the street outside all speaking of the Member of Parliament from England who is to address them. One boasted that he worked at the hotel where the Englishman was staying! But Harriet – listen to me, your father does not matter. I will save you, I will marry you, I forgive you.'

At that moment it struck Harriet that he knew.

The blood rushed to her face and she heard a singing in her ears. She sat there, at the table, but she could not speak, she could not look at him. *Somebody knew what her father had done.* She closed her eyes, so great was her terrible shame, so that she could not see the world. *Somebody knew what her father had done.*

Ralph seemed to observe none of this, so great was his exultation. 'Say that we shall be married tonight, my darling Harriet. I have crossed the whole world to find you. I shall not lose you a second time.' Her eyes were still closed but she was aware of him looming above her, above the table. He pulled her to her feet, took her again in his arms and then he held her shoulders tightly, so tightly that he hurt her, *he held her like her father held her.*

Somewhere in the distance a crowd was cheering.

'My darling, you know I will protect you always, the past will seem only like a dream and you will easily forget it ever happened. Let us marry now, tonight! And you shall travel home with us and I shall take you to Kent as my wife, as the new mistress of the Kingdom estate and fortune and there you shall live in safety for the rest of your life!'

She saw the cold, high-ceilinged rooms.

She could go with him now. She could go out past Peters, out of the Barratt's Hotel, out of her misery and her shame and her fear. In her mind she saw the embroidery bag and the cloak in the alley, under the window. All she had to do was say yes, and she could pick them up as they passed by to her new life. The handsome, wealthy, eligible Lord Ralph Kingdom would carry her embroidery bag and she would tell him that it contained her life. Still his arm held her too tightly, still her shoulders were trapped, and then, as he held her even closer, she felt the hardness of his body, pressing on to hers.

'No,' she said quietly.

'Tomorrow then – or the next day! Whenever you like.'

'I cannot marry you.'

He looked down at her: he had not heard her, he thought. He loosened his grip slightly and she was able to free herself.

'Lord Ralph, forgive me. It is not possible for me to marry you.'

He did not believe her.

'What are you saying?'

'I am – I am most conscious of the honour you bestow upon me. But it would be wrong of me to marry you.'

'But I *know* about your father. About the terrible wrong he has done you. I forgive you, Harriet.'

'You forgive me.' She stared at him then and he was conscious of something else, something different in her eyes, and then she repeated his words: you *forgive* me?

'Yes. Yes I do.'

Still she stared. And then she said quietly, 'I could not marry you, Ralph.'

It was as if she had said something absurd. '*You* could not marry *me*?' His voice was incredulous.

'I could not.' She did not elaborate.

Still he stared at her, unbelieving.

Still she stood, in the room that held such terror for her, decided. He saw from her face that she was decided. *She had refused him.*

Lord Ralph Kingdom suddenly felt his world, of which he had been so sure, smash into a million pieces. Without another word he turned, throwing his cloak over his shoulders, and strode blindly, wildly out, past Peters, along the corridor of Barratt's Hotel, out into the night.

Peters came into the room at once. 'Don't think of telling your father that Lord Kingdom was here,' he hissed across the room. 'For I will say you had arranged it, and he will believe me, not you, you little whore.' She heard the key turning in the lock.

For some moments she could not move.

And then suddenly, all in one movement, she opened the window and jumped down into the alley. She heard her dress tear, she felt her bones jolt, but she landed on her cloak. On her knees she felt round in the dark. Her embroidery bag was there. She threw on the cloak, snatched up the bag, and ran: ran along the foreshore, away from the crowds and the raised voices and the flickering lights of the settlers' meeting, in the other direction towards the *pa*, the Maori village. The wind whipped at her cloak and her clothes and her hair, her mouth filled with dust and sand blowing along beside her but she ran on, her breath coming now in harsh gasps, right to the edge of the town. She tried again and again to catch her breath as she approached the carved gateway. It seemed quiet and deserted: all she could hear now was the wind and the sea. Had she seen, from the hotel, the shadows of natives gathering quietly in the darkness? She thought she saw a fire flickering in the distance, partly sheltered by a wooden palisade. She quickly entered the gateway, hurried unseeing past strange carved figures and approached nervously, but there seemed to be nobody there, by the fire. She looked about her, saw only shadows of canoes, moving in the wind at the water's edge. There must be someone. *There must be someone. Someone must be here. I must have a horse.* She thought she could smell tobacco on the wind.

Something moved in the firelight and she jumped, let out a little gasp. Beside the fire in the shadows an old man stared up, smoking a pipe. Harriet quickly, nervously drew closer. 'Good evening,' she whispered. There was no answer. She looked again. Perhaps it was an old woman. The lower part of the brown face was tattooed and it looked foreign and fearsome as it stared at Harriet without expression.

'Good evening,' said Harriet again. Her voice shook.

Perhaps the old woman heard it. She looked past Harriet, saw that she was alone. She stared at the white visitor a little longer and then she said, '*Tena koe.*'

Harriet tried. '*Tena koe,*' she answered and in the firelight she saw shrewd eyes studying her face. She knelt down by the fire. Still the old woman said nothing more, still the small, dark, watchful eyes in the strange, foreign-looking face observed her.

Harriet leaned towards the old woman, felt the warmth of the embers burning her face. 'Please, if you have any heart, please help me. I want to buy a horse. I have money but I must have a horse.'

There was a sound behind her, she screamed, turned in terror, convinced it was her father or Peters or Lord Ralph. But it was a much younger Maori woman wrapped in a kind of mat. She was perhaps not much older than Harriet.

She spoke in English. 'You came with the *pakeha* to buy a horse. You want a horse now, girl?'

'I must have a horse,' she heard her voice gabbling. 'Please, I must have a horse.' And she pulled money from her purse, held it out to the younger woman, sovereigns spilled to the ground. Harriet, scrabbling at the ground in confusion, burst into tears.

'Oh please,' she said, she heard her own voice saying, 'please help me. I have used up all my strength.' To her horror she could not stop crying. All the unshed tears of the day that had started with her wearing a blue dress and scrubbing a pot poured down her cheeks in great convulsive sobs.

'Please excuse me, I am so sorry,' she tried to say politely to them, still trying to collect up the sovereigns. Visions of her father holding her, *this is your punishment*, hitting her, pressing her to him, filled her head like a scream, her head screamed. *Marry me tonight I forgive you*, said Lord Ralph, pressing against her, *You little whore*, said Peters and locked the door. 'I am so sorry, I am so sorry,' Harriet Cooper tried to say.

For some time, from the Maori *pa*, there was only the sound of the sea breaking on the shore and the sound, somewhere in the shadowy darkness, of a woman crying. Occasionally the two Maori women spoke softly in their own language; at last the younger woman moved to Harriet and put her arm around the desperate, weeping girl so that the *pakeha*, the white girl, would have a shoulder there, to cry on.

'I will apprise Her Majesty's Government, and the Prime Minister, of your feelings.' Sir Charles's florid handsome face was lit by the ever-moving lights as the settlers crowded round him: energy and excitement flashed across his face as he spoke. 'It is clear to me that self-government by people here who know the situation and live in this country is preferable to rule from thousands of miles away by those who do not.' The crowd applauded, Sir Charles bowed slightly. He knew he would soon be gone from this godforsaken place, his colleagues might do as they wished. *Let me go now to my darling girl.* And he felt a surge of wild exultation run through his body. Then into the excited chatter of the crowd and the flickering lights a great cry filled the air from nowhere and, hearing it, the crowd shuddered uneasily and became silent and even the wind seemed to abate.

'*Tihei Mauriora!*'

And the cry seemed to be answered from all around them in the darkness by other voices, '*Tihei Mauriora! Tihei Mauriora!*' The settlers looked about them apprehensively, could see no-one, only the black hills, and yet the voices were everywhere, seeming to echo over and over in the night, *Tihei Mauriora!*

And then just one Maori, an old man with a strange marked face and carrying a staff made from a tree, stalked through the crowd and climbed on to the platform. Even Sir Charles Cooper could not but be impressed just for a moment: the man was tall and the strange patterns carved on his face gave him an ominous look as the lanterns flickered all around him. He and the Lieutenant-Governor greeted each other in a curious way, hands clasping, noses touching briefly. He looked also at Sir Charles but did not offer his hand, nor did Sir Charles make any gesture of politeness to a native: for a moment the two men stared at each other and the crowd seemed to hold its breath.

And Benjamin, standing on the outskirts of the meeting, watched, almost mesmerised. *And where is Harriet?*

And then the native spoke. He had a deep, resonant voice, deeper than Sir Charles's; uttered a few words in Maori. His English, when he reverted to it, though accented, was understood by everyone.

'The Lord is my shepherd. I shall not want. He leadeth me beside the still waters. He restoreth my soul. We have signed a treaty with your Queen, Queen Victoria, who has become our Queen also. We offered her our loyalty, she offered us her protection over our lands. But all over our country, all over *Aotearoa*, we are now, in great sorrow, losing our land.' He turned now to Sir Charles and the Lieutenant-Governor. 'I wish you both to advise Queen Victoria that her loyal subjects, *ko nga Maori o Aotearoa*, follow the teachings of the missionaries as she well knows. But we cannot forgive them who trespass against us. We will not stand by and see the land of our *tupuna*, our ancestors, destroyed, any more than your Duke of Wellington would have done when Napoleon marched to battle.' Sir Charles shot a surprised glance at the Lieutenant-Governor and raised his eyebrows.

The Maori chief's gaze took in the white, angry, upturned faces, *how dare he mention our own beloved Duke*, and then he seemed to look beyond the crowd, to somewhere else in the darkness. And then he said, so quietly that many people did not hear, '*He iwi rua tatou,*' and a sigh seemed to echo from somewhere in the hills.

And then he stepped down from the platform and stalked away again and was almost at once lost in the darkness where the lanterns did not shine.

'What's that? What did he say?' Sir Charles leaned towards the Lieutenant-Governor who was looking anxious as the crowd murmured angrily.

'He was quoting what we said when we signed the treaty with them. The Governor said then, I expect he got carried away, that we, the British and the natives, were one people. The chief has just said,' and the Lieutenant-Governor looked apprehensively towards the hills, 'that we are two.'

Suddenly one of the settlers leapt on to the platform brandishing a shotgun: Sir Charles and the Lieutenant-Governor quickly moved away slightly. 'We have been cheated by the New Zealand Company,' shouted the newcomer. 'And now the British Government with no understanding of our situation is hindering our growth and our prosperity. They send us soldiers but they do not want the soldiers to fight the natives. From London they indulge these Maoris. They do not understand their shiftlessness, their trickery, the way they try to take back the land that we have purchased in good faith. But we understand the natives only too well, and with the help of God we – every man here – will deal with them ourselves.' The Lieutenant-Governor, alarmed now at the turn the meeting had taken, muttered to Sir Charles that he thought they might withdraw but the settler added loudly, raising his arms in triumph, '—with or without the assistance of our Lieutenant-Governor and the soldiers of Her Majesty's 65th Regiment!' and he fired his gun into the air.

The crowd erupted, a hundred lanterns raised into the night, a hundred shouts of agreement, so that the new shot was not heard. It caught the darkness by surprise, someone on the platform fell forward suddenly to the ground below.

Pandemonium exploded. Soldiers fired into the air, women screamed, settlers ran in all directions. A space was cleared round the wounded man, a doctor came forward, knelt down. Benjamin moved towards the platform. He saw the Lieutenant-Governor kneel also, saw the wounded man try to rise, heard quite clearly the wounded man say, 'My daughter. Send for my daughter.' And then fall back, as the doctor probed the wound. A soldier pushed Benjamin away with his gun, then saw his attire, realised he had pushed a gentleman, apologised, moved on to push other, less well-dressed people. A group of soldiers passed, dragging natives. People held lanterns for the doctor, the face was seen to be deathly pale, there was much blood on the ground. The wind blew and Sir Charles whispered, 'My daughter. I must have my daughter.'

But it was Peters who appeared. He whispered to Sir Charles but Sir Charles could not hear. In his agitation he tried to sit up, but could not.

'Where is she? Where is Harriet?'

Peters still had to speak much louder than he would have preferred and Sir Benjamin Kingdom and others beside him heard Peters say, with terror on his face as he looked at his master, 'She has disappeared again, Sir Charles,' and they saw Sir Charles fall back. And then there was a loud, angry cry of anguish which was caught by the wind and echoed round the harbour and into the hills.

'MY HARRIET!' cried Sir Charles Cooper.

Benjamin felt rather than saw someone very close behind him; turned to see his brother Ralph, wild-eyed and without his cloak, staring down at the man, and at the blood that seeped into the mud and the sand along the quay.

And then the eyes of Sir Charles Cooper opened.

Harriet opened her eyes suddenly, as if she had heard something. For a moment she wondered where she was, wondered if she had fallen asleep. She realised with deep embarrassment that *the native girl was holding her*, could smell the oil on her hair; she pulled away, heard the sea, heard the native language they spoke: the girl, the old woman, saw their faces in the firelight. *What is happening? Was I asleep? I must hurry. I must hurry*, yet her body felt somehow heavy. Her mouth tasted sand and tears, still she could smell the oil of the girl's hair.

The Maori girl, feeling Harriet move, waited for a moment and then spoke to her.

'My grandmother asks: *the person who has been your mother has died?*'

Harriet gasped in surprise. At first she could not speak at all. *Did I fall asleep and say something? I must have said something, I must have fallen asleep and said something.* She stared at the old woman and the old woman stared back across the firelight from old, unreadable eyes. Harriet took a deep breath. 'Yes,' she said slowly. 'Yes. The person who has been my mother has died.' And then suddenly her face was close to their faces across the dying embers of the fire: 'I must escape from my father. Please help me.'

'*Hoatu he hoiho ki te wahine pakeha.*' And then the old lady looked away altogether, as if Harriet was no longer there.

'Come,' said the girl.

'Hurry!' said Harriet.

The girl moved quickly across the windswept, seemingly empty village, past shadowy huts and piles of flax. Harriet followed, clutching her precious embroidery bag. She did not see the little faces, the small, curious, silent faces inside the huts that watched her go by. Behind the huts some horses were corralled within a fence of branches, there was a whinnying and stamping in the wind. The girl spoke softly to them in her language, threw a rope round one of them; its neck reared up as she caught it but still she spoke softly and at last the dark horse allowed itself to be led away from the others.

'Where's your saddle, girl?'

Harriet looked confused. 'I have nothing. I must buy a saddle.'

'We don't sell saddles. No-one has *wahine* saddles here.' She looked again at Harriet. 'Could you ride a man-saddle?'

'I could ride anything I think, if I try. But I must hurry. I cannot wait.' Far down the quay she thought she saw lights moving.

'You give me a petticoat. I lend you my brother's saddle.'

Harriet looked astounded. 'My *petticoat*?'

'I don't think you can ride man-saddle with all the petticoats. I will have your petticoat. I will lend you my brother's saddle but you must return it.'

'I might be gone a long time.'

'Never mind. Give me your word-on-the-Bible.'

'I give you my word-on-the-Bible. But hurry!'

'Now give me your petticoat.'

Harriet quickly took off the biggest black petticoat underneath her skirt.

'What is your name, girl?'

Harriet suddenly froze. 'Forgive me. I do not want you to know my name. They will come looking for me.'

'Give me your petticoat, *koreingoa*,' said the girl and she grinned at Harriet. Then she disappeared into one of the native huts with the petticoat and returned almost at once with a man's saddle and a bridle. She quickly put them on the horse, at last taking the money from Harriet, then helping her up. The horse shied slightly as Harriet, for the first time in her life, put one leg right over the horse; she would have fallen if the girl hadn't steadied her. She saw that her biggest petticoat would indeed have been a hindrance; her corset dug into her hips. The horse turned and tossed its head, feeling a stranger, feeling someone unsure; Harriet tightened her hold on the bridle, tried to balance sitting in this new way on the prancing animal.

'What is that word you called me?' Harriet stumbled over it. '*Kore – ingoa?*' It could not be worse than whore. The horse stamped and shook its mane, the Maori girl handed up the embroidery bag, Harriet placed it in front of her as the horse moved off. Again Harriet pulled at the bridle.

'I am calling you No-name. If they come I will say No-name hasn't been here, at *Pipitea*.'

For the first time Harriet managed to smile. 'Thank you. And – I should know your name,' she said, 'for I will return the saddle.'

'My name is Piritania of course. After your country.'

And then, becoming still for a second, as if she heard something, the girl was quite suddenly gone in the darkness and Harriet Cooper was left alone in the night with her impatient horse. She turned it quickly past the carved statues at the entrance but as she came out of the village she heard shouting in the distance. Suddenly her instinct told her that there were other people here, quite near, that Piritania had heard them. Yet she could see no-one. Fear made the hair at the back of her neck suddenly quiver. *I must go now.* She knew that the road north, the one she had taken with Edward and Hetty and Miss Burlington Brown, ran along behind the native village to the sea. In the dark she had only the windswept moon to guide her; quickly she turned towards the dark coast road away from the town; as she turned she heard more shouting and then suddenly the sound of shots.

The horse whinnied and reared: figures appeared out of the darkness, men running on silent feet, towards her, past her, melting away again as they turned into the *pa*.

Suddenly Piritania was again beside the horse. 'Get off, girl, get off.'

'What is it?'

'Quickly! You cannot get away now. There are soldiers everywhere.' She helped Harriet dismount, slapped the horse's side hard, it disappeared at once. Harriet stood clutching her embroidery bag, realised she was not wearing the big petticoat, her dress hung oddly. Piritania grabbed her arm, dragged her down on to the shore away from the village and on to their knees in the sand where they would not be seen; they heard horses' hooves, soldiers appeared with lanterns, they saw they were carrying guns. Still Piritania held her, motioning her to be silent.

There were scuffles and shouts, then a gunshot nearby. Soldiers were pulling some of the natives away. Then Harriet thought she heard her own name being called in the distance and she turned to Piritania in terror. The voices called out of the darkness along the quay.

'Harriet Cooper! Harriet Cooper! Where are you?'

'Don't let them find me, don't let them find me.' She clung to Piritania.

'Harriet Cooper, Harriet Cooper! Your father has been shot!'

'Dear God,' whispered Harriet. *Dear God, dear God, dear God.*

It was as if Piritania understood. 'Now go back, girl,' she whispered. 'I will keep the horse for you.'

'*Harriet Cooper!*' called the voices all over the town.

'Go now,' whispered Piritania.

And Harriet moved forward into the light of the lanterns.

'I am Harriet Cooper,' she said.

The soldiers escorted Harriet back along the quay; in all the confusion no questions were asked about where she was going, where she had been; nor was her torn dress or her lack of a petticoat observed in the excited, charged night. A soldier carried her embroidery bag.

She asked only one question.

'Is my father dead?'

The Regimental Officer looked embarrassed. All they had were carts, they could hardly place her in a cart; if only they had a carriage, a closed carriage to take her, as they would have in England. 'He has been taken to the Government House, Miss Cooper.'

'Is my father dead?' she repeated, as if he had not spoken.

And now the Lieutenant-Governor himself came hastening towards the little procession. 'Oh my dear, I am so very sorry, so very sorry, these are troubled, troubled times,' and he took her arm as they hurried back the way he had come.

Ralph and Benjamin Kingdom stood in the shadows and saw the pale and beautiful figure of Harriet Cooper, who had brought them so far, being escorted in the moonlight along the unpaved road. But they did not call, fell back into the shadows until she had passed.

Then the two brothers turned to a boatman down on the shore, called to him quietly to row them back to the *Seagull*. As the oars splashed, phosphorescent light rippled outwards along the dark water. Lord Ralph Kingdom shook; he did not stop shaking when Benjamin gently put his own jacket around his brother's shoulders.

And Benjamin understood the premonition at last.

THIRTY-TWO

Wellington town could not sleep. The lights continued to flicker along the beach and on to the quay, nervous lanterns could be seen everywhere, settlers stood about in excited, angry groups planning reprisals and revenge. The Maori villages were dark, silent and uneasy at each end of the town. The 65th Regiment was on full alert, soldiers stood on corners in the night, their guns ready. The wind dropped.

Then the news came: three natives had been arrested and charged with murder, justice would be done.

But the settlers muttered sullenly as they slowly made their way back to their rough houses and their sheds and their land and their farms along unfinished roads; many were men like Edward who had come with high hopes: this was not how they had foreseen their lives.

The sea, calmer now, broke gently on the shore.

Out in the harbour the *Seagull* waited until dawn.

In the Government House, at midnight, in a dark formal room at the back that was used only for very important official occasions, Harriet Cooper said goodbye to her father.

She was not alone: they did not feel she should be, nor had she asked to be: the Lieutenant-Governor's wife and Mrs Burlington Brown stood beside her, to give her support.

They saw that Harriet did not cry, that she stared down at the body of her father with a strange look that they could not read. But they knew, and said to each other later, that grief takes many forms.

And then Harriet closed her eyes and they moved slightly, looked away, in deference to her prayers. For some time Harriet could not form any words. At last she prayed.

> Dear Lord,
> forgive us our trespasses.
> As we forgive them
> that trespass against us.

They were near enough, both women, to hear a small, light sigh.

> Dearest, dearest Mary.
> I am free.

And then if the kind ladies had been looking at her they would have seen just the ghost of a smile.

To be continued next week.

THIRTY-THREE

In the fresh morning air a dog barked in the distance.

The Lieutenant-Governor's house was full of people but few of them were known personally to Harriet, though Mr and Mrs Burlington Brown were there, and Miss Eunice, and the vicar; somehow Edward had been sent for, across the harbour. Messages had been sent to the Governor-in-Chief in Auckland about the death of Sir Charles Cooper and the uneasy situation in Wellington. Armed soldiers were everywhere, the natives had now been forcibly confined to their villages. The Maori chief who had spoken at the settlers' meeting had been to see the Lieutenant-Governor, they had been locked in his study for some time and raised voices were heard. It was agreed that the funeral of Sir Charles Cooper should be held as soon as possible in order for it not to be used as a rallying point for angry settlers: he was to be buried that afternoon. Fortuitously, although it was cloudy, they did not anticipate (which would turn the new cemetery to mud) rain. Harriet, of course, was not expected to attend the burial.

There was much discussion at Government House as to what was to be done with Harriet. She was so pale. She had not wept. She had lost her sister, and now her father. She must of course go back to England as soon as possible but should she be put aboard the *White Princess* next day as arranged by her father and sent back to London at once to the charge of her brothers? Or would such a journey be too soon after such a terrible shock? Mr Burlington Brown took it upon himself to speak to Harriet alone since he knew her so well; he spoke to her of her duty to her brothers and to God: Harriet nodded politely but did not speak, not at all.

A black petticoat had been found for Harriet at Government House and the rest of her things sent for from the hotel: no-one questioned her confusion at hearing the terrible news and not dressing properly; no-one thought of Peters bending to Sir Charles and saying that Harriet had disappeared. Peters was placed in the servants' quarters in Government House until it could be decided what should be done with him; in his boot lay two sovereigns from Lord Ralph Kingdom.

Harriet was permitted to walk alone in the garden where a few last English roses, deep yellow, still grew along the low wooden fence. The dog barked, nearer, but Harriet did not hear, so deep in thought was she as she walked.

She only looked up when Quintus jumped the wall and ran like an arrow towards his old mistress in a wild, remembered joy.

Her face registered total disbelief.

'Quintus?'

But of course it was Quintus, thousands of miles from Bryanston Square, his tail wagging madly, his ears back in sheer delight as he danced about Harriet. As she looked up from him she saw the Lieutenant-Governor escorting more guests upwards towards the door of Government House; Lord Ralph Kingdom and Sir Benjamin Kingdom walked gravely; behind them came her old maid Lucy, holding a small boy by the hand.

Just for a moment Harriet was so disoriented that the hills above her whirled. Lucy? *What was her maid Lucy doing here?* Lord Ralph had not mentioned Lucy. Or *Quintus*. The figures vanished into the Government House.

But Quintus stayed with Harriet. He leapt and barked, and from a window Benjamin saw the beautiful, beautiful girl at last kneel on the Lieutenant-Governor's lawn and bury her face in the dog's coat.

Visitors arriving were escorted by footmen and tea was served at once.

Sympathy was expressed to Harriet on her great loss.

Guests took Harriet's hand, gave formal condolences. Harriet bowed her head, did not speak at all.

Lord Ralph Kingdom bent low over Harriet's hand, his face haggard. He did not look at her.

Sir Benjamin Kingdom held her hand gently, his grey eyes sombre.

Lucy curtseyed.

The boy, George, was sent to the garden with Quintus; the terrible fate of the *Cloudlight* was discussed by the men in hushed, serious voices in the Lieutenant-Governor's study that still smelt faintly of the Maori chief. Lucy, in the kitchen, regaled the other servants with her adventures (but did not speak of Annie jumping from the rocks) as they prepared funeral meats; she ignored Peters who sat distraught on a barrel of flour. In the drawing room guests spoke in low voices of the murder, of the difficulties of getting servants in the new colony; cast quick, appraising glances at Miss Harriet Cooper. She soon asked to be excused and went to the room she had been given in Government House.

There she sat, her face blank.

Edward arrived by boat just in time, slipped quickly into the church with his hair smoothed down and his earnest face deeply disturbed; looked in disbelief at the presence of Ralph and Benjamin; stared in distress at his pale cousin, having had as yet no chance at all to speak to her. Miss Eunice Burlington Brown, manoeuvering herself (in becoming black) to Edward's side in the church, was mortified to see that he looked at her blankly before at last realising who she was and bowing apologetically. The vicar prayed for everlasting life for Sir Charles Cooper.

The small procession, escorted by red-coated soldiers, left the church on the hill and wound upwards to the cemetery at the back of the town. Sir Charles Cooper's body was carried on a cart. No prancing horses with waving plumes, no lines of carriages of the rich and influential: many of the mourners like Lord Ralph and Sir Benjamin were not even wearing black, having no mourning clothes among their possessions. But all wore black armbands as they toiled upwards. The sky was overcast and grey, the Wellington wind blew softly across the town. Trees on the hills bowed and sighed and the scent of *manuka* hung in the air.

And for some reason Harriet had insisted on attending: it was not at all the thing for a lady to do in these circumstances but none had liked to forbid her, so strange was her manner, so cold and still. Lord Ralph, pale-faced, had finally offered her his arm: she looked at him so blankly, as if she was in a trance, that he drew back; it was Lucy who helped Harriet over the uneven earth tracks to the burial ground. (Benjamin suddenly remembered the small, desolate figure in the chapel at Highgate Cemetery, forbidden to follow her sister to her grave, and his heart contracted, understanding now that desolation.)

The Maori chief and several of his men stood above them as they came up the track: the procession stopped in alarm, the soldiers felt for their guns. But the chief's head was bowed: finally, at a sign from the Lieutenant-Governor, the procession moved onward to the new grave.

The vicar spoke a few more simple words, the body was lowered into the ground, watched carefully by Harriet. But it was Edward Cooper, not Harriet, who threw some handfuls of earth into the final resting-place of the Right Honourable Sir Charles Cooper, MP.

In the distance could be heard the eerie sound of wailing of native women.

Tea was served at Government House, and plates of food.

The drawing room was crowded with people: Harriet suddenly could not breathe, escaped to the garden. The boy George was there with Quintus who, seeing Harriet, ran towards her, barking, looking up at her face. He seemed almost to be smiling. George too watched Harriet for a moment as she stood looking at the sea, calming her breathing. He had heard the people talking. Then he said:

'Did your father die, lady?'

For a moment she did not answer him. George tried again, most persistently. 'Lady, did your father die?'

'*Yes!*' Harriet let out a long, long breath at last. 'Yes. Yes. Yes. My father died.'

'My father died. And my mother. Did you cry, lady?'

Harriet shifted focus at last: looked at his scrubbed and anxious face.

'I did cry,' she said. 'When my sister died. But that was a long time ago.'

Quintus stood between them listening, his ears cocked.

'My good friend has told me not to cry and to be a man and not to think about dying but in the night I think of them.'

'You cannot help it,' said Harriet gently. 'You cannot help remembering.'

George spoke very fast. 'They did drowned in the water and there was screaming and waves and the waves went over me and my mother held on to me and I can read now but I want to see my mother before I go to heaven where she is, I want my mother now, I heard her screaming in the water and I ain't never going in the water again.'

The Lieutenant-Governor was at her side. 'Now, young George, off you go and play, do not bother Miss Cooper today,' and he took Harriet's arm firmly, moving her away from the boy and the dog. 'A little walk around the garden,' he said determinedly, and for a moment or two they walked in silence.

'You see the remains of our roses,' he said at last. 'But I fear it is a long way from England, all the same. You will be glad, my dear, to be Home again after such terrible tribulations.' She did not answer.

'But my dear Harriet, out of sadness joy sometimes comes. It is with great pleasure that I have understood that Lord Ralph Kingdom wishes to speak to you.' Harriet stopped walking. Surely, *surely*, Lord Ralph Kingdom, here with his brother, and somehow her maid, and her dog, would not speak to her again of marriage? Had he not told them she had refused him? She took a deep, trembling breath, and reminded herself that, for the first time in her life, she was free.

I will not marry.

I will not go back.

'I just want you to know,' continued the Lieutenant-Governor, encouraging her to walk on, 'that my wife and I will of course do everything in our power to assist you in any of your arrangements. This has been a quite dreadful time for you; that your father should have been caught up in the difficulties we are experiencing here is most terrible and I cannot say how distressed I am at the turn of events. I shall remember always the look of pride and affection upon his face when you played the piano for us, only yesterday. Ah my dear, my dear. You will, of course, need someone to look after you.' He sighed and shook his head. 'In the end they are uncivilised, the natives – primitive, savage and malign. I believe they have been provoked by the foolish actions of a minority of the settlers, but that of course is no excuse. We believe we have found the perpetrators, who will be summarily dealt with; there will be executions of course.'

'It was the Maoris who killed my father?'

'I am sure so, but unfortunately we cannot identify the gun. Your father was killed with a bullet from a pistol. It is regrettably true that there is trade with the natives in firearms – but muskets, not pistols. We do not sell pistols to natives. The native chief – whom I believe to be an honourable man, on his own terms of course – tells me he knows of no pistols. But of course black-market trading goes on all the time and we will find the gun, and so the murderers.'

'It was definitely the Maoris?' She kept getting odd flashes in her mind, Piritania holding her as she wept, the smell of the oil in her hair.

'My dear Miss Cooper, we are in a primitive, barbarous land, but we are men of England. Who would kill someone like your father, if not a native? They were looking for trouble last night. The old chief insists they were merely gathered at the back of the town in support of his speech, and it is true, I have learnt from experience, that there is a certain *theatricality*, sometimes, about their formalities. He said they were all there because they had planned a big gathering of their own later in the evening, but I have it on good authority that the *pas* were empty, on both sides of town.' Again the Lieutenant-Governor sighed. 'Ah – forgive me, my dear, this is men's talk. But I wanted to assure you, Miss Cooper, that every effort will be made to bring the killers to their maker and all the reports that go to London on the *White Princess* will, of course, tell how your father died in support of his country while with his beloved daughter. And if, after such sadness, you are to leave New Zealand with the prospects of joy, my wife and I will be delighted.'

Handsome, debonair and pale, Lord Ralph Kingdom was striding towards them, across the grass: in this public place, on the day of her father's funeral, she could do nothing but allow him to lead her down the lawn.

*

They sat on a bench, overlooking the harbour. Above them, on the flagpole that usually intimated ships' arrivals, the Union Jack flew at half-mast. Occasionally it was caught by the wind, flapped against the pole.

From the drawing-room window they could be seen in the distance. Benjamin, making polite conversation with the Lieutenant-Governor's old aunt, moved away from the windows. But the aunt, a rather grand lady of much social pretension (who thought Sir Benjamin Kingdom most marvellously presentable and hoped he would stay for the good of the new colony's many unattached young ladies), was nevertheless enthralled at the prospect of a proposal going on under her nose and kept observing, during her conversation with Sir Benjamin, the couple under the flagpole. They had been there for some time: they seemed not to be speaking a great deal; Lord Ralph did not seem to look at Miss Cooper, he looked rather at the sea and the hills.

Lord Ralph Kingdom's tone was formal and cold as he stared outwards.

'I presume, Miss Cooper, that you have not changed your mind.'

'I am sorry, Lord Kingdom, for your long journey and I am conscious of the honour you do me. But as I told you last night, I could not marry you. Nothing has changed.' She made as if to rise but his hand detained her even though he did not look at her.

'Nevertheless they think I am proposing to you now so we shall have to use up the time. People have been informed that I came to New Zealand to propose to you, and propose I must. It is not known by anyone but my brother that I was ashore last night.'

'Why is that?'

He answered her in a low voice, as if they could be overheard, although there was no-one near.

From the window the Lieutenant-Governor's aunt saw the girl's head whip round suddenly so that she was staring at her suitor.

'*What did you say?*' said Harriet.

He repeated the words. 'I shot your father. He did not deserve to live, he had no right to live. He has destroyed my happiness and I have no regrets about what I have done.' He continued to stare outwards.

She simply stared, white-faced herself, at the white face of Lord

Ralph Kingdom, one of the sons of England, and at the wild eyes where, they said, women drowned.

It was as if the barbarous country made barbarians.

Her hands began to shake. For some moments she held them across her mouth and rocked backwards and forwards slightly and he heard that she made little gasping sounds. But if he feared she would run screaming to the house he gave no sign. After some time she stopped shaking and her hands returned to her lap.

'Who else knows this?' she said in a low, low voice.

'About last night? Only my brother Ben. And he knows the reason. Lucy told us.'

'*Lucy?*'

'She was afraid. She guessed your father might be here. She thought I should know—' he still did not look at her, 'what your father did to you.'

There was a long, long silence. Some small birds with tails like open fans flashed past them and into a big tree in the corner of the garden. Distantly, from the harbour, men shouted and carried barrels and logs across the sand. The Union Jack made a hollow sound as it suddenly flapped against the flagpole.

At last Harriet felt able to speak. 'Forgive me, Lord Ralph, but *why* is Lucy with you?'

'She was coming to New Zealand of her own accord, to bring you your dog.'

Harriet made a small, odd sound. Lord Ralph did not know if she was crying, or laughing. He would not care, he told himself as he watched the sea, either way. Tomorrow he would be gone from here.

From the window, the Lieutenant-Governor's aunt saw Harriet lean across so that her head was very close to her companion's although she was not looking at him.

'Ralph, I have to explain something to you,' Harriet said in a low voice. For some reason she wanted to speak truthfully to him, to try and explain something to him, perhaps to make him understand. She perhaps owed that to the man who had crossed the world to find her, and then saved her life, even if she did not love him. She paused as if to gather unspeakable words together; he waited as if transfixed, suddenly staring at her: *had his action made her change her mind?*

'Ralph, you must understand that I have never, never spoken about this, about – my father – to another living person. Even with my sister Mary, she knew of course, there was no need for words, and there were no words for this. I did not know that Lucy guessed. If I have the courage to talk to you now of what is, literally – unspeakable – it is because – of what you have done.' She stopped for a moment. 'And because, now, we both have – secrets.' She felt him staring at her, she took his look, swallowed several times and continued doggedly.

'Ralph – I would like you to understand something. I think my father has damaged me. Not in the way that perhaps you have—' she stopped and then made herself continue, 'imagined – but in another way. I think he has made it impossible for me to—' she felt her face flush but still she forced herself go on, 'to wish to – perform my duties as a wife.'

Her words shocked him: this was not how any respectable woman spoke, or thought. But something in her face touched his heart, made him understand that she was bravely pushing away the way women spoke, because she was trying to tell him the truth. For just one moment he let down his guard, as if her honesty had triggered his own.

'Something happened to me on the journey here, Harriet. I was happy.'

For just a moment their eyes met in something like closeness. And then as if he had already said too much he moved away from her slightly. This time at least she would remember him as a gentleman.

It never occurred to him for a moment that she would remember him as a murderer.

They sat in silence and watched the harbour. The *White Princess* was already loading, small boats plied to and fro from the shore's edge, carrying flax and timber. It was Harriet who finally spoke.

'Peters knows you came ashore last night. I would not trust Peters.'

'I will employ Peters, and he will remain grateful,' said Lord Ralph. 'I know how to manage people like Peters.'

The timber and the flax crossed the sand, a group of native women laughed with some of the crew from the *White Princess*, the laughter echoed upwards.

'You will return to England of course? Your father will have made provision for you.' Harriet saw that he spoke matter-of-factly, there was no irony in his words. 'Your brothers will be responsible for you. You will need the protection of your brothers.'

She answered him slowly. 'No, Ralph. I want to stay here.'

Again she had shocked him. '*Why?*'

She paused before she answered and then she said, 'I feel at home here. There is something about the space and the air that makes me feel as if I belong.'

'But you belong, surely, in England, in a civilised country. You could not be happy here for long.'

'I shall try.' And she smiled at him, that old remembered smile that lit up her face, and he turned away in pain. He could not know what she was thinking. *In this uncivilised country I have become free.*

They sat for some time on the bench in the garden. Dusk was falling. He could not help himself.

'You will always remember me,' he said. It was a statement, not a question.

She nodded. 'Yes, Ralph. I will always remember you.'

So at last he said, 'It must be reported then, that you have refused me.' With a touch of his old panache he added: 'They will not believe it.'

'No,' said Harriet gravely. 'They will not believe it.'

A little later, watched from the drawing room, the two of them walked slowly, not arm in arm but close together, towards the Government House. They made an extraordinarily handsome couple. The wind caught Harriet's hair. She put up one graceful arm to the side of her head, walked with her hand beside her pale face, holding back her dark hair.

From the window Benjamin, looking out at last as a frisson of excitement shivered over the drawing room at the couple's return, thought he had never seen anything so beautiful as Harriet Cooper at that moment.

He turned away.

THIRTY-FOUR

Two things were arranged, even if the hoped-for betrothal was not: Sir Benjamin Kingdom would not be returning to England in the meantime, he would walk into the interior of the southern island and see if there was any sign of the existence still of the fabled tall bird, the *moa*. And Lucy was employed, until she got to know the new country and found ways of finding her own dreams, as Harriet's maid.

The Lieutenant-Governor's aunt felt extremely angry at Miss Cooper's foolishness and made so bold as to mention to the world in general that London society might never forgive her. Surely to refuse the proposal of the mighty Kingdom family was unforgivable?

'I dare say, ma'am,' said a banking official recently arrived from London, 'that her brothers will have inherited a great deal of money. Sir Charles Cooper was a very rich man and Miss Cooper will have friends enough.'

'Not,' said the Lieutenant-Governor's aunt in her grandest manner, 'the people who matter,' and Mrs Burlington Brown nodded sagely.

Edward Cooper, loyal Edward, bemused by everything that was happening, bowed coldly to the aunt.

'My cousin will always have the support of her family, ma'am,' he said stiffly, 'and her decisions are her own affair.'

Harriet did not go down to the harbour to farewell the *White Princess* on its way to Sydney. Such was the disappointment of her hosts, the Lieutenant-Governor and his wife (not to mention the disapproval of their aunt); such was the incredulous disbelief of Mrs Burlington Brown and Miss Eunice who had never known such an extraordinarily handsome man as Lord Ralph Kingdom, that Harriet deemed it more politic to stay in her room in Government House. (Mr Burlington Brown felt some kind of personal glow, his protégée would stay under his personal care and guidance.) But the others all seemed to imply that it was her *duty* to marry Lord Ralph, she had failed in her duty. They tried to be kind, they tried to put her unfeminine behaviour down to grief; tried to understand that she might want to stay, however briefly, in the country where her father was buried. But everybody felt she had made a most terrible mistake in not accepting Lord Ralph Kingdom's proposal of marriage, one he had travelled so far to offer. Her cousin Edward particularly, despite his public support, remained uneasy: he felt that there was something else in all this, in the extraordinary appearance of the Kingdom brothers, in Lord Ralph's pale silence, in Harriet's containment, that he did not understand. He hurriedly wrote page after page to his family, letters to be sent with the *White Princess*, trying to make sense of all that had happened in the last days. He wrote letters of condolence to Richard and Walter on the loss of their father, to add to Harriet's brief notes.

And all the time Miss Eunice Burlington Brown watched Edward, hoping for some small sign, her hopes fading as she saw he simply did not notice her. She had read from the newspaper to him, that delicious intimacy: they had been happy. She jealously wondered if Hetty Green still languished round the harbour, her arm tied to a cricket bat. But then she pulled herself up. What was she thinking of? How could she feel jealousy over a *servant*? Edward would not, of course, be thinking of a *servant*: he was kind merely, he had healed her arm. But she had understood that the strange idyll in the little house (it seemed to her an idyll) had bewitched them: all of them in that small rough room in a storm,

Harriet seeming to think she could speak of 'women's rights', Hetty drying her hair. Her brother was quite right (and Miss Eunice's mouth pursed in disapproval): it was *even more important* in a colonial situation for standards to be maintained, for the lower classes to be kept in their place. At least so she tried to comfort herself. But slowly, as Edward did not notice her, as he made plans for his move north to his new piece of land, her hopes faded; miserably she turned her thoughts to living forever, more and more a spinster, with her brother and his wife in this godforsaken, miserable colony, and in private she held her arms around herself, and wept.

On the shore, as they were being loaded, as Quintus ran everywhere, barking with delight (but keeping well away from the sea), the boy George began to scream. He simply refused to go back on the water, nothing could make him set foot in the small boat that rowed them out to mid-harbour: when Ralph tried to lift him he fought and kicked and screamed like an animal possessed.

Finally Benjamin said, 'Leave him, Ralph, for God's sake. He is terrified of the sea. I will arrange something.'

'Nonsense,' said Ralph, 'he must learn to be a man. That is what I will teach him.' And he nodded to the big, burly boatman in waterboots, who picked up the screaming boy bodily, placed him under his arm, and walked out to sea. George was unceremoniously dumped on the bottom of the boat beside a portmanteau of clothes; his piteous screams could be heard as the man rowed imperviously onwards to the *White Princess*.

Ralph and Benjamin embraced. They did not speak, for there was too much to say.

Benjamin and Edward stood together on the beach, hearing the capstan begin noisily to raise the anchor, seeing the white sails fill with wind. They waved as the barque turned; Edward thought of his letters, making their way to his dear family; Benjamin thought for a moment of the boy George, back so soon on board ship; waved again to the small, almost invisible figures on the *White Princess*.

Somebody called and they turned away from the harbour. The natives were to take Benjamin south that day, the stores were being loaded on to a schooner, there was some question to answer. The two friends shook hands, then Edward went off to arrange nails and Benjamin, his business completed, walked back to the Government House with the Lieutenant-Governor, then excused himself to find Miss Cooper and say goodbye

She sat by the flagpole, watching the *White Princess* intently: did not see or hear Benjamin until he sat beside her.

For a moment neither of them spoke. Then Benjamin said, 'What shall you do now?'

'Lucy and Quintus and I are to join my cousin Edward. He has been given new land.'

He nodded. 'Edward seems very relieved at another chance to settle. I am glad.'

'So am I,' said Harriet. 'But I will have to learn many things.'

The same bright fantails darted across from tree to tree in the Lieutenant-Governor's garden; still the flag flapped at the flagpole; Quintus could be seen in a far corner, chasing something with delight.

Then Benjamin said softly, 'Will you be – all right?'

She looked up at the grey eyes, remembered at once how he had asked her that question in the bookshop in Oxford Street, in another life.

She smiled at him: the smile that took away the strain, and the pain, of what had happened to her.

'I think I will be all right,' she said. 'Thank you for your – kindness to me, Ben. Then. And now.'

They called for Benjamin and he was gone.

And Harriet, shading her eyes from the white Wellington light, watched from the seat in the garden above the harbour the sails of the *White Princess*; saw the barque, tiny now, turn towards the heads and the open sea and then quite disappear. She turned her head slowly towards the hills behind the town, where the rough cemetery lay.

In four months perhaps, the news of the death of her father would reach England, and it would be real.

THIRTY-FIVE

Quintus tore across the field, through the big wooden gate, past the house, to where Harriet was sitting in the long grass, brushing at little insects, balancing her ink bottle, and writing. He came up to her barking and panting and wagging his tail, checking she was there, the way he often did. She rubbed his ears and laughed, his wet nose caught her cheek and then he was off again, haring back to the gate. There was so much to do, not just rats but sheep, but he seemed to be smiling.

Harriet was writing a letter to Mr Dawson, of Dawson's Book Emporium in Oxford Street.

Dear Mr Dawson,

I am writing to send you my very good wishes, to hope that you are very well and to ask you if you will prepare a parcel, or parcels, for me of all the books that you use in all your classes at the Working Men's Institute. All the books. I have had come upon me a hungry feeling that I want to read everything. I want to read all the philosophy books and all the language books (ancient and modern) and all the history books and all the books on religion and all the novels and all the poets. I include mathematics in my list. All these subjects I at least have spoken of with my dear sister

Mary: I will be grateful to be guided by you as to how to proceed further. The only way I can describe my hunger is that I want – if this does not sound too odd – to learn everything in the whole world! I enclose a letter of authorisation for Coutts Bank. I will return to London at some time and come to see you but please in the meantime send me everything you think I will benefit from. I will watch for the ships' arrivals and wait, every week, to hear from you.

Your friend
Harriet Cooper

PS I would be glad if you would give my greetings to Mr Cecil Forsythe who, like yourself, was so very kind to me, when I was most in need.

She read the letter over. And then, at last, she slowly picked up the old pale notebook that was lying beside her on the grass, the one that her brother Walter had given her, and began to write.

TO THE DEAR READERS OF MY JOURNAL
30 November 1851

Yesterday my cousin Edward married Hetty Green at the little wooden church in the valley, and I baked my first cake. And I wondered, as we sat eating cake and cold mutton in the warm spring sunshine, what Aunt Lucretia would have said, had she been here. Edward has recently had mail from her: '<u>Which</u> Greens?' she enquired most anxiously, several times (for he had written of his intentions). But dear Edward told us all that he had written back yesterday to say he was now a married man, a farmer, and the happiest man in New Zealand. Yet Aunt Lucretia will one day discover that her son has married beneath him and she will be mortified, and in my heart I know that I too have much to learn, and that I still struggle to come to terms with the new ways of this new world.

    I think of Hetty as I first met her aboard the Amaryllis. She seemed to me then not only a servant but a 'naughty' girl, with that – overflowing energy, and her immense attractiveness, and her eye for the sailors, and the things that she said. Some of the things she said disturbed me always. But over this last year and a half I have seen how she has used that same energy to assist and support and encourage Edward: on the land, in the house, from dawn to dusk she has been indefatigable (as is he: they are marvellously suited in that way). I see that sometimes, as he walks past her, he brushes her arm and I have seen how he looks at her, with a kind of wonder – and I do not dare to interpret that wonder too deeply. But I know that Miss Eunice Burlington Brown, a more acceptable choice in many ways, could never have delighted Edward in the way that Hetty Green has delighted him.

But I do hope that it will not be something Edward comes to regret, for I feel they will never be able to go home, to England. I think of his family, my dear relations, around the table in the dining room at Rusholme and I cannot see Hetty, sitting there, with Alice and Augusta and Uncle William and Cousin John. And Asobel. Uncle William said, with tears in his eyes: the sun never sets on the British Empire, let us hear proud things of you. And he would be proud: of how hard Edward has worked, success at last with his wheat, and with his new sheep: financial gain already. But Uncle William would not expect Hetty. Yet I know that <u>without</u> Hetty, Edward would not have thrived so well and so happily.

Edward and I have never, in the end, spoken to each other of the things within our hearts. I know that part of him still disapproves of my coming to New Zealand alone, that it has never been satisfactorily explained to him. And I would have liked to ask him if he had realised he could never again sit at ease with his family, with Hetty. But it would have seemed like disapproval also, and I do not mean that. Only that it is hard to be the first to break society's rules (especially while Mr and Mrs Burlington Brown are the arbiters of its moral and social register!) and I know that he will find it difficult, even here.

Or – perhaps I am wrong. Perhaps this country will teach other ways, just as it is teaching me. This is the country where I became free. And perhaps, in another way, Hetty (and Edward) feel the same.

When Edward and I and Lucy and Quintus rode over the hills here to the Wairarapa; when we saw the flat, fertile land stretching out before us from the bridle path at the top of the hill, down there beside the shining lake, I believe Edward nearly wept in relief. Everybody wanted to be seen to be doing their utmost for the nephew of the recently deceased Sir Charles Cooper, MP: the New Zealand Company assured him that they owned the acreage involved and so Edward would travel no further. (Recently we have found that the intricacies of the land purchase from the natives are unclear but Edward is too involved now to back out. He paid the New Zealand Company: that is certain and documented; he has acted always in good faith and we hope that all will be well.) So Lucy and Quintus and I stayed in the tiny settlement at the bottom of the hill and Edward went back to collect his belongings, of which – it soon became clear – Hetty Green was now part. (She still wore the cricket bat on her arm; it did its unlikely work well and now Hetty uses it for banging stakes into the ground or chasing the sheep, for Edward has one hundred and fifty sheep which I am proud to say I assisted him to purchase.)

The first winter in particular was very hard and our pioneering life was no longer a romance (as perhaps I had seen it at first). I of course did not understand that just the business of living, and being, is such hard work if other people are not doing much of it for you. We have had many terrifying experiences also and I have been frightened, but I do not find rats or wild pigs as frightening as the things that frightened me earlier in my life, nor the appearance late one night of an escaped convict from Australia, nor the odd comings and goings of the – sometimes immensely kind, sometimes undependable – natives, nor the rumbling sound in the distance that heralds another earthquake. But although I often wished that I was warm, or dry, or comfortable, or that my arms and my legs would not ache so, or in particular that there was time to read, or simply to think – never once did I wish I was back in Bryanston Square. But there have been three women in our little family, and no children, which is quite different from most families. Two women in this tiny settlement have died in childbirth. For women with children, and having more children, life is often difficult and dangerous and heartbreaking. (But I see, too, that Hetty faces her future with joy: some small boy will play cricket with that cricket bat.)

We lived much at first under tarpaulin; it was colder than we expected and it rained a great deal and Edward had immense trouble trying to build another house because the weather was so unpredictable. But he employed a gang of natives to help and then Benjamin Kingdom appeared on his way to look northwards for his elusive bird and turned out to be a most practical man (for an ornithologist). He is also extremely erudite and taught me many things in the time he was here: I found myself discussing the strangest matters with him — rocks of course, and birds, but also telescopes, and Latin, and balance (we were on the roof trying to unblock Edward's chimney), and God, and Henry VIII, and shoes!

In our new house Lucy can cook and sing at the same time, Hetty seems to be able to do anything at all, Quintus chases rats for all the world as if he were in Bryanston Square, and I attempt daily all the things that other people once did for me. I have, for instance, learned to hang the clothes I have washed with my own hands outside to dry in the fresh air, even undergarments, without so much as a blush to my cheek.

Lucy wishes to go back to Wellington to work in one of the hotels, where she will meet (she is quite certain of this and so am I!) a hard-working husband. Although she has not said so I think the marriage of Edward and Hetty has disturbed her also, disturbed old certainties that have sustained her. She would be too polite to say so but she does not really approve of me doing the washing, for instance, it makes her own role unclear and she does not like that. I encourage her to make her own life, of course, for I am constantly aware that it is because our roles are less strictly defined that we both have the chance to grow. But I shall miss her abrupt kindness more than I can say. And her singing! I woke this morning to hear her high clear voice echoing back from the fields, she sang that she would be seventeen come Sunday, and indeed she soon will be sixteen at least! There are many things unsaid between us. It still moves me (and makes me laugh at the same time) to think of her bringing Quintus to New Zealand. And in a way she saved my life, but she does not know that.

It is now two years since the Amaryllis left the English coast at last. Sometime I will have to go back to England to, as they say, sort out my affairs. For ironies abound (I sometimes see Mary's face still, that quizzical smile). I have received letters advising me

*that my father left me a great deal of money 'if she is living with
me at my death and has not married' and there we were, as the
Lieutenant-Governor no doubt advised the lawyers and as it says
in the hotel register, living at Barratt's Hotel, Wellington. Of
course I expected him to leave me to the care and charity of my
brothers. But my father no doubt thought that I should have,
unmarried, served him well before he died.*

*It feels so odd to think of England, and that life. Asobel writes of a
huge exhibition in Hyde Park which is inside, so she says, 'a palace
made from glass and there were exhibits from New Zealand which I
studied, Harriet, to learn as much as possible, until I should come'.*

   *Whatever happens I will return here. I want to live here. I feel
there is a better chance here for women to have some sort of say in
their lives, if they wish it. But there is something else. I have
changed a great deal, I no longer have to look about for my safety
in the way that I did. And like my sister Mary I now find that it is
not enough just to <u>be</u>, I want so much more than that, even though
I will never have to worry about money again.*

   *It is almost a new year, with new hopes: 1852! I want a new life
and I want my life to be useful. Oh – I feel like Mary felt, there is
so much for me to <u>learn</u>: to read, to understand. I know I am still
in great want of education and I am so, so hungry to be taught. I
suppose I, too, am now too old for the Ladies' College in Harley
Street, in a few months I will turn twenty! But I have written to
Mr Dawson in his Book Emporium and he will advise me. And
then, when I have at last been properly, truly educated, and opened
my mind, I might be useful, somehow, in this new land.*

   *My thoughts about what I might eventually do are so
unthinkable (even to me) that I hardly dare write them down: yet I
believe in them. It was true what my father said: he owned us, my
mother and my sister and me. He owned us because we were
prevented from being educated and owning ourselves. So we were
owned by my father and only a quirk of fate has prevented me now
from being passed on to, and being owned by, my brothers. There
is much agitation here for self-government, and for working men
as well as gentlemen to be given the vote. And what I have been
considering is this: why should not <u>women,</u> whose lives here are
not easy, but without whom good men like Edward could not*

*survive, <u>be given the vote</u> also? Why should they not, without
having to get permission from a father or a brother or a husband,
make decisions for themselves, own property themselves, earn
money for themselves? <u>Why not?</u>*

*These are heady thoughts indeed, but surely I cannot be the
only woman in the world who is thinking them?*

*Benjamin Kingdom makes me laugh. For some reason I trust him,
even though I realise he knows very much about me. He has a very
droll view of the world, rather as my sister Mary did. And the more
I laugh, the more I remember laughing with Mary when I was
younger, before things changed. I feel almost as though I have at last
become – myself: my mother's daughter. (I am aware that I show
great want of character in writing about myself so portentously in
this way but my life has changed so much that I feel I need to try
and make sense of it all. I mean only to say that fear prevented me,
earlier, from growing. One cannot grow if one is frightened. I shall
however desist from such portentousness from now on!)*

*Benjamin told us he has had mail to say that Lord Ralph
Kingdom has become engaged to a young girl of sixteen, a distant
relation of the old Duke of Wellington, and that Lady Kingdom is
ecstatic at the match. The boy George has been sent to Eton,
sometimes Lucy and I speak of him, and wonder how he will fare. I
could not help being delighted with the news of Peters and I hope
the Lord, who knoweth all things, will forgive me for such
unkindness and lack of charity. He was bitten by a poisonous
snake in Sydney.*

*Benjamin has been gone now for some months. Perhaps he has
found the fabulous bird up in the north or perhaps he has left for
England, which he said he must. Perhaps I shall see him there.*

*He and I spoke, just once, about the night my father died.
Benjamin told me that three natives were imprisoned in the
Wellington Gaol for some time and there was much agitation for
their execution but they were, finally, released.*

I am glad of that, dear readers of my journal.

The notebook and the letter fell gently to the grass where Harriet
lay. She closed her eyes in the warm sunshine and undid the top
button of her blouse, where it felt tight at her throat.

It had been so long since she had thought of London. She saw Mr Dawson in his Book Emporium, surrounded by knowledge. She remembered what he had said about Mary: 'I believe she saw life in smiling terms . . . tha must take her with thee.' *And so I did.* She saw Cecil in his squashed top hat lighting the lamp on his cab in Oxford Street, agreeing to take her luggage to Gravesend, and whistling. She saw the one oak tree, her oak tree, in Bryanston Square. And she saw her brother Walter, standing hesitantly at the door of her room with the notebook in his hands, 'Will you write a Journal again, Harry?'

She supposed she must be asleep. That it was the sun that caressed her eyelids so gently. She felt the warmth of the summer morning and she sighed with the pleasure of it. And for some reason an echo of Hetty's curious words aboard the *Amaryllis* whispered to her from far, far away, the way they sometimes did. *Ain't you done it? Don't you miss it?*

She began to dream: strange, languorous dreams. She dreamed of her beautiful mother, telling secrets of Mary Wollstonecraft and women, amid the laughter in the rose garden and the scent of the flowers. She dreamed of her sister Mary, dancing in the dark fields after Alice's wedding. She dreamed of Asobel reading 'Robinson Crusoe' with wide eyes. And then she dreamed of Seamus, the little red-headed Irishman, so lovingly giving his sister Rosie a little bit of quietness. The sun seemed to caress her cheeks, and then moved gently across her lips. She thought she heard her Maori horse pulling at the grass, somewhere near. She dreamed of Piritania, named after Britain, holding her as she wept, and the smell of the oil in her hair.

All her dreams caressed her, like the sun that seemed, somehow, to be very gently smoothing her hair from her face.

Harriet opened her eyes.

Benjamin Kingdom sat beside her in the sunshine with his wild blond hair and his grey thoughtful eyes, as if she had conjured him. The same feeling that she had had in the bookshop, that winter's day so long ago.

'Good heavens,' she murmured but for some reason that she did not quite understand she did not move.

'Are you – all right?' said Benjamin.

And she smiled up to him. 'I'm all right, Ben,' she said. 'I'm just lying here dreaming.'

He smiled back at her and said nothing.

'Have you come to the wedding? You are too late.'

'Are you married?' Something flickered across his face.

'Edward and Hetty were married yesterday.'

'Were they?' he said. He did not sound surprised but for a moment or two he did not speak. Then he said slowly, 'I saw that there was much between them. I think they have made a wise decision to follow their hearts rather than social convention for I believe there will be many upheavals in this country.'

'Do you mean, by upheavals, social upheavals such as theirs?'

'That, certainly. But I meant something else. I think there will be war, with the natives.'

Harriet looked at him carefully. 'Over land?'

'Over land. Not yet. But eventually. I saw it on my travels.'

'Edward's land?'

'I am not sure. Possibly.'

And they stayed without speaking for a long time. And Harriet saw the embers of the fire, and the old woman's carved face, and the silent shadows in the darkness along the shore, the night of the death of her father.

'I made a cake for Edward and Hetty,' she said at last, 'in that camp oven we carried over the hills last winter. It is my greatest triumph.'

He smiled down at her, and she smiled lazily back. 'I was dreaming before you came,' she said. 'I was dreaming of sunshine.' She saw herself reflected in the grey eyes. Somewhere a bell-bird sang its high, joyous song. 'Did you find the *moa*?'

'No,' said Benjamin. 'The *moa* proved elusive, as, I expect, a fabled bird should do. But I have found some wonderful, wonderful old bones.'

Harriet laughed; she could not help it.

'And kiwis. I have seen kiwis in the bush. Funny little things. This is a kiwi feather.'

For a moment she tensed as he leaned forward. And then he began, very gently, to again run the feather over her face and down her neck to her uncovered throat. After a moment she closed her eyes.

'It feels so peculiarly – beautiful, Ben,' she murmured, her eyes still closed. 'It is a feeling I do not quite – understand.'

Very, very gently Benjamin undid just one more button of the high-necked blouse.

He felt her tense.

And then he saw her face.

By a supreme effort of will she had not jumped up. But her face had completely changed: her eyes were open, the colour had immediately gone from her cheeks, and her face as she stared up at him showed horror, and pain, and memory.

Benjamin, dismayed, sat back. 'My dearest Harriet,' he said in a low voice, 'I am so very sorry.'

Very slowly, in the sunshine, Harriet's face cleared again, her breath slowed, finally her eyes closed. Benjamin sat very still, the stillness he had learned from watching strange and beautiful birds that had come to rest on the branch of a tree, who may, or may not, have sensed his presence.

The sun was warm, again the bell-bird sang in the trees. There were other sounds: the humming of insects, a horse shaking its mane somewhere near; in the distance Quintus barked.

After a long time she spoke.

'Is this something I could learn, Ben?' said Harriet.

In September 1893 New Zealand became the first country in the world to give the vote to women.